W9-AJM-659

TALLGRASS

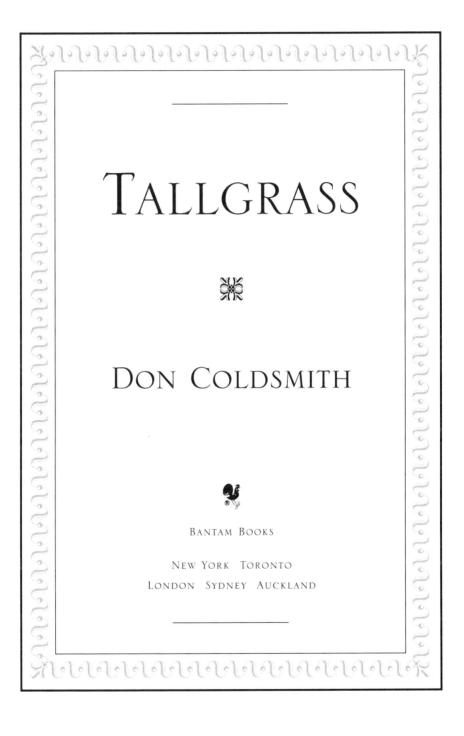

TALLGRASS

DON COLDSMITH

BANTAM BOOKS

NEW YORK TORONTO
LONDON SYDNEY AUCKLAND

TALLGRASS
A Bantam Book / May 1997

BOOK DESIGN BY ELLEN CIPRIANO.

MAP DESIGN BY GDS/JEFFREY L. WARD.

Library of Congress Cataloging-in-Publication Data

Coldsmith, Don, 1926–
Tallgrass : a novel of the Great Plains / Don Coldsmith.
          p.   cm.
ISBN 0-553-10632-5
1. Indians of North America—Great Plains—Fiction.
I. Title.
PS3553.0445T35   1997
813'.54—dc20   96-19672
                          CIP

Published simultaneously in the United States and Canada

PRINTED IN THE UNITED STATES OF AMERICA

BVG   10 9 8 7 6 5 4 3 2 1

*To the Kansans who have made this story
possible, natives or newcomers of whatever
heritage, who have loved our land.*

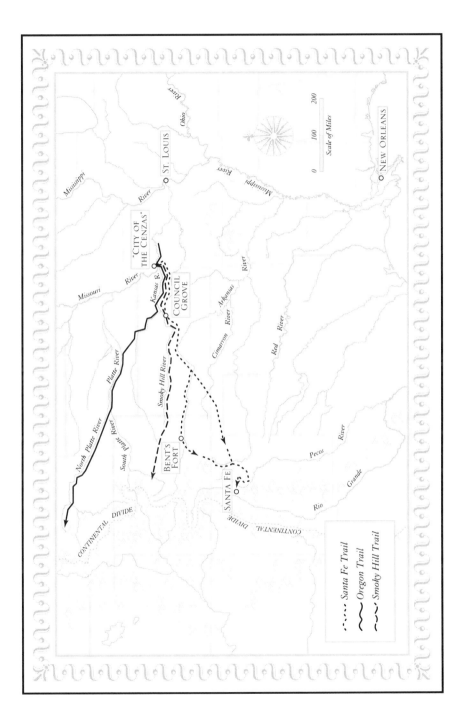

INTRODUCTION

There are four major areas of grassland on planet Earth: The steppes of Russia, the African veldt, the pampas of Argentina, and the Great Plains of North America. These prairies with their complicated, fragile ecologies have been used for thousands of years in the same way. The crop is grass, used to fatten grazing animals for human consumption. It is still so, though encroachment of other uses has reduced or damaged much of the former areas.

In the course of history, a series of civilizations and cultures passes across such an area, using its bounty, modifying it. And in turn, being changed for better or worse, by its spirit.

This book takes place in the central Great Plains of North America. Here, all the major prehistoric trails cross, though in more recent times they have borne new names bestowed by Europeans. Now there are only numbers, as part of an interstate highway system.

The area involved cannot be contained in a map. The inhabitants were (and are) constantly moving, the picture changing. A wise person once referred to boundaries as a "white man's disease." Let us consider instead a circle with a two-hundred-mile radius. Its center may be anywhere in the area where the trails of the westward expansion cross each other . . . The Great Plains. It could be called the Circle of History, because it will contain more early American history than any circle of similar size on the continent.

Parts of this circle have been claimed by six modern nations: Spain, France, Mexico, the Republic of Texas, the Confederate States of America, and the United States. The first European incursion is usually considered to be Spanish, in 1541. It is worth noting that Henry Hudson, "discoverer" of the New York river that bears his name, had not yet been born. By the time he reached Manhattan Island, Spain had sent several major expeditions into the tallgrass prairie. It would be another eighty years before the Pilgrims set foot on Plymouth Rock.

By the early 1700s, Spain and France were carrying on international trade across this area, from Santa Fe to French forts around the native city they called the Chez les Canses . . . "City of the Canses" . . . Kansas City.

The region bears a name today that has been applied to it for at least five centuries, in one form or another. It is derived from the name of a people, the People of the South Wind, since a prevailing south wind is a prominent feature of the land. There have been many variant spellings, because originally, with no written language, it was totally phonetic. Konzas, Kensas, Kenzas, Censas, Canses, Kanzas . . . At least sixteen spellings are noted in an 1883 *History of Kansas.* These varied pronunciations occurred as the name rolled from the European tongues of outsiders. They came to trap, trade, farm, ranch, preach, and build.

At the age of sixteen, my grandfather, Ezra Willett, drove a covered wagon and an ox team into the fertile soil of the prairie. I grew up listening to his stories of the land he pronounced "Kenzas."

Stories are bits and pieces of history. Some involve major historic events. Some are minor experiences of everyday people, as they related to such events. However, the situation is much like that in wartime. A "minor skirmish" in a news release may seem quite major to those involved and to the families of the dead.

I have attempted to portray, as best I could, the feelings of the individuals who peopled this prairie, red, white, brown, or black. All were people, with hopes and dreams, joys and disappointments, who laughed and cried and loved, were hungry or full, warm or cold.

Many of these individual stories have been told before, but some only by oral tradition. I have talked with some of the people who experienced them, or with their descendants. I listened for hours to a charming lady with nearly a century of stories, who remembered how she felt as a child when the president was assassinated. President *Lincoln.*

Are these stories true? Of course. True, at least, in the minds of those who lived them. . . . History is written by the survivors. In the case of this volume, it is the story of the land itself, a mosaic of different cultures melding on the frontier. If these stories did not happen to identifiable people, I still maintain that they *could* have, within the framework of known historic fact.

But now let us return to a day before the inhabitants of the Great Plains saw their first metal weapons and armor, the first horses . . . 1541 . . .

Don Coldsmith
1997

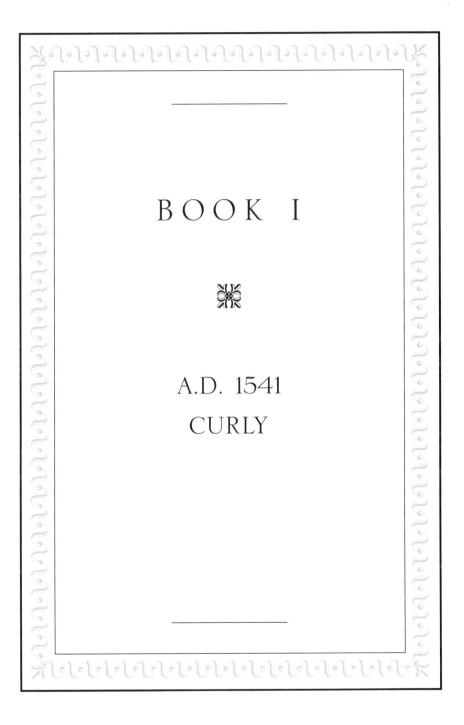

BOOK I

A.D. 1541
CURLY

1

Heron Woman stood outside the lodge, looking to the south. There was excitement in the air. A traveling trader had stopped briefly only yesterday to tell of an approaching column of strangers. Many of them . . . hundreds, maybe.

A hunting party? No, it seemed not. A band of one of the tribes who were always moving their skin tents from one place to another?

"No," insisted the trader, using mostly hand signs, "you do not understand. They have no women and children with them."

"Ah! A war party!" said Weasel. "We will teach them!"

"No, no. These men are different. They grow fur upon their faces. They have come from far to the south. Many sleeps . . . many moons, maybe. They have a great herd of animals like elk that they ride upon."

There was a roar of derisive laughter, and the trader flushed angrily. "It is true! You will see!"

He turned away, and Bull's Horn called to him. "Wait, friend. Tell us more. Here, sit and smoke with us."

A bit reluctantly, the trader set his pack aside and joined the circle of men that quickly formed. He was persuaded to continue, using hand signs and some of the words of the People, the *Pani.*

He told of the appearance of the strangers, how they wore a smooth garment as silvery and shining as the sides of the minnows in the stream. The animals of which he had spoken must be dogs, it was presumed, because some carried burdens. But as big as an elk, and yes, he insisted, some were ridden by warriors with spears. In fact, farther south, he had been told, some had seen them and believed it to be all one creature: four legs, but with the upper body of a man!

There was a chuckle around the circle. Ah, this was becoming a good story! Not to be taken seriously, of course.

"How many of these elk-dogs are there?" someone asked.

"Hundreds, maybe."

"You have *seen* them?"

"Only at a great distance. We were afraid, my wife and I. We hurried away."

The People were beginning to take the trader a bit more seriously now. He and his wife, who sat a little way apart from the circle, seemed genuinely concerned. There was fear in the eyes of the woman as she sat waiting.

"What is their purpose?" someone asked. "A war party?"

"No one is sure," the trader admitted. "They do not attack towns. Mostly, they travel. They are coming this way."

"How soon? When?"

"Two . . . maybe three days. The big dogs on which they ride travel fast."

This time there was no laughter. The trader rose.

"We must go on," he said.

"Where?"

"Downriver. We will stop with the Kenzas, maybe."

"You go east, then?"

"For now, yes. . . ."

The trader and his wife shouldered their packs and were quickly out of sight. It was strange, a trader who did not want to take the time to trade. . . .

There had been much discussion after the trader left. Some were inclined to disregard any significance to his story. Are tall tales not a part of a trader's way? Others took it more seriously. This man and his wife had been traders for many seasons, and had stopped here before. They were of the nation of Arapaho, the Trader People, and had traveled to many strange places. And *they* had shown fear.

Not that there was any real concern for the safety of the town. The men of the Pani were respected and feared in the whole region. Their hunting parties went where they pleased, and were avoided by their neighbors.

Heron Woman was aware of all of this, of course. There was no fear in her. In this, her eighteenth summer, she had settled into her marriage quite comfortably. There was no child yet, no pregnancy, even, after the ten moons of her marriage to Beaver. She was reasonably happy, though a trifle bored sometimes. She envied the wife of the trader, who had traveled to exciting places and seen wondrous things. The mountains . . . she could not envision such a thing as a hill that could be seen from many days away.

There was a sameness to her life that she saw no way to escape. There had really been nothing different in any season since she could remember. The People planted the corn. Some of her earliest memories dealt with that. Beans and pumpkins, too, but these did not have the religious significance of the corn.

Each year, after the second hoeing of the corn, the Pani went on a summer buffalo hunt. Then there were different chores, the drying of the meat and dressing of skins. In all of these tasks, Heron had participated since she could remember. Even small children can shoo away flies and birds from drying meat.

Sometimes strangers came to trade and that was always interesting. Some of the nomadic hunters who drifted in and out of the area would have an especially good hunt occasionally. Then they would come to trade meat and robes for the vegetables and grain of her people.

Her marriage had been an exciting distraction at first. New living arrangements, with Beaver moving into her family's lodge. . . . She was proud to introduce him into the extended family of some forty people who lived there. The marriage bed and its associated activity provided a new and wonderful experience. She had expected a pregnancy, but none had happened yet. The older women reassured her.

"Sometimes it takes a little while. It will happen soon enough."

"You could try another man," suggested her aunt. "Beaver's brother? He is a handsome one!"

Heron shook her head. Not yet . . . she had not been with another man, and was quite happy with Beaver's ways. Some of her friends had taken other men occasionally. The rules were very strict, however. A woman must be able to guarantee the parentage of any child she bore. The father would be responsible for its support. Of course, the only way to be *sure* of the father's identity was to have no other man for that entire moon, until her next flow. Not even her husband. . . . Heron was not ready to do without Beaver's nightly attentions for anything like a month. She would wait and see. Maybe this would be the moon in which she would conceive.

Meanwhile, the excitement of the approaching strangers was a pleasant diversion, a thing to anticipate. Heron did not know how much to believe. Especially about the great dogs, large enough to be ridden by men. Well, they would see if the trader told truth.

This morning she had risen with the dawn to go outside and empty her bladder. Some people were stirring, but the usual bustle and activity of the town had not yet begun. It was a time of quiet, one that she always enjoyed. The night creatures were becoming silent and seeking their lodges, their songs replaced by those of the creatures of the day. An owl floated soundlessly across the hillside and sank out of sight into the heavy timber along the river below the town. She heard the calls of a couple of crows as they dropped after him in their noisy pursuit. She smiled as the words of a childhood song came to mind, *"You hunted too long, Kookooskoos . . ."*

But the main thoughts in her mind were those of the approaching intruders. Her gaze tried to stretch beyond the cornfields, across the rolling prairie to the south. In another day it might be possible to see such a large party. Sometimes in the spring a migrating herd of buffalo could be seen for a day or two as they made their way northward, following the greening of the grasses. The really big herds usually followed a route farther west, it was said. It varied from season to season, she thought.

From where she stood, she could easily see across the tops of the growing corn. The first hoeing was completed, and a rain three days ago had stimulated the spirits of the corn to a spurt of growth. There were a few weeds. Not many yet, but soon it would be time to hoe again. Heron hated that task more than any. To spend a day swinging the heavy stick with a buffalo's shoulder blade lashed to it. . . . Ah, she would rather butcher or dress hides!

The corn was doing well, she noted. Separate fields for the

different colors. They must be kept pure. Yellow, white, red, and blue, each area paced off and designated by the priests. There were the other types, too. That for meal, that for eating fresh, that for popping. Most beautiful to look at, she thought, was the spotted corn. Snow white, each ear was, but each individual grain bore a tiny black spot.

Odd, how her mind kept wandering today. She would be thinking about the coming of the strangers with their strange dogs, and the excitement of being able to see new things. Then her mind would wander to something like the corn, the crop with special meaning to the People.

The People . . . every group calls itself the People, each in its own tongue, she had heard. Would that be true also of the approaching strangers? Probably, she decided. But each tribe or nation has also a name by which others call it. Her own, the Pani, or Horn People, after the hair style of the men. This was borne out also in the hand sign for the Pani, and was proudly accepted. A tall warrior, his head shaved except for the lock of hair that was plaited and twisted into a horn-shaped projection . . . how handsome they looked! Fierce, too. Her blood always raced with patriotic pride when the men dressed and fixed their hair for a ceremony. Yes, with physical desire, too, she had to admit. It was a stimulating thing to observe the proud warriors of the People.

Heron suspected that the other women had similar feelings, too. After one of the ceremonial occasions there were always the sounds of increased activity in the darkness of the big lodge.

The sun was rising now, and more people were moving around outside, going for water, carrying wood, attending to the duties of nature. A scout trotted in from the south, and some of the town's leaders gathered to meet him. The young man paused to catch his breath and to wait for a man or two who hurried from their respective lodges. Heron Woman drew near to listen.

"We have seen their campfires," the scout reported, still breathing heavily. "We are made to think that they will be here tomorrow before dark."

2

That night they saw the fires of the approaching strangers on a distant ridge. When this was discovered, practically everyone in the village trooped out to the little rise south of the lodges. One must see for oneself.

The number of fires scattered along the ridge told of many people. It was a little frightening, since all, or nearly all, were said to be warriors. There were also the tales of the strange creatures, the giant dogs that ate grass like an elk. *Could* there have been any truth in the story of the trader . . . the one about the men being *part of* that mystical animal?

Heron Woman was inclined to think that the trader himself did not really believe that one. It was told in a tone like that used in the Long-Ago stories. Stories of Creation, when all animals and even Man spoke the same tongue.

There was no doubt, of course, that the trader and his wife were alarmed, frightened over the advance of this party of outsiders. But this did not prevent his passing on a good story when opportunity offered. And it must be admitted, a tale of an animal that comes apart and becomes two creatures, one a man and one an elk-dog, is quite a story.

The men were talking of the many fires now, estimating the number of fighting men they might represent. Even if five or more people used each fire, this was a large number. Hundreds . . .

"Unless," an old woman observed sarcastically, "they burn many fires just to impress you!"

That was a possibility, of course. It would be a clever move, to worry an enemy before a battle. But there would seem to be no cause to do so in this case. According to the trader, there had been no battles with these strangers. No skirmishes, even. They were simply traveling, looking . . . but for *what?*

Regardless of their purpose, it seemed prudent to be prepared. The men decided to ready themselves ceremonially, for anything. This would include the prayers and blessings called down by the priests, and ritual songs and dances. Some of these would begin immediately.

Heron Woman had helped her husband dress his hair, combing and waxing it with tallow mixed with pigment. It was then twisted and knotted and drawn up into the horn-shaped projection that gave the People their name of Pani, the Horn People.

She was proud when he finally stood ready for the ceremonies. The horn added at least a hand's span to his height, and he was tall already. It would be a fearsome thing, Heron thought, to face a war party of horn-men, tall and handsome in their paint and finery.

The strangers would arrive tomorrow in the afternoon, it was estimated, allowing for their more rapid pace as described by the trader. They would probably camp near the village, and no one was certain how long they would remain. A day or two, maybe. If they sought no conflict, they would probably trade a little, hold council with the priests and elders, and then move on.

Having helped her husband prepare for the ceremonial meeting, Heron began to think about her own appearance. She looked at her image in a still pool that next morning. She was not entirely pleased with what she saw. What woman, no matter how beautiful, is ever completely satisfied with her beauty? Heron was tall and long legged. Those same legs, spindly and thin, had earned her the childhood name, Heron. It had been a bit derisive at first, maybe. But, as womanhood approached, the calves of the long legs began to bulge attractively. It was said that she moved with the deliberate grace of her namesake, the great blue heron. She began to develop a certain degree of pride in all of this, and to glory in her height. She had no objection to the transformation of her name from the teasing childhood name Heron to Heron Woman. When puberty made the corresponding changes in her body she began to see the young men in a different light.

Their courtship had been quite short and simple. Beaver had joined the lodge of her family. She had found much pleasure in the physical side of her marriage. Some of the strange urges that had seemed so illogical to her as she matured were now understood, and satisfied. Not permanently, of course. Such urges return frequently, and she was pleased that her husband's urges were similar, or at least compatible with her own.

But now was no time to think of such things. Until after the council met, Beaver must remain ceremonially chaste. A mild disappointment, because she had just completed the unclean time of her moon, and they had not yet resumed marital activity. This, coupled with the excitement of the approaching visit by the strangers, gave an urgency to her desire.

No matter, she told herself. When it was over, and the ritual abstinence behind them, Beaver, too, would be ready and eager. She smiled to herself as she thought of some of his favorite caresses, and how she would use them. The emotional excitement of the ceremonial dances always stirred their desires and made resumption of the marriage all the sweeter. After the council, yes. She began to plan just how she would entice and excite him. She could make it worth the delay for him. For them both . . .

For now, she bathed in the stream, washed and carefully plaited her hair. She would wear her other dress, of soft buckskin. She had worn it only a few times, for special occasions. It was a bit more revealing than the everyday dress that she usually wore. A low-cut neck, but tight across her breasts. She liked the feel of it, and it turned heads. It was a little shorter than her usual garment, too, showing her long legs to best advantage. She had seen how the men looked at her when she wore it. And after all, did she not owe it to Beaver to look as good as possible for this special occasion? She would make him proud. And, of course, amorous.

.   .   .

It was early afternoon when the advance party approached and halted, a bowshot away from the greeting party of the People. Heron saw with wonder that it was true. These men *did* ride on the elk-dog animals. The five or six who drew up to meet the Horn Men were each sitting on one of the beasts! The creatures were of different colors. One black, several a blue-gray shade, and one that was a reddish brown with black mane, tail, and feet. These animals did not seem dangerous, but quite calm. They gave an occasional blowing snort, which was quite disconcerting at first, but seemingly no threat. And she saw a thing not mentioned by the trader. The elk-dogs seemed to wear a turtle on each foot. The trader had not been close enough to see that, she supposed. Nor to see how the animals were controlled, with ropes or thongs around their heads, somehow.

She saw, too, the bright garments that had been mentioned by the trader. He had not seen those at close range, either. Hard, smooth, and shining, they appeared. She had seen a few ornaments of copper, worn by a trader's wife. The woman had permitted Heron to touch one. It was cold to the touch, and very hard. These garments appeared to be of a similar material, but silver in color rather than reddish. Some of them had headdresses of the same material, too, round and shiny, with a crest running from front to back.

There was another thing, too, one that the trader had mentioned. Heron had completely forgotten it in the wonder of the whole situation. Most of these strangers had fur on their faces! Black, soft fur, leaving bare only the area from the forehead to below the nose. She wondered if their entire bodies were covered with such fur. This idea sent a sensual thrill through her, and brought on other thoughts that she pushed aside quickly. Strange thoughts . . .

The two parties were beginning to talk now. The strangers had brought a man who was apparently not one of them, but knew the hand signs for talk. Someone from a tribe farther south, she supposed.

The men exchanged greetings and the open-hand sign for peace, and then began to get down to serious conversation. These men, the interpreter explained, were looking for something. He showed some small objects that Heron could not see well, but that appeared to be of yet another shiny metal. This time, *yellow*. It was apparent from the respect with which the strangers handled the objects that they must have great religious significance.

Her eyes and her attention wandered to the ranks behind those who were holding the conversation. They were drawn up a few paces behind the leaders and the interpreter.

The first impression was that these strangers all looked alike. It was only when she began to study them as individuals that she saw it was not completely true. Some were older than others, and yes, some more handsome. That thought struck her as humorous. How could one suppose that a man whose face was heavily furred could be considered more or less handsome than another with heavy fur? Yet it was so. What makes a man handsome, or a woman beautiful, anyway? Is it not a look in the eyes, a sense of confidence, pride, and dignity? These things were still observable in the way the strangers looked as they sat and waited for the leaders to finish their conversation.

Some, she noticed, were showing a bit of gray in their hair. "The snows of a few winters," the People called it. It was interesting to see that there was gray, too, in the facial fur. She wondered . . . No, better not to wonder about that. She did not even know whether they had body fur, anyway.

Her eyes roved on down the line of those who sat on their elk-dogs behind the leaders. Then she noticed one. . . . Ah, how had she not seen him before? Young, handsome, strong looking, with a look of eagles in his eyes. His mount was different in color pattern, too. Mostly white, with black spots over its entire body, the size of a duck's egg. Could these be *painted* on? It did not look so. She wondered whether such an animal might indicate something of the importance of the man who rode it. This man, though young, carried a demeanor of authority about him. A subchief, a rising leader, probably.

Now the dialogue was breaking up. There were gestures toward a level meadow to the southeast, and Heron assumed that this was where the strangers would camp. For how long? Tonight only? A day or two? Maybe Beaver would know. Surely there would be many rumors sweeping through the village within a short time. It would be a matter of sorting out the best and most likely. Her glance fell on her husband, straight and tall in the ranks of the Pani warriors. She was made proud by his appearance.

She looked again at the ranks of the strangers as they moved out to begin preparations for their camp. For some reason her eyes searched for the rider of the spotted elk-dog, though she could not have explained why. Possibly she was reluctant to admit the attraction she felt. An odd, thrilling attraction . . .

Ah, there! She saw him pull on one of the thongs attached to his mount's head. To something in its mouth, actually. The animal turned obediently. *So that is it,* she thought. *Some object that they put in the mouth of the elk-dog lets them control it!*

Just then the young man turned to look over his shoulder and their eyes met. Heron was startled and a bit embarrassed. She would have dropped her eyes, but she could not move. Despite the distance, she knew that he was looking at her. Maybe looking *for* her. He smiled. At least she thought so.

It seemed ridiculous as she thought of it later, that she could have seen a smile at such a distance, and under so much fur. But she had felt it, the reaching out of his spirit, searching for hers. There was no question in her mind. It was confusing and a little alarming, the way she felt.

The same confusion assailed her again when Beaver told her that the strangers would be here a day or two. Their elk-dogs were growing thin from so much travel, he said, and they needed to take a day of rest to allow the animals to graze.

After dark, as they sought their sleeping robes, Beaver reached for her, his hands roving over her body. For reasons she could not explain, she pushed him gently away.

"But I was made to think . . ." he began, confused.

She stopped him, a gentle finger on his lips.

"No," she told him, "I was wrong. It is not yet time."

Then she lay in the darkness, her thoughts racing. Why had she done that? Earlier in the day she had been almost frantic with desire.

It was a long time before she fell asleep, to dream of making love in the darkness with a half-supernatural spirit-creature that was covered with soft, warm fur.

3

The visitors had laid aside their shiny garments and hats when they camped. They all wore shirts and breeches, it was seen. But, without the metal outer garb, they appeared much like normal men. Except, of course, for their hairy faces.

Some of the Pani developed a theory that the metal must be for protection as well as appearance. Would not the hard shell turn the point of an arrow or spear, much as a bullhide shield did?

"It would be very uncomfortable," someone suggested. "See how clumsily they moved when they wore it?"

Some of the strangers also wore a sort of shirt that appeared to be woven of tiny rings or coils of metal. It was flexible, and made an odd jingling noise when they moved. That garment, too, appeared heavy and uncomfortable. It was little wonder that as soon as they camped, they laid such things aside to enjoy more freedom of motion.

Many of these facts were reported by the boys who followed the strangers to their camp a few bowshots from the village. That had not been long in happening. Although there were dire predictions and warnings from the old women, the natural curiosity of the young prevailed. Cautious at first, they found that the mysterious strangers were much like other people. Some were gruff and forbidding, but some smiled at the youngsters and playfully teased them.

By dark, much was known about the visitors. One question, that of whether the fur grew only on their faces or on the entire body, was partially solved. Boys who had watched them bathe in the stream reported the answer.

"Some are hairier than others."

Their purpose in being here was still obscure. At a council that first evening, their leaders seemed preoccupied with questions about the shiny yellow metal. They even became angry and frustrated when the Pani denied any knowledge of its source. It appeared that they did not believe such answers to their questions, and there was some argument among themselves.

Some indecision, too, possibly. During that next day, there seemed to be some doubt as to what they would do next. Their leaders met in conversation, and talked a lot among themselves. Very quietly, although sometimes vigorously, it was noted. The rest, the lesser warriors, loafed around the camp, waiting for whatever would come next. Some wandered into the village by twos and threes, watching the activities of the People with curiosity. They seemed to present no threat, and the initial uneasiness soon passed.

Yet it was a distraction, a departure from the normal, and most of the People would be glad to see them gone. Some of the old women still clucked their tongues in disapproval and warned of dire consequences as a result of these strangers' visit. But the People, inclined to take each day as it came, paid little attention to such gloomy predictions. There were those who actually enjoyed the diversion that the presence of the strangers presented.

Perhaps Heron Woman was one of those. Maybe it was purely coincidence. No matter, when the encounter came it was a complete surprise. Or at least she believed so. Maybe, she thought later, he had contrived it. Or possibly, even, *she* had. . . .

Heron had gone down the slope to the stream to gather wood for the cooking fire. She was returning along the path, and was no more than halfway back, perhaps a long bowshot. There was a sharp bend in the path, and a clump of bushes that obscured the view. As she rounded that obstacle she suddenly found herself face-to-face with one of the hairfaced strangers. She was startled and caught off guard, and in her confusion missed her footing. Her left foot stumbled against the protruding root of a nearby sapling, she toppled forward, and her armful of sticks fell and scattered along the path. Heron would have fallen flat, but the stranger reached out quickly, catching her elbow and halting her fall.

The young man helped her to her feet and they stood back for an instant, looking into each other's eyes. There was a moment of panic, but then he smiled. A friendly, amused smile. It was a moment before she realized that this was the rider of the spotted elk-dog. Their eyes had met before. He was even more handsome at close range, and now he stooped to help her pick up her scattered firewood. At the same moment she, too, bent forward and their heads collided with a sharp bump.

Heron jumped back in surprise, and straightened to face the stranger again. There was a startled look on his face, too, and in a moment both of them burst out laughing. The young man rubbed his head and frowned in an exaggerated grimace. Now Heron began to relax a little. The stranger actually seemed quite human, and rather pleasant.

They stooped again to gather her spilled firewood, more carefully this time. Heron nodded her thanks and returned his smile. His hand rested on her elbow for a moment, gentle yet firm. She felt a thrill of excitement at his touch.

Then, haltingly, he began to use hand signs. It was obvious that he was not experienced in such communication. But such things are not complicated, and convey ideas, and words. The young man pointed to her and to himself, then to the ground where they stood. . . . This place . . . and then made the sign for "moon" and pointed to the east. All of this was followed by the sign for a question.

It was her first encounter with a person who shared not a single word in the tongue of either of them. Heron was a bit surprised that the young man was able to make his meaning so clear. Maybe she had been looking for such meaning, even wanting it, but there was no question as to what he had tried to convey:

Meet me here, when the moon rises. Will you?

Confused and uncertain, Heron turned and fled. One glance over her shoulder from a few steps away showed him standing exactly where he had been. He was watching her, and smiling.

Heron was embarrassed. She should have signed *No.* Or *Maybe.* But she had been confused and off balance. Her arms were full of fuel. How could she have signed anyway? Surely he would realize that. She felt a flicker of anger at him, that he would put her in such a position.

But it was no concern of hers anyway. She tossed her head indignantly. *Let him wonder! It is his problem,* she thought.

Heron told no one of her chance meeting on the path. She had no particular reason. She even planned how she would tell it later. It was quite a funny story, actually, how she had fallen and dropped the wood, and then they bumped heads in the confusion. But she wanted to think about it a while, turn it over in her mind. She kept remembering the feel of his hand on her arm, firm yet gentle. That part of the story she would not tell. Nor of his clumsily signed invitation. Certainly she had no intention of meeting him again, and she would not even mention that part. Well, maybe after the strangers were gone. An amusing thought crossed her mind. Her friends would probably not believe that part. No matter, since she would not go to meet him at moonrise anyway. It had been an exciting moment, a flattering experience, that encounter on the path. One to be remembered. Nothing more.

She went about her daily tasks as if nothing had happened. Nothing did happen, she told herself fiercely, trying to drive the event from her mind.

Then she would find herself counting the days since the full moon. No more than two or three . . . the moon would rise awhile after sunset.

Heron shook her head to clear it of such thoughts. She pounded the corn in her grinding stone with extra vigor to work off the excitement that was seething in her.

Heron lay in the darkness, unable to sleep. Beaver had not approached her tonight. She knew that she had been acting strangely, and was sure that he had noticed. Probably he thought she was not feeling well, and assumed that her menses were prolonged and difficult this time. She had implied that when she rejected him last night. He had understood, and had made no objection. He *could* not, of course.

Now he lay snoring gently, and she lay awake. She could wake him now and initiate some marital activity. Beaver would be surprised. Pleasantly surprised, because she had misled him into expecting nothing. Yes, that would be good. It would relieve her tension, too.

Pretty soon, but not yet. She was enjoying the excitement of the day's events. She would think about it a little longer, then wake him.

Maybe she should empty her bladder first. Now that such a thought had occurred, she could think of nothing *but* the need to empty her bladder. She wondered how she had waited this long. She shifted her position to relieve the pressure, but that was only temporary.

Well, she could rise and leave the lodge without waking her husband, she thought. If she accidentally woke him, he would be ready for her attentions when she returned. If not, she would rouse him when she returned, and relieve the tensions and concerns of both.

Heron slipped out of the robes and made her way to the doorway. There she paused for a moment. The dying fire gave a soft, flickering light as she looked back at the sleeping forms around the periphery of the big lodge. Clearly she heard a gentle snore from the area where she and Beaver lived. She recognized that snore from close familiarity with it. There was no doubt. That was Beaver, and she had not disturbed him. When she returned . . .

She stepped into the cool night air, and moved toward the area used by the women for this purpose. The night was dark, and the stars bright overhead. She attended the call of nature and felt better, placing a hand on her now-flatter belly.

Starting back toward the lodge, she paused for a moment to enjoy the night sounds. A fox barked somewhere in the growth along the river, and a coyote's call sounded in the distance. The haunting cry of a night bird floated up from heavier timber downstream.

She was about to turn again toward the lodge when her eye caught something to the east, and she turned to look. Somehow it was a surprise, though it should not have been, to see a thin sliver of blood red moon lying along the distant horizon. She watched for a little while, admiring its beauty as the slim stripe fattened and became fuller, brighter. A little longer . . .

Heron realized but was reluctant to admit the timing that had drawn her out of the lodge. It was pure coincidence, of course. Or was it? Was there purpose in her being outside to answer nature's call? Had she willed it so?

Of course not, she told herself indignantly. She often rose to empty her bladder, did she not? Did not everyone? Even the strangers, probably.

Her mind reached down the path to the bend with the clump of bushes. Was he waiting there? *Of course not.* She had been clumsy and foolish and had not even given him the courtesy of an answer to his question. Such a man would not waste his time standing alone in the dark, in the middle of the night. Not for someone who had appeared so ridiculous at their only meeting.

Still, he *might.* Curiosity nagged at her. All her life she would wonder whether the handsome stranger had actually gone to see if she would come. Maybe she could take a look just to see if he did. She really should know. In years to come, whether he did or not, to know would make a better story.

Trembling a little, both from the night's chill and from excitement, she turned and started down the path. Just to look would do no harm. . . .

4

Heron had had in mind to approach stealthily, but that would have been hard to do. The moon was shedding more light with each passing moment. She made her way down the path, peering into the darker shadows and feeling for her footing. Her heart was beating wildly, her palms sweating. She tried to stop her trembling, which was only partly from the night's chill.

Ahead of her, she saw the clump of bushes, but saw no waiting figure. Maybe she had misunderstood his halting use of the hand signs. It was almost a relief that he had not come. It removed all responsibility from her, and it was over. She turned to start back toward the lodge.

But wait . . . a shadow separated itself from the shadow of the bushes and moved into the moonlight. He approached her and gently reached for her hand, drawing her back into the darkness. She saw that he wore a sort of cape around his shoulders, and now he drew it around the two of them. Possibly he realized how she was trembling, and wanted to shield her from the chill of the night. Its warmth felt good, but she still trembled.

It was odd, not knowing exactly what he wanted or how he

would go about it. They had no words in common, only a few hand signs. And physical attraction, of course. The feel of his muscular arm around her shoulders was exciting.

Deeper into the shadows, he circled her with both arms and drew her to him. The feel of his body against hers was good. But then he bent his head and placed his mouth on hers. She experienced a moment of fright at this strange and unknown custom. For an instant she wondered what else he might expect to do. She wanted to pull away, but she was encircled in his arms. Not roughly, but firmly. His hands were gentle. . . . Besides, after the moment of startled shock, the touch of his mouth on hers was good. Sensuous and exciting . . . she found her own lips eagerly responding, and she wondered what other customs the strangers might have. There was the unfamiliar feel of his facial fur on her cheek. Not really unpleasant, just different.

He removed his cape and spread it on the soft grass, gently drawing her to him as they sank down together.

Heron reentered the lodge some time later, wondering if she had been missed. She would pretend that she had only gone out to empty her bladder, and stayed to watch the rising of the moon. All of that was true, of course. She would tell Beaver the rest later. Just now she did not want to think about it. About telling Beaver, that is. Her head still whirled with the realization of what had happened, and the ecstasy and excitement of it all. She could have done better, she was sure, if she had known the ways of the stranger, but all things considered, it had gone well. Another time . . . but there might not be another time. Probably not. The strangers would depart tomorrow or the next day. And this stranger, whose name she did not even know, was her selected mate for this month. She had not quite realized until now that she was firmly committed. Under the laws of the People, she could have no other man, even her husband, until the next full moon.

Heron moved through the lodge, listening to the deep breathing and soft snores of the sleepers. It seemed entirely likely that she had not even been missed. She lay down beside Beaver, and he half rolled toward her, throwing an arm across her. She snuggled against him, realizing that he was not fully awake. The familiar feel of her own bed and of Beaver's body against hers was good. She wanted to wake him, to share her love with him. But that could not be. And the time until the next full moon would seem very long.

. . .

Next morning the strangers prepared to leave, trailing back the way they came. Heading a little more westward, maybe. They did not say, did not even hold a final council with the Pani, and no one ever determined what their real purpose was. It must have had something to do with the yellow metal ornament they had shown to the priests and elders. A quest of some sort. There was a strong impression that this quest was unfulfilled.

Riders were rounding up the hundreds of elk-dogs and starting to push them down the trail. It was fascinating to watch the motions of the ridden animals as they moved to the command of the riders. Heron watched for one rider, the young man on the spotted stallion. She finally realized that those working with the herd were some of the younger men. Lesser in prestige than the one she sought, probably. Yes. He would have more status, that of a subchief, maybe.

Then she saw him. He had donned his armor and headdress and was riding his elk-dog toward the group of earth-bermed lodges. He appeared to be looking for something or someone. She felt a bit of concern. Could it be that he was possibly looking for *her*? Heron wanted to run and hide, but could not. Even more, she wanted to watch him. He was more handsome in full daylight than by moonlight, if that was possible. She admired the way his muscular body balanced on the spotted animal. She had wondered before whether the facial fur covered the entire bodies of the strangers. There was the partial answer by the inquisitive boys, *Some are hairier than others.* This one, she now knew, was not one of the hairier ones.

Now he seemed to recognize her, and turned the elk-dog's head toward her. There was a dignified look on his face, yet a trace of the friendly smile. Their eyes met, he nodded ever so slightly, and touched the front of his metal hat in a sort of salute. She nodded in return. This must be a ceremonial sign, she thought. Its exact meaning was vague, but there was unmistakably a spirit of respect and friendship. Her heart beat faster. Why must he go? He was hers, Heron's, for this entire moon. And she, his.

No matter. He was leaving, and she would never see him again. She would have pleasant memories to bring back to mind for the rest of her life.

He turned and rode away, joining the departing column. She

watched his broad shoulders until she lost sight of him among the other riders.

For the rest of the day the Pani could see the dust plume as it grew smaller in the distance. Things could now return to normal. But for some of the People, nothing would ever be the same again.

Beaver approached her that night with more determined romance in his heart. His hands caressed her body, and she was tempted. But no, it could not be, not now. To be with any other man was forbidden until her next menses. And she must tell him. She owed him that. Besides, she could not put him off very long.

"Beaver, I cannot yet," she whispered.

There was concern in his voice. "Something is wrong? You are not well?"

It had not occured to him what might be preventing their conjugal activity.

"No, no, it is not that," she told him.

"Then *what*?"

"Beaver, I . . . I have been with another man."

There was a long silence before her husband spoke.

"Because I have not given you a child?" he asked seriously.

"No, no . . . well, maybe . . . Beaver, I . . ."

"My brother?" he guessed.

That would have been the logical choice, a close relative in her husband's family. A relative of her own would be forbidden, of course. Rules against incest were very strict.

"No. You do not know him, Beaver."

And I do not know him either! she thought frantically.

"But . . ."

He would quickly reason it out, she thought. There was probably no one in the village that he did not know. Therefore . . .

"One of the visitors," she told him.

"The hairfaces? Heron, what—"

"I do not know, Beaver," she said quickly. "Maybe I will be able to explain it later."

She wondered whether she could ever explain it, to him or to herself. It was something that had happened. Why? The young man had been there, had been available. It had helped that he seemed strong and masculine yet kind and gentle. And handsome . . . just to think of him now stirred her desire all over again. The way they had met, the bumped heads as they worked together to pick up her firewood. . . . They had had something in common for a little while. Something shared.

She would always remember him. It might be that she would never have another man, except Beaver. She would have no need. And a strange thought came to her. She wanted Beaver now, more than ever, maybe because she knew that she could not have him now. Not for the rest of this moon.

"It will be a long moon," Beaver said as if in answer to her thoughts.

Her heart was heavy for him. For *them*. She regretted her impulse that had taken her down the path in the moonlight. Yet, not really. Ah, life had seemed so simple when she was a child. Now it only became more and more confusing.

Heron wondered if it would have been better to say nothing to Beaver about her tryst. She thought that no one else knew. The man was gone, and would never return. What difference would it have made? Yet, she could not have done that. It would have been wrong. She, Heron, would know. She would have lived the rest of her life with a lie, and with the knowledge that she had violated her marriage. Not by the alliance with the stranger, but by resuming relations with her husband during the same moon's cycle.

Another thought came to her, and she now voiced it in a whisper to him.

"Beaver, shall we say nothing of this to the others?"

"Why?" he asked.

"Well, I . . ." She was not sure why she felt this way. "You know how some women are," she said haltingly. "I would not want it thought that I was boasting about it."

"Of course not. I know you would not boast, Heron. I will say nothing."

She felt that he really did understand. At least about that part, the bragging.

"Thank you, Beaver."

"It is yours to say," he went on. "Your choice, all of it."

He sounded a little hurt.

"It is not that I care for you any less, Beaver."

"I know. It is all right, Heron."

There was a long silence now, and she wondered if she had hurt him more than she realized. But most husbands were not as sensitive as hers, maybe.

His next whispered comment filled her with mixed emotions.

"Of course," he said, "if you are with child by this man, I may have to boast about your accomplishment. But who would support the child?"

She knew that he was teasing her, and it was good. Things would be the same between them. Not the same, maybe, but the old spark was there, the friendship and good humor in their marriage that others seemed to envy.

The other part of his comment was more disconcerting. *If you are with child . . .*

She had not seriously thought of that.

5

$\mathcal{S}$urely she could not be with child. It was only one time, and very early in her moon. And she had never been pregnant, even with ample cause. No, it was a very slim possibility. Yet it *could* be.

This made Beaver's half teasing comment much more serious. *"Who will support the child?"* It would be the responsibility of the father to provide for the child of such a union. In this case, the father would not be there, and might as well not exist.

Heron thrust the idea aside. It was highly unlikely that she would have to face such a situation.

The days dragged slowly on through the Moon of Thunder. Noisy storms rumbled across the plains, dropping the needed water for the crops. The corn sprang to life and grew so rapidly that it seemed one could watch it grow. Pumpkin vines groped among the stalks with their curly tendrils, stretching, reaching as they grew. Beans, too. The flowering of the vines produced a heavy set. It would be a bountiful year, unless . . . but one should not speak or even think of such things as the possibility of hail or grasshoppers.

The second hoeing of the cornfields was finished. Heron Woman was glad when it was over, because it was hard, exhausting work. She would have been too tired, she thought, to accept Beaver's advances even had it been within the rule of the Pani marriage. Beaver was tired, too, of course. Everyone was, during the second hoeing. The weeds were always tougher and more resistant at this time. It was good, Heron thought, that everyone was tired. There would be less notice that in the living area of Heron Woman and her husband there was no lovemaking.

She was very conscious of this. They had told no one of her tryst with the stranger. She could not have explained her reluctance to do so. It was her right as a woman to make such a choice. There were probably women who would boast of having taken advantage of the opportunity that the strangers' visit offered.

Now it was time for the summer hunt. Most of the men would go, and many of the women. Especially young women with no small children, and those whose children were old enough to be of assistance. She would be expected to go, and she looked forward to it. It would be a diversion while she waited for the coming of her menses. Then her life would be back to normal, and she and Beaver would not have the obstacle that now kept them apart.

The hunt was good. The scouts had found many buffalo grazing on the lush grasses of the surrounding valley. The same rains that nourished the crops had made the prairie grasses heavy and nutritious. It would be a good year, one to remember.

There were those who attributed the fine season to the visit of the strange outsiders and their obviously powerful medicine. No one had ever seen a mere man control large animals like the elk-dogs. Of course, there were others who insisted that the good year had been *in spite of* the presence of the outsiders. Still another faction felt that, strange and powerful as the visitors had seemed, their power could not compare with that of Morning Star and his Pani priests. Had the strangers not departed in some confusion, and arguing among themselves? Ah! You see?

Heron Woman had no opinion about this. She dreamed sometimes about her romantic interlude with the stranger. Sometimes she would waken and lie there thinking for a moment, wondering if it *had* actually happened, or if it had been all a dream.

No, it must have been real. She could remember the sensation of his facial fur on her cheek, and the firm yet gentle touch of his hands. It *did* happen, or she would not have told Beaver, and gone into the period of separation from him that was so frustrating.

Well, only a little longer. The moon was growing fatter each night, and would soon be full. Her time would arrive, and the cycle would be over, and it would be as before between her and Beaver.

But the moon became full and began to wane and nothing had happened yet. She tried to tell herself that it was because of the heavy activity. Hoeing of the corn, butchering, skinning, drying meat. Yet that would not account for her sudden episodes of irritability, sometimes followed by tears. Or for her bouts of nausea when she rose too quickly in the mornings. In her heart, she knew. . . .

"Should your time not have come just before the full moon?" Beaver asked one night.

"That is true," Heron admitted. "But we have been working hard. Maybe I have been too busy to start. Anytime now . . ."

But nothing happened, except that she became more moody and her tendency to nausea in the mornings became worse. She became impatient with Beaver when he showed concern, and sometimes burst into tears over nothing when she was alone.

"What is it?" he asked one day, noticing a tear in her eye.

Heron flew into a rage. "If you do not know, how can I tell you?" she shouted at him. She stalked away, swinging her body indignantly.

Ah, how can a woman express so many things merely by the way she walks? Pride, anger, sensuality, any other emotion, merely by the swing of her hips. It must be something with which she is born, because she is a woman. What chance has a mere man against such power?

There are other things about a woman's walk, too. Some are noticed only by other women, especially older women. Sometimes even before a young woman herself realizes she is with child, the old women are nodding to themselves and sometimes telling each other: *"Yes, that one . . ."*

Heron Woman finally realized that she should seek the counsel of an experienced woman. Not her own mother. Somehow she did not want to start there. Later, she would enjoy sharing her secrets with her mother, but for now, someone else. She had always been close to Fox Woman, her mother's sister. This aunt, a little older, had been a source of advice, wry humor, a comfort in time of trouble, and some-

times even an ally in mischief. Yes, she would talk to Fox Woman.
There were questions she must ask.

It was a day or two before she could draw her aunt aside for a
private conversation. Even then, she did not know how to begin. After several false starts, Fox Woman took charge of the conversation.

"Yes, Heron, tell me. What is it? You are pregnant?"

"What? How . . . how did you know?"

"Ah, child, what else? You and Beaver have been acting
strangely. You cry easily, tire easily. The way you walk . . ."

"The way I *walk*?"

"Of course. That is the first thing an old woman sees."

"But *how*? How is it different?"

Fox Woman shrugged. "I cannot describe it, child. But you
watch. You will see. A little different slant of her body, a bit more
aware of her belly, even before it begins to grow. You cannot see it in
yourself, of course. But no matter, now. Here! Come and sit with me.
Tell me about it. What is it that bothers you, child?"

Heron blurted out her story, all the details about the timing of
the full moon, and her mood swings, her irritation with Beaver. She
did not mention yet about the handsome stranger, though she could
not have said why.

Fox Woman nodded as the story unfolded, a pleased smile on
her face.

"Yes . . . yes . . . of course! See, it is as I said. I am made to
think that you are with child. Now, let us see when. The last full
moon? Not the one just past?" She was counting on her fingers. "Ah,
yes! About the Moon of Awakening, after the Moons of Snows and
Hunger. It is good! You will join the new life of the season with one
of your own."

Heron, on the stone ledge where they sat, said nothing. She
stared at the ground, head down.

"What is it, child? Do you fear this?" asked her aunt.

"What? No, no. It is not that. . . . I . . . I . . . Fox, it is not
Beaver's child!"

Her aunt laughed, loud and long. "Ah! So *that* was the cause
for Beaver's moods. But who? How is it that no one knew?"

"We have told no one. Fox, it was only once, and I thought it
unlikely. . . ."

"Wait! Only once? Why? Heron, when a woman chooses another man for a moon, she should . . . ah, a *forbidden* man?"

"No, no, not a relative, Fox. I would not do that!"

"I thought not. Then, something was wrong?"

"No . . . Fox, it was one of the hairfaced strangers. He was gone, the next day."

The older woman's jaw dropped.

"One of those . . . *aiee!* Which one?"

"The one on the spotted elk-dog. I do not know his name."

"Ah, I remember *that* one. A handsome man. Heron, you did well!"

"But Fox, I will never see him again. There will be no one to support the child!"

"True. But do not worry about that. There is much honor and prestige in bearing the child of one of those. Do you suppose it will have fur on its face?"

Heron was irritated at her aunt's flippant attitude. She said nothing.

"Does Beaver know?" Fox Woman asked.

"He knows about the man. We have not been together since. Maybe he suspects about the child. I have put him off, but he probably knows."

"Ah, this does explain his moods. But he will be good about it, Heron. He is a good husband."

"That is true. But I should probably tell him."

"Yes. Heron, this is exciting! You are probably the only woman of the People to be honored in this way. I know of no others."

"No others who were with one of the hairfaces?" Heron asked.

"No. There are one or two, that I know of. They are boasting. You have not heard? But no, I meant with child. I know of no other."

Heron was not certain yet that this was an honor she would relish. It was a very complicated situation, and she was not sure of Beaver's reaction. Aside from his teasing comment about a child's support, that possibility had not been mentioned. She must talk with him.

"Fox," she requested, "I would be grateful if you would say nothing about this yet. I would talk with Beaver first."

"Of course, child. I understand. But you will wish to tell him soon."

"That is true. He once asked who would support such a child."

"Ah, then you *have* talked?"

"No, that was when I first told him about it. That I had been with another. But he was joking. Neither of us suspected then."

"I see. Yes, I am made to think that Beaver deserves to know. I will say nothing until you tell me."

Heron felt better. It was good to share her questions and her feelings with another woman. She would plan how to tell her husband now. That would not be easy.

They rose from the rock where they had been sitting, and Fox Woman spoke again.

"Heron, tell me," she said, her eyes sparkling with mischief. "This handsome hairface of yours . . . *was he good?*"

6

I t was not easy to approach Beaver with her news. Heron could, of
course, choose her time and place. She selected an evening when
the day's heat was giving way to cooler twilight. The stars were
beginning to appear, and the south breeze was stirring gently, promising a comfortable night.

"Let us walk," Heron suggested.

They strolled out of the cluster of lodges, westward a little way
along the crest of the hill overlooking the river. From the trees below
came the cry of a night bird, and downstream a raccoon whickered
softly.

"Here, sit." Heron pointed to the rocky ledge where she and
Fox Woman had talked.

The two sat, close together, watching one star after another
become noticeable against the darkening sky. It was always an event
that fascinated her.

"Look, there is another. . . . And there . . ."

"Heron," said Beaver finally, "you did not bring me here just to
count stars."

"That is true."

"Nor to make love," he suggested.

Heron was silent. She did not know how to approach her subject.

"So," Beaver went on, "you have something else to tell me. You are pregnant, maybe?"

Heron gasped. "How . . . Fox Woman told you?"

"No, no! But what else could it be? You have not started . . . *aiee!* Fox Woman knows? Who else?"

"No one, Beaver. I had to talk to a woman. I . . . ." She found herself without words.

Her husband, too, sat silent for a little while. Finally, he spoke, slowly and thoughtfully.

"Heron, I must tell you how I feel, and I do not know, myself. I have missed you, of course."

"I, too—" Heron blurted, but he held up a hand to stop her.

"Let me go on. We have missed each other, then. There are other things to think of here. The support of the child . . . I thought I was only teasing you when I spoke of that, before."

"I know. I thought so, too."

"I will support it, of course."

Tears came to her eyes, and she could not speak.

"I am made to think," Beaver went on, "that you have accomplished a very special thing. I know of no other. There are two women who boast of having bedded with the visitors, but none except you is with child."

"That is what Fox Woman told me."

"So, Heron . . . among all the People, only *our* child will carry the blood of the strange visitors. All women will envy you!"

She had not thought of it in that way. But, if this was to be Beaver's attitude, maybe . . . Heron began to feel a sense of pride in accomplishment.

"You really think so, Beaver?"

"Of course. Heron, I am made to think that this is one of the most important events among the People for many lifetimes. I am proud of you."

She leaned her head against him, tears flowing freely now.

"Do you think," Beaver asked mischievously, "that it will have fur upon its face?"

.   .   .

There was much discussion in the village when the fact of Heron's pregnancy became public. A great honor, most considered the circumstance. Not only to Heron Woman and in turn to her family, but to the People, the whole town.

There were detractors, of course. One of the women who claimed to have bedded with the strangers refused to believe it at all.

"Heron is pregnant by her own husband," the woman jeered. "Nothing more. She lies! She was not even with one of the visiting warriors. If she had been, she would have told it at once."

Fox Woman was indignant. "You are the liar!" she accused. "*You* are not even pregnant, so who are you to talk?"

"We will see," sneered the other woman. "I will believe it when I see the facial fur on her child!"

This opened an entirely new subject of discussion and argument. It was generally conceded that such a child might not have facial fur as a newborn, but might acquire it later. Some men of the People were hairier than others. As was the custom, Pani men plucked their facial hair with clamshell tweezers. And this was seldom necessary before the age of thirteen or fourteen summers, anyway.

But might it not start earlier, to produce a shaggy crop like that of some of the visitors? And the body hair of some . . .

"Do you suppose," someone suggested, "that their *women* are hairy, too?"

This was a sobering thought. One that led to many questions that could not be answered, and to a whole assortment of ribald jokes. It would go on, Heron realized, until the baby was born. Probably, a new wave of discussion would begin then. Sometimes she felt that the honor connected with the child she carried was not worth the gossip and jokes and doubting speculation. She wished that she could simply forget the whole thing.

That, of course, was not possible. The fullness in her belly, though it did not really show yet . . . the tenderness in her breasts . . . her mood swings, from laughter to tears to anger for no apparent cause. . . . All of these things told her that she was now committed to this experience.

Heron did regret that there were those who thought she lied. That was a hurtful thing. In a way, she wished that this *was* Beaver's child. Then there would be none of this public discussion, debate, and speculation. Only the few expected ribald jokes. But it was too late to think of that.

The Red Moon of summer passed, more hot, sticky, and misera-
ble than usual, even. She longed for the cooler weather of autumn. It
was one of her favorite times of the year, with the colors of the tall
grasses turning to reddish and yellow and pink, and waterfowl starting south in long lines across the sky. The flowers of autumn bloomed
in profusion, gold and purple in contrast to the gentler colors of
spring. The warm, hazy days and cool nights, the smells of autumn
. . . and this would surely be one to remember, marked by her pregnancy.

The morning sickness was better now, and her moods not so
unpredictable. Once her mind and body had become accustomed to
the idea, and she was sure of Beaver's reaction, she felt much better.
There was a feeling of anticipation, a longing to finish what was
started, and to bring this new life into the world. What would it look
like? The moons ahead seemed very long.

Fox Woman laughed at her over this. "Heron," she reminded,
"you are nearly halfway through the pregnancy. Have you felt it move
yet?"

"No, I do not think so."

"Well, at any time!"

It was true. Only a few days later she was sure. She realized
that the tiny flutter that she had noticed from time to time had meaning. While she had thought it only the squirming of her bowel, she
now understood. *That was it!* She tried to remember when she first
noticed. Maybe half a moon ago! No matter. Now she knew.

Days were shorter now. The squirrels in the timber along the river
were frantically hurrying to store nuts and acorns. Some said that
would tell how heavy the winter to come. Heron wondered if the
creatures simply store more nuts in a season when there *are* more nuts.
But then, is such a *season,* with bountiful crops of nuts and other seeds,
itself a sign of hard moons to come? Surely there was some meaning
in the whole sequence. She would let the holy men worry about it.
Maybe the stars would tell them.

It *was* a hard winter. Heavy snows drifted over the village, and it was
difficult to get from one lodge to another. There was no reason to do

so anyway. There were enough people, some fifty in each of the big half-buried structures, to provide social contact.

Twice the snows were so heavy, and the drifting so bad, that no one could get out at all. For several days each time, day and night could only be told by the square patch of sky at the smoke hole. The doorway, when the hanging skins were pushed aside, revealed only a vertical wall of white.

Each time, after the blizzard subsided and the smoke hole turned from gray to blue, the People tunneled out. The sun on snow was blinding after days and nights in darkness, but it was good.

The Moon of Long Nights, the Moon of Snows, and now the Moon of Hunger. There was no real danger this season, because supplies were plentiful. The People had taken an example from the squirrels, and stored in abundance. Still, it would be a relief to see the end of the winter season. There was always the possibility of an unexpected late winter storm. If that happened, supplies *could* become scarce very quickly. The Moon of Hunger could become a reality. It had, in past generations, earned its name.

The Moon of Awakening was heralded by a few warm days, the beginning of a new year for the people of the prairie. Buds began to swell on the trees, and the willows along the smaller streams began to stir into life. The color of their twigs seemed to change from dull gray-green to bright greenish yellow overnight.

And the blanket of snow began to melt. A wet puddle here and there, rivulets running across the smooth surface and cutting tiny canyons. All of these small streams joining as they flowed downhill, becoming larger. The tinkling voices of the smaller tributaries joined in a louder chorus and swelled to a shout as the combined streams rushed down the slope to pour into the river.

The river's ice, which had been safe to walk upon until now, was rotten and treacherous. But the sky was clear and bright, and the long lines of geese headed back to the north, honking their way to faraway unknown lands.

And Heron Woman was very pregnant. Large and ungainly, she was becoming impatient now. When would this end? Fox Woman had estimated the Moon of Awakening, and that time was here.

But still she seemed to grow every day. She moved clumsily and with difficulty, off balance and unsure. It was a task to sit or to get up, and there was no comfortable position for sleep. Her legs, long and slender and curving attractively at the proper places, had been a matter of pride for her. Now they looked fat and ugly. She could not see them well around the bulging of her belly, but she could tell that her ankle bones were invisible, buried in the puffy flesh that covered them. They were painful to the slightest pressure.

"Prop them up on something," her mother advised. "I had that with you."

Others had other ideas. "Drink more water," Fox Woman said curtly. "It will wash away the fat ankles."

That made no sense to Heron. None of it did, but she tried both bits of advice. She could not really tell which might have been effective, and could not see that either made any remarkable change.

"It will not be much longer now," Fox Woman assured her.

That would certainly be good, thought Heron. She was sure that when she sat on a flat surface, she was sitting on the child's head, it seemed so low.

"Women of our family have easy birthing," Fox told her another time.

"It is good," Heron retorted angrily, "but what good is that until I can *start*?"

7

Heron woke in the night. She had not slept well. Not for two or three moons, it seemed. She changed positions a time or two, but all were uncomfortable. Her belly was so full now. Maybe she should go and empty her bladder, but she hated the thought. It seemed like a major effort to rise and go outside, only to return to her bed and the lack of comfort that she now felt constantly. Well, she must do *something*.

She sighed deeply, rolled over and rose to hands and knees, struggling to stand. Beside her, Beaver stirred and settled back, disturbed for only a moment. The lodge was dark, the fire down to a few coals. The square of sky above it was pale with the coming dawn.

Just as she stood, there was an unexpected sensation in her abdomen. She put both hands on it, and was startled to feel the texture. Hard as a rock. For some time, she had noticed that the now-prominent bulge varied, sometimes soft and sometimes hard and firm. But it had never been like this! Still, could it be? *Is this how it starts?* she wondered.

But just then, the bulge of her belly softened again. There was nothing unusual about the way she felt. Except, of course, for the clumsiness. She feared that she would never again enjoy the lithe grace that she once had. She walked to the doorway, feeling heavy and poorly balanced. She had just pulled aside the inner doorskin when she felt her belly harden again. Startled, she placed a palm on the rounded surface. *Yes . . . hard . . . rocklike*, through the tight-stretched skin. *This must be it!*

Heron turned back. No, she should go on to empty her bladder. *Then* back to alert Fox Woman, who would act as midwife. She struggled against the pressure that she now felt. Instinct told her to stand still or lie down until it was past, but she stepped outside and straightened in the morning air. There was a red glow in the east, and it was light enough to see the mounded tops of the other lodges. As she moved toward the designated area the hardness faded again and she hurried on.

It was on her way back to the lodge that her water burst, showering her inner thighs and legs with warm fluid. She giggled nervously at the unfamiliar sensation, and quickly moved on. At least, it had not happened in their bed.

Someone had placed small sticks on the coals from last night's fire, and the new flames were lighting the lodge. Instead of going to the area of her bed, hers and Beaver's, Heron turned toward the area occupied by Fox Woman and her husband. Fox quickly awoke when Heron spoke.

"Fox . . . wake up! I am made to think it is my time!"

The older woman rolled quickly out of her robes, mumbling questions.

"When? How?"

"My water has burst." Heron paused as her belly hardened again. "Here, feel."

Fox placed a hand on the hard surface and uttered an exclamation.

"Ah! Of course! We must get ready!"

The woman flew around the lodge, moving people and possessions and hanging robes to curtain off an area for the event.

The contractions were coming more strongly now, and with more discomfort. *But I want it to stop now!* Heron thought in a moment of panic. It was good to have Fox Woman with her, serious and intense yet still joking, coaxing, reassuring, steady.

·   ·   ·

Finally it was over. There was a cry of protest from the newcomer at his rude introduction to this new and colder world. Fox Woman tied the cord and slashed it in two, wrapping the infant in a soft skin to place him on Heron's now-flatter belly.

"A boy!" Fox chortled. "And no facial fur! Ah, are you glad he was not wearing his father's metal hat?"

"He is beautiful!" Heron said softly. "But does he not look much like babies of the People?"

"What did you expect?" Fox retorted. "Do not all babies look much alike?"

"No, not this one," Heron assured her. "This one is special. And look, Fox! Does not his hair appear curly?"

"Maybe. But it is wet, Heron."

"But hair is not curly. On a buffalo, maybe, but not on people."

"Wait!" Fox Woman said thoughtfully. "Was it not that some of the strangers had hair that was curly? Did you notice that of yours?"

"No . . . I . . . it was dark, Fox."

"But you saw him before that."

"Yes . . . I am made to think he wore his hat before, though." Fox laughed. "Did he wear his hat? . . . No, never mind."

"No, he did not!" Heron snapped.

"But you did not notice if his hair was curly?"

"No. Does it matter?"

"Maybe not. But there will be those who try to say that he is not from a union with the strangers."

"I do not care, Fox. He is mine. *Ours,* and he is the most beautiful child ever born."

"Of course. Here, put him to breast. Come here, Curly, have your first food!"

It is of such incidents and chance remarks that names and nicknames are born. The child became "Curly."

There were those, of course, who did not accept the lineage of this child. The curly hair was dismissed as an accident, a variation from the usual. Are not the facial features of one person different from another? Their height and body build? Some have darker or lighter skin color, too. No, this was the child of Heron Woman and Beaver, they insisted. Nothing more.

It did not matter to Heron, happy with the joy of her baby. She knew, and Beaver knew, and Fox Woman was eager to handle any argument that arose about the child's parentage. Most people accepted her interpretation, and there was indeed a measure of prestige for Heron's child.

It was several years before anything could be determined about facial hair. Even then, there seemed to be no spectacular difference as the boy attained puberty. His body was not excessively hairy, but then that had been true of some of the strangers.

Like the other young men of his age, the boy learned to pluck his facial hair. His head was shaved as he ceremonially came to manhood, and he learned to dress the scalp lock with tallow and paint. It was drawn into the horn-shaped projection that identified him as a man of the Pani, the Horn People. This, of course, obscured the fact that his hair had remained curly.

Even so, the name stuck. He had remained Curly through childhood and adolescence. Though it was usual to change a name as a child entered a new part of his life, this name seemed to fit, and there appeared no urgent reason to change it.

The young man maintained his prestige by his actions and skills, and it was acknowledged by all that there was something special about him. Here was a potential leader, a man of whom the Pani might be proud.

It was many seasons before more of the hairfaced strangers visited the village. The connection of the son of Heron to such visitors was remembered, but no longer carried the importance that it once had.

But times were changing. The sight of wild horses on the prairie was not uncommon. Some of the nomadic peoples were using them in the hunt and to transport the covers and poles of their skin lodges.

In another generation or two the People still remembered a prominent man called Curly. And some of his descendants were proud when their children's hair exhibited this trait.

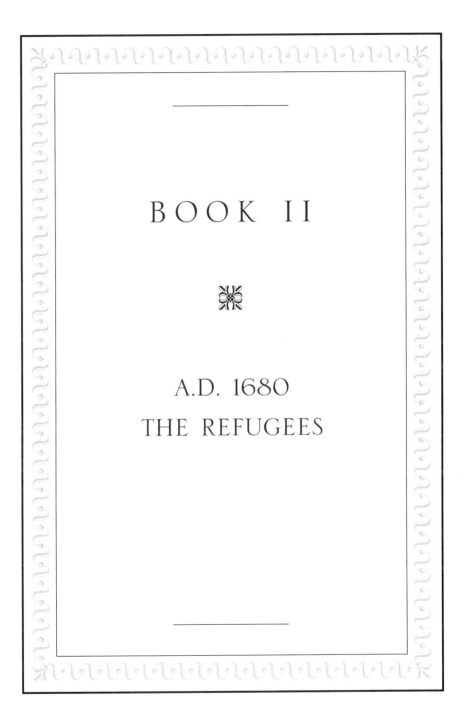

BOOK II

❁

A.D. 1680
THE REFUGEES

1

No one had spoken for some time. There was no special reason. It was only that there was no need. This was a time of comfort and fellowship.

It was warm in the kiva, and Magpie was pleased with the day. He watched a swirl of bluish smoke. It writhed in the shaft of sunlight that shone down through the hole in the roof and across the floor near the ladder. A lazy, drowsy day . . .

He discovered that his pipe had gone out, and rose to knock the dottle out into the fire. He refilled and relighted the pipe and sat down again next to Spider, who was weaving on a small loom in front of him. The design was beginning to form, a pattern in the earthy tones of the fibers Spider was using. Magpie nodded in wordless approval and Spider grunted in acknowledgment of the compliment.

Magpie looked on around the room at the familiar faces. He was somewhat younger than most of the men. It had been a few seasons since he came of age and entered into the loose brotherhood of the kiva. Well, more seasons than he realized, he now thought. His own children were growing up rapidly. Rabbit must be ten, maybe eleven! Ah, time passes . . .

Around the circle in the kiva there sat about a dozen men today. Not by any intent. It was only that these were the ones who had happened to drop in. It was a retreat from the cares of the world, a symbolic return to the womb of Earth. A chance to smoke, to talk, and enjoy the fellowship of the other men.

Old Painted Rock, an elder of the Turtle clan, could always be counted on to be present. It was joked that he *lived* in the kiva. That was understandable, Magpie thought. A man with so sharp-tongued a wife as that of Painted Rock would need a place of retreat.

There were other regulars. Face Like the Sun, Limping Coyote . . . Coyote was well along in years, and had great stories. He was the man who had been designated to lead the war party the last time the village had been involved in a conflict. It was long ago, before Magpie was old enough to remember. The People, normally peaceable by nature, had become tired of annual raids by their more warlike neighbors. It could not be tolerated, the loss of the hard-earned crops of corn and beans and pumpkins.

They had planned carefully, and set up an ambush. Ah, how many times he had heard old Coyote tell of the cleverness of it. The surprise had been complete, and the enemy had retreated in confusion. It had lent great prestige to Coyote and to the Brotherhood of the Bow. There had been no trouble since.

Across the circle sat Stargazer, the Galaxy Priest. He could see and feel things in the movements of the stars that were beyond the understanding of most. To his left, Snake, elder of the Bird Society. Others . . . Blue Corn, Little Tree . . . all the familiar faces that one might see in the kiva on a warm spring day. *Life is good,* reflected Magpie.

He was concerned a little bit, and he knew others were, too, about some of the stories that filtered out of areas where the Spanish had settled. It was hard to understand, especially at a distance, what these outsiders wanted and why they behaved so strangely. The Spanish holy men seemed to have a bizarre idea that everyone should think and worship exactly as they did. Magpie did not see how this could be, or why. He had had little personal contact, although there were parties of Spanish horsemen in the area. His own village had not been affected much, being somewhat removed from events at larger towns like Taos.

Theirs was not a town as large or as well known as that of

Taos. Magpie had been there once. Many people . . . he remembered the beauty of the place, and the way the clear stream divided the town in half. It was unique, too, in the way the houses were stacked one atop the other. Taos Pueblo, the Spanish called it now.

There was another place, too, where the Spanish had built a town. Large houses, several of them, it was said, at a place they called Sennafay. They did not even live in these houses, though, but used them to gather in. Like a kiva, maybe, but above ground. Magpie was mildly interested in all of this, but it was far away and of no concern.

Still, in the back of his mind came a nagging whisper of warning sometimes. If a man believes that everyone must think exactly as he does (a preposterous idea), how far will he go? It would be a great bother to have someone want to argue about such a thing. Ah, well . . . in the unlikely event that he was ever faced with this, he would simply refuse to listen. *I think as I think,* he would say. *You cannot tell me what I think.*

He relighted his pipe again and shifted his position to let the sun warm his back more easily. A good day. . . . The air was still damp from a gentle rain last evening. A warm, slow, soaking rain, a female rain, as opposed to a noisy man rain with thunder and lightning. This one carried nourishment and helped prepare the ground for the planting soon to come.

Across the circle, Limping Coyote began a retelling of his story of the ambush of the enemy raiders. Everything seemed as it should be.

There were voices outside, and a man swung a leg over the ladder and started down into the kiva. It was No Tail Lizard, who dropped the last step or two and turned to the seated men.

"Ah, my brothers, some of the Prairie People come!"

"Are they here?" someone asked.

"No, no! Still a day away. They will be here tomorrow, maybe."

He took out his short pipe, filled and lighted it, and joined the circle.

The coming of the buffalo hunters from the plains had become almost an annual event. They brought furs to trade with the Spanish, whom they called the Metal People, for knives and arrowpoints and other goods. The traders were welcome because they also brought small gifts and dried meat and robes to trade for corn and meal and beans. Most of this was merely gift trading, but it was an amusing and interesting diversion. It was well understood that the primary purpose of the pack train was to trade with the Spanish.

"Is it Red Sunset?" asked someone.

Lizard shrugged. "Who knows? They are too far away yet. Probably. But they all look alike anyway, no?"

A chuckle ran around the circle, and there was a relaxed silence for a little while. Almost every spring for several years the same party from the plains had paused here. Friendships had arisen. It would be good to see Red Sunset, thought Magpie, and to hear news from other places. It was always a time of storytelling, too. The two groups had entirely different stories. At the time of Creation they had come into the world in different ways. Both from inside the earth, up into the sunlight . . .

But the Prairie People told of being summoned from the earth by one of their deities, a mischievous being they called the Old Man. He sat astride a hollow cottonwood log that jutted from the earth, and pounded on the log with a drumstick. Each time he struck, another human being crawled through. There was a joke in that story, too. A fat woman, it was said, got stuck in the log, and no more could come through, so theirs had always been a small tribe.

The storytellers of the village always responded with their own Creation stories. Not only that of the climb out of the *sinapu,* the "Hole," but other stories, too. Why the Coyote's eyes are yellow . . . how the People stole fire from the Sun . . . how Man was given the gift of corn. . . . It was always an interesting time, the exchange of stories. Tomorrow they would do so again, maybe, unless the Prairie People were in too much of a hurry. Surely they would take time, though, to visit and smoke and tell stories. Everyone loves a good story, no?

Except the Spanish, of course. That was a puzzling thing. Their storytellers were their holy men, who loved to gather a large crowd of listeners and tell their Creation stories. Magpie had not seen one of these gatherings, but there were many tales of odd incidents in some of the other towns.

A dark-robed priest of the Spanish, it was said, had gone to a small town north of Taos to tell his stories. They were good stories, too, said people who had been there. One of the Spanish gods had made a figure of a man out of mud and caused it to come to life. Then he made a woman out of one of the man's ribs. These were First Man and First Woman.

There was more to the story, too, according to those who had been present. It was very complicated. The god became angry at the man and his wife and drove them away. Yet much later, when there were many more people, that same god married one of their women and had a son, who became a most important man.

Yet now came the strangest part of this thirdhand account. The Spanish holy man had finished his story, or had at least paused. The local storyteller rose to thank him and congratulate him on a good story, as would be the custom.

"And here is *ours*. The People lived in caverns deep in the earth, and there was no sunlight—"

But at that point, the Spanish holy man had flown into a terrible rage, and had screamed at the listeners in his own tongue. He had been very impolite, and had refused to listen to any of their stories at all. Naturally, the listeners rose and departed. How can one deal with the embarrassment of such rudeness? Who can even understand it?

Some said that the minds of the Spanish had been poisoned by the yellow metal-rocks that they craved. They seemed to place far more importance on such ore than it deserved. The metal was pretty, but not very useful. It was too soft to cut with, and too scarce to use for arrowpoints.

There were stories about it, nonsense stories that had become mixed with the tales about the Foolish People. Foolish People stories were for the young, of course, to instruct by bad example. Yet it was easy to change such a story slightly, and adults always enjoyed such a tale anyway.

A man had a horse that was worthless. In the original, he convinced a man of the Foolish People that the swayback and spavined legs were desirable, and that a horse needs only one eye anyway. His teeth? Ah, a horse with few teeth eats less, so is easier to keep, no? So he made a good trade. But, in the new version, the owner of the horse approaches a Spaniard. The real value of this horse, he explains, is that it defecates not dung, but gold nuggets. The Spaniard gives virtually all his possessions to acquire such a horse, and everyone is happy.

But that was only a story. Magpie was uneasy about some of the odd and illogical actions attributed to the Spaniards. He could not have said why. The People of this town had had infrequent contact with them anyway, so it should be of no concern. Or should it?

No matter . . . he would much rather think of the pleasure that the visit of the Prairie People would bring tomorrow. *They* understood the proper exchange of stories. Maybe they would have some new ones from neighbors of theirs far away along the ancient trail that led here across the plains and mountains.

2

It seemed a short visit, the time spent with the party from the prairie. There were five men, counting the young son of Red Sunset, leader of the group. Two of the wives accompanied them.

As usual, the Prairie People brought small gifts to show their goodwill. Arrowpoints of flint from their own area, furs of small creatures unknown here, a bit of tobacco, a very important gift because it is a thing of the spirit.

And they talked of the weather, the hunting of the Prairie People and the crops of those here. They exchanged stories and the women talked of women things and the evening was good.

In the several seasons they had met in this way they had learned some of the languages, each of the other. In addition, the people from the prairie used a system of hand signs that made communication easier. In their own country, and farther north and east, they had said, all tribes and nations used these gestures. Such use was spreading with the increased contact, and it was relatively easy to learn the signs.

The next day the visitors departed and the People returned to the routine of the village. Planting time was near, and there was much to do.

·   ·   ·

It was on their return trip half a moon later that the visitors stopped again. This time they bore news of importance. The Spanish in Sennafay had seized several of the holy men in the area and had put them in cages in one of the buildings there.

"But *why*?"

"We do not know," Sunset told them. "It was very strange. A test of power, maybe. The Spanish holy men caused it, I am made to think. You know, the ones with the dark robes who wear the fetish like this. . . ."

He raised crossed forefingers to illustrate. "The warriors of the Spanish tied the captives' hands and dragged them off."

"Ah! To treat a holy man so?"

"Yes! We were told it was *because* they were holy men. The Spanish holy men seemed to have no respect for these. This is why we thought that it must be to show the power of their own spirit-gifts."

"But," argued old Crane, "to use warriors shows nothing of their spirit-gifts' power."

"That is true. These are strange times, my friends. We were glad to leave when we finished trading."

It was the very next morning that a messenger arrived, verifying the news. He had more details. Yes, it was as the Prairie People had said. The Spanish had imprisoned several holy men, merely for *being* holy men and for giving instruction to their own people.

"The Spanish holy men want no instruction but theirs," the messenger related. "None at all! They are saying that all other holy men are evil."

"They want everyone to pray alike?" asked Magpie. "How could that be?"

The messenger shrugged. "That is what they say. There is no good but that of their god. All else is evil. Everyone must pray to their god, and to his mother."

"Does their god know about growing corn?" someone asked.

There was a nervous chuckle around the circle. Without the appropriate rituals and prayers, crops surely would not prosper.

"Well, they will not come here, will they? We can still plant in our own way."

The messenger shook his head in doubt. "Who knows? Their ways are very strange."

Magpie thought about it for a long time after the messenger left. There was much that the Spanish had brought that was good. It had been many generations since they came, with horses and metal tools and sheep and cattle, to build at the place they called Sennafay. They had been there since the time of Magpie's father, and before.

He did not understand why times were changing so. Maybe because there were more of them, more Spaniards. In several places, it was said, a family or two had built houses and shelters for their animals out away from the Spanish towns. He wondered if there were so many Spanish now that they needed more space. They had settlements near most of the larger towns like Taos.

It was only a short stretch of thought to wonder if now they would come here. So far, Spanish contact with the town of Magpie's people had been limited. It was small, it was off the main trails, and isolated. The People were not antisocial, but they had always depended much on the old ways and were slow to change because although they worked hard their life was good. Probably, he decided, the village had simply been ignored. But now with times changing, would there be more contact?

The thing that really bothered him, maybe, was that of the holy men. He had heard of the stories of the Spanish priests and how they demanded that people listen. He had heard some of their stories from people of other towns who had followed the way of the Spanish gods. Some carried the crossed-stick fetish like that of the Spanish holy men.

Their god, it was said, had married that human female, though she had a husband also. She bore a child who was half-god and half-human, and she was called the Mother of God.

Then when the half-god grew up he was killed by his own people, fastened to a structure like the crossed-stick fetish. Why this had happened was unclear. Some power struggle, Magpie supposed, though the killing of one's own would be completely unacceptable to the People.

But then came the miracle in the story. After three days, the spirit of this god-man, which had crossed over, *came back*, and he recovered!

Well, it must be admitted that this would indicate great power, a very powerful medicine. Magpie wondered some about how a body could recover from three days of rotting and still function. It implied strong magic. But what about the rules against touching the dead? The People had strict customs against this. Either the Spanish did not, or somehow these taboos had been canceled when their god recovered. Would his flesh have been restored? Ah, it was too complicated to think about.

Yet the biggest mystery of all remained. Why would the Spanish holy men insist that no other story be told? They had a good story. Yet did they have no confidence in it, so that they *feared* the stories of others? If what the trading party had said was true, the local holy men had been put in cages merely for telling their own stories, those of their own people. The whole thing made his head hurt to think about it.

The days passed, the corn grew tall. Little more was heard for a while of the doings in Sennafay. Maybe it was because the People were busy with the crops. Other villages were also. Still, there was an occasional bringer of news. There had been a few incidents.

A detachment of Spanish soldiers had stopped a ceremony at one of the kivas south of Taos, and taken one of the holy men prisoner. They burned the roof of the kiva to make it collapse. This was an insult to the Kachinas, of course, and there was a great dread of what might happen. The spirit-power of offended gods was unpredictable.

"Has anything bad happened yet?" asked Lizard uneasily.

"Not that we know," the messenger answered. "But, what may be caused by this, and what might have happened anyway?"

The men nodded. The storm a few days ago . . . a vicious male storm, with lightning and loud thunder and wind and hail that had damaged the crops . . . one should not offend the gods!

"But *we* were not responsible for that," protested one of the younger men.

"That is true," agreed an older and wiser man, "but when such power is released in anger, everyone will suffer."

It may have been only coincidence that there were two incidents that summer and fall involving skinwalkers. A young girl who had ventured outside after dark to retrieve a forgotten toy encountered a man she did not know. He stared at her for a moment with burning yellow eyes that frightened her. Then he dropped to all fours and changed into a wolf, who ran with supernatural speed into the night and disappeared. The terrified girl was questioned by the elders, and it was agreed that she must have seen a skinwalker.

In the other incident, a huge owl flew at a young man when he stepped outside. Again, it was after dark. He should have known better, it was said, because the spirits of darkness and evil travel then. But he *had* stepped out, and the bird struck at him, its eyes glaring into his and its talons raking at his face.

Terrified, he struck out with a stick of firewood he had just picked up. His blow struck solidly, and the owl fell, flopping in the dust.

People came running with a torch when the youth cried out. But there in the dust lay an old man, not a dying owl. The stranger rose stiffly, angrily accusing the youngster of attacking him. There was a bloody welt across his neck where it joined the shoulder.

The old man whirled and stalked off, still muttering to himself. There were those who later claimed that he had disappeared in front of their eyes *before* he reached the edge of the circle of firelight. However it had happened, he was gone. He had disappeared into the darkness. No one had recognized him as anyone they knew, and there was a concerted movement back into the relative safety of the houses. Most were certain that they had seen and heard a skinwalker. A few really wanted to deny it, but did not seem completely convinced.

As the light of the torch faded, Magpie had stooped to pick up an object from the ground at his feet. He said nothing to the others, because the shock was too great. There was no point, anyway, and people were hurrying back inside. They did not want to stop to discuss anything at the moment.

Magpie had raised his hand and opened it to let the thing be carried away on the gentle night breeze. He hoped devoutly not to see it again. It was a soft, fluffy feather, a breath-feather from the breast of a great hunting owl.

The moons passed, and there was a heavy uneasiness in the air, an expectation that bad things were about to happen. Messengers came more frequently from other towns, telling of atrocities by the Spaniards. More kivas had been destroyed in villages here and there. Still it had not come to the People of Magpie's town.

There were stories of resistance, or at least planned resistance. A young holy man called Popé was trying to establish communication with all the towns in the area. He was from Tewas Pueblo, but was now living in Taos, trying to persuade others to join his resistance movement.

The People were reluctant. Their town had not been bothered. By nature they were a peaceable people, not easily roused to violence. Yet this was true of all of the people of the pueblos.

"You will think differently when it comes to your kiva!" warned the messenger. "But no matter. We will keep you informed anyway. We are all brothers in this, no?"

They watched him depart, and the heart of Magpie was very heavy.

3

There came a time when the messenger trotted into the village with a very different look on his face.

"Call everyone to the kiva," he panted hoarsely. "Things have happened."

He was weary from long travel and seemed nearly ready to collapse. Streaks of sweat had made rivulets of mud through the dust on the skin of his face, neck, and chest. It was apparent that today he carried news of great importance.

It took only a little while for the men of the village to gather and to seat themselves in the circle of the kiva. The messenger had been given water to drink, and had sponged the dust of the trail from his face. His breath came more easily now.

"Everything has changed," he began, glancing around the circle at the attentive faces. "They have killed three of the holy men."

There was a murmur around the circle.

"Who? Popé has killed the Spanish priests? Where?"

"No, no, no!" the messenger said quickly. "They, the Spanish, have killed *ours,* with ropes."

He paused to take his hands and circle his own throat with his fingers.

"They put ropes around the necks of the holy men, and hung them from a tree."

There was a gasp of horror from the circle.

"But . . . their spirits . . . they were strangled?"

The messenger nodded. "Yes! It is as you say. Their spirits cannot escape to cross over."

A stunned silence settled for a moment over the kiva. Then old Painted Rock cleared his throat to speak, and everyone looked to him to voice wisdom.

"This is very bad, my friends. To kill a holy man is a bad thing anyway, and very dangerous. The Metal People should know that. But this other . . . such a thing has never been!"

"What will happen, Uncle?" asked Lizard. "To the spirits, I mean."

Painted Rock shrugged. "I do not know, my friends. The spirits are trapped. . . ."

"This is as Popé says," the messenger nodded agreement. "These spirits cannot escape from the bodies because of the rope around the neck at the time of death. They are caged in the rotting corpse!"

Magpie shuddered. Such a fate was unheard of.

"For how long?" he asked, and was startled at the thin huskiness of his own voice.

"No one knows," said Painted Rock. "This should not have happened."

The messenger nodded. "Popé says this may be *forever,*" he said dramatically.

"What is to be done?" asked Face Like the Sun.

"Now hear me. Popé has a plan. Nobody must do anything yet."

The very pose of his body now seemed to take on an air of conspiracy.

"This is the way it will be: When the time comes, *not before!* We will begin to kill all the Spaniards. We will destroy everything that they have brought to this, the land of our People."

"Everything?"

"Yes, so Popé is made to think."

"But some things are good. Metal tools, horses, sheep!"

"And this is the problem, Popé says," the messenger went on. "These things, which have seemed good, have made us forget the old ways."

"We must listen," said Painted Rock. "I am made to think that nothing this important has happened to the People since we crawled out of the Hole."

The messenger nodded. "It is as your elder says. Now . . . for now, we do nothing. We say nothing. We *know* nothing, if the Spanish ask. This is important, and could mean the lives of many of us. Wait for more news, which will come by messenger. But be ready."

"Ready for what?" asked Lizard.

"To kill Spaniards!" spoke the frustrated messenger. "What did you think?"

"But there are no Spanish here!" protested Lizard.

The messenger laughed, but it was an ugly laugh, without humor.

"There will be enough, my friend. Enough for all. The main battle will be at Sennafay, where their strength is. But when the day comes, we will kill *any,* anywhere."

"How will we know?"

"It is as I have said. You will have a message. Remember—for now, do *nothing.* It is important that it happen all at the same·day, everywhere."

"Will we have time to prepare? A day or two?"

"Oh, yes. More than that. Maybe half a moon. It will be well planned. And now, I must go on. There are others I must see, and tell."

The men left the kiva, and Magpie watched as the runner trotted on along the dim trail that led to the north. A great change was coming in the life of the People. At least, he was made to think so.

The shock and horror of the hanging of holy men by the Spanish had cast a shadow over the People. Over the entire area, actually. To kill someone, although not common among those peaceful agricultural people, was not unknown. Sometimes it was in defense of the crops, sometimes for other reasons. It might be justified.

But this . . . if the Spanish felt that they had reason to kill, they certainly had the power to do so. They had shown it many times.

While one might not argue with their reasons, it was the way of things. People live and die and it is the way of the world.

But this . . . surely to kill a holy man was a bad thing, as well as dangerous to the killer. And it seemed that these holy men had done no wrong. The Spanish merely wanted to stop them from teaching their own people. Such a thing was beyond understanding in itself. Then in addition, the worst of all, the manner of the deaths . . . strangling with a rope.

Magpie had developed a theory about that. If a holy man with much power in his gifts was killed, might not his spirit stay near to seek vengeance on his killers? Particularly if the killing was unjust? Maybe the Spanish recognized this. To protect themselves from such vengeful spirits, maybe they had taken this action. Death by strangulation . . . no chance for the spirit of the dying to come up out of the body and escape through mouth and nose to cross over. It might possibly be an effective defense against reprisal by the spirits, but would it really? The deed itself carried so much evil that Magpie doubted that this would control the vengeance that was due.

Messengers came more often now. Men were gathering in the mountains, preparing for the day when everyone would attack the Spanish in his own area. There would be a concerted push against Sennafay. The proper day would be decided by Popé, the holy man. On that day, everything Spanish was to be destroyed. The People would return to the old ways, and everything would be good again.

The situation remained tense in the days that followed. There were rumors and reports of more Spanish patrols, more destruction of kivas in other towns. Still it had not happened here. As a precaution, many of the objects that pertained to the ceremonies were hidden. The Kachinas, the garments worn by the Clowns in the dances.

Then, many things started to happen. A platoon of Spanish horsemen entered the village and rode to the kiva, where they proceeded in a very methodical way. They had done this before elsewhere. Two soldiers descended into the kiva with brush and tinder to start a fire. Others brought more fuel, and soon a greasy smoke began to billow through the hole in the roof. The men inside retreated up the ladder, and then pushed the ladder itself over toward the section of the roof that was beginning to burn.

The People, who had retreated to a safe distance, stood and watched, their faces expressionless. Nothing could be done. Their more precious religious objects were hidden. The kiva could be restored, with a new roof and a new ladder. The Hole in the ground could not be burned. It could be cleaned out later.

Magpie watched with anger and resentment. How could anyone try to destroy the religious belief of another? It could not be done, anyway, without killing the other. More to the point, why would anyone want to do such a thing? It made no sense to him at all. The kiva was still there. At least the excavation. To try to destroy it was futile, for it could be dug again. It was like the Hole that it symbolized, the *sinapu*. It would always be there, because it was a part of Creation. Its exact location was vague, but that did not matter. It was somewhere, and would remain for all eternity, despite efforts by the Spanish outsiders.

Magpie had talked of this whole situation with his wife. Some men, he knew, did not talk with their wives to any extent. But he and White Flower had always talked of many things. At most times he would rather be with her than with the men in the kiva, if it were not for the prestige of the kiva fraternity and the Societies. Well, he would not dwell on that. There were times, no matter how good a marriage, when it was only prudent for a husband to absent himself from the house and to retreat to the kiva. These are the things a man learns . . . how to discern when talk is futile, and absence more rewarding. . . . Such things are gained only through experience, and cannot be taught.

But in usual times, he did talk with White Flower, and her thoughts were often good. She, too, was concerned with the way times were changing.

"What will happen, Magpie?" she asked him one night after they retired. "Can they really kill all the Spanish?"

Apparently some of the other men talked to *their* wives, too. All the women knew of the plan by Popé, holy man of the Tewas. They had discussed it, as the men had.

"I do not know, Flower. But I am made to think this—men with weapons will not let themselves be killed easily. They will fight, and many on both sides will be killed."

"Will you join them?" she asked, cuddling provocatively against him.

"I do not know," he answered thoughtfully. "But I do not have to decide at this moment."

He gathered her in his arms.

Rumors continued to fly. There was a tension, a feeling in the air that it would not be long now.

There was one possibility that had been nearly forgotten. It came to mind with a jarring recall. The annual visit of the people from the prairie, Red Sunset and his train of pack horses, eager to trade with the Spanish.

"Ah, it is not a good time for them to be here," said old Painted Rock. "We must warn them."

The warning did little good. The Prairie People simply did not understand the seriousness of the actions of the Spanish.

"We have friends among them," protested Sunset. "The trading has been good for us and for them. They will not bother us. Gomez, the trader, will vouch for us."

They felt obligated at least to hint at the sort of trouble that was coming, but the visitors did not really understand.

"It will be a war," Coyote explained. "But you must say nothing. Even we will not know when until the time comes."

"But we are not involved," Red Sunset insisted. "We are not enemies of your people or of the Spanish. We will keep it that way."

"But," said Painted Rock as the visitors prepared to leave, "there will be many who do not know that. On both sides, maybe. You must be very careful."

"Of course, Uncle. We will be sure to do so."

They watched the Prairie People wend their way across the hills toward the Spanish stronghold, and Magpie wondered whether they would ever see them again.

The situation was looking worse by the day, and he saw nothing that could be done to avoid it. Many would be hurt and killed, no matter what. Worst of all, Magpie did not know, even now, what he would do when the time came.

4

Days passed, and the tension grew. Finally, when Magpie thought that they could wait no longer, there came another messenger. This one, however, carried the means to determine the day of the uprising. He took a knotted string made of twisted yucca fibers, and handed it to Sky Watcher, leader of the Clowns. The Clown, being close to things of the spirit, would bear the responsibility of keeping the string and interpreting the meaning of the knots.

"Our kiva was burned, you know," Sky Watcher told the messenger.

"So I saw. No matter. You can hang the string somewhere in a public place. Or keep it yourself. Just so it is known to all. But if the Spanish come, no one is to know anything about such a string. Now, each morning, you must untie or cut off one knot. Then, when none are left, that is the day for the attack."

"But there are no Spanish here!" someone protested.

The messenger nodded. "That is true. But they might come here. Or some of you may want to come to Sennafay to help with the fighting there."

Although it was a matter of concern, few of the men were eager to go. Coyote was among those most militant, but he was too old to go himself. Magpie noted that it was easy for the old warrior to talk fight when he would not personally be involved.

"You have a war chief?" asked the messenger.

"Yes. Limping Coyote, there."

A look of doubt that was almost despair flickered across the messenger's face.

"We have not fought for many seasons," explained Painted Rock.

"Of course." He turned to Coyote. "I am sure you are a strong leader, Uncle," he said diplomatically. "But you could help them select another if you wished to do so."

Coyote nodded, flattered with the attention, and the messenger prepared to move on.

"I have other places to go," he said as he turned toward the trail. "These are brave times! May we meet in Sennafay!"

He moved on in the running dogtrot for which such runners were famous, and was soon out of sight in the rolling hills. Magpie wondered where the darkness would find him, and whether the man would be in danger from the spirits that move in that darkness.

Magpie had other concerns, too. It would surely be impossible for the followers of Popé to kill *all* the Spaniards in the area they called New Mexico. There would be survivors, who would probably bring more Spanish warriors and more bloodshed. These would be very dangerous times, the next year or two.

A more immediate concern now, however, was the trading party of their friend Red Sunset. Magpie counted the knots on the string that hung limply on a post for all to see. How still and unimportant the object looked, hanging there. Yet it carried a secret that would determine the day of dying for many people. That day was ordained already by the number of knots in the cord. And one thing was apparent to Magpie. The killing would take place while Red Sunset's party was in the city of Sennafay.

It would be very dangerous for them. When the fighting came, the Spanish would not trust the Prairie People because they were natives. Yet the followers of Popé from around the territory would also be a danger. *They* would not trust those who were in Sennafay to *trade* with the Spanish. Red Sunset's party could easily be killed by either side, through misunderstanding.

Magpie did not know what to do. He talked to Flower, who was also concerned, but they saw no way to help.

"How many knots in the string?" she asked. "Ah, Magpie, you could hardly reach there in time to warn them now."

It was true. He had thought of it too late. Now a mantle of guilt fell over him. He might be responsible for the deaths of friends.

He went to talk to Blue Corn, who was somewhat older and wiser.

"I have thought of this," Corn admitted. "I see nothing that we could do now. I am not made to think that we should go and fight. But look, Magpie, Red Sunset is a good leader. He will take care of his people."

"Have any gone to Sennafay from here?" he asked.

"I think not," answered Blue Corn. "Some have talked of it. Let us think. . . . How many knots? Five? Oh, only four? Days pass quickly! Well, there is time to reach Sennafay if you wish. You would have to travel for one night, maybe. If others want to go, there would be less danger in the night travel."

"You do not think we should take part in the fighting, Uncle?"

Blue Corn was silent for a little while, and finally gave a deep sigh.

"There was a time," he admitted, "when I would have thought so. I was with Coyote at the battle he loves to tell."

"Ah, I did not realize that."

"I do not speak of it often, Magpie. I was very young. I killed a man. Shot him with an arrow, here."

He touched the soft part of his chest, in the vee of his ribs, and continued.

"He was looking into my eyes, as close as you are now, when I loosed my arrow."

"But he would have killed you, Uncle!"

"Yes. He had an ax. But still I dream about the look in his eyes. When the arrow struck, he knew he was dead, though he could still see and hear and feel for a little while."

It was a clumsy moment, and the younger man did not know how to respond. Finally Blue Corn broke the silence.

"Let us talk of something else, Magpie. After this is over, what? You know, Popé and his followers will not be able to kill *all* the Spanish. And even if they drive them away, they may come back, no?"

Magpie had not really thought beyond the day when there were no more knots in the string that hung on a post by the ruined kiva. He had supposed that the People would rebuild it, but there were no plans yet.

"What do you suggest, Uncle?"

Blue Corn was one of the more respected men of the town, though very quiet and thoughtful. It was apparent that he had thought deeply on this, but as far as Magpie could recall, had never expressed an opinion until now.

"I am made to think," said Corn, "that there must be places where there are no Spanish. They came from the south, it is said. They seem not very active north of here. Maybe we could go north, along the edge of the mountains, and build a new town."

Magpie was astonished. Not in the memory of anyone alive had such a thing been considered.

"But Uncle, we do not know that country. Will it grow corn?"

"I do not know, but we can find out. Our Prairie People friends might know. They travel through there, no?"

"That is true. We could ask them."

Another thought struck him. *If they are still alive after the day of the uprising.*

"I am made to think, Uncle," he said slowly, "that I must go to Sennafay."

"To warn them or to talk to them?" asked Blue Corn.

"Both," Magpie answered.

What a clever man, he thought later. Blue Corn knew that this must be done. Yet he had quietly allowed Magpie to think the matter through and make the decision, as if it had been his own idea all along. *I have underestimated this man,* Magpie thought.

But now he looked across the fire at the others in the little party. After his talk with Blue Corn he had decided to seek out those who had expressed interest in Sennafay and the uprising. Coyote had encouraged them, but did not go himself.

"I would only slow your journey," he said quite truthfully. "My old legs could not keep up. And you will have to hurry. One night's travel, and four days, you say?"

"We are made to think so. Part of each night might be more dangerous from dark spirits than one night's push."

"Yes, that is true," agreed Coyote. "You will travel through tonight?"

"Tomorrow, probably," Magpie answered. "We will get the feel of travel and camp today and tonight."

"It is good. May it go well with you. You will be war chief?"

Magpie had not even thought of that.

"No, no, Uncle. I am not skilled in such things."

"No, but you have started the party. No one is really skilled anymore."

Coyote seemed sad about it, but Magpie realized his feelings. Someone *should* be equipped to lead in such a thing. Usually it would be in a defensive fight.

"We will select a leader at our night camp," he suggested.

"That is good," agreed Coyote.

Magpie had the unpleasant feeling that since he had been the one who made inquiries, the others would assume that he was the leader, as Coyote had.

Now they sat around the fire, trying not to stare into the darkness and the evil it might conceal. They had traveled well, the excitement of the adventure sending blood coursing through their bodies.

Coyote had suggested an alternate dogtrot and walk, with a frequent rest for a short while. It had proved a ground-eating pace, but tired muscles complained of unfamiliar use. Magpie studied the others. Seven in all, mostly younger than himself. Some he knew well, others barely by name. Badger, White Feather, Antelope, One Horn Deer, Fat Snake . . . all were eager, but inexperienced. He wondered how many would . . . well, he must not think of that.

The distant cry of a great long-tailed hunting cat echoed across the mountain like the scream of a woman in torture. Everyone jumped, and a nervous chuckle ran around the fire. Somebody tossed another stick on the flames and it flared up brightly, pushing back and widening the circle of light. Everyone knew that the great cougar seldom attacks humans, but the scream was nerve-racking, though probably not so dangerous as the unseen spirits out there. Magpie had offered a pinch of tobacco when they kindled the fire, to appease any local spirits. It was always done by the Prairie People, Red Sunset had told him. And were not the Prairie People more experienced in campfires and strange places than those who lived in adobe houses?

The thought crossed his mind that maybe the cougar who had

just screamed could be a skinwalker, a human in animal form. He tried to ignore the thought, and wondered who else in that circle had thought of it. He must turn his attention, and that of the group, to other things.

"Now," he said, trying not to let his voice sound tight and nervous. "It is time. We must select a leader."

There was a look of surprise on the other faces.

"*You* are the leader, no?" asked Fat Snake.

Others nodded.

"No, I only passed the word," Magpie protested. "We must choose."

The men looked at each other, undecided, and then back to Magpie. Finally one spoke.

"I am made to think," said Badger, "that you are our leader. What say you others?"

There were nods around the circle, but no dissent.

"So be it, then," announced Badger.

"But . . . but I . . ." Magpie started to say, but then fell silent.

He was not certain how the party might accept the fact that his agenda was quite different from theirs. Magpie had two goals, the first to warn their friends from the prairie, the second to talk with them about the possible move. Neither of these seemed to coincide with the goals of Popé and his followers, or with those of these new recruits. He did not know how they might respond to such an admission on his part. They might be disillusioned, possibly angry, maybe even discouraged, or demoralized. To go into battle with such an attitude might be very dangerous, and he had no wish to place these young men at a disadvantage that might threaten their lives.

He took a deep breath and nodded.

"So be it," he agreed.

5

The next night, their night for travel, went well. They saw no skinwalkers. At least none that they recognized as such.

There was the owl who sailed overhead on silent wings and disappeared into a clump of trees, but it seemed only an owl. There was nothing threatening about its behavior.

Probably they were too busy thinking of the journey and their aching bodies to worry much about evil spirits and skinwalkers. For these men such unfamiliar activity called for the use of different muscles, new motion of joints. Magpie's bones had seen a few more winters than those of the others, and his body did not hesitate to remind him. He gritted his teeth and kept going. Pride would not allow him to complain before the younger men.

The next day found them in unfamiliar country, but the trail they traveled was plain, and becoming more so. They were traveling at an easier pace now out of necessity. The stiffness of their bodies as well as the weariness of a sleepless night's travel demanded it. Rest stops were more frequent.

At one point, where a less-traveled trail joined theirs, they met three men from one of the other towns. After a few moments of suspicion and distrust they all realized that they must have a common purpose—the coming war with the Spanish. One of the newcomers had seen Popé, the holy man, and had heard him speak. He was loud in his praise of a great leader, and at each rest stop talked at great length.

"We must return to the old ways, destroy and reject all that stands for the Metal People. Then everything will be good again. The crops will grow better, times will be good. Popé has said it."

The excitement in the man's voice and the manner of his speaking were contagious. Others began to feel it, too. It was a time of great happenings, but privately Magpie wondered if the opportunity to be a part of such events might be a curse or a blessing.

Once, as they traveled, they saw a platoon of horsemen approaching on the trail ahead. The soldiers were still some distance away, and it appeared that they had not yet been seen. It seemed only prudent to disperse, and the party scattered, disappearing quietly into the rocks and junipers.

Magpie watched the horsemen pass, bright uniforms gleaming in the sun. Each carried a long spear with a shiny metal point. He could plainly hear the jingling of their equipment, even the squeak of the leather saddles and stirrups. They rode close together, and he did not think that they even suspected that the rocks and brush of the hillside concealed a force almost equal to their own. Strange times . . .

The soldiers passed on out of sight, and the sounds of their noisy equipment faded. The People began to come out of concealment and reassemble on the trail.

"We could have killed them all!" chortled the talkative one of the strangers. "Did you see them? They did not even know we were here!"

Magpie was uneasy over the man's attitude. He could hardly wait, it seemed, for the bloodshed to begin. It might be necessary, of course. If need be, Magpie would not hesitate to kill. But this man and his companions seemed *eager* to begin the killing and the destruction. It made his heart heavy to see it.

As they neared Sennafay, it became apparent that something was in the air. A still, heavy, foreboding spirit lay across the hills. There were people, many of them. Some moved around, some sat by themselves or talked quietly in small groups. Spanish patrols ventured out from time to time and those who ringed the city faded silently away into the rocks and junipers like shadowy ghosts, to reappear again after the horsemen passed. It was not the time yet.

Magpie fingered the knotted string from his pouch. He had carefully copied the one that hung on the post beside the ruined kiva. A string to carry, to be sure that the traveling party understood which day the attack was expected.

Each day at dawn he had cut off and discarded one of the knots. Now the string was short, and only one knot remained. A fear gripped him for a moment. Had he cut off a knot for the night they traveled? Was this correct? Was he a day too short or too long? Forcibly, he steadied himself. It must be right. Tomorrow blood would flow and men would die. Both Spanish and native, he knew, though some of the younger men seemed not to realize it.

He sighed. At what point does a young person begin to realize that he is not immortal? He sees others die and cross over, but cannot apply it yet to his own existence. Many would be forced to do so tomorrow, he feared.

It was nearly evening when the party reached an area overlooking the Spanish town. First, a place to camp, and then look for their Prairie People friends . . .

The dark spirit of foreboding and dread was very heavy here. All afternoon as they traveled, they had seen camps of small groups of men camped in the hills, waiting. Tomorrow . . .

Magpie was puzzled at the scarcity of Spanish patrols, but as he considered the situation he began to understand. The Metal People must realize that something was going on. There was too much activity, too many men moving around. It was quiet, unobtrusive movement, but anyone could see that it was there. Even the Spanish.

He inquired at several of the scattered camps as to where they might find the Prairie People, but was met only with blank stares. No one seemed interested. They were preoccupied with the thought that at dawn the attack would come. He could not, of course, let it be known that he did not intend to take an active part in the fighting. The safety of his unsuspecting friends was uppermost in his mind. Yet this might be deeply resented by those who were eager to draw Spanish blood. Ah, what a time of confusion!

They made a dry, fireless camp, as twilight purpled the canyons and low areas between the rolling hills. It would have been good to have a fire, but no one else did. Apparently word had been passed by the messengers of Popé that there were to be no fires within sight of the town.

Except for one . . . as darkness fell, Magpie saw a campfire blossom on a flat area overlooking the town. He was puzzled at first. A signal of some sort? But then he realized. The Prairie People would not know of the coming attack, and would be camping according to their custom. Only one fire. It must be that of Red Sunset and his people. He rose, told the others of his theory, and walked in that direction.

A fire at night is often farther away than it looks. Twilight is deceiving anyway. It was some time before he approached the fire. As he did, he could see an argument in progress. A stocky, well-armed warrior was arguing with Red Sunset, partly in words, partly in hand signs.

"There are to be no fires!" the angry man was insisting.

Red Sunset, also irritated at the insistence of the other, was trying to explain. "It is not my problem. We always have a fire. We were here last night, and had a fire."

"But Popé has said it. No fires within sight of the town tonight. The attack is at dawn!"

"Attack?"

Now Magpie felt obliged to enter the conversation.

"I can explain, Sunset."

"Who are you?" asked the other man in surprise. "You know these?"

"Yes. They are friends. They do not know. They are here to trade."

"Trade? You trade with the Metal People?"

Red Sunset's anger was rising at the arrogance of this man, and Magpie hurried to explain.

"They have stopped at our village to the north of here for several seasons. We know them. They are from the plains to the east."

"But they come not to fight?" The man turned accusingly to Red Sunset. "You are friends of the Spanish, who have killed our holy men!"

For a moment, it appeared that the two would begin the fighting right here at this point. Magpie stepped between them.

"Wait! They only *trade* with the Metal People. For knives, arrow points, fire strikers."

"Yes! The things that we must destroy! These are the cause of the evil!"

"But they are outsiders," Magpie protested. "This is all none of their doing. They did not even know of it."

"Is this true?" the man demanded arrogantly of Red Sunset.

"What are you talking about?" Sunset snapped. "I know nothing of your political problems!"

The man from Popé stood staring numbly for a moment. Finally he spoke.

"You really do not. This is a new problem."

"Look," said Magpie quickly. "I can explain it to them."

"But if they are here, they must fight!" insisted the other. "And they must put out the fire."

"I am made to think," said Magpie carefully, "that it is theirs to decide about the fighting. But about their fire . . . would it not seem strange to one watching, to see them build a fire and then put it out? Why not let it die out as usual? It would attract less attention."

"That is true," agreed the other. "But let us explain to them about the attack."

"It is good," Magpie said. "You tell them, because you know more of it than I."

The other nodded, and they all sat, as if for storytelling.

"My brothers," began the messenger, "these are very bad times. The Spanish have taken away our holy men, killed three of them by strangling, cut off the hands of others. They destroy our kivas, and try to stop our ceremonies and prayers."

"Why?" blurted the astonished Red Sunset.

"We do not know. They want everyone to follow their ceremonies and their gods."

"How strange," Red Sunset said slowly. "What sort of gods?"

"Yes, theirs is a strange story. Their main god is half-human, sired by a higher god and born to a human female. He was killed by his own people, but came back to life again, they say."

"*Aiee!* Where is he?"

"He was taken up into the sky later, we are told."

"Then there are two of them, father and son?"

"So they say. But three, really. And Maria, the mother of the one. And she remains a virgin."

"Aiee! Three?"

"Yes. The other one is spirit only, they say. But they are all the same."

"How can three be only one?"

"Never mind . . . it does not matter, anyway. We will kill them tomorrow. Now I must go."

He rose and started away, then turned back.

"Leave your fire," he said. "And your choice, to fight or not, is yours to decide. But you will not contact the Spanish tonight, or we will kill you."

6

There was little sleep that night. Magpie and Red Sunset sat up for a long time, talking near the fire. Magpie tried to explain the circumstances that had led to the pending bloodshed. The man from the prairie was astonished as the story unfolded.

"But why would they try to stop your worship? I do not understand."

Magpie shrugged helplessly. "Who knows what the Metal People think?"

Sunset shook his head. "Your people had told of this, but we did not know it was so bad. *Aiee,* my friend, one does not fight over *religion*!"

"That is true. But there comes a time . . . you know about the killing of the holy men? Yes, we spoke of that. But to trap the spirit so that it cannot escape to cross over . . ." Magpie shuddered.

Sunset nodded again. "Who is this Popé who leads the fight?"

"I have never met him. A holy man of the Tewas, it is said. He has been in Taos, planning this attack to rid us of the Spanish."

"But your people are peaceable. *You* will fight, Magpie?"

Magpie gave a deep sigh. "I do not know, even now. We came

partly to warn you. Some of our young men are eager to shed blood, though. And how can I let them go in while I stay here in camp?"

Sunset nodded sympathetically. "I will go with you," he offered. "But it is not your fight."

"That is true. And we have friends among the Spanish. We are not finished with the trading, either. Our furs are in the trading store of Gomez."

"It will be dangerous to go there. The soldiers . . ."

"Yes, I know. Look, let us go in together, you and I. My companions, like yours, must decide for themselves what to do, no? But we can watch, and help if needed. Now I should tell my Prairie People of the things we have said between us. They do not know all that is happening."

It was explained to the outsiders, with the predictable results. Two of the younger men were eager to take part in the action, others were more reserved.

"But why would the Metal People want to stop your worship?" one asked.

"We do not know. Not all of them do, maybe. Their holy men with the long robes are the worst. They have captured and killed *our* priests, with the force of their warriors," Magpie explained.

"But one does not kill another because their worship is different!"

"*They* do."

"Then your people should kill only these holy men, who misuse their power, no? But is that not dangerous?"

Magpie, more confused than ever, shook his head sadly.

"That is true. We risk both the weapons of the soldiers and the power of the holy men's medicine."

He wished that he could go back to the simpler times of his childhood. At least, the world had seemed simpler then.

He drank some water before he retired, so that his bladder would waken him early. Even as he did so, he realized that there was little chance that he would oversleep. Or sleep at all.

Afterward, Magpie was never certain how it began. There were men, hundreds of them, moving into the town. He moved along with them, unsure of his place in all this, wishing that he could be somewhere else. But as the one who had been selected as leader of his little party, he felt a responsibility to the others. Red Sunset and his party went along, mostly out of curiosity.

The sun was rising blood red in the east as they made their way along the wandering streets toward the open square of the plaza. Everyone was trying to be quiet, but it is difficult for hundreds of men to move quietly. Somewhere ahead there was a surprised cry of alarm, followed by a scream. Perhaps a sleepy sentry had managed to give the alarm before he was cut down. There was the flat crack of matchlock muskets from nearer the center of the town.

"What is it?" asked Magpie.

"Thundersticks!" said Sunset.

Then pandemonium broke loose with a mutter of sound that quickly became a roar. Repressed anger rumbled through the streets, unleashed in all its fury.

A squad of lancers managed to ready themselves and mount an attack. Perhaps they had been preparing for a routine patrol when the crisis came. The horsemen charged into the crowd, which fell away before them and closed behind them, effectively swallowing the attack. The long lances were ineffective in the closely packed throng. Brightly uniformed soldiers were dragged from their horses by innumerable hands. They fell into the dust of the street, and were hacked and stabbed to death, some with their own weapons.

A dark-robed priest stepped into the street in front of the church, hands raised for attention. No one could hear his demand that they cease this activity. He was seized, beaten, and carried aloft by a crowd now gone crazy in its frenzy for vengeance. Magpie could not tell if the limp body still held onto life.

It did not matter. Other priests were captured and brought to the church as the frenzy of killing and burning gained momentum. At the suggestion of some who appeared to be Popé's followers, the church became a focus of violence. Captive priests were mutilated and killed, some on the altar itself, and the bodies piled high.

Other warriors herded sheep and pigs into the building, and began to pile furniture into a giant funeral pyre in front of the altar. Someone brought a burning brand to ignite the blaze. Everything Spanish that could be tossed, crammed, or herded into the structure was added. Finally the smoke and flames made it necessary to close the heavy doors.

Magpie was astounded at the violent hatred that ran rampant through the streets. He was sickened by the killing and destruction, and it was not yet over. A horseman thundered down the street and across the plaza, trying to reach the comparative safety of a big building along one side of the square.

"What is that big lodge?" Magpie asked Red Sunset.

"Their meeting place," his friend answered. "Like your kivas."

"But their place of ceremonies . . . there!"

He pointed to the church, where greasy smoke poured from the windows and now through a hole in the roof. The smell of burning flesh hung heavy in the air.

Red Sunset nodded. "Yes. I am told they meet in one place, and hold worship in another."

"But why?"

"Who knows, my friend, what a Spaniard thinks? But today, he is afraid!"

The fleeing lancer, his weapon gone and his horse already wounded, almost reached the safety of the thick adobe walls. But a hail of arrows knocked him from the saddle, and his crippled horse floundered until it fell by the wall.

The scene was changing to one of celebration now, men singing and dancing through the streets and the square. Then a sound like the crack of thunder . . . a puff of cottony white smoke billowed from a small window in the wall of the Spanish building, and a warrior in the street stopped his dance in midstride and fell limply to the dust. The plaza cleared quickly. It was not over yet, and the celebration seemed premature. The People discreetly withdrew from the fortified buildings of the Spanish, taking their dead and wounded. Spanish wounded were killed, and the bodies left lying in the streets. Magpie saw the corpse of one of the long-robed holy men crumpled against the outside wall of a house. The right hand was missing, in symbolic vengeance for the torture and mutilation of the holy men of the kivas. He moved on.

By dusk the campfires had blossomed in a great circle around the town. There was singing and dancing and much waving and display of trophies and souvenirs.

As darkness fell, Popé himself visited each campfire with words of praise and encouragement. He had a wild charisma about him, an urgency, yet a haughty demeanor that spoke with authority. He was quick to point out that *everything* Spanish must be destroyed. Even the scraps of uniforms, saved as trophies. Any stray livestock must be killed.

"What about horses?" someone asked. "Are they not Spanish?"

This was a great dilemma. The horse had made a major change in the past few generations. Of course, so had the sheep, pigs, and poultry. There were some who might view the demands of Popé as excessive.

"I am made to think," said an old man, "that the People once had horses. They were lost to us for a while, until the Spanish brought them back."

This did not seem to sit well with Popé, but the attitude of most was clear. The horse would stay. Of sheep, there were those who said no more, but had private opinions as to their usefulness, regardless of Popé's demands.

"It is not over," Popé cautioned. "We have just begun. They will now leave the town and go back from where they came."

"We let them go?" someone asked.

"Yes, their power is broken. Let them go if they will."

Even so, it would be half a moon before the besieged survivors of the town were able to straggle forth to begin the long trek back to Mexico.

Word trickled into the camps of victories in other areas and towns. Whole Spanish families had been killed in remote areas, and their houses and barns destroyed. Some straggling columns of survivors had been allowed to leave, headed south under the watchful eyes of the People.

The circling campfires around the town of Sennafay were fewer now, as the People began to remember urgent tasks at home.

"You will start back to your prairie?" Magpie asked Red Sunset.

"Yes. There is nothing we can do here. Your people do not need our help. Our furs are lost, and one of our young men was killed. But we have mourned for him, and he has crossed over."

"My heart is heavy for your loss, my friend."

"It is the way of things. We will go back. There are buffalo to hunt, and more furs this winter."

"But where will you trade?" Magpie asked.

"*Aiee,* not here! Maybe we will have nowhere to trade."

"That is true. But things can never be the same for us, either."

"How is that?" Red Sunset was puzzled.

"I . . . I am not sure. I am made to think that it will be much different now. We have lived with the Spanish for many lifetimes. Now, to give up all they have brought. . . . No one is really sure anymore what *was* brought by them."

"Ah! I see. Tell me, Magpie, is this Popé a good leader?"

Magpie was quiet for a little while. *Yes, that is it!* he thought. So many demands by the followers of Popé. . . . *"You must do this, you cannot do that. . . ."* He thought sometimes that the everyday activities of the People were being dictated now more strictly than under the Spanish.

The world in which he had grown to manhood would certainly never be again.

7

The surviving Spanish settlers, soldiers, traders, and a few priests started the long trip to Mexico. They were carefully watched and escorted by a column nearly as large as their own. Mounted warriors, followers of Popé, rode alongside at a little distance, parallel to the course of the refugees. They would make certain that the column kept moving and did not try to return. It would be nearly a decade before the power and prestige of the charismatic young holy man was lessened, and Spanish settlers and traders began to move back into the area.

But for Magpie, there were other concerns. In his remote village, there had not been much trouble with the Spanish. Well, until the kiva was destroyed.

He had grown up with many of the advantages of things brought by the outsiders, without realizing it. The People had, through the generations, accepted that which was good, and made it their own. Now Popé was demanding that it be not only rejected but destroyed. He would never forget the horror of the events at the holy meeting place of the Spanish. The burning flesh, the slaughter . . . he would see it in his dreams. Forever, maybe.

When it came down to it, there had been, in Magpie's own life, more interference, more demands, from those who followed Popé than from the Spanish. This troubled him greatly, as he and the others traveled back toward the village with the Prairie People.

It was a much more relaxed time, it was true. There was no hurry now. Magpie could talk with his friend Red Sunset. They had become closer from their shared experiences.

"You will start home soon?" he asked.

"Yes, maybe. We have nothing left to pack and make ready, so it is easy, no?" Red Sunset smiled grimly at his dark joke.

"That is true. Tell me of your country, Sunset."

The other man hesitated. "What do you wish to know?"

"Oh, what grows there?"

"Buffalo . . . elk . . . deer and antelope, of course. Some small game. Rabbits, squirrels."

"No . . . what plants?"

"Grass! It is what makes good hunting. My friend, I have seen grass in the autumn, the seed heads taller than my horse here. And the short buffalo grass farther west. Not tall, but good food for buffalo."

"You have no crops?" Magpie asked, shifting his position to try to find a more comfortable seat.

He was not accustomed to a horse. None of his party were, but Sunset had offered the use of his packhorses for Magpie's party to ride, since they had no loads now.

"Crops?" Sunset was saying. "No, we are hunters, my friend. In the spring we burn the dead grass, and the buffalo come back to eat the new green."

"Then no one grows corn?"

"Yes, the growers do. We trade with them, meat and robes for corn and pumpkins."

"Ah! Then there are those who plant!"

"Of course. But it is not our way. We hunt."

"It is good, Sunset. But tell me more. Are there other crops?"

"I do not know, Magpie. Several kinds of corn. Oh, yes, beans. But why do you ask these things?"

Magpie was hesitant. He was not certain that he was ready to share his idea.

"You will say nothing of this?"

Red Sunset looked at him in surprise. "If you wish it so. What is it?"

"Sunset, I am made to think that there are hard times ahead."

"But your war is over, no?"

"That is true, but you saw. There are those who would tell us what we must do. *'You must do this, you cannot do that. You must kill and burn that animal. . . .'* This is not good. Worse, maybe, than the Spanish."

"I do not understand."

"Nor do I. But what I am thinking . . . Sunset, is there room for a few families of my people in your country?"

The man from the prairie stared at him in surprise.

"I . . . I am made to think so. You would do that? Leave your homes here?"

"I would think on it, pray about it. Could it be, Sunset?"

"I can see no reason why not. We could ask some of the growers. Not too close to Pawnees . . . Kenzas are easier to deal with. I will think on this."

"I, too."

"You would go back with us?"

"No, no. We could not go now. Our crops are growing. We would have to carry seed from this season's harvest."

"*Aiee!* I had not thought of that. You cannot move at all from the time of planting until autumn? It is a strange way."

Magpie laughed. "As is yours to us. But it is good to have differences, and to trade, no?"

When they reached the village, they saw that the men who had remained there had begun to restore the kiva. The charred poles that had been the rafters had been cleared away, the pit cleaned, and debris removed. New poles were in place and smaller sticks and matting were being positioned.

"You will be moving on?" Magpie asked Sunset.

"A day or two. We will let the horses rest and eat. They are thin."

It was a pleasant time with no immediate pressures, and the horrors of the killing in Sennafay behind them. The stories of things seen and done there were told and retold, growing somewhat with the telling, and taking on a life of their own.

Before the departure of the Prairie People, Sunset sought out his friend Magpie.

"I have given much thought to the thing we talked of," he began. "It might be done."

Magpie was interested at once. "Tell me."

"I am made to think that there are two things to consider. One is that of which I know nothing. You spoke of it . . . it must be that you move only when you have seeds?"

"That is true. After the harvest. Late summer."

"Ah, yes. And our seasons are a little different from yours. But the growers in our country speak of the 'Moon of Gathering.' That would be the time, no?"

"Yes, maybe."

"But you need to make shelter for winter. Could it be done? If you leave here as soon as you can harvest?"

"I do not know. How many moons?"

"Three moons, maybe."

"I am made to think so," Magpie said thoughtfully. "The place must be found."

"That is the other thing," said Red Sunset. "It should be decided before. Even we do that. Our council decides where we will winter while we are in summer camp. But no matter . . . let us talk of this. What sort of place you need. You can grow your crops anywhere?"

"Some places are better than others."

"Of course. You need water?"

"Yes. A place not too rocky."

"A place like this!" Sunset laughed.

"Yes, maybe so."

"And with neighbors who will not bother you?"

"That is true," Magpie agreed.

"I have thought about that. It is important. You should ask permission, maybe. Not too near Pawnees. They are warlike. They steal girls sometimes, too. So, not too far north. And there are fewer people of any kind to the west of us."

"How far do we speak of, Sunset?"

"For travel? Maybe half a moon. A little more. I am made to think that someone could go back with us, find a place, then lead you there when your seeds are ready."

"It might be done! I will talk to some of the others. You leave tomorrow?"

Sunset shrugged. "Or the next day. When it is time."

•   •   •

They met in the nearly restored kiva, to consider. There were those who were violently opposed, but several showed great interest.

After much argument, it was decided that it would be good to send someone to look at the possibilities. He could return with his findings before the harvest was complete, and final decisions made at that time by each family. If, of course, the report proved favorable.

"Now, who will go?" asked Magpie.

The men looked from one to the other, and at last Blue Corn spoke.

"You should go, Magpie."

"I? But I have a family!"

"Maybe that is why. This is your idea, no? A better place, without the killing we have seen?"

Others were nodding.

"Well, yes . . ."

"We will look after your family," Corn went on. "Go, find out. If it looks good, I will join you in the move."

Several others nodded agreement.

Sometimes a leader arises who is merely in the right place at the proper time. And a good leader is often reluctant at first.

"But I am not . . ." he began, and paused to look around the circle. Some were opposed to the plan from the start. Some were too old, too young, or too foolish. His gaze finished the sweep of the circle and returned to Blue Corn, who sat waiting. There was really no one else on whom the burden should fall.

"I will go," he said. "But I ask the prayers and blessings of you all. I will need them."

AFTERWORD

1692

Some twelve years later, a Spanish expedition under Diego de Vargas returned to Santa Fe, and met with no opposition. Popé was dead, and was little mourned. He had become a tyrant to his own people, and lost his prestige and the power that accompanied it. The farmers of the pueblos had resumed their peaceful ways.

In 1720, an expedition from Santa Fe under the command of Pedro de Villasur, vice-governor of the province, made its way into the central plains. They found, in an area now known as Scott County, Kansas, a small village of adobe bricks. They invited the farmers of the town they called El Quartelejo to return to their traditional home, but were refused.

"We are doing well here."

Villasur's exploring party had a secondary mission. There had been rumors of natives in Tejas attacking Spanish settlements there. They were led, the rumors said, by French officers and carried French weapons. France and Spain, though recently trading in the New World, were now at war again in Europe. Villasur was to determine whether France was expanding into the central plains.

He encountered no French, but was killed by Pawnees carrying French weapons, probably on the Platte River. A few survivors straggled back to Santa Fe to tell the story.

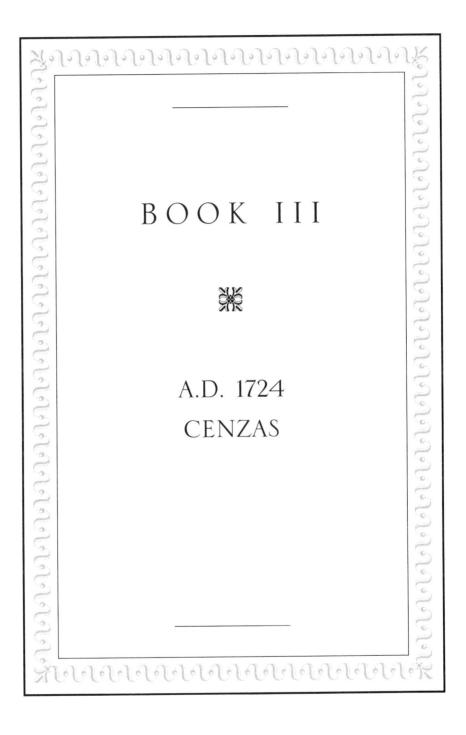

BOOK III

A.D. 1724
CENZAS

1

This, the journal of Pierre Rivier, lieutenant in the service of His Majesty, King Louis XV . . . Of July the second, A.D. 1724, Fort Orleans, Louisiana Territory . . .

Pierre laid aside his pen and stared at the page. How could he record his thoughts and feelings as he prepared to embark on this monumental journey? The excitement and adventure of exploration, the knowledge of its importance . . .

There would be danger, but that was a given fact. His parents understood that. Had his father not followed a military career? They were proud when he enlisted. There had been some influence through his father's contacts, he knew, in acquiring his commission. Was that not the way of such things?

Until now, his military service had been rather uneventful. The brief struggle for power after the death of the king had been while Pierre was still a youngster at home. He remembered the talk of it, and his father had been away most of the time for a year.

That unpleasantness was now sometimes called the War of Succession. But Phillip, Duke of Orleans, had proved his right to rule as regent. Louis XV, great-grandson of the dying Louis XIV, and heir to the throne of France, had been only a child. But on his dying bed, the king had decreed that Orleans serve as regent until the young king came of age.

France had been politically unstable during the transition. After all, Louis XIV, the Sun King, monarch of the longest reign in Europe, had occupied its throne for over seventy years. There were some who said, although very quietly, that the monarch had all but bankrupted the country with his patronage of the arts and his interests in exploration of the New World. Others referred to his reign as the Golden Age of France. It was only prudent, with this political instability, for a young lieutenant to leave his political position unstated, and to support the Crown, though inconspicuously.

Yet that was another thing. . . . The boy king, still only fourteen, had just been declared of age by the Council of Regents.

In the midst of all of this, Lieutenant Rivier had met, at a party in Paris, a remarkable man, Etienne Veniard. The man seemed somehow above all the intrigue of the royal court, though well informed and a bit amused by it. During the course of the evening, the two had talked at length. Light conversation, at least at first . . . Bourgmont had mentioned some of his adventures in the New World, his military service at a place called Detroit. There was mention of a number of leaders among the savages, with whom Veniard seemed personally acquainted. It seemed that the man was tossing out bits of information that might startle the listener, in order to see the reaction.

Pierre had shown interest, but tried to avoid revealing his fascination with the tales from the New World. Then the other man blandly stated that he had spent some years as a *coureur des bois,* one of the lawless "woods rangers" in the frontier forests. The young lieutenant still felt that he was being tested, somehow, and a faint warning sounded in the dim recesses of his mind. He remembered the advice he had received at the military academy from another cadet: Be neither the best nor the worst at anything, and never volunteer. But he could not conceal his interest in this opportunity to learn, and he had asked questions about the frontier in the New World.

Now, two years later, the memory of that evening that had changed his life seemed remote. It was a blur of color and sound, a dreamlike mix of dances and perfume and food and good wine. . . . That probably accounted in part for the dreamlike blur. He had heard from the lips of Veniard the names of strange and romantic places— Mishi-ghan, Missi-sepee, Missourie, Cenzas. The whole region was called Louisiana, after the monarch. Somehow he had not noticed that Veniard's interest seemed to lie with political expansion in the name of the Crown, and that this was somewhat out of character for a lawless woods ranger.

Pierre Rivier had wakened next morning with a splitting headache and a bad taste in his mouth. It was as if a platoon of horse cavalry had marched across his tongue. He could still hear the hoofbeats. . . . No, that was someone beating on his door, not on his skull. . . . He crawled out of bed.

A uniformed lackey stood outside, timidly preparing to pound again. Under normal conditions, perhaps "tapping" would have been a more appropriate term. The noise may have been converted to pounding by his own indiscretion last night. *Sacre bleu,* had he made a fool of himself, talking to that big Norman officer? What was the man's name . . . Ven-something?

Still nursing his self-afflicted discomfort, he tried to make sense of the messenger's words. The lackey was holding a card out toward him.

"Captain Veniard is waiting," the man was saying. "I have a carriage outside."

Bewildered, Pierre tried to focus bleary eyes on the card.

"Etienne Veniard," it read.

"He is here?" he blurted.

"No, no, Lieutenant. He wishes you to come to his house. I will take you there."

"But . . . I . . . may I dress and shave?"

There was a suggestion of a contemptuous curl of the man's lip. "But of course, m'sieur. I will wait." He turned and started down the hall toward the outside door of the bachelor officers' quarters.

It was quiet. *No formation today . . . Sunday,* he thought. *And a good thing, too.*

But what could this summons mean? Had he made a complete fool of himself? Well, very likely, but to the extent that he might be in trouble? No, he thought. If that were true, he would be under arrest, and carried to Bourgmont in irons. Maybe merely for a reprimand?

Quickly he shaved, trying not to cut himself with his trembling, and pulled on a fresh shirt. *Go slowly,* he told himself. *Be calm, now.*

The shiny, perfectly matched team drew the ornate carriage through the streets of Paris toward his unknown destiny. The combination of headache and the bumping of carriage wheels on cobblestones was not comfortable, but the fresh air was clearing his senses somewhat. He closed his eyes and tried to breathe deeply.

The carriage drew up before a rather unassuming house, and the lackey jumped to the ground and opened the door.

"Come with me, sir," he said with a polite bow of his head. More like a nod, actually.

Pierre followed the man up a short curving walk of flagstone, and up a few steps to a door with an ornate brass knocker. The lackey lifted the knob, in the shape of a grotesque gargoyle's head, and thumped three times. It was only a moment until the massive door swung open on well-oiled hinges to reveal a butler in a velvet suit with prominent ruffles and lace at the cuffs and collar. The eyes of the two servants met briefly, and they exchanged the slightest of nods before the lackey turned back toward the coach.

"This way, sir." The butler motioned with a white-gloved hand as he turned down a hallway to the right.

Only a few paces . . . the butler stepped aside and ushered the guest through the doorway into a large, richly appointed room with soft, thick carpet beneath his feet. The walls were lined with books, and there was a warm look in the polished wood of the shelving and trim.

Near the window stood a huge desk, ornate with inlays of exotic woods, ivory, and shell. And behind this desk sat Pierre's drinking companion of the previous night, seemingly none the worse for wear. He looked up from the clutter of papers on the desk.

"Ah! Rivier!" said Veniard with a smile. "Good! Please be seated."

He gestured toward a well-upholstered chair by the desk, and Pierre sat, feeling clumsy and out of place in such a room. The young man had been unprepared for such a display of wealth and opulence in a house that had seemed rather unassuming from the outside. It was larger than he had expected, somehow.

Now the captain fumbled among some rolled parchments in a case behind him and selected a couple. He untied the ribbon from one of the tubes and unrolled it across the desk, weighting the ends with a book and a container of blotting sand.

"Now, take a look!" he said, smiling. "What do you see?"

Pierre Rivier struggled for a moment to focus his eyes, and

began to study the symbols and shapes on the map before him. Here were some of the names he had heard from the lips of this big adventurer the night before. He began to remember more details now, struggling up through the self-inflicted fog and the dark taste in his mouth. He would never drink again, he told himself, knowing that he lied. He took a deep breath.

Mishi-ghan . . . Missi-sepee . . . Missourie . . . Cenzas . . . the places of which they had talked.

Pierre sat staring at the compass rose on the map's upper corner. It was beautifully rendered in hand-illuminated color. The slightly longer point, which indicated north, was actually gilded.

"A map," he murmured, and promptly felt stupid in his obvious answer. "A map of the New World."

Veniard chuckled, as if to acknowledge his visitor's recovery, and nodded.

"Yes, but not all of it. See, here are the Great Lakes . . . Detroit . . . I have served there, you know. . . . Here, the Missi-sepee, the 'Great River' of the Missourie nation . . ." He paused and studied the visitor for a moment. "You know, Rivier, of the theory of a water passage to the China Sea? Both we and England have searched for it."

"I have heard it discussed."

"Yes . . . well, I am made to think that it does not matter."

"Does not matter?"

Veniard nodded.

"But why?" blurted the young lieutenant. "The trade—"

"Of course!" Veniard interrupted. "And there may be such a passage. But there is the immediate possibility of trade with Spain at a city they call Santa Fe. Here."

He pointed with a forefinger to a point far to the southwest in an area largely unmarked by inked patterns. It was nearly on the edge of the parchment.

"The great sea to the west would be here." He gestured at empty air beside the desk. "Now, look . . ."

He leaned forward with a conspiratorial air to point again.

"Here is a river, almost as big as the Great River itself. They join here, at this point. This other river flows from the west. Some are calling it the Missourie River. Oh, yes, the savages call it Big Muddy. Now, I have been westward as far as this point. . . . This Missourie River takes a bend to the north, there. A large town . . . Cenza, the natives are called. . . . South Wind People. And a somewhat smaller river joins it from directly west. We may think of that as the 'River of the Cenzas.' "

"But . . ." stammered Pierre, "what has this to do—"

The captain waved the question aside before it was finished.

"Now from here, where the two great rivers join, to the city of the Cenzas, is no more than eighty leagues by land. A little farther by water, because the river winds and wanders. But it is *navigable*. So is the Cenzas River, I am made to think. If it continues westward, it could bring us to within maybe eighty leagues or so of the Spanish in Santa Fe."

"But what has this to do with me?" blurted the confused lieutenant.

"Oh!" Veniard's eyes were large and round and glittered with excitement. "Did I not mention, last evening? I have a commission from the Company of the Indies, an arm of the Crown. I am to explore this area, make peace with the savages. 'Indians,' some call them, though that is mistaken, of course. I am preparing to form an expedition, a party to build a fort on the frontier, and establish a French presence there. If Spain wants to trade, well and good. But if they prefer territory, we will defend the interests of France."

Pierre was still confused, and now Veniard seemed to notice this for the first time.

"Did I not mention?" he asked seriously. "I want you to accompany me."

2

Pierre sat staring at Veniard, trying to organize his thoughts. He had already been confused, off balance, and self-conscious about his appearance and his behavior of the previous evening. But in his wildest imaginings he could not have guessed the purpose for which he had been summoned there on that morning.

"Well?"

Veniard's voice lent a certain urgency. He obviously expected an answer.

"I . . . I am honored, monsieur, but I . . . my allegiance must be to my duty as an officer. To the Crown."

The captain tilted back his head and roared with laughter. That in turn caused considerable discomfort in the throbbing head of his guest. Then the big man stopped, leaned forward, and spoke in softer tones. Perhaps he recalled mornings when his own head had felt like that of young Rivier.

"Lieutenant," he said gently, "as I have just told you, this *is* a mission on behalf of the Crown. It supersedes your present commission. All that I have to do is to send a request to your commanding officer. You will be relieved of your present assignment immediately and assigned to me. But I do not want you against your will. Now, will you do it? Or do you need more time? We are limited to some extent, for there are preparations to make."

Pierre was thinking quickly. As quickly as possible, that is, in his confused condition. It seemed unfair that he must make such a decision while still suffering from the effects of the previous evening's pleasures.

I must not appear indecisive, he thought. *My answer is of the utmost importance.*

"I am honored, sir, to be chosen. When do I leave?"

The broad smile on the face of the other told him that he had spoken well.

"Good! I depart on Monday next. Can you be ready?"

"Of course. Are there supplies, provisions I should obtain?"

"No, no. Only personal effects. You will be relieved of your present duty as of today. You may want to visit family, friends. You will be gone for some time."

Pierre hesitated to ask, but felt that he needed to know.

"How long, sir?"

Veniard looked at him sharply, but then realized that it was a reasonable inquiry.

"I would say three, possibly four, years. Agreeable?"

"Of course. I only—"

"Yes, yes. I had not told you much about my commission. Let me explain more fully."

Veniard turned to the map again, and pointed to a spot about halfway between the Great River and the junction of the two other rivers, which he termed the Missourie and the Cenzas.

"Here," he said, "we are to build a fort. It will be farther west than any other French fort. That will provide a base for our operations. Then we will proceed with a party of Frenchmen and a larger force of natives upstream, toward the towns of the Cenzas. Then on westward, mapping the river. The one here, that we call by their name."

"Are the tribes hostile there?" asked Pierre.

"They have been, at times. That is part of the mission, to bring them to peace with us. And with each other. I hope to bring back a few of their leaders, to show them the sights of Paris, and that Paris may see them."

For a moment, the thought crossed Pierre's mind that the man was mad, and that he, Pierre, had just agreed to be a part of a ridiculous scheme. The personal charisma of Veniard was so great, however, that such thoughts were gone in an instant. After all, did not this man have the sanction and support of the Crown? Doubts were unthinkable.

"You mentioned, Captain, that these tribes have been at war with each other? Is that not a problem?"

Veniard thought for a moment, then answered directly and to the point.

"Traditionally, they raid each other, steal horses, children sometimes."

"Children?"

"For slaves. Sell them to other tribes, to Spain, to us."

Pierre was startled. "I had not been aware of this, Captain."

Veniard shrugged.

"Slaves must come from somewhere, no? These people have enslaved each other for centuries."

Pierre felt somehow that there was more to this than met the eye. *This man is not quite comfortable with this,* he thought. What was it? There were those who opposed slavery as a matter of principle, but his perception was that somehow this was not the position of Veniard. *Slaves must come from somewhere,* the man had said. Was it that he felt a difference in *these* natives? In France there were many *nègres* slaves. From Africa, Pierre supposed. There were in turn many of mixed blood, with varying shades of skin coloration. He understood that the so-called Indians were also moderately dark skinned, but had not seen any. At least, as far as he knew. But it appeared that Veniard—his thoughts were interrupted as Veniard spoke again.

"I am made to think that their raids for slaves are a hindrance to trade. I hope to convince them of this. And of course, both we and the Spanish must stop providing a market for their slave raids."

That explanation answered the question to some degree. But there was still a subtle something, something felt but left unsaid. Pierre would recall this and think about it later as events unfolded.

Pierre's parents would be understandably concerned. They were a day's hard travel away, but he borrowed a horse and made the ride. He could do no less. And he must let them know what sudden turn his life had taken.

His father was proud, and his mother cried, but she was accustomed to such departures. She had long lived with the knowledge that such a parting might be the last, each time her husband had left with his troop. Pierre spent the night in their modest home, and left early in the morning. It was another hard day's ride back to Paris.

His father took him aside for a moment just before his departure.

"Be brave, be loyal, but mostly, be careful," the old soldier advised. "I envy you, my son. There are wondrous things to be seen and done. And you should keep a journal. *Write* your doings as they happen, because you will forget. Someday, this may be important."

Now, two years later, he sat staring at a page of that journal. He had stopped at a little stationer's on his return to Paris, just to buy such a ledger. It was bound in warm brown calfskin, but had only blank pages. These pages somehow drew him, called out to be used, written on, to display something of importance. It was frustrating, but he had nothing of importance to write. He had inscribed his name and the date on the first page, and another entry on the day they left Paris.

From that time, his entries in the journal were irregular. It was difficult sometimes on the long sea voyage to lay hand to ink and a pen. Once a small bottle of ink leaked and spoiled some of his clothing. Another time, he prepared to write and could not find a quill. He could have asked one of the ship's officers, of course, for such an item. Or even Veniard himself. But his pride would not let him. Embarrassed and angry, he stuffed the leather-bound journal back into his valise, and abandoned it for the duration of the voyage. It would be better on land, he told himself.

But it was not. They reached New Orleans, procured boats, and started upriver. Although there was more to see, that portion of the trip was harder. It was no longer possible merely to sit back and watch sailors carry out their tasks. The traveler must take an active part here. In all of this, there was little time or opportunity to write in his diary. He would bring it up to date later.

At Fort de Chartres there were people who expected Veniard, and had made preparations for his arrival. Sometimes it was little short of amazing, how the plans seemed to fall together. Pierre realized that it was all due to advanced planning. Veniard was assembling a party of picked men, several of them specialists with particular skills.

Most impressive of these was a man introduced by Veniard as "M. de Renaudiere, an engineer of mines." This man's bearing and appearance suggested something of great importance, but it seemed obscure to the young lieutenant. Mines?

There was also the surgeon, Dr. Quesnel, whose function was more apparent, and a chaplain, Father Mercier.

They were joined by a platoon of about twenty soldiers, who would build the proposed fort at a site chosen by Veniard. But where? They traveled up the Great River and up the Big Muddy, the Missourie, stopping at native towns and villages occasionally.

It was during these stops that Pierre Rivier began to notice a rather strange transformation in their leader. Veniard, now dressed in the soft-tanned leather garments of the natives, was exhibiting a familiarity with their ways beyond that which would be expected. True, he had mentioned a period of time that he had spent as a woods ranger. Pierre had almost forgotten that. But now the natives they encountered seemed to recognize Veniard, and to consider him one of them. After some time, and after several occasions where native towns welcomed Veniard like a long-lost brother, Pierre made bold to ask about it.

"These are Missourie," answered Veniard. "I lived among them."

Later, he seemed to relent, and offered more detail.

"There are many of these Indian nations," he explained. "To the north, between here and Detroit, Sac, Fox, Illinois. These, Missourie. South of them, Osage, who are their allies. I have spoken of Cenzas, who are also known as Caw. But farther west of them are Pawnee and Padouca, or Comanche. They are the ones who range all the way to New Mexico and the Spanish. It is those with whom we must negotiate."

It was at about this time that Veniard had also suggested that Pierre would be more comfortable in native garments. That was easily accomplished with the aid of Veniard's fluent use of the native tongue. Also during that portion of the travel, he prevailed upon the young lieutenant to begin to learn the native hand-sign talk.

"You will find it quite useful," he advised. "Any of these nations communicate with each other in this way, even without speaking. It is quite simple, actually. Here, I will show you."

There followed Pierre's first lesson in the use of native hand signs. It was relatively easy, he found. *You, me,* were obvious. Then *man, woman, speak, eat, water,* and the universal sign for any question, *Why, what, how, where.*

Pierre fell asleep that night with a strange thought that made him smile as he drifted off to sleep. The question sign was perfect for anyone who wondered about their leader, Etienne Veniard.

3

For several days they traveled upstream from the junction of the Missourie with the larger Missi-sepee. Pierre did not understand why it should be called Big Muddy by the natives. It seemed no more so than the other rivers they had seen. He ventured to ask Renaudiere about it.

The engineer smiled. "I have never seen it, Rivier. This is my first trip into the area, too. But I am told that it is a springtime and early summer phenomenon. Much muddier then."

"Why would this be, sir?"

"Such a thing suggests an annual, seasonal event, no? Spring rains, far upstream? Yet I think that this will not entirely explain it. But the natives tell of mountains, many leagues to the west."

"Yes, so I am told." Pierre did not see the connection. "But what—"

"Snow melt!" explained the other. "Imagine, Rivier, mountains so great that the melting of their snows each spring roils the waters a thousand leagues downstream!"

"We will see such mountains?" asked Pierre.

"Ah, I do not know. Probably it depends only on how far westward we go. The area is largely unexplored, you know. Except for the Spanish to the southwest, of course. That is part of our mission, to map a portion of it. But we will go nearly straight west. This river, the Missourie, Veniard says, comes from the northwest. We will follow another, the River of the Cenzas, which comes from due west. And, I suspect, from a very long distance. Ah, we may see wondrous sights, Rivier, but maybe not those far mountains."

Pierre thought of asking about the strong impression he had that Veniard was well known to the natives of this area. Somehow it did not seem appropriate, so he said nothing. After all, it was only logical. The Missouries had assisted in the war against the Fox nation and had helped to defend Detroit. Veniard had become acquainted with many of their leaders at that time. He had apparently been so impressed by these people that he had lived with them for a time. A man with Veniard's energy and the sheer size of his physical stature would surely be remembered. So maybe it was logical, after all.

Besides, there were greater concerns. They had been traveling since June, when they left Paris, and it was now autumn. The first goal of their mission was to select a site and build a fort on the Missourie River. But they continued to travel. Nights were cold, and a rime of frost often coated the grasses when they woke at dawn. Would there be time to build adequate shelter before the snows came? And what sort of winter could be expected here? He had no idea, but Veniard did not seem concerned. Well, so be it.

Meanwhile, there was much to enjoy. There came a time of a week or more when the days were still and cool and the sun warm. He had never seen the sky so blue. The leaves of the oaks and maples along the river turned from green to glorious red and yellow and orange. Trees and shrubs of varieties completely strange to him blazed forth in colors unfamiliar.

Long lines of geese honked their way southward, high above. It was much like the season called Second Summer by his countrymen at home, especially those who lived in areas where their lives revolved around the changing of the seasons. Crops would be harvested back there now, winter vegetables stored, fuel for winter seasoned and stacked.

There was the scent of autumn in the air, too. Slightly different from that at home, but nonetheless an autumn smell. Pungent, rich, and warm. It was a season that he loved, and it was a thrill to experience it here, in a new world of adventure.

There came a day when they approached a town on the south bank of the river. Missourie, Pierre noted. He was learning to recognize differences in structure of the dwellings of various tribes and nations. And without a doubt, this was a town of the Missourie nation. He supposed that Veniard would call for a stop, though it was only a little past noon.

True to his thoughts on the subject, Pierre saw the leading boat in which Veniard rode swing toward the shore. People gathered to meet them, calling out a recognition in the manner to which they had become accustomed. The other boats, too, turned toward the shore.

Still, Pierre was not prepared for the next event. The first boat had hardly grounded when Veniard leaped ashore. Instantly, a beautiful native woman ran to him and into his outstretched arms, smothering the big man with hugs and kisses. Veniard was returning the affection enthusiastically. There had been no such display at any of their other stops.

Renaudiere, riding in the second boat where Pierre sat, chuckled.

"That must be his wife!" he said calmly.

"His *wife*?"

"Yes. You did not know about that?"

"Well . . . I . . . no, monsieur, I did not."

The engineer chuckled again. "Nor did I. But I am not surprised. Many of the *coureurs des bois* take native wives, I have heard. Probably most of them. And Captain Veniard spent some time among these people, you know."

"Yes, so he said. But I had not thought . . . a *wife*!"

This helped to explain the familiarity and respect that was so apparent among the Missouries they had encountered.

Now Veniard beckoned to the leaders of his party. Renaudiere, Quesnel, Pierre, the ensign, de St. Ange, and the three noncommissioned officers, Sergeant Dubois and Corporals Rotisseur and Gentil.

"Here," Veniard stated with a dramatic sweep of his arm, "here we will build our fort. Fort Orleans, in honor of the regent. Long live the king!"

It was now a race against time as the days grew shorter and the nights colder. Renaudiere chose the actual location for the fort and staked out the first of the buildings. It would be on the north shore of the river, across from the village.

Soldiers meanwhile began to fell trees and drag the logs to the building site. First, a barracks, to shelter the entire party. That would be followed by a structure for officers' quarters, and small houses for the priest and for Veniard. For the present, they all camped as they had during their travels.

Except for Veniard, of course. He promptly moved into one of the native lodges with his wife and a lanky youth whom he introduced as his son. The boy was perhaps twelve or fourteen years of age, and showed his mother's fine bone structure and his father's height. His eyes were an odd gray-green color, showing his mixed blood.

Pierre had an odd feeling of envy as he saw this unexpected family unit. Veniard was certainly fortunate to have such a wife, one of the most beautiful women Pierre had ever seen. Her smile, the way she moved, and her obvious adoration of Veniard made plain his reasons for hurrying back to the woods. The young lieutenant would lie in his blankets, trying to stay warm by the campfire. He thought of Veniard across the river in a warm lodge with a warm and loving sleep mate. Ah, well . . . it would be warmer when the barracks were finished.

Christmas came and passed, and construction continued. The New Year arrived, 1723. Pierre Rivier tried to enter the event in his journal, but his ink had frozen and broken the bottle. There were snows, and sometimes it was impossible for the builders to work at all. But after the roof closed the first building against the weather, things became more tolerable.

Meanwhile, he extended his use of the hand signs and began to learn some of the language. He discovered that the natives loved stories. Before the really bad weather of the winter months began, on many evenings there would be a "story fire." The people would gather and one of the few who were apparently professional storytellers would speak.

The first time that this happened, he assumed that it was a council of some sort. Veniard, who was in attendance with his wife, explained.

"No, it is just for the telling of stories. For enjoyment. I am

made to think this, Rivier—since they have no written language, this
is their history. Notice, each story fire begins with Creation and comes
toward the present, a brief history of 'the People.' But wait . . . I
forget! You do not know their tongue yet. Well, you will see."

Since most of the other French of Veniard's party were also
unskilled in the Missourie language, few were interested in the story
fires. But somehow, with the insight given him casually by Veniard,
Pierre's interest grew.

It was helped along by his understanding of hand signs. An old
storyteller began to use hand signs one evening in accompaniment to
his spoken story. Apparently it was for the benefit of a trio of visiting
outsiders. They were Osages, whose use of the Missourie tongue was
limited. But it greatly helped the young lieutenant, who began to understand the stories much more clearly. In turn the storyteller, noting
his interest, continued to use the signs. This, too, helped his progress
with the spoken language.

Veniard seemed to approve. He appeared pleased that the
young man attended the story fires and took an interest in the ways of
"the People." *His* people.

"I am made to think that this is good," Veniard once said.

Pierre recalled that he had heard the big man use this expression before. In fact, several times. *I am made to think* . . . not "I
think," or "I believe," but "I am made to think."

Strange. Veniard's demeanor had changed when they arrived in
the country of the Missourie nation. He was no longer the polished
aristocrat whom Pierre had first met in Paris. The transformation was
complete and he was again the woods ranger, the *coureur des bois* of
his other life. He was even phrasing his speech differently, and it was
apparent in this one phrase. *I am made to think* . . . it was a conces-
sion, a recognition of the spirit-forces at large in the world, the world
of the People. Forces that influence human destiny from outside, and
over which mere humans have no control.

Pierre found that he had no problem with this idea. In fact, he
found it rather comforting. The mystic connection of the spirit with
the spirits around him seemed perfectly logical.

He had noted earlier that at each new campfire where they
stopped, Veniard would take a pinch of tobacco and toss it into the
growing flames. Pierre inquired about it.

The other man looked at him strangely for a moment.

"It is a custom here," he explained. "It says to the spirits of a place 'I am here! Here I intend to camp tonight.' Maybe it is a recognition, and a request. Permission to stay the night."

They did not talk of what Father Mercier might think of this communication with spirits, but Pierre thought that it might not merit the priest's approval.

He did ask another question of Veniard during this period of learning the ways of the People.

"Do they celebrate a Sunday or Sabbath?"

"No," replied Veniard. "They do not need it. They are in contact with their God every day."

Maybe, thought Pierre, *this man is more Indian than the Indians themselves.*

4

December had been called the Moon of Long Nights by the people of Veniard's wife. It was followed by the Moon of Snows, which was aptly named.

The soldiers struggled to complete the log structures of the fort. There were days at a time when they could accomplish no outside work at all. The wind howled through the timber and across the ice of the river like the moans of a living thing. The Indians stayed inside during those days and played games of chance, smoked socially, and told stories. On better days, they ran trap lines, harvesting beaver, fox, mink, and otter for their furs.

Once the first barracks building was completed, it was a little better for the soldiers. They, too, now had shelter from the howling storms of winter. It was apparent, however, that there were fewer of them than when they left New Orleans. Pierre noticed this with some alarm. There had been two deaths from pneumonia, according to Dr. Quesnel, and one man killed by a falling tree during the construction. But as Pierre thought about it, and took a rough head count, there must be . . . *ten or twelve* that he could not account for! Alarmed, he reported to the commander.

Veniard merely shrugged. "They run away."

"Desertion?"

"Oh, yes. Some of them are conscripts, you know, and leave at the first opportunity. We lost some, probably, before we reached Fort de Chartres."

"But what will happen to them?"

Veniard shrugged again. "Some will try to go home. But most will become *coureurs des bois* and join the natives. It happens."

He seemed to show little concern, and Pierre felt a strong suspicion that the former woods ranger had a certain amount of sympathy for the deserters. The circumstances of Veniard's own resignation of his command at Detroit had never been completely clear to young Rivier. Now he wondered even more.

"What is the next moon called?" he asked the big man.

Veniard chuckled, a deep-toned grunt of amusement.

"That is the Moon of Starvation."

It was a chilling thought. Or would have been, if they had not been already constantly chilled to the bone. Pierre could not remember when his feet had been actually warm.

"Starvation?"

"Yes. Supplies run low. There must be enough seed corn saved for the spring planting. Beans and other crops, too. Seed must be saved. Hunting is poor, if at all. It is a time of hunger. Some deer die, or are pulled down by wolves. This removes the weaker. It is the way of things, Rivier."

Again, Pierre saw in Veniard a reflection of the ways of his wife's people. *He is one with them,* the young man realized. *He thinks like an Indian.* One day at a time, accepting what cannot be changed, yet willing to change what can be. It was an odd combination, a fatalism that seemed out of place in a man with the grandiose schemes of Veniard.

"What is next, monsieur?" Pierre asked.

Veniard looked at him sharply.

"The next moon? The Moon of Awakening."

"No . . . I meant, what do we do next? But . . . the Moon of Awakening?"

"Yes. The world awakes, buds open, things begin to grow. It is the beginning of their New Year."

"Ah! I see."

"But to your question—we finish the fort. More of the buildings. Meanwhile, make contacts. Councils, talks with other towns, tribes. Begin to plan our expedition west. But that will not be until next season. There is much to do."

Contacts, councils . . . Veniard knew what would be necessary to bring about the treaties he would seek. Pierre's respect for the man continued to grow. What other Frenchman anywhere would have the broad knowledge as well as the leadership ability and the charisma to carry off such a scheme? He mentioned this to Renaudiere.

The engineer nodded. "That is true, Rivier. And this was all his own idea, you know. He approached the regent with his scheme."

"Ah, I had not known that, monsieur."

"Yes, so I understand. The nation has some economic problems, you know."

"No, I . . . I have never dealt with such things," Pierre stammered, embarrassed.

He felt that the conversation was over his head. Such matters were not a subject of casual conversation in the world where he had grown up. In short, he was reminded that he and all his family were commoners. Matters such as the economic state of France were completely foreign to their lives. Now he was in a situation where he was in contact with the aristocracy. Evidently both Veniard and Renaudiere would feel quite comfortable even in the presence of royalty. Probably Dr. Quesnel would, also.

How odd to think of this at this time. Here were men with whom he had shared hardships and camaraderie, heat, dust, mud, and cold. They were as human as he, though he had great admiration for them. Yet they had carried on conversations with key figures in the world of royal politics and intrigue. Thinking back to the night he had met Veniard at a party, he could see how that could be.

"It is like this, Rivier," the engineer went on. "King Louis, may he rest in peace, had done wonderful things for the arts. Music, literature, art . . . he also was fascinated by North America, the New World! Colonization, trade. Competition with England and Spain for the wealth of a continent. A great and a wise plan. But no one realized how very big it is, this land. More riches, maybe, but much more expensive to explore because of distance. Pay and supplies for troops, support for colonies . . . it has cost much, and our monarch reigned, you know, for over seventy years! The royal treasury is low. So this scheme of Veniard's to stimulate trade with Spain makes sense. Trade *here,* let the Spanish bear the expense of shipping furs back to Europe."

For the first time, Pierre began to see the reasons for this mission. Until now, he realized, he had been thinking only in terms of the adventure.

But Veniard must see both the adventure and the economic benefits, and enjoy both, as well as the political intrigue. Yet what would be his reward? Beyond the enthusiastic joy that the man seemed to derive from everything he did, of course.

As if in answer to his thought, Renaudiere continued in a slightly lower tone.

"I am not one for gossip," he said uncomfortably, "but it is said that if he is successful in our mission, our leader will receive a title of nobility."

"A *title?*"

"So I have heard, though not from him. It is a part of his contract with the regency and the Crown."

"That is how it is done?"

"In this case, yes. A title is earned by great service to the Crown, and is then handed down through the generations. Certainly in this case, it will have been earned, no?"

Both men chuckled.

"Say nothing of this, of course, Lieutenant. Ah, we have been gossiping like fishwives!"

"Not really, sir. It was in admiration of our leader, was it not?"

Pierre's confidence was returning.

"True," Renaudiere responded. "And of that, we have plenty!"

Progress on the fort continued. With the thawing of spring, it was possible to caulk the cracks between the logs of the buildings, plastering with clay. Ah, how that would have helped during the winter, to have had a more weathertight structure! But it was good to think of how much better the next winter would be.

Fort Orleans had been skillfully designed by Renaudiere, and in great detail. He showed Pierre some of the sketches. Actually the plans envisioned a complete community, with a fortified retreat at its center. There were crop fields and pastures, houses, a church, a powder magazine, storage for crops and for trade goods, even an ice house.

"It is much like a standard plan," admitted Renaudiere modestly. "Marshal Vauban, the king's military engineer, devised such a plan for colonial outposts. See, a square of thirty or forty places, defensible in case of attack, into which the community can retreat. Bastions on each corner. From those firing points, extended and raised, an enfilade can be directed against attackers along any or all four walls. The design is good."

"But surely we do not expect to be attacked," Pierre protested. "Are not these people, the Missouries, our allies?"

"Of course! But *they* have enemies. Think . . . if they were engaged in a war, which *could* happen, we would be drawn in. That would be no time to think of building a fort!"

Pierre had to admit that such reasoning made sense. To plan ahead is to survive the unexpected dangers.

It seemed also that this fort was extremely well planned. A means for defense when needed, provision for self-sufficient maintenance and growth. If things went well, expansion in the surrounding area. More houses, families, farms, a town surrounding the original site of the fort . . . if not, Fort Orleans was still a well-designed and easily supplied outpost at the frontier of expansion.

Pierre thought from time to time of bringing his journal up to date, but the opportunity never seemed to occur. He had not replaced his ink bottle, frozen and broken in the first hard storms of winter. He would have to beg or borrow from one of the leaders of the party, and was reluctant to do so. His lack of insight had resulted in the loss of his own writing equipment. How could he admit such shortcomings to men who had planned ahead for such possible mishaps? It was easier to defer the task of keeping his journal. He choked down the slight feelings of guilt at not following his father's advice, and put the matter behind him.

Veniard had continued to live in a native lodge, but as warmer weather set in, a house for his quarters as commandant was constructed. It would be somewhat different in design. It was still of unsquared logs, set upright in the ground like the palisade walls of the fort. The roof was of heavy thatch, after the fashion of French country houses. The walls were plastered with *bousillage,* a mixture of clay and straw. This, applied both inside and out, lent a substantial air of gentility to the fort.

The church received similar treatment, and more such structures were planned, to be completed later for the fort's officers and their families.

Crops were planted with the advice and help of the Missouries, and colonization seemed well under way.

Meanwhile, Veniard was planning his push westward. With the flair of a showman, and to impress the tribes they would encounter, he was planning a spectacular expedition. Not one, but two parties, he described to his officers. One was to travel by boats on the river, the other overland with horses, at least for the initial leg of the journey, to the junction of the Missourie and Cenzas rivers. They would be accompanied, he said, by as many as a thousand natives, of the Missourie and Osage nations.

This large a delegation, and in the cause of peace, would make a spectacular impression, he felt. It was easy to agree. The enthusiasm and excitement of Veniard was a contagious thing. A listener could be swept along with the sheer energy radiated by such a leader.

Of course, he cautioned, this is not until next season. June, maybe, the Moon of Roses. It must not interfere with the planting, either that of their allies here, or that of those they would encounter on the upper Cenzas River.

5

Now the time for the journey westward was finally here. Pierre could hardly control the excitement that he felt over the monumental thrust into the wilderness. It amused him to think that two years ago he had considered *this* the wilderness. And it *had* been, though it was much different now.

He looked down the slope from where he sat, at the neat outlines of the fortified square, its stout log walls, the heavy gate. From this angle he could see just the tip of the roof gable at the north end of the barracks. There was a feeling of pride in all they had accomplished since he had arrived here with Veniard, fresh from France.

Across the river were the houses of the natives. His attitude toward them had changed, too, he now realized. He was not sure when or how that had happened. Possibly the relationship that Veniard held with these people had affected Pierre. He admired Veniard as a leader, and the big man's easy acceptance of the Missouries and their customs had impressed him from the first. It was a short-cut, maybe, a hastening of his own insight into the ways of these people. In turn, Pierre had been quickly accepted. Partly that was due to his association with Veniard. But his own interest, too, in the customs, the hand signs, and the language of "the People" gave him a great advantage. He, too, had become accepted, probably to a greater extent than any other of the garrison at Fort Orleans. With the exception of Veniard himself, of course.

He looked down at his journal again, at a loss. What should he say? Was this to be a formal report, like the ledger kept by Renaudiere? Or a more personal record, like a diary? Or even a series of letters to his parents, to be sent home when opportunity offered? He wished that he had asked more of his father before he left Paris. The elder Rivier had impressed on his son the importance of keeping a record. And yes, there was still some guilt about that. The same guilt had driven him to borrow writing equipment from Renaudiere at least to make a start.

But now, what more to say? So far, his name, a date, and a place. ". . . of July, the second, A.D. 1724, Fort Orleans, Louisiana Territory . . ." Nothing more. Well, he must produce something.

> "We are about to start on an expedition to the west," he wrote.
>
> Our leader, Captain Veniard, is under contract to negotiate with the Indians of the plains, to allow safe passage for trade with Spain in a town that they call Santa Fe. The tribes or nations that we are to contact include the Cenzas, (who are presumed to be friendly), the Pani, and the Snake People, known also as Comanche. The latter two are of questionable deportment, being often at war with each other and with the nations to the east of their range. There may also be others we will encounter.
>
> We will be in two parties, one by boat and one by horse and on foot. The two will meet at the city of the Cenzas where the river that bears their name joins the Missourie River. From there we shall proceed westward along the Cenzas River into the country of the Panis. Some thirty French will be involved, accompanied by a force of natives friendly to us, mostly Missourie and Osage. Captain Veniard expects as many as a thousand, which will be a show of force if necessary.
>
> The first detachment, that by water, departed Sunday last, at noon, being about twenty-two men, under the

command of Ensn. M. de St. Ange, Sgt. Dubois, and Cpls.
Rotisseur and Gentil. There are eleven soldiers, and five
Canadians, including the priest, Fr. Mercier. Two men,
Toulouse and Antoine, who are in the employ of M.
Renaudiere, accompany this river party.

I take pen in hand this day of July the second to
record that we shall depart overland, by horse and on
foot, on the morrow. There are, in this overland party,
some ten Frenchmen, and a Canadian drummer Hamelin
to mark the marching cadence for the troops. There will
be with us also the son of Captain Veniard, and a
hundred Missourie warriors, including most of their
important chiefs. Some sixty men of the Osage, allies of
the Missouries, will also be with us.

It was a bright summer morning, the third of July. With considerable fanfare, drums beating and banners flying, Veniard mounted
his horse and turned toward the trail. At his side, his son, tall and
proud. Close behind, Pierre Rivier, riding with Renaudiere, the engineer. Behind them, the military detachment, led by the pennant bearer
and Hamelin, beating the march. Behind, in front, and among the
French moved the escort of nearly two hundred natives, Missouries
and Osages.

They would follow the old trail, used for centuries by the Missouries. In general, it followed the river, though not closely. The river
itself wandered, looping and turning and sometimes almost meeting
itself. In addition, it had often changed its course during seasons of
flooding. Across the generations, moccasined feet had found the going
somewhat easier and more efficient a little distance from the river
itself, on higher ground. In places, the stream was close at hand, not a
bowshot away. In others, it would be seen at some distance, or even
completely out of sight for a little while.

With the fort and the village behind them, Veniard called for a
cessation of the drum and the march and ceremony, and the soldiers
were allowed to fall into an easy route step. This would be far less
tiring than the stricter tempo, though not as showy. Veniard's years as
a woods ranger would stand him in good stead.

The party traveled well, and when they stopped to camp for the
night, Pierre estimated that they must have traveled seven or eight

leagues. He was in good physical condition, but not accustomed to long distances on horseback. His legs, which he had thought to be numb, now denied that theory. The last part of the day's travel had been the longest. Apparently Veniard wished to push forward to this, his preselected camp. For whatever reason, he had not called for a rest stop in some time.

Pierre stepped down stiffly, and his right foot struck the ground with a sensation like that of a hundred tiny needles. He almost fell, but gritted his teeth and took a step or two. Self-consciously he looked around at the other horsemen. Renaudiere, somewhat older than himself, seemed to be having similar problems. Veniard, however, was striding around the camp as if he spent long hours in the saddle every day. His son, with the agility and exuberance of youth, was trotting around, gathering firewood.

"I fear we shall be stiff tomorrow," Renaudiere suggested, swinging his legs to restore circulation.

Both chuckled. It would be a day or two before their muscles became accustomed to the change in activity.

"We have been impressed by the things we have seen," Pierre wrote in his journal after their second day of travel. "There are herds of deer, turkeys, and many trees bearing nuts. Hazelnut trees especially, heavy with nuts, grow in profusion along our way."

He was still stiff and sore, but tolerating it somewhat better now.

They continued to travel well. The weather cooperated, and in only three days the party had reached the first goal, their contact with Cenzas. The Cenzas, of course, had been expecting them. Such a large party cannot move unnoticed. It was apparent also that they were friendly. Veniard had sent messengers ahead, and a great gathering of Cenzas waited on high ground several leagues to the northeast of the junction of the rivers.

Veniard rode forward, holding aloft a peace pipe, and was met with cheers and greetings. The time of their arrival had been well estimated, not only via the messengers of Veniard, but those of the Cenzas. The party traveling by water had arrived at the village some days before, the Cenzas related. These runners had been shuttling back and forth for the past two days. A great feast had been prepared. There were elk, buffalo, and venison, waterfowl of all sorts, turkey, rabbit, and squirrel.

The council mats were spread, and discussion began, with ceremonial smokes and speeches and statements of friendship. The leaders of the Cenzas pledged their assistance in Veniard's cause. The day was done and purple shadows fell across the valley of the Missourie River before the festivities were over and each participant sought his blankets.

"The next day we crossed the river," Rivier wrote.

It required most of the morning, even with the help of the Missouries. They showed us the fords where the depth is not too great. Even so, it was necessary to swim the horses for a short distance at one point. Some of the men, too, swam across. Boatmen carried our supplies and those who did not swim.

The party moved on, and arrived at a village of the Cenzas on July 8, the next day. There they were reunited with St. Ange's party, and received with another celebration. People from other towns were arriving. It seemed that Veniard's boast that a thousand men would follow him westward was not unlikely.

After a day of discussion, rest, and planning, it was decided to move on. According to the Cenzas, there were villages of the Panis along two rivers that flowed from the west. Veniard preferred to try the more southerly of the two, the Cenzas, since his goal was contact and trade with Spain in Santa Fe. The other river, he feared, arose from too far to the north.

There was yet another stream, the Cenzas told him, even farther south. They referred to it as below, or downstream from this, the Cenzas. In their tongue, the river was called the Ar-Cenzas. This river too had a trail, a southwest trail, used by travelers for many generations. There was some discussion, but Veniard had apparently already decided on the trail along the Cenzas. Both trails were virtually the same for a few days' travel, they told him. Then the southwest trail branched southward from the other and led overland toward the Ar-Cenzas River.

"Are there Pani towns there?" Veniard inquired. "We must contact them."

"No," he was told, "the Pani country is to the west and northwest."

Veniard shook his head, displeased. "And the Comanche?"

"No towns. They move around."

"Ah, yes. I have heard! They camp in skin tents, no?"

The Cenzas nodded. "That is true."

"We must talk with both Panis and Comanches," Veniard explained.

The others nodded. "Then this way, along the Cenzas River."

"How far?"

"To the Pani, the Horn People? Maybe six, seven sleeps."

"Why are they called Horn People?" asked Veniard.

"That is their name."

"Buy *why*?"

"Oh. The men have a horn from the top of their head, here."

At this point even hand signs began to break down. There was a confusion of signs for head, hair, and horns. The conversation was finally abandoned, with assurances by the Cenzas that "You will see."

This was somewhat disconcerting to Pierre. Could it be that a race of humans could possess a *horn* like that of a unicorn? The hand sign indicated a single growth from the center of the head, not one on each side like those of an ox. Well, as their Cenza hosts assured them, they would soon see.

6

The fine weather held. There were occasional storms, which swept from the west with noise and lightning and pelting rain. On these occasions the expedition would camp for a day and then move on. It seemed that these passing summer storms served to wash both the prairie and the sky. The return of the sun always produced a brilliance in the green of the grasses and the blue of the heavens. Life was good.

They saw great herds of bison, elk, and deer, more wild turkeys, and quite a variety of fur bearers—beaver, otter, mink, and fox, as well as the larger wolves, which constantly circled the flanks of the buffalo herds.

Veniard, familiar though he was with the frontier, was greatly impressed with such bounty. This open prairie was a new experience for him. He would stand gazing across the rolling hills during each rest stop as if his spirit could reach out ahead in its eagerness.

"A beautiful land," he would murmur, half to himself. In the evenings he would often write in his journal.

This is the finest country and the most beautiful land in
the world; the prairies are like the seas, and filled with
wild animals, especially oxen, cattle, hind, and stag in such
quantities as to surpass the imagination.

He organized an impromptu buffalo hunt to provide meat
for the now large party. It only added to his prestige when he
amazed their Indian escort by shooting buffalo from a running
horse.

Unexpectedly, Veniard fell ill with a fever. Dr. Quesnel examined the big man, and recommended that they camp for a day.
Veniard would not hear of it. By evening, however, his fever was
raging. Still, he insisted that they travel.

"It will soon be over," he snapped irritably as he swung into the
saddle and led the way westward.

By that day's end he was swaying in his seat. The next morning
he was too weak to climb onto the horse. This would force him to rest.
Or so thought the others of the party, but they had not considered his
stubborn singleness of purpose.

"Make a litter," he commanded weakly. "A couple of stout fellows can carry me. It makes no sense to waste a day's travel, and I will
ride tomorrow!"

Dr. Quesnel shook his head in despair, but advised in the construction of the litter.

There was much slower progress in travel with soldiers carrying the sick man. His great height and muscular build made the litter
a heavy load. The carriers had to trade off frequently.

He was not able to ride the next day, or the next. Instead, he
became weaker. Dr. Quesnel pleaded with him, but to no avail.
Veniard only became angry.

Finally he became delirious, however, babbling irrationally. The
doctor called a council of the officers.

"I fear this will kill him," he admitted. "His mind is gone, and
he does not even know his name."

"What do you suggest, Doctor?" asked Renaudiere.

"First, that we stop here. He *must* rest. I am not certain that he
could survive the trip back to the fort. Who is second-in-command?
St. Ange?"

The ensign nodded. "I suppose so."

"Then let us camp here and see what another day brings. Agreed?"

The others nodded agreement. It was a somber mood that evening under the prairie stars.

The patient appeared more stable after a day's rest, but there was little actual improvement. Another informal council was held.

"We must take him back to Fort Orleans," the doctor announced. "He must have bed rest and proper care. Even so, the trip . . . I am not certain that he will arrive with life still in him!"

But that night as darkness fell, the fever reached its peak and broke. The big man was now seized with a chill and drenched with sweat.

"It is good," grunted Quesnel. "The crisis is past!"

However Veniard remained too weak to hold up his head, much less to protest. A plan was devised. A small advance party under the command of Gaillard would proceed to contact the Comanches and explain the situation. A recruit of Renaudiere's, Gaillard had previous experience in negotiating with Indians.

The main party would return as rapidly as possible to Fort Orleans, carrying the ailing Veniard. St. Ange would be the nominal commander, relying heavily on the advice of Quesnel in the care of the patient. But hearts were heavy. The great adventure had failed.

It was mid-August when the now-shattered expedition arrived back at Fort Orleans. There the ailing Veniard received badly needed rest and care. The ministrations of his adopted people and the ceremonies and potions of their medicine men undoubtedly played an important part in his recovery. Even so, the process was painfully slow.

"This malady would have killed a lesser man!" Dr. Quesnel observed.

Veniard, now rational though extremely weak, immediately began to plan for a fresh start.

"We can still reach the Padouca by summer's end," he insisted.

Within days he was sending messengers, organizing again, planning, estimating a day of departure. All of this, of course, was to the dismay of his physician. But the overwhelming enthusiasm and vibrant life force of the man made it difficult to keep him down. They struck a balance of agreement, and Veniard resigned himself to a moderate degree of cooperation.

Even so, it was a month before the big man was strong enough to attempt a new start with any rational expectation of success.

"Of September the 19th, A.D. 1724," wrote Pierre Rivier in his journal.

Tomorrow we start again. Our commander is well recovered, although still not back to his fullest capacities. I pray that he will follow the advice of Surgeon Quesnel, and take some care for his personal welfare.

The beauty of early autumn had crept across the land during their enforced delay. Pierre had watched it happen the previous year, but now had more time to enjoy. Wild flowers bloomed in abundance. In contrast to spring's assortment of soft shades of color, this season seemed made of gold and purple. Brilliant sunflowers taller than his head turned their faces toward the rays and followed east to west each day. A variety of smaller types in the same brilliant color grew in profusion along small watercourses and in open meadows.

Here and there, spikes of bright purple liatris thrust upward, blooming in their strange pattern from the top downward as the season progressed. It was a time of great beauty.

Nights were beginning to be cool, sometimes with the threat of things to come, but the days were wonderful. Long warm afternoons with the clear blue of summer sky overhead. Pierre was becoming restless. Would there really be time to accomplish their purpose before winter descended? He did not yet have the feeling of what to expect in this climate. Yet somehow the weather did not create a sense of urgency. Maybe he was beginning to take each day as the Missouries did, one day at a time.

There was something comfortable about it, a simplicity in the way of living. Not only the Missouries but the other tribes he had met seemed to have a similar philosophy. *When* will it happen? The ever-present demand by his own culture seemed absent here. The answer was a nonchalant shrug and a careless remark: *When it is the time for it.*

Pierre began to see some of the conflict that must seethe inside of Veniard. There was a need to meet the terms of his all-important contract, yet there was the pull of his wife's people, his adopted nation. *When it is time . . . it does not really matter.*

However, Veniard was now back in his military mode. He pushed the party to its limit. Rather, to his own limit. It may have been that a lesson had been learned. Veniard seemed more willing to listen to the advice of the doctor, and handled himself accordingly.

Of October the second. This day reached the village of the Cenzas, from whence we started earlier. Dr. Renaudiere has recommended a few days' rest, and our commander, though impatient, seems willing to comply.

Of October the seventh. Tomorrow we start again into the western prairie. We have held important council with the Cenzas, who were already friendly. Many of their warriors, along with our Missourie and Osage, will join us. Captain Veniard's expectation of a thousand men may not be far off.

Travel was good, the land open and the trail plain along the River of the Cenzas. They made good time, and paused for a day at a village of the Pani. These seemed quite a different people. The appellation "Horn People," echoed by the hand sign, became quickly apparent. The heads of the men were shaved, except for a circle perhaps a hand's breadth across, just above the forehead. This tuft of hair was allowed to grow long. Twisted and plaited, it was drawn up into a horn-shaped projection, and waxed heavily with tallow and red pigments. This made the Pani men, already tall, appear even taller. It would be a fearsome thing, Pierre decided, to face a charge of such warriors.

"But they are easiest of all to scalp," one of the Osages confided. "You skin off only that one patch of hair."

Pierre saw the twinkle in the warrior's eye. He was beginning to appreciate Indian humor. He smiled, waiting.

"Of course," the Osage went on, "he may be one of the hardest to put down."

There was a healthy respect for each other by these different nations. Sometimes there was some personal resentment over past differences. Yet all groups seemed to realize that to stop the warring and slaving and to open trade would be good for all.

It helped, perhaps, that Veniard was well supplied with gifts to bestow. This seemed to make a great impression. In addition, Gaillard had apparentiy done his job well. His advance contact had produced much goodwill. There was feasting and storytelling and many pledges of friendship.

"It is to be hoped," Veniard observed to his officers, "that Gaillard has done as well with the Comanches. They are the ones who concern me. I suspect that they trade with the Spanish."

"But will this not depend much on the attitude of the Spanish?" asked Renaudiere.

"Of course. That is what concerns me," Veniard answered. "But look!"

Several of the Pani men carried flintlock muskets of Spanish pattern.

"These are gotten by trade?" he asked in hand signs.

The bearer of one of the muskets smiled. "No. By war," he signed.

"You are at war with the Spanish?"

"Not really. They came here with warriors."

"When?" asked Veniard with the universal hand sign for any question.

"Three, four seasons. We killed them."

"All?"

"Most. Nearly all. A few went home."

Veniard was obviously uneasy, but it was hard to say how this would affect their mission. There were also French muskets here, from trade with the *coureurs des bois*. Well, this might indicate either a neutrality or a trend toward France. Either would be acceptable. But what about the Comanches? Apparently there was an openness of mind here. The Pani, it seemed, would be ready to fight them or trade with them, whichever seemed best. But the slaving must stop.

There were a few other things of note about the Pani. Their women seemed quite available to the visiting French, and quite openly so. Some of the women, at least. Others were quite obviously *not* available.

"It is a woman's choice," a Pani man explained to Pierre in signs.

He found this quite intriguing.

"At all times?" he asked.

The man nodded. "But only for one moon at a time. Next moon, new choice."

Confused, Pierre made the question sign.

"She must prove the father of any child she may have," the man answered.

And that is the only way, thought Pierre. *She must be with only one man during any one moon.*

"Does she not have a husband?" he asked.

"Of course. She can be with him next moon."

Another strange thing . . . he noticed one or two women whose hair seemed slightly wavy rather than straight. He inquired about that.

"Yes," his informant signed. "One family, mostly. It is said that they had an ancestor, a subchief called Curly."

7

They quickly moved on westward. Veniard was anxious to contact the Comanches.

Pierre noticed a change in the grasses through which they rode as they moved westward. For the first few days they marveled at the height of the growth. The tallest variety, which bore a three-pronged seed head, ("turkeyfoot," the natives called it), was often taller than a man on a horse. A man on foot could be hidden completely from view.

As they moved farther west, however, they noticed another change in the flora. There was a short, gray-green grass here that grew no more than a few inches tall. It was thick and tangled, however, a mat in which nothing else grew. The scattered bands of buffalo seemed to graze this plant eagerly.

Quesnel tasted it. "Sweet," he remarked. "This may be a very nutritious plant for these cattle. But the taller types must be, too. Look at the vast numbers!"

"Why is there such a change here?" asked Pierre. "A whole new set of grasses and plants and trees."

Renaudiere shrugged. "There must be a difference in the

amount of rainfall. Some plants favor dry land, and cannot grow in a wet place."

"The river grows smaller here," the young man noted.

"Yes, but that is different. That is because it is *shorter*. It drains a smaller land area than the great rivers. At least, that is my guess," the engineer explained.

The greatly enlarged party now traveled entirely by land. It would have been impractical to have boats, traveling at a different speed, attempting to match that of the column. Veniard had decided that on the earlier attempt, after talking to the Cenzas. However, it appeared that the Cenzas River *was* navigable for some forty leagues west of that point. For small boats and canoes, even farther.

Gaillard was now leading the way, having traveled it before.

"The country flattens to the west of here," he explained. "Still many days to the Comanche country."

"They are expecting us, though?" Veniard asked.

"Yes, of course. It was my impression that they welcome our visit."

"Is there a place designated? The Comanches move around, it is said."

"That is true. But they know we are coming, Captain. And they do stay in one area for some time. I told them we will follow the river. *They* will find *us*."

They had followed the river since leaving the Cenzas. It flowed almost directly from the west. They had been advised to follow the south bank, because all streams of any size entered the main river from the north. This had proved to be true. Any stream they encountered was small enough to cross without difficulty. There was a trail of sorts most of the way. Even when it was indistinguishable in the heavy summer's growth of the grasses, the river was in sight. From time to time, a sizable stream was seen to empty into the river from the other side.

Renaudiere explained. "We are apparently on a high prairie, a divide, though we cannot see that it is so. A few leagues to the south, there will be another river, with streams draining into it from the north. Or maybe from both directions. That would be the one called Ar-Cenzas, maybe."

"Then the major rivers here run from west to east, all of them?" asked Pierre.

"One might say so. At least, in this area. Think of it this way,

Rivier: The land slopes west to east, but also north to south. Remember the biggest river, the Missi-sepee, runs from the north. The gentle roll of these hills prevents our seeing it. But we know of mountains to the west, no? Had you thought about this? Their western slopes also drain to the *other* side. A whole system of rivers. Ah, Pierre, this must be a *huge* continent. Bigger than Europe!"

It was difficult for Pierre, with a somewhat limited education, to grasp. Still, it was easy to catch the excitement of the more learned engineer as Renaudiere interpreted their findings. He could see the excitement in the older man's eyes. "Pierre, this will be very important in the future!"

Of October the seventeenth, A.D. 1724. Tomorrow we are to meet with the Comanches. There is great expectation. Some of their messengers have already joined us, and will guide us to their village or camp. It is said that these people live in tents entirely.

They had seen a few of the conical skin tents before. Apparently this sort of shelter was practical and versatile enough to be utilized occasionally, even by those who lived in permanent dwellings.

Pierre was not prepared, however, for the sight that lay before them. Hundreds of lodges were scattered along the prairie, apparently in a random manner. Yet all the doorways faced in the same direction, to the east. Pierre was curious.

"Why is this?" he asked Gaillard.

"I am not sure," the other answered. "It is always so. It seems part of their religion. The rising sun in the doorway, maybe."

His curiosity was not satisfied, but he set that question aside.

"There are hundreds of lodges here, Gaillard. A big camp."

"Yes. The ones I saw before were in a smaller band. See, there seems to be a cluster of the lodges in the bend of the river, there. Another in the meadow to the west. Those appear to be the ones I talked to."

Renaudiere joined them, and now entered the conversation as they rode on in.

"I believe," he noted, "that the size of such a camp is limited by the available forage for their horses. They can gather like this for only a short while, and must then move on when the grass is all eaten."

Of course! Pierre thought. He had noticed the hundreds of horses on the prairie to the south, loosely herded by a few mounted riders. He had not paused to realize the immense amount of forage that such herds would consume.

"That is true," agreed Gaillard. "We had first thought of food supplies as the limiting factor, but we have seen so much game. The hump-backed cattle, too many to count. But you are right. The limiting factor must be food for their animals, not for their people. They have gathered for a short time here to meet with Veniard."

"They seem peaceful enough," noted Pierre.

Gaillard chuckled. "Do not be deceived, Lieutenant. These are some of the most dangerous fighters on the prairie. And you can figure two warriors to every lodge. Older boys learn to hunt and fight alongside their fathers."

"But why do they seem so pleased to see us?"

Gaillard laughed. "Veniard instructed me to tell them that he will bring many gifts."

"*That* is how he will impress them? Not with his force?"

"It is his way. He has lived among them, you know. I think sometimes he has begun to think like a native. The great numbers with him show that he has *friends.* That he has strength, too, of course. But these people will feel that there must be a reason for so many friends, no?"

Pierre nodded, still not quite convinced. One cannot really buy friendship with gifts. Maybe it was simply Veniard's manner, his personal excitement and enthusiasm. They had seen it many times. The big man could enter a room or a group of people and make each person there feel that it was a personal visit to *him.* Veniard was aggressive and even somewhat demanding in his relationships. Yet one always felt *honored,* somehow, to be selected for the work and sacrifice that these demands required. This, Pierre decided, is truly the mark of a leader. The gifts were only to attract attention at an initial meeting.

Whatever the means, it was apparent that a warm welcome awaited them. There were cooking fires everywhere, and the rich smells of roasting bison and elk hung over the encampment. There would be feasting tonight. . . .

The parlay itself was simple. Partly in sign, partly translated by interpreters. Veniard spoke to the assembled Comanche leaders, promising friendship and trade. He opened the bundles of gifts from the pack-horses, taking out knives, mirrors, trade beads, ornaments, and trinkets.

One of the Comanche chieftains stood to make a speech of welcome and acceptance. The dignified old man used hand signs as he spoke. A younger man translated into the Cenzas' tongue, understood to some degree by most of those present.

"We are honored to welcome you to our camp. Your gifts are good, not like those of the Spanish, who give none or very poor gifts. You are our friends, and are welcome in our lodges."

Veniard responded with pledges of continued friendship and trade.

"But there is no reason," he went on, "why we should not all benefit by trade. We would trade with the Spanish, and wish to pass safely through your hunting lands. We would trade with our brothers the Comanches, also. Let there be open trade with all . . . Missourie, the people of my wife, with Osage, Cenza, Pawnee, and Comanche. Is it not better to trade than to war and to sell slaves?"

There were nods of agreement.

"And to eat together?" Veniard went on, spreading his arms wide and with a broad smile on his face.

This time there were cheers.

"I would speak of other things, too, before we depart. I wish for some of your chiefs to visit in my country, to meet my chiefs. But for now, enough! My nose tells me that the meat is ready!"

It is hard for men who have eaten together to consider warring, and a man such as Veniard was well aware of this. The breaking of bread, long symbolic in his culture, was comparable to the sharing of meat among his wife's people and the others of the prairie. "Come, join our fire, we have meat," was an often-repeated invitation on that October evening as the setting sun painted the western sky and the crisp chill of early autumn descended. The diplomatic skill of Veniard was reflected in the evening campfires.

Pierre Rivier, along with the rest, gorged himself. The richness of broiled hump ribs of buffalo was not entirely new to him, but he had never tasted better. Full and content, he lay back on an elbow and watched the stars appear in a velvet sky so broad that one could see forever. Somewhere a night bird gave a plaintive cry. A coyote called, and its mate answered from a distant ridge.

It was only then that Pierre had the feeling that he was being watched. It is a strange sensation, one without description. There are none of the senses that really report such a feeling. It is a thing of the spirit, maybe. How odd, that in this camp of a thousand people, he would feel a single pair of eyes upon him. He turned to look, though he felt no threat or discomfort, only curiosity.

There was no question as to the direction. His gaze moved to the next campfire, where he looked directly into a pair of the most remarkable dark eyes he had ever seen. He was thrown off guard, embarrassed, and for a moment had not even the presence of mind to smile.

Then the owner of the dark eyes did so, revealing even rows of white teeth. Both the eyes and the smile were set in the most beautiful face in the world. Tiny wrinkles of humor crinkled at the corners of her eyes, and there was an unspoken invitation in her smile.

There is nothing more intriguing to a man than an attentive approach by a beautiful woman. His heart beat faster and his palms were damp.

8

The girl was somewhat younger than he, but fully mature in every way, it seemed. At least in every way that he could see. He had seen a variety of women in the past two years. But none, he thought, could begin to compare with the beauty of this lovely creature. She saw him watching her, and smiled. His heart melted.

Maybe he had been preoccupied with the hard work of travel and the discomfort of summer's heat on the plains. Maybe the women he had associated with had been less forward, less inviting than this Comanche girl. Maybe it was only that there had been no available women for a long time. Perhaps, though, it was as he believed at that moment. He was surely looking at the most beautiful girl in the world. Her form and figure were perfection, Pierre thought.

Many of the Comanches were fairly short of stature. The French had already noticed one thing, however: While a Comanche warrior might appear unimposing on foot, on horseback he was to be reckoned with. The horse had more than made up for the genetic tendency to short legs among some of the Comanches. Pierre had watched the young horsemen, and considered them some of the finest cavalry in the world. He marveled at their ability to swing from one side of the horse to the other, to shoot to the front, rear, either side, and even *under the necks* of their mounts.

The young woman he was watching, however, was not of the short-legged build. She was tall, with long, well-shaped calves and thighs. Her ankles were slim and trim. The thought crossed his mind that maybe this was one of the examples of intermarriage. Possibly, even, a girl of another tribe, who had been kidnapped or sold as a slave to the Comanches.

It was no use to wonder, he decided. She was purely Comanche now. Her hair, dress, and moccasins said so. And her bearing was not that of a slave.

Very quickly, the next thought came to him. *What are the marriage and sexual customs of these people?* Was this girl available?

He tried to remember. Different tribes and nations in this new land varied widely in their customs. Some were quite similar to European cultures, except for the multiple marriages. Even that was understandable, with the dangers experienced by the men in war and in the hunt. There were always more women than men, and the age-old answer to this inequity has always been the same: plural marriage.

Beyond that, though, there had been a time when Pierre, along with most Europeans, had considered the women of the new world to have very loose morals. Now, after two years in close contact with the Missouries, he had come to better understanding. It was not a matter of ethics or morals, but of *difference*. Women possessed a quite different status among all the tribes with whom he had met. They carried far more influence and power than the women of Europe. Among some groups, even, the principal leaders were women.

He had completely misunderstood the function of the moon lodge at first. Each month at the time of her menstruation a woman must leave her own lodge for a few days for the good of her family. Her spirit-strength at that time was so powerful as to make her dangerous. But only she knew when she must go to the moon lodge. This gave her control of her body and her sexuality in a way completely unknown to European women. In turn, among most of the tribes he knew, it gave the woman the choice of whom she would bed.

This was not to be confused with morality. Among some of the tribes the rules were extremely restrictive. Among Pawnees, he had learned, a woman must guarantee the father of any child she bears. This can only be by complete restriction to one man during an entire moon cycle. But it is *her* choice, in contrast to the loose promiscuity of the European male-driven morality, or lack thereof.

All of this half-formed understanding caused his head to whirl in confusion. He would have known the rules and customs for a potential courtship among Missouries, Cenzas, or Osages. But what about Comanches? And of course the status of the woman might make quite a difference. Married or single, slave or free? He might have to deal with the girl's *owner,* in which case an entirely different set of rules would apply. He did not think, though, that her demeanor was that of a slave.

Finally he realized, as he stared and the girl smiled back, that regardless of all else, he must allow her to take the lead. She knew the rules, he did not. He must also trust her. If she did not stay strictly within the rules of her own people, then both might be in great danger. But he was dazzled by her beauty and her smile. He found himself ready to do anything she wished, regardless of the consequences. He smiled back, and the girl seemed pleased. Now, contrary to the customs of his own people, he would wait for her to make the first move. Of course, he would take care to be quite visible and available to any such move. Just to be sure, he raised his right palm in a subtle hand sign of friendship. Her smile broadened, and she returned the sign. So far, this was going well. . . .

The council was to last for a few days, with the fine weather of Second Summer still holding. Over all, however, was a certain sense of urgency. Veniard was eager to complete his mission and hurry back to Fort Orleans. Originally he had thought to travel all the way to Santa Fe to open the trade route. But this goal had been thwarted by his illness.

Now it was a matter of completing his negotiations with the Comanches and hurrying back before the onset of winter. There seemed to be no other tribes to the southwest who would present an obstacle to the proposed trade route. As a part of the present council Veniard inquired in detail about this. He was assured that there were none who would present a problem. Besides, the French traders would have the protection of the Comanches, no? And who would dare to challenge such might? The lavish gifts that Veniard bestowed seemed to cement this relationship.

Still, it seemed only prudent to gather information about tribes farther west, and Veniard was thorough. A mere mention of a town or village that was new to him piqued his curiosity. Mention was made of a town of growers to the west, who lived in permanent houses made of blocks of mud. Instantly he was alert.

"How far?"

"Six, seven sleeps."

Veniard shook his head. "Too far! Damned sickness . . . too late in the season," he muttered, half to himself.

A travel of seven days, another of council and seven more to return to this point would be unacceptable. It would delay the return journey by more than two weeks, and in turn, the departure for France.

"But tell me more of these people," Veniard requested. "They live in mud lodges?"

"That is true," the Comanche leader responded. "They grow corn, pumpkins, beans. We trade with them sometimes."

"They have been there always?"

"No. They came from that way . . . southwest. In my father's time. There was a war with the Spanish."

Ah, yes, thought Veniard. Had there not been an uprising of some sort? These could have been refugees. Maybe it would be possible to send a small party to make that contact. He summoned Renaudiere, and outlined his idea.

"We could send Gaillard or Rivier with a small party," he suggested. "The Comanches would provide a guide."

"Captain," the engineer protested, "you are talking of a journey of a hundred leagues. If our main party starts back on schedule, this scouting party could not overtake us before it is time to board ship."

"That is true," Veniard agreed. "I forget . . . the distances here in this land! Well, it was a thought. But this brings another. Our main purpose was to open trade to Santa Fe. Is it practical? How long would such a journey take?"

"From Fort Orleans? Mmm . . ." the engineer mused. "Yes, I think so. The distance, maybe three hundred leagues . . . sixty days, another sixty back. Somewhat slower with a pack train . . . four or five months, round trip. Yes, it can be done."

Veniard nodded impatiently. "Yes, yes, of course. But you are right. It is not practical to send a party now to this town they tell of. What is it called?"

"It has a Spanish name, m'sieur. *El Quartelejo.*"

"They are *Spanish*?"

"No, no. They are natives. The Spanish call the town by that name."

"Yes, I see. Well, we will stop there next time. This season draws to a close too quickly, no?"

Part of the time Pierre had watched and listened to the negotiations at the council. It was moderately interesting, he thought. But there was another interest on his mind. The girl.

He had seen her only the one time, on the previous evening. He had hoped that she would contrive for them to meet again, perhaps that same night. In this he was disappointed. He went to his blankets and lay awake for a long time, staring at the stars, watching the slow circle of the Big Dipper as it swung around the polestar. The Seven Hunters, his Indian friends called the constellation. Each night they circled their base camp at the North Star. It was a convenient way to estimate how much of the night had passed.

A considerable portion of the hunters' nightly arc had been traveled before Pierre fell asleep, to dream of dark eyes, an inviting smile, and a soft yet supple body. . . .

He looked for her the next day, but did not find her. He watched the council, wandered among the lodges, and went to check his horse. But the dark-eyed beauty was nowhere to be seen.

He wondered if he had been wrong about her status. Maybe, after all, she was a slave, and had fallen under a threat not to associate with the visitors. Somehow he could not believe that to be the case. There was the "look of eagles" in her eye, a spirit that would not bend under the yoke of slavery. He viewed this with mixed feelings. If she *were* a slave, it might be possible for him to buy her. Such a thing had never occurred to him, but his heart and soul had gone out to this girl. He would have risked anything to free her from such status.

Even as such thoughts occurred to him, he knew that it was ridiculous. He had never met the young woman, had not even spoken to her. There was only that smile, the hand sign. . . . Yet their eyes had met, and there *had* been a communication of the spirit. He was sure of it.

There was another possibility, one he did not even want to consider. She might have a husband. He did not even want to think of her in the arms of another man, even a husband. *Especially* a husband.

But that could easily be the answer to the puzzle. A husband, seeing her interest in one of the strangers, might forbid her to leave the lodge. If, of course, that sort of authority was the custom here.

And that, he did not know. So he wandered, looking for her, not finding her. He could not even think of a way in which he could inquire.

Frustrated as evening drew near, he climbed a little rise behind the encampment, alone. They would be leaving in the morning to return to Fort Orleans. He would have only the memory of a smile. He was irritated that this should disturb him so. Was the world not filled with beautiful women? *But none like this one,* came a whisper in the dim recesses of his mind.

The sun was setting in a blaze of glory. The prairie sunsets under the big sky were like none he had ever seen. He sat down, trying to concentrate on the beauty of the western sky. All the colors of a dream . . . the brightness began to fade, and the evening star, not visible a few moments ago, appeared. It was silvery white against the orange of the fading horizon.

He sensed motion in the edge of his vision, and turned to look. Someone was approaching. A woman, alone. *The* woman . . . she smiled and sat down beside him. A beautiful dream? No, he could feel the warmth of her body near him, and smell the faint woman scent of her.

"I search for you," she signed.

"It is good," he signed in answer. He was still slightly annoyed that she should seek him out only now. "But where is your man?"

Her eyes showed a shadow of hurt in the gathering darkness.

"I have no man," she signed.

His heart soared like the eagle.

"None?"

In answer she only moved closer to him, leaning her warm body against his. He drew her to him, kissed her gently, and they sank to the dry grass together.

And it was good. . . .

9

The next morning Veniard and his entourage left the Comanche encampment on the return trip to Fort Orleans. There was a chill in the air, a reminder of the coming of winter. It appeared that the warm days of second summer were over for the season. Soon it would be the Moon of Falling Leaves.

Pierre rode in brooding silence. The experience last night had been a time of wonder and delight. Yellow Flower (that was her name, he had learned) had lived up to the promise in her smile. Not just in a physical way. . . . Her laugh was like the murmur of the breeze in the cottonwoods. It matched her sense of humor, and they had laughed together, often and well.

Communication had been a slight hindrance, but even that slight problem had been a joy to solve together. Initially, their communication was largely physical, with the urgency that transcends all human speech. It was a little later that they discovered that both had a fair working understanding of the Cenza tongue. Between that and hand signs they quickly adjusted. It must be noted, also, that there was a force of the spirit at work. Thoughts came easily, and in the slight struggle to find vocal expression, each would finish the thoughts of the other. It was as if they had been together always.

Flower's mother had been an outsider, he learned. Her background was largely Cenza, hence her daughter's use of the language. The girl herself, however, had been born Comanche and considered these her people. Her father, whom she described as a brave warrior, had been killed last season in a battle with Pawnees. After appropriate mourning, Flower and her mother had moved into the lodge of a relative. The mother became a second wife. Flower herself had been expected to take a husband, because she was of age.

"But you have not done so?" he asked.

"I have been courted much," she said, showing a shyness that he had not seen before. "None have interested me. Not to make me want a lodge with them."

She took a deep breath. "My mother's husband becomes impatient. I think he wants me, but that cannot be. Mother and daughter . . . one must leave."

Though the language was difficult, Pierre thought that he understood. Customs varied, but in all groups there was a dread of incest, with varying definitions of such a taboo.

"What will you do?" he asked.

The girl shrugged. "I do not know. Choose a husband . . ."

The subject changed, they were distracted by other matters. They watched the moon rise, a little past full. They listened to the night birds in the thin strip of timber along the river. Kookooskoos called his hollow cry from a huge cottonwood above the camp. A pair of coyotes, striving to sound like a dozen on the next rise, nearly succeeded.

The gray of the false dawn was showing in the east when they rose. Pierre drew her thick buffalo robe, which had sheltered them, around Flower's shoulders. Both shivered in the morning chill. The weather was changing. . . .

Now Pierre rode dejectedly in the column, well behind the leaders. In front with Veniard and Renaudiere were several of the chieftains whose influence they sought. Even after two years in Veniard's service, Pierre was amazed at the way the man could influence others. There was an aura, a charisma about him that made even men of other cultures want to follow him. It had little to do with the lavish gifts he bestowed. Veniard could walk into a council and make everyone there feel important. It was as if each person was feeling *He came to see me.*

Tasks must be assigned in a quasi-military situation such as this. But rather than resenting the daily chores, the men of Veniard seemed to cherish them. His personality and leadership were such that it often seemed a privilege to be asked to carry out some menial assignment.

And this feeling crossed cultural lines. There could be no other explanation for the immediate loyalty demonstrated by leaders of the various native groups. Veniard's goal was to take back to Paris perhaps a dozen leaders of various tribes, to show them the wonders of civilization.

Well, riding ahead there, flank to flank, were chieftains who had promised to go. Men of the Comanche and Pawnee nations, sworn enemies by birth and tradition, now eager to follow Veniard. Beside them, a Cenza interpreter, an Osage chieftain, and a brother of Veniard's Missourie wife.

In the company of perhaps a thousand who rode with them were men of all the above tribes, as well as a few Illinois. One of their chiefs, old Chicagou, or Skunk Water, had already agreed to be part of the diplomatic mission to Paris.

Pierre Rivier himself would have followed Veniard into the jaws of hell. Why, then, did this return trip weigh so heavily on him? He kept thinking of the dangers, the long ocean voyage. . . . Odd, that had only been an adventure on the outbound trip. Was it that he regretted that the great adventure to the New World would be over, once back in Paris? A few weeks . . .

By the time they reached Fort Orleans, it would be the Moon of Madness. He realized that he had been thinking in terms of the natives' concept of the seasons. But time *was* flying past. Was he ready to return to the mundane life he had lived before? He did not know.

He thought often of that last night among the Comanches. There had been little sleep, and he had paid dearly all that next day, dozing in the saddle as he rode.

And then there were thoughts of the girl. . . . Yellow Flower. All of his senses were affected. The smooth touch of her skin and the silkiness of her hair . . . the faint scent of her nearness. . . . Her chuckling laughter beckoned to him in the whisper of the cottonwoods. The vision of her loveliness, the beauty of face and form . . .

ah, what a vision! These things kept recurring to his senses, asleep and awake.

He would have thought that such memories would be good. He had loved and left before, and had fond memories of some of these experiences. Why, then, did he feel only sadness over this one-night encounter? It made no sense to him. After all, this had been only a native girl, a harmless flirtation within the rules and customs of her people. And *she* had initiated it, had she not?

Now he began to resent his own feelings. She had no right to affect him like this. Then his flare of resentment would cool, and be replaced by guilt that he should feel so. It was not her fault. His own stupidity was bringing such feelings. He should have sent her away when she first approached. Then his memories would jerk him back. How wonderful that he had *not* sent her away.

He had no appetite, and ate poorly. Maybe some bad water . . . he wondered if he might be coming down with the malady that had stricken Veniard earlier in the summer.

By the third day he was swaying in the saddle. At the evening camp the doctor approached him.

"You are not feeling well, Rivier?"

"What? Oh, yes. I am fine."

Quesnel studied his face. "Of course. But you seemed to sway a little bit."

"A little tired, maybe. It has been a long summer, no?"

"That is true."

Some time later, Dr. Quesnel reported to Veniard.

"I see nothing really wrong, Captain. He denies any problem."

"Then why is he so quiet?"

The doctor shrugged. "Who knows? But you know that he spent the last night with a Comanche woman?"

"Ah! You think he has *that* disease?"

Quesnel laughed. "No, no, not the one you mean. No, I think his is not of the genitals but of the heart, Captain."

"What? *Rivier?*"

"Why not? Surely you can understand such a thing."

Veniard gave him a sharp sideways glance. "You are being sarcastic, Quesnel!" he accused.

"No, no! Pardon, Captain. I intended no disrespect, no offense."

Veniard studied him a moment and then smiled. "None taken," he grunted. "But about Rivier? I will talk to him."

The doctor nodded. "Someone should."

"And as you have so artfully pointed out, *I* should understand, no?"

Now both smiled.

It was yet another day before the opportunity arose. Veniard approached his lieutenant, who sat a little aside, eating halfheartedly. He had noticed that the young man had formed this habit. Rivier was no longer the sociable young man he had been. Evening camps found him withdrawing, avoiding companionship.

"May I join you?" Veniard began.

"Of course, Captain," the younger man muttered.

Veniard sat cross-legged and began to eat from his own tin plate.

"What are your plans, Rivier?" he asked conversationally.

The lieutenant looked up. "What . . . I do not understand, sir."

"When we reach Paris. What then?"

"I do not know. . . ."

At this point, the young man was completely confused. He was not certain what his leader was asking. *Is he telling me that my services are no longer needed?* he wondered.

There could be several possibilities. It might be that Veniard was trying to determine his interest in further service. On the other hand, maybe this was the big man's way of beginning to let him down gently, and suggesting that he look for other employment. He could, of course, return to his military service. His commission was still good.

Somehow, though, it had never entered his mind to wonder what would happen next. Beyond the return to Fort Orleans, that is. The very magnitude of their present mission had overshadowed all else. He had envisioned their triumphant return to the fort, and the celebration of success. He knew, also, of the plans to take the native leaders to meet the royalty of Europe. Yet he had never quite seen himself as a part of that operation.

But now, that operation was actually in progress. They would return to Fort Orleans, then immediately on to board ship for France. It was the way Veniard would do things.

Now it occurred to him that Veniard had not actually offered options. Maybe this conversation was merely that, a friendly conversation. With this reassurance, such as it was, Pierre took a moment to think. He had been with this prince of diplomacy for two years now, and had surely learned *something*.

"What of yourself, Captain?" he asked.

Veniard looked startled. "What?"

"Your own plans. Will you stay in Paris?"

The older man seemed confused for a moment, and then chuckled.

"Well done, lad. Yes, I must take the native leaders to Paris and see that they return safely. My plans are not complete, so how could I ask of yours?"

Pierre waited, and finally Veniard spoke again.

"I was wondering, though. Do you have any specific goals, now that our primary mission is drawing to a close?"

Be very cautious, now, Pierre told himself. Aloud, he spoke in question.

"What are my options, m'sieur?"

Again, it appeared that he had caught Veniard off guard.

"Well . . . you could stay at the fort, or come with me to help show the chiefs Paris. You could resign at any time, of course. Go back to the army. . . ."

Or none of these, thought Pierre. He could not even think of such things when his thoughts, his dreams, were still occupied with the sweet memories of the beautiful Yellow Flower.

Now his companion startled him with a comment.

"I am told," Veniard said casually, "that there was a Comanche girl for you."

Pierre flushed. "It . . . it was not like that, Captain."

"Then how *was* it?" the other asked pointedly. "Tell me how this was different."

Pierre found his anger rising.

"Captain, this was not merely another romp in the blankets. It was more."

"*What?* Tell me!"

"I was . . . well, you know how they talk of spirit. . . . I am not sure how to say this, Captain, but our *spirits* were one."

Veniard smiled, and his intense look changed to one of benign approval.

"So . . . you do not wish to go back to Paris? You would stay at Fort Orleans?"

"But that would not . . ."

"Or go back to *her?*"

Now that it had actually been said, a feeling of immense relief flowed over the young man.

"Rivier," Veniard said gently, "I once found myself with a similar problem. All I can tell you is this. I am made to think that your heart will tell you what to do."

The sun had set, and purple shadows were filling the low areas along the stream with twilight. Pierre saw the evening star appear against the orange sky. He had been given permission, somehow, to feel as he did. And now he felt that his heart not only told him what he must do. His heart soared, like the eagle.

AFTERWORD

Etienne Veniard did return to Paris the following year, 1725, to accomplish his mission. His company of several native chieftains and their families were presented at the royal court. They performed their native dances at the Paris Opera, and demonstrated a deer hunt on horseback in the royal preserve, to the delight of the young King Louis XV.

Pierre Rivier was not with the party.

Veniard received a title of nobility, Sieur de Bourgmont, as a reward for his accomplishments. He did not return with his native emissaries to their homes, but settled in Paris, married a rich widow, and died in 1730, at the age of fifty.

His love for the land he called Cenzas is reflected in his journal:

> This is the finest country and the most beautiful land in
> the world; the prairies are like the seas, and filled with
> wild animals, especially oxen, cattle, hind, and stag in such
> quantities as to surpass the imagination.

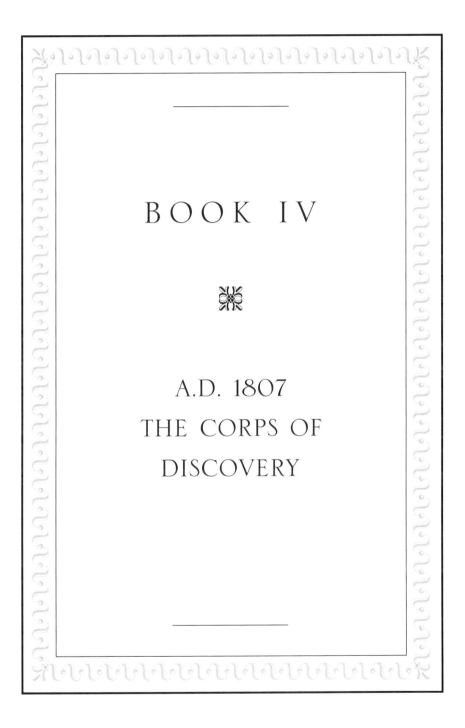

BOOK IV

A.D. 1807
THE CORPS OF
DISCOVERY

PROLOGUE

The two men still sat at the rough table, talking in animated tones. It was late, and all the other patrons had departed. The barmaid leaned in the doorway, watching them, hoping they would leave soon. Then she could retire to her crib in the slanting attic space up under the eaves.

Earlier in the evening, when the two young officers had entered the inn, she had eyed them with a great deal of interest. Both were handsome, yet in entirely different ways. She would not have resisted the attentions of either of them. They were by far the most interesting of the travelers in the inn tonight. She was not above flirting a bit, and contrived to brush against one or the other from time to time as she served them. Finding little response beyond a friendly smile, she showed a little cleavage as she reached across the board to refill their tankards. Still nothing. Well, maybe they were more interested in each other. With that idea in mind, she backed off to observe them. It was a slow night anyway.

The two had come in the door together, but she had the impression that they had met just outside. Yet they were talking like old friends. Yes, like comrades in arms who have not seen each other for a while. Before long, she decided that was it. They had planned to meet here to spend an evening in talk and army stories. Or possibly had met accidentally on the turnpike. Either way, their earnest conversation and their preoccupation with talk told one thing plainly: These two were not looking for girls tonight.

She felt with a woman's intuition that there were times when either of these *could* be. The way they talked and looked at each other was excited, but not toward each other, beyond the common bond of soldiering and man talk. She would watch them and maybe when they tired of that she could catch the eye of one or the other.

The taller one was a rough and outdoorsy type, a Kentuckian, maybe. Handsome in a rugged way. She could see the muscles in his shoulder tighten under his shirt as he moved. A strong man, probably, but powerful as a cat is powerful, like a steel spring, ready to pounce. That one wore the insignia of a lieutenant.

The other was a captain, yet she could see no attitude of deference on the part of the frontiersman. No, these two regarded each other as equals, despite the formality of rank. The captain was handsome, too, yet in an entirely different way. He had the look of nobility about him. He had been raised as a gentleman's son. Not soft . . . no, far from it. She felt that this one could be every bit as strong, or as dangerous, as the other. A dreamer . . . yes, she thought, a dreamer, a romantic. He would be gentle, attentive. That one would recite poetry to a woman while . . . she would prefer him, she thought. Some might prefer the other one. She shook her head to clear it. No, she would be sleeping alone tonight. Just as well. She was tired.

She was convinced now that their conversation was the goal of the two men. Nothing more. They were drinking and talking politics. Man talk . . . the frontier, the West. She found that interesting, and began to listen.

"I tell you, Will, this is my most exciting assignment ever," the captain was saying.

"And this is because you knew him before?" the other man asked.

"Well, yes. Our two families were neighbors in Virginia. Albemarle County."

"But I thought you grew up in Georgia?"

"Yes, Will, that is true. My father died when I was small, my mother remarried and we moved to Georgia."

"Yes, go on."

"When I was old enough, I came back to Virginia to manage the family land. Tom was good to me, and we neighbored often."

"You call him *Tom?*"

"Not as a rule, Will. At the office I call him . . . but let me go on! I could see his house and barns from my window. Sometimes he would want to talk, and would take a mirror and flash the sun at my window. I would walk over and he would share his theories, his ideas, and dreams."

"I can't believe, Lewis, that you knew him. You never said . . ."

"What was to say, Will? He was a man, a smart man. A friend."

"But he was ambassador to France."

"Yes, a bit later. But even back then, he had this dream, to explore the *western* half of North America. Did you know . . ." He paused and chuckled. "Will, one time in Paris he met an adventurer and *hired* him to try a scheme that we had talked about. Ledyard, the man's name."

"What was the scheme?"

"Well, Tom thought, because of the distance, that it might be closer to go north from France, through Russia and Siberia, across the Bering Strait to Alaska and down the coast to California."

"Really?"

"Well, it was an idea. Nobody has crossed from here to the coast, you know. How far is it?"

"That's true, Lewis. What happened to the mercenary?"

"I'm not sure. He got a good start. Some three thousand miles, into Siberia. The Russians thought he was a spy, and jailed him. The empress is not to be angered, you know."

"Incredible!" the other man murmured.

"Isn't it, though? But then he tried again."

"Siberia?"

"No, no. This was at home. He was Secretary of State by that time, and it was before I joined the army. There was a Carolina man with good credentials, Micheaux, I think his name was. He was to go west under the employ of Tom as a private citizen, to explore the French region, Louisiana. I wanted to go with him, but they wouldn't let me. Just as well. It turned out this one *was* a spy, but for France."

The two men laughed and slapped their knees.

"But why . . ." the lieutenant began, "why did France want to spy?"

"Who knows? Nobody trusts anybody. And you know, that area has belonged to France, then Spain, then France again, for a hundred years. Nobody even knows how big it is. Maybe a million square miles. And what's out there?"

"Well, furs . . ."

"Exactly. Maybe other things, too. Gold, silver . . . but he's probably more interested in the science of it. New birds, animals, plants. He's fascinated by the Indians' crops. Did you know he's growing tomatoes?"

"Love apples? Aren't they poisonous?"

Both men chuckled.

"*He* eats them," said the captain.

"Yes, so do I. But Lewis, there could be anything out there. You've heard some of the French stories. A race of little demons a foot and a half tall, tribes of Amazons, hairy elephants."

"I know . . . unicorns!"

They laughed again, and then settled back, quiet for a little while.

"Seriously," said the one called Will, "somebody will go and see. Wouldn't that be great?"

"Of course. But back to reality. I'm just starting on this job. It was mere chance that we had this opportunity to meet, Will. But I wanted to tell you about a couple of things. This was one, the job."

The other man shook his head. "I still can't believe it. . . . *You,* secretary to the president."

The captain brushed it aside. "I'm sure, Will, that Jefferson will want to explore that French country, if he can do it. He'll only regret that he can't go himself. But more immediately, his concern is that between England and France, the fur trade leaves us—the United States—out of it. We need a seaport nearer the fur country."

"But what for?"

"Think about it, Will. New Orleans, a shipping point for furs, timber, cotton."

"But that's *French.*"

"Of course. But Napoleon has been spending his country into debt with his militarism. There's a good chance that they'd sell the Port of New Orleans. Say nothing of this, of course."

"Of course."

"Now, the other . . ." He lowered his voice, but the barmaid was no longer interested anyway. "This is really confidential, Will, but the president has asked me to do some thinking on it. If he can manage to get it funded, he wants me to lead an expedition into the western territory, and I would get to pick my men."

Lieutenant Clark shook his head in amazement and envy.

"Lewis, I don't know how you do it. What an assignment!"

"Isn't it, though? And Will, it's pretty speculative yet, but stay in close touch. If it happens, I'll want you for my adjutant."

In 1803, President Thomas Jefferson, negotiating for purchase of the Port of New Orleans, was astonished to find that France would give up all her North American territory under the same treaty. For fifteen million dollars the size of the United States was doubled with the Louisiana Purchase.

Jefferson's secretary, Captain Meriwether Lewis, was commissioned to explore the new land west of the Mississippi, with Lieutenant William Clark as his adjutant. Their Corps of Discovery, handpicked frontiersmen, became the cadre of experienced mountain men who guided others, opening the West.

1

Liberty sat at a table, alone, watching the crowd that ebbed and flowed in the smoky room. Yellow light from the lamps barely reached the dark corners, and did nothing at all to dispel the shadows in the rafters. Or in his mind . . .

Normally, with the amount of whiskey he had consumed, he would be pleasantly drunk. This time he was only depressed. There are times when one's mood requires only a minimum quantity of alcohol to achieve the goal, he reflected. Other times, there is not enough in all of the country to do the job.

He was not certain just what the problem might be, except that he had nothing to look forward to. But why should that bother him? He had *never* had anything. It was a puzzle.

He took another sip of the raw whiskey and began to take stock of his life. Maybe that was the problem. What was there to do? It was winter, but he had a place to stay, and a little money, even. *That* was a first. His pay from the corps had been hoarded. Well, not really. He had been lucky at cards. And that wasn't really luck, but experience. He had watched every gambling trick in the world all his life. It had enabled him to see through that crooked game and take advantage of the situation. Not a huge win, just enough to gain a few dollars without rousing suspicion.

He pulled his thoughts back to the task at hand. What was he doing here in St. Louis? It was 1807, and he was not yet twenty. As far as he knew, anyway. He'd never been sure, because he didn't know for sure who his mother was, much less his father. His earliest memories were of being a small child, in a high-class brothel in Philadelphia. He remembered a certain amount of pride about that. He had been kept carefully segregated from the patrons of the establishment, but had seen them come and go. Dignified gentlemen, well-groomed younger dandies. There was always a certain amount of gossip among the girls. More properly, ladies. He had ignored most of it, because it really was not very interesting.

All of the ladies had mothered him, and for the first few years of his life he assumed that everyone had several mothers. The one to whom he answered for discipline was Madge, who also mothered the girls as well as the kitchen staff and Samuel, the Negro butler and handyman. He was relatively certain that Madge was not his mother. She had once told him that his mother was dead.

His closest friend was Maria, younger than most of the others. She was pretty, with dark silken hair and large deep eyes. She was not his mother, either. There were mixed emotions when she left Madge's establishment to marry one of her frequent customers. There was a bittersweet going-away party for her, and everybody hugged each other and cried a lot and Maria held him close against her chest and cried some more.

"I wish I could take you with me, Lib," she snuffled. "It just wouldn't work."

That had been when he was about seven, he figured. He never saw her again.

He had the idea that probably he had been born to one of Madge's girls who had either moved on or died. The others had taken him to raise. No one had ever mentioned who his father might have been.

The girls had given him his name, Liberty. He knew that it was a good name, because of the Liberty Bell and the cause, and all. Usually Samuel called him Lib, and the others did, too, sometimes. Madge always called him Liberty. She taught him to read and cipher, too. His last name, Franklin, seemed to be partly a joke, partly to honor the great Benjamin Franklin, also of Philadelphia.

A few years later he began a spurt of growth. His voice changed, and a thin fuzz began to show on his upper lip. His reddish blond coloring made it nearly invisible for a while, but soon he would have to begin shaving. Some of the girls began to make lewd remarks and flirtatious moves. Liberty felt a strange stirring in his loins when one of them brushed past him in the narrow hall.

Then had come the night when he overheard a conversation not meant for his ears.

"It ain't right, Miss Madge," Samuel was saying. "You don't want to let this happen to him. You got to get him out of here!"

"Yes, I know, Sam, I know. But it's hard. Do you think? . . ."

"No!" The old Negro said firmly, much to Lib's surprise. Sam had always shown a great deal of deference to his employer. "He deserves a chance, Miss Madge. You been good to him. And to me, of course. But he's got the whole world out there. You and me, we've had our chance. Give him his."

Madge sighed deeply. "You're right, of course, Samuel. But he's developed so young! He can't be but twelve or so."

"Thirteen, maybe," Sam said.

"Well, I'll see about it."

Liberty had slipped away, to spend a sleepless night of worry about what they meant.

He learned, a day or two later, when he was summoned to Madge's private parlor.

"Liberty, put on your best clothes. I want you to come with me in the carriage."

That was always a treat, but this time there was a dread of the unknown. He met a sallow-faced man called Reverend Whitworth, who smiled with his mouth but not with his eyes, and did not seem to have met Madge before. They talked about his learning a trade, and how big he was for his age, and the weather and things. He stopped listening, and was shocked a little later to learn that he was to stay there to go to school.

Not only that, it was not merely a school but an orphanage. There were about thirty other boys there to learn a trade and to save their immortal souls, though not necessarily in that order. Liberty developed an immediate dislike for the Reverend, whose ideas of salvation of souls seemed to revolve around pounding on the other end. His favorite quotations were based around "Spare the rod and spoil the child," and "This hurts me more than it does you."

Liberty suggested that he'd be glad to trade places, which was not received well, and earned him five more whacks with the rod.

He ran away once, back to Madge's. He was returned to the Reverend's tender mercies by Samuel, who urged him to behave until he had learned a trade. There were a few more whacks.

Mrs. Whitworth was a pale, thin woman with a sad face and no color in her cheeks. Liberty wondered if she'd never heard of rouge. He thought of telling her about it, but with the lack of logic here, it might mean more whacks. Besides, a little color might make Mrs. Whitworth's life a bit more pleasant. And, it appeared that pleasantness and the salvation of immortal souls were completely foreign to each other.

He found that some of the boys had a deck of cards, and they organized a game in the barracks-style dormitory. They were caught, and Liberty was blamed. More whacks . . .

At least he was learning a trade. He could already read and cipher better than any of the others, but was assigned to hard labor as a farmhand because of his size. He found that he liked the outdoor work, ate well, and became heavier and well muscled.

There was an extra benefit of being in the detachment assigned to farm work. Those boys were "farmed out" for a week or two at a time, away from the Whitworths' orphanage. He didn't realize for some time, though, that the Whitworths were being handsomely paid by the farmers for their services. In addition, they solicited funds for their operation in the cause of salvation.

He had learned not to rock the boat, and kept quiet until the proper time, which was nearly a year. Then one night he bundled his meager belongings and slipped out of the dormitory. He ran right into the arms of the Reverend, who grabbed at him. Liberty lifted a coal scuttle and with a wild swing leveled the man, breaking his jaw. Lib fled into the night.

He stowed away in the back of a big Studebaker freight wagon, headed for he knew not where. He didn't care. He worked for various farms and apprenticed to a blacksmith for a little while.

Then came a big break. He saw a line of men talking to an army officer seated at a table. Curious, he asked some questions. A party was being recruited, he was told, to explore the new country to the west. Men with special skills were needed.

He was now fifteen, but looked seventeen, with heavy muscles and beard. He was nearly six feet tall. He lied and said he was nineteen, going on twenty, and was a blacksmith, which was partly true. He had also heard one of the other applicants tell about his skill with plants and flowers, and decided to toss that in, too. He *had* harvested a lot, and had once helped Miss Madge plant some petunias in her flower boxes.

In this way, Liberty Franklin became one of the elite Corps of Discovery.

When the clerk wrote his name, he looked up from the paper to ask with a grin, "Any kin to Ben Franklin?"

"Not that I know of."

There was a chuckle among the others.

"Might as well claim him, kid. You know how he was! You never know."

Now there was general laughter, and Liberty was embarrassed.

That was a lifetime ago, though only a few years by the calendar. He had traveled with Lewis and Clark, and was proud of their accomplishments, and of his part in it.

Maybe that was the problem. What more was there to do now? He'd "seen the elephant," and the future. The rest of his life appeared pretty boring from where he sat.

He rather envied John Colter. On the way home last summer, the corps had met a couple of trappers, out to find new beaver country. They had wanted to hire Colter as a guide. The captain thought it might be a good plan, and gave Colter permission.

Captain Lewis was adamant, though. He would excuse no one else on an early discharge until they reached St. Louis. No one tried to leave. Lewis had nearly had Moses Reed shot when he tried to desert back when they were among the Otoes. He had settled for a flogging instead.

Lib wondered where Colter might be tonight. It would be cold, wherever he might be camped on the upper Missouri. Maybe he would have a Mandan or an Arikaree girl to warm him, though. They had certainly proved eager and amorous. . . . Maybe that's what he needed.

He poured another drink, and was distracted by a conversation at one of the nearby tables.

"Yah, I seen it mineself. The Glass Mountain," one of the men was relating. "Captain Lewis, he shot at dis elk, und it just kept grazing. He reloaded, vent closer, und shot again. Still, nottin'. Anodder time, no heed from dat elk. So we valked toward it a vays, and here vas a mountainside of clear glass, clear as air, and dat elk vas on the other side of it. We vent hungry."

Liberty looked the man over. He was a big fellow, in a heavy buffalo coat, talking to three others at the table. One wore a well-tailored suit and a top hat, and seemed to be the one whom the talker was trying to impress. Liberty had never seen the big man before.

He scooted his chair around, facing the other table.

"You were there?" he asked the man in the buffalo coat. "I was, too!"

"You vere?"

"Sure! Remember at the Burnt Cliffs, where we saw all the little people, this high? Mean and evil, they was!"

"Sure vas . . ."

The big man looked puzzled.

"And the unicorns was interestin', wasn't they?"

The big man sat, openmouthed, but nodded uneasily.

Liberty slapped his knee as he chuckled. "I tell you, though, I don't want no more of them warrior women. That's plumb crazy, the way they cut off their right tits so they don't get in the way of the bow string, ain't it?"

"Vell, I . . . uh . . ."

"Fat man, I don't know who you are," Liberty went on pleasantly, "but you weren't with the Corps. I was! I never saw you before, and none of what I just told is true."

The other rose from his chair, pulling his coat aside to reach for the knife in his belt. Liberty was faster, and all his pent-up frustration came out with a rush. He grabbed the lapels of the buffalo coat and pulled it back and down over the man's shoulders. His arms pinned and helpless, the impostor stood swaying for the fraction of a second that it took to land a crushing blow to his face. The man swayed and dropped like a poleaxed ox, blood streaming from his flattened nose. The knife clattered to the floor, loud in the silence.

"You were with Lewis and Clark?" asked the man in the silk hat.

"I *was,*" Liberty declared. "He was *not.*"

"And what is your name, sir?" asked the other.

"Franklin. Liberty Franklin."

"An honor, Mr. Franklin. I would be honored to talk to you of a job in a project of mine."

2

The sudden excitement that had gripped the tavern for a few moments was quieting. A couple of men were assisting the now-subdued impostor toward the door. They cast backward glances at the still-smoldering Liberty Franklin, but seemed to want no more trouble.

Now the well-dressed gentleman spoke again. "Come, let us talk."

He led the way back around a broken chair to the small table in the shadows where Liberty had been sitting alone. As he moved, he raised a gloved hand to signal the barkeep for service. Yet he did not even look to see whether his request would be honored. Liberty was struck by this confidence, and took a moment to study the man.

The stranger was not a big man, but carried himself well. One whose stance and posture gives him dignity also gains the illusion of height. Such was the case here. Liberty might have overlooked the man on the street, having seen by his clothing that here was a pampered dandy, with ruffled shirt, tailored coat, and expensive boots of fine leather. But a second look at the way the man moved and spoke, and the utter confidence he exuded suggested that actually he was completely out of place here in a waterfront tavern in raw young St. Louis. Lib had been too preoccupied with his own thoughts to see all this before.

The stranger adjusted his chair to face the room at a better angle. Then, before seating himself, he deposited his cane on the table, removed his gloves, and laid them beside it.

The cane caught Liberty's eye, and he studied it while his companion casually brushed imaginary dust from the chair before seating himself. It was made of a highly polished dark wood. The handle was topped by an ornate knob with the face of a gargoyle. It had a dull yellow sheen, and Liberty wondered if it was gold. If so, and it was solid, there was quite a value there. Was it not foolish to carry such an inviting treasure to a place like this? There were probably a dozen men in the room who would cut a defenseless dandy's throat for such a prize.

Then, as the man seated himself, he ran his hands smoothly over the head of the cane. Liberty did not see exactly where the button or latch might have been, but the device seemed to come apart under the touch of its owner just a little way, a fraction of an inch. But it was enough to reset the latch mechanism. Then the soft-looking hands just as smoothly pressed the shaft of the cane back onto the hilt. There was a slight click, no more audible than the tick of a well-oiled clock.

Liberty was startled. A sword cane. The apparently defenseless gentleman was actually well armed. Not only that, but the grace with which he handled the weapon told of familiarity with its use. And, unsuspected, the man had been ready to enter the fight if needed. The whole thing had been done so smoothly that Lib doubted that anyone else in the tavern had noticed, even now. Here was a man of deceptive appearance. A powerful man, a dangerous opponent or a valuable ally in a fight. It would not be surprising to learn that there was a dirk or even a small pistol hidden under that plum-colored coat.

"Now," the gentleman began, "my apologies, sir. Let me introduce myself. You were rather busy before." A smile flickered around the corners of the handsome mouth as he extended a hand. "Alexander Andrews."

Liberty shook the hand. He had expected it to be soft and feminine, but here, too, he was deceived. Smooth, yes, but there was a hard strength here.

"Liberty Franklin," he murmured.

"Yes," said the other. "Any kin to Ben?"

Liberty had been asked that many times. Sometimes it was irritating. This time, it was plain that Andrews understood that, and sympathized. *He understands,* Lib thought, *and he has a sense of humor!*

"Not that I know of."

Both smiled at the inside joke, and it was as if they had known each other forever. There was a difference in their ages. Andrews was perhaps thirty, well past Lib's age, but a kinship lay between them.

"Now," Andrews said again, "to business."

Liberty had no idea what this might entail. He had never talked "business" before, and was completely puzzled at what might come next.

"Do you know Manuel Lisa?"

Whatever he might have expected, that was not it.

"The outfitter?"

"Yes."

"I know *of* him, yes. I have seen him, I would not say I know him."

"Did he not outfit the Corps of Discovery?"

Here was a very ticklish decision, how to answer this question. What if this Andrews turned out to be a partner of Lisa's? Or was the man pumping him for information? He should be cautious, now, despite his good feeling for Andrews. He knew well what Captain Lewis thought of the outfitter, "that damned Manuel."

"Yes," he said carefully. "That is my understanding. At least, part of the outfitting."

Andrews's eyes narrowed confidentially.

"And was it quite satisfactory?"

He knows something, or is trying to find out more, Lib thought. *Careful, now . . .*

"That would not be mine to say, sir."

Andrews gestured impatiently. "But surely you have some idea of the attitude of your captain," he pressed.

Liberty was quite uncomfortable. He liked this man, wanted to trust him, yet Andrews was trying to induce him to gossip. It angered him slightly.

"You would have to ask him yourself, sir. I could not speak for the captain."

Andrews seemed pleased, and settled back comfortably. The barkeep brought another bottle and glasses and set them on the table. Liberty, who had been on the verge of departing in anger, settled back, too. He was curious now. There was something here that he did not understand. Andrews poured each of them half a glass of whiskey and lifted his own in an unspoken toast. Lib followed suit. It was good whiskey, considerably better than what he had been drinking. This man, then, was well known to the bartender.

"That," Andrews said, "was what I had hoped."

"What?"

"Your answer. It told me much about you."

"I do not understand." His head was a little fuzzy from the evening's drink, but he was sobering rapidly. The pressure of the one-punch fight and the even greater stress of Andrews's pointed questioning was forcing him back to reality.

"You revealed much about yourself," Andrews went on. "First, you know that Manuel Lisa is a scoundrel, but you do not know *me* well enough to say so. Next, you would not betray your captain. You know that *he,* too, knows Lisa, but you were unwilling to put the words in *his* mouth. Am I close?"

Liberty nodded in wonder. This was a very clever man. He, Liberty, had just been tested, without even knowing.

"Close enough. You were testing me, then?"

"It is sometimes necessary."

"I guess I passed muster?"

"Close enough," Andrews grinned. "Now, down to business." That word, again.

"You know," Andrews went on, "that there will now be a push to open the fur trade to the west."

Lib hadn't thought about it much. "I guess so."

"Of course. Several have already gone up the Missouri to trap. The French have been trapping there for a century. More properly, they have been buying plews from the Indians. A few of the *coureurs des bois* trap for themselves and sell to traders, you know."

Liberty nodded.

"Now, did not one of the corps go *back* with some of these new beaver men?" Andrews asked.

Jesus, thought Liberty. *Does he know everything?*

"How did you know about that?" he blurted.

Andrews brushed it aside, and Lib let it drop. He'd get nothing from Andrews that the man didn't *want* him to have. But Andrews must know about Colter. Colter hadn't returned yet or everybody would know. So Andrews must have some contact with some others of the corps, who would know that John Colter had gone back to the wilderness.

Another thought was forming. If Andrews had talked to any of Lewis and Clark's Corps of Discovery, he had known all along that the man in the buffalo coat was an impostor. Alexander Andrews had been listening attentively to tall tales that he knew to be untrue. *Why?*

His train of thought was interrupted again as Andrews continued.

"You know Manuel Lisa is preparing to go west himself?"

No, he had not known. He shook his head. What could Andrews be leading to?

"Lisa wants to build a fort on the upper Missouri. He's trying to find a member of the corps to take him."

Liberty was uneasy again. Was Andrews trying to recruit *him* for Lisa?

"No, I—" he began, but Andrews again waved him aside.

"I'm not interested in that," Andrews went on. "There are already trappers heading up the Missouri. I'm looking at other areas. May I show you a map?"

Without waiting for an answer, he extracted a rolled parchment from somewhere in an inside pocket. He glanced around the room and seemed to make a quick decision. He rose.

"Come," he said. "Bring the bottle."

He led the way among the tables toward a back room, signaling to the barkeep as they passed. They had no more than entered the dark room when the barkeep followed them in to set a lighted candle on the table. He closed the door on his way out.

Liberty set the bottle and glasses on the table. Andrews pulled two chairs closer together, sat in one, and pointed to the other. He slipped a soiled red ribbon off the rolled parchment and spread it on the flat surface.

"Here, hold that edge. You read, Franklin?"

"Yes . . . cipher a little."

"Good. Now . . . recognize this?"

It was a map, very similar to the one with which he had seen the leaders of the expedition occupied. Was this the one? If so, how had he—?

"No, not the same one," Andrews said, as if reading his mind. "But the captain allowed me to sketch his."

So. That might explain much. This was a friend of Captain Lewis. And since Lewis's map was government property, apparently a very close and trusted friend.

But now he saw major differences in the map. This one did not include the entire route of the Corps of Discovery. The far western leg of the journey was missing. But there was detail directly west of St. Louis, and on toward the mountains, which were indicated as a wall of peaks running north and south.

"That is not where we went, sir," Liberty stated apologetically.

To his surprise, Andrews smiled approvingly. "Yes, I know. Now, show me where you *did* go."

Liberty followed the route with his finger. From St. Louis up the Missouri River. "Here, another river, a big one, enters. There are towns there, a people called Kenzas. We followed the Missouri northwest. The Kenzas River flows from nearly straight west."

"Yes . . ." Andrews was still smiling with approval. "Now, did you see beaver in that area?"

"Of course."

"Exactly. Now, Franklin, this is my point: Dickson and Hancock, with Colter's help, and now Manuel Lisa . . . all are going up the Missouri."

"Yes, but . . ." *He does know everything!* Liberty thought. *I did not mention those two.*

"Now," Andrews continued, "suppose a party set out for the mountains, straight west along this, the river you call the Kenzas. Would that not be a source of furs and peltry, and much *closer* to civilization?"

Lib studied the map. "Yes, it would seem so. Can this map be trusted?"

That was always a question worth asking. There were many maps that were less than worthless, being downright misleading. Andrews understood that, and was not offended by the question.

"I think so," he said. "I have combined sketches of your expedition with some I have obtained from the French."

Liberty longed to ask how, but by now he realized that Andrews would tell him what he wanted to tell, no more, no less. He rather admired that.

"This route," Andrews went on, "is a trail followed by a French party nearly a century ago. A nobleman called Veniard. He hoped to trade with Spain at a place called Santa Fe."

"This is *Spanish* territory?" Lib blurted.

"No, no. Not this part. This is part of the Louisiana Territory. Jefferson *bought* it."

"I have no knowledge of such things, sir," Liberty murmured, ill at ease.

"Of course, Franklin. I understand. But why should you? I want you for what you *do* know. I want you to help me lead an expedition up the river of the Kenzas."

Liberty was too overwhelmed to ask how he should address his new associate.

Now another thought struck him. The burly liar, telling of an expedition he had never seen . . . could it be that the whole thing had been a test? Was the man in the buffalo coat *hired* to rankle the young corpsman, to see his reaction?

From what he had seen of Alexander Andrews, it was possible. Well, if so, Andrews had gotten his money's worth, and more. And if so, Lib hoped that the impostor had been paid well to play the part. *He* had certainly earned it.

3

The two men talked until far into the night. In essence, Andrews's plan was simple. As soon as the coming of spring made travel feasible, he proposed an expedition to explore the possibilities of his theory.

"Let the others travel two thousand miles up the Missouri," he chuckled. "There are thousands of plews within half that distance."

His eyes glittered with the excitement of the possibilities. He pointed to his map again. "Straight west, here, along the Kenzas River."

The man's enthusiasm was infectious, and Liberty's interest began to rise.

"How many men would it take?"

"For the original scout? Half a dozen, maybe. Nothing like Lewis's corps. Will you assist?"

Liberty, even though he was becoming fascinated by the idea of going out again, was cautious. There were a lot of questions that remained unanswered. First, about the expedition itself.

"Is it known what Indian nations might be in that area?" he asked.

Andrews looked at him, somewhat startled. "You are afraid?"

Liberty looked at him without an answer for a few moments. Andrews was caught off balance for the first time since they met.

"Forgive me, Mr. Franklin. That was poorly phrased. I do not question your courage, only the nature of your inquiry. No offense intended."

"None taken. But it would be foolish not to be prepared, and informed as well as possible."

"That is true. Now in answer to your question. Initially, the Missouris and the Kenzas. Both are traditionally friendly, and have long traded with the French. Osages, allies of the Kenzas, at least most of the time. A bit farther west, Pawnees. Something of a question."

"A moment," Liberty protested. "Where do you learn these things?"

Andrews smiled. "An honest question. In effect, how accurate is my information? Fair enough! I mentioned the explorer, Veniard, and that I had made sketches of his map. I have some French acquaintances, through my mother's family, going back before the War of Independence. I had a copy of Monsieur Veniard's journal. In French, of course. Do you speak French?"

"No . . . a few words."

"Pity . . . but never mind. Back to your question . . ."

Despite Andrews's tendency to ramble, Liberty saw that the man's mind was orderly and purposeful. In many respects this man reminded him of Captain Lewis.

"West of the Pawnee, which Veniard often spelled 'Pani,' are Comanche and Cheyenne. I believe that these may be more unpredictable. They are nomads, living in skin tents rather than in towns, and moving often. You know of such tribes, of course."

"Yes. Blackfeet, Absaroka, Lakota . . . Lakota are called 'Sioux' by the French. All live in tents."

"Oh, yes, Franklin. I meant to ask, are you fluent in any of the Indian tongues?"

"Afraid not. We were on the move, you know. But all of them use the hand signs."

"Ah, yes, I have heard. You can use those?"

"Pretty well."

"Good. Could you teach me?"

"Certainly. It's pretty simple. Logical. A few hours and you'd have enough to get by."

"Marvelous! But back to our purpose here. How was your corps able to deal with the Indians?"

"With gifts. We carried a lot of trinkets and small useful items. It helped, of course, that both our leaders are sincere and open men. The Indians can see and respect that."

"Good. I had assumed as much. But there was some talk of a skirmish."

Liberty nodded. "You probably heard of the misunderstanding with the Blackfeet. Not really a skirmish, I'd say. One of their warriors was stealing a gun. He refused to give it back and Captain Lewis shot him. His people did not take it well, and we moved on."

"No matter. Apparently there are no Blackfeet this far south."

"Forgive me, sir, but where would you expect to sell plews? If the outlook is favorable, of course."

Andrews looked at him quizzically. "That is far ahead, Franklin. First, to explore the territory. It would be next year and into the spring before we would have furs to sell. Then, probably here, St. Louis. There is the possibility of trade with Santa Fe, of course, but . . . well, look—the French traders have bought furs from the Indians. So have the Spanish. Then they ship them out, with a great increase in value. But if I can arrange to *trap* the beaver—to employ trappers, that is, or to buy from freelance trappers, Indians, anyone— then I am closer to a shipping point. Let Lisa build his fort. My furs are still half the distance away."

"I do not understand, sir, exactly my part in all this. What is it that you want of *me*?"

"Oh! Forgive me, Franklin. I find myself carried away with the enormity of the undertaking. First, to recruit a few stout fellows for our expedition. Then, to lead it. Then, depending on the outcome, we will see. By that time, we shall see how we get along, you and I. And, of course, where your aptitudes and interest lie. Now, can you find me a few good men?"

Liberty thought about it. He had always been pretty much of a loner, had not formed lasting friendships with other men. There had been a special bond of comradeship, though, among the men of the corps. These were men he could trust in an emergency. Their reliability had been proven over two years and eight thousand miles. They were a *family*. At least someone had said so. Liberty had never known the feeling of family. Except for the mutual concern and support that Madge's girls had shown for each other and for him, of course.

Now he wondered. How many of the Corps of Discovery were still in or around St. Louis? It might be possible to inquire in the taverns and along the waterfront. Colter was still on the Missouri, as far as he knew. Ah, he would have liked to have John Colter! But there might be others, some who were experienced frontiersmen who had *not* been with Lewis and Clark. Well, he would see.

"I think it can be done, sir."

"Good. You may start selection at once."

"What will you pay?"

Andrews shrugged. "You know more than I about what is appropriate. Oh, yes! Give me a list of supplies and the trinkets you mentioned."

Liberty felt somehow that he was still being tested. "How many men do you want?"

"Five or six. Besides ourselves, that is."

"*You* are going?"

"Of course. I would not fund such a thing and leave others all the pleasure of discovery!"

Liberty had not been thinking along these lines. He viewed this revelation with mixed emotion. It would be good to have someone else with the final responsibility. Still, it could backfire badly. What if it turned out that this well-dressed dandy was helpless in a more primitive setting? That thought was short-lived, however. He had seen the readiness of Andrews after the brief encounter in the tavern.

"Very good, Captain," he smiled.

"Captain? Why do you call me that?"

Liberty was embarrassed. He had not realized what he had said. Perhaps the qualities that he admired in Captain Lewis were visible in this dynamic young man. He flushed.

"Sorry, sir. I did not . . . I guess it seemed appropriate."

Andrews thought about it for a moment, amused.

"I rather like it," he admitted. "Better than 'sir,' at any rate. Well, shall we call it a night? Meet here tomorrow about sundown?"

The candle had burned low. They returned to the front room. Andrews tossed a gold coin on the bar. Liberty thought it must be a substantial tip, judging from the bright smile on the face of the sleepy barkeep and his surprised "Thankee, sir!"

"Oh, yes," he said as the two men stepped out into the snow. "What is our transportation?"

Andrews nodded. "Of course! There are too many things to discuss. I had a keelboat here. Which way to your residence? Ah, same direction. Let us move on. What are your views?"

Liberty was not accustomed to being asked his views, and paused to think a little.

"Well . . . on the lower river, the keelboat worked well. But farther upstream, it was horses, you know."

"Yes, so I heard."

"Six men might become a small crew for a keelboat."

"There is no urgency to decide tonight," Andrews said as their boots crunched through the new snow on the street. "We will talk of this later."

They shook hands and parted in front of the rough boarding-house where Liberty slept. Andrews's place of abode was in a slightly more affluent hotel some distance beyond.

Liberty had a nagging doubt about the safety of a well-dressed man of means on the dark street at this hour. Then he thought again of the incident at their meeting, and smiled to himself. Probably any doubts should be over the safety of any thug who accosted Andrews. Besides, it was probably too cold for any evildoers to be abroad.

Possibly by sheer coincidence, a story circulated around the waterfront the next day. Early risers had found a trampled area in the new snow, some of it bloodied. There was the severed half of a human ear and a large butcher knife lying nearby. A trail of blood led toward the waterfront, but disappeared as the injured party apparently was able to stanch the bleeding. It must have happened sometime shortly after midnight when the light snow fell. It was scarcely a stone's throw from the rough boardinghouse where Liberty Franklin slept.

But knife fights were common in the boredom of late winter in St. Louis of 1807. The incident was soon forgotten, by all but the unknown participants, and by Liberty Franklin, who had an idea as to the identity of one of the participants.

Ultimately, it was decided to use horses for transportation. Alexander Andrews recalled Veniard, who had headed into the same area both with boats on the river and a party by land. The French explorer had decided that horses were more practical in the country involved.

"Besides," Andrews pointed out, "the tribes toward the west, Pawnee, Comanche, Cheyenne, use horses more than boats, do they not? They are buffalo hunters, according to the French."

So it was decided, and preparations began in earnest.

4

As the two men became better acquainted, Liberty Franklin was given increasing authority. He was given a line of credit at one of the outfitters, (not Manuel Lisa's), and began to assemble a pile of supplies in a corner of their warehouse.

Meanwhile, he quietly spread the word that he wished to contact members of the Corps of Discovery. In the town of St. Louis, however, there was little that could be done quietly. Rumors spread like a prairie fire. In no time it was known that a party was forming to proceed to the West, and that a man named Franklin was one of the organizers. Andrews was also mentioned, and few were certain as to the connection between these two, or whether this was one expedition or two.

To add to the confusion, Manuel Lisa was recruiting for his proposed fur-company fort on the upper Missouri.

It was of some concern that a young Lieutenant Pike and twenty men had departed more than a year ago to explore the mountains of the Louisiana Territory. He had not been heard from for some time.

Add to that the fact that there were lone trappers by ones and twos heading into the former French territory. It was enough to fan the flames of the wildfires that the rumors had become.

Andrews and Franklin discussed this at length over breakfast one morning.

"My guess," confided Andrews, "is that the army unit under Pike has met with trouble from the Spanish. Spain has always been jealous of her borders."

"Is that land not well to the south?" asked Liberty.

"One would think so. But there are few maps, and the border is indefinite, you know. Pike's mission was probably to *find* the border. I do not propose to go that far south. At least for now. Tell me, have you found any capable men for our party?"

Liberty smiled ruefully. "Only one that I really want. He was with the corps, so I know him. He has a cousin, whom he will vouch for. I am to see him today. Most of them are adventurers with no skills. Romantics, drunks, or dreamers, sir."

"Well, no hurry. Concentrate on the supplies and equipment. And did I not mention about the 'sir'? If we are to travel together, we should dispense with formality. Now, what are you called by friends?"

Liberty was embarrassed. "Liberty. Sometimes just Lib."

"Very good. Liberty . . . a good name."

"It was given to me by the woman who raised me."

"The one who taught you to read?"

"Yes. And how should I address you?"

"Alexander or Alex. 'A rose by any other name . . .'"

"'. . . would smell as sweet,'" finished Liberty.

"Ah, she also taught you some of the classics!"

"Yes. I probably had a better education than I realize."

He saw no need to go into all the details at this time, and moved the conversation along.

"Four more men, you think, or three?" he asked.

"Depending on who you get, I suppose," Andrews mused. He sipped his coffee and leaned back in his chair.

A figure approached the table, and Liberty recognized the buffalo-coated bully from the tavern encounter. He tensed and half rose to meet any expected attack. But the man appeared to present no threat. He stopped, a bit embarrassed, hat in hand. He nodded respectfully to Andrews, but spoke to Liberty.

"Mr. Franklin? May I speak with you?"

Liberty was somewhat surprised, but nodded.

"I vant to tell you . . . you treated me fair, the odder night."

"What?"

"Yah, I was outta line. It vas whiskey talkin', and you call my bluff. I drawed a knife on you, and you could've killed me, but you didn't an' I admire that."

Liberty was confused. Surely this hulk of a man had not sought him out merely to apologize. He took a moment for a better look at the man.

A burly giant, light Nordic hair and eyes, well over six feet in height. Legs like massive posts of oak, hands like great paws, each as big as a small ham. The buffalo coat hung open, revealing a torso resembling a whiskey keg. There appeared to be no fat on the giant frame, and Liberty took a slow, deep breath. He had been very lucky. If he had not been drinking he would not have dared to challenge such a man. And, if his one first punch had not accomplished its purpose, this hulking beast would have broken him in two.

He nodded in acknowledgment of the apology, and the man hurried on.

"I heard you're the von to see about a trip up the river."

Now Liberty was even more astonished. He glanced at Andrews, who sat sipping his coffee, an expression of mild amusement on his face. Lib recalled that he had wondered afterward if that confrontation had been engineered by Andrews. Maybe he would ask about it later. Just now, he attempted to maintain his composure.

"We are looking for another man or two," he said casually. "What is your experience?"

To himself, he was thinking that it would take a large horse or an outsize canoe to transport such a hulk.

"I've vorked as a boatman. Been in the voods a lot since I vas a boy. I'll rassle any man in St. Louis. I can throw a knife or a 'hawk, and shoot purty goot."

"Do you know hand signs?"

"Yah, enough to get by. I've trapped a little, some west of here."

"How far west?"

"About six sleeps."

That told much. This man had enough experience but not enough guile to use casually the Indian term for distance. Very likely his story was exactly as stated.

"What is your name?" Liberty asked.

"Schmidt, sir. Gustav Schmidt."

"Well, Schmidt, come by the tavern this afternoon, and we'll talk further of it."

The big man nodded. "Thankee, sir," he said as he turned to go. "I be there."

Schmidt lumbered out the door into the street, ducking his head as he went through the door frame. Liberty turned to Andrews.

"Did you know him before?" he asked bluntly.

Andrews looked surprised. "You mean . . . before the other night? No, I . . ."

Suddenly the depth of the question seemed to dawn on him, and he roared with laughter.

"You thought I . . . my God, man . . . no, I did not set you up. I never saw him before that evening." He paused to laugh again. "But it did work out well for my purposes. No, I *was* there to watch *you*. You had been pointed out to me, and I wanted to observe you a little."

Liberty smiled ruefully.

"Are you going to hire him?" asked Andrews.

"Probably. You know, it took some character to come in here, apologize, and ask for a job. You have any objections?"

"No, it's yours to say. Of course, it will be expensive to feed him."

Liberty saw the smile flicker around the corners of Andrews's mouth. He was beginning to appreciate the man's sense of humor.

"I don't know, Alex," he mused. "A deer or a small buffalo every day or so . . . and he's said he shoots well. He can supply *himself*."

They chuckled.

"Seriously," Andrews went on, "would he not make a great impression on the natives?"

"Yes, unless somebody shoots him for a bear. But he won't wear the fur coat in summer, I suppose. I'll talk to him some more."

"Good. I rather like him. Glad he didn't kill you the other night."

"I, too! I was lucky."

"True. But also, quick. Isn't there something about 'the quick and the dead'? It seems that here on the frontier there are those two kinds of men. Quick or dead."

.   .   .

Liberty had wondered about a horse large enough to carry the massive weight of Schmidt. As it turned out, it was no problem. The German had his own mount.

"A mule?" Liberty asked in some surprise.

"Yah. His mudder, a big mare. His fadder, a Spanish jack. For me, he ist goot."

Liberty looked the animal over. The dam must have been one of the massive animals like those that pulled freight wagons back in Philadelphia. This mule carried her large frame, and the long ears and voice of his donkey sire. Red in color, with a lighter shade around the nose—"mealy-nosed," a desirable characteristic, Schmidt insisted.

Lib had learned much about the use of horses while in the corps. He was impressed by the bone structure and strong legs of this animal. Very likely Fritz would be as durable an addition to the party as his rider. As an extra bonus, they learned that Gustav Schmidt had experience with pack animals. They would need several.

The former corpsman did bring his cousin, and as Liberty had hoped, the man seemed well qualified. The two carried the same surname, Williams.

Their last recruit was a complete surprise. Liberty had finished his breakfast one morning and stepped out the door of the restaurant to see a Negro standing beside the steps.

"Mistah Franklin?" the man inquired. "May I speak with you?"

It was a warm baritone, with cultured accents. An educated darky! Lib looked him over. He was neat and well groomed, despite obvious wear to his garments. Even the ruffles of his linen shirt at the neck and cuffs were clean and orderly.

"Yes?"

"I have been told, sir, that you seek a man or two to explore the frontier."

"Well, I . . ."

Lib was completely taken aback. What could such a man contribute to the expedition? His accent showed enough influence to mark him as a Southerner, even though one with culture. His skin was a rich golden brown. Probably a half-breed, Lib supposed, maybe sired by a plantation owner or overseer. But what could he want here?

"I believe that you know a Mr. York, a servant of Lieutenant William Clark?" the Negro asked. But it was a statement, not a question.

"Of course," Liberty replied.

How could he forget the big black man and his contribution to the effectiveness of the corps? The only Negro among the seventy, but a memorable individual. Lib remembered the strange reaction of the buffalo-hunter nations on the plains. They had reacted to the man's dark skin with awe. It had become apparent that the natives thought that he had blackened his skin intentionally as a ritual. With York's curly hair, it seemed that he resembled the buffalo, a creature sacred to them. When they discovered that he had been born that way, they were even more impressed. York had reveled in the attention, but did not hesitate to use his prestige to assist in councils and negotiations when needed. A good man.

But now the Negro spoke again. "My name is Washington," he stated. "Mr. York sends his greetings, as does Mr. Clark."

"How do you know them?" Liberty asked.

"I grew up with York," the man replied. "We are kin, probably."

There was a trace of bitterness or sarcasm in his tone.

"Then you serve Lieutenant Clark, too?" Liberty asked.

"No, no!" Washington spoke proudly. "I am a freeman. I have my papers, if you would like—"

"No . . . but what do you want?"

"Let me explain, sir. I was traveling toward the frontier, and encountered my friend York and his employer en route. York believed you were still in St. Louis, and asked me to wish you well."

Liberty nodded, still puzzled. He had caught an undercurrent here in the use of the term "employer." Lieutenant Clark had always referred to York as his servant, and their relationship seemed easy and relaxed. But Liberty had always had the impression that York was a slave, nothing more or less.

"When I reached St. Louis," Washington continued, "I heard that you were going back out. Since my friend spoke well of you, I thought to ask, do you need another man?"

Liberty was startled again. He had gotten along well with York, possibly because of memories of Samuel, the black handyman at Madge's. Samuel had been kind to him as a child, had been his friend and mentor in many ways. But Lib had made no special effort, and he was surprised at York's reaction.

Ignoring the last question, Liberty blurted out a denial. "But I don't understand. I did nothing for York!"

"Oh, yes, sir, you did. You treated him as a man, treated him with respect."

But not intentionally, Liberty thought. Sometimes the simplest things, which seem to have no consequence, influence the lives of others. And in turn, our own. Liberty had not been aware that he had treated York differently in any major way, yet here was evidence that to York, it was important.

"Well," Lib began, trying to regain his composure, "what are your skills?"

"I am well educated," Washington began. "But largely, I am adaptable. I am able to improvise, *because* of my varied background. My skills might be considered the same as those of Mr. York, common daily tasks like cooking, making camp, simple survival, but with education besides."

Liberty found that he rather liked this man. There was no bragging or exaggeration here, merely statement of fact. But did they *need* a man with this sort of formal education? Washington had more culture and book knowledge than anyone in the party, possibly even Andrews. While he was still thinking about it, the Negro took from an inside pocket a small packet of papers carefully wrapped in oilskin and tied with a string. He drew one out and extended it toward Liberty as he returned the packet to his coat.

"From Lieutenant Mr. Clark," he said simply.

Lib unfolded the slip of paper and smiled. There was no doubt as to its authenticity, for it bore the unmistakable stamp of Clark's poor spelling.

"This man, Washingtonn, is a freman as he sez. A gud man, and can do any jobb he tryes. W. Clark."

Liberty smiled. Clark, a thinker and doer, had never seemed to have time for mundane things like correct spelling. There was no doubt as to the genuine origin of this note, or of Clark's feelings about the man.

It might be hard to justify the hiring of Washington, an odd paradox on the rough frontier. But Liberty had a good feeling about it, even without the assurance of Clark's note. He handed the note back.

"Here, you might have need of this. But yes, let us give it a try!"

5

The reaction of Alexander Andrews to the hiring of Washington was a mixture of humor and puzzled wonder.

"A freed slave?" he chuckled. "Why?"

"Because . . . well, wait until you meet him. He is hard to explain. But he carries a note from Lieutenant Clark, whose opinion I respect."

"Remarkable! But what is the interest of an educated nigra in the frontier?"

"I do not know. He just seems fascinated by it all."

"You know, Franklin, that this is just the sort of interest that we agreed is undesirable?"

"The romantic adventurer? That is true. This is different, somehow. Well, talk to him. See what you think. Now, do we want one more man?"

"Let's see . . . the Williamses . . . Schmidt, this Washington of yours, you and me . . . that should do it. How is the assembling of supplies going?"

"Quite well. Schmidt has his own mount. We should make sure of our horses and pack animals soon, I think. One of the Williams boys is good with packing, in addition to Schmidt. They've both been helping with the selection. I'm afraid that when the weather opens up, everyone will want to go and look for a place to trap beaver, so horses will be scarce."

"Good. Continue, and I will look forward to meeting this Washington."

It had been an easy winter, but the gods of ice and snow mounted one last assault. It was March, and buds were swelling on the trees. The willows along the river were changing from their dull gray hues to yellow-green, even though no leaves had yet appeared. Green sprigs of grass were appearing in sheltered areas. In places there were optimistic splashes of color as violets made themselves known.

Overhead, long lines of geese honked their way across the clear blue of the spring sky, and men became restless to move. What is it in the call of the wild geese that excites in man an urge to follow them? Some primitive migration instinct, maybe, a wanderlust that against all reason nudges quietly at the soul: *it is time to go.* . . .

Liberty Franklin had felt it before. It may have been a factor in his sudden decision to escape from his servile existence with the Reverend. It returned each spring, but never more strongly than this year. He walked restlessly, and spent much time alone. On a little rise at the edge of the bustling town, he would stand and watch the geese, and wonder what sights they would see before they reached their destination.

It was on one of those occasions that he noticed a thin gray cloud bank in the northwest, maybe the last storm of the season. Samuel, back in Philadelphia, had had a saying that applied here. A March storm can be bitter and tough, but will be short. In a few days, though, they could begin to think of leaving. He turned back toward the town.

The storm came in gently, in an unusual way. When he woke the next morning the air was still and the sky was overcast. It was not uncomfortably cold as he walked to breakfast. When he left the restaurant, there was a fine mist in the air, enough to dampen his coat and his spirits. Not quite cold enough to snow, or wet enough to rain. Just soggy and still.

He turned along the street to the livery to check on their horses, and noticed that there was a rime of frost on a dead clump of tall grass in a narrow space between buildings. He noted in passing that its flocked appearance was rather pretty, and thought no more of it.

On the way back, after looking at the horses and visiting with the stable boy, he noticed a change. There was a glistening wet sheen on each twig and blade of grass. On a fence that he passed, small icicles were forming along the rail's lower edge. *So,* he thought, *a little colder and a little more drizzle, and it could become icy.*

By evening there was a coat of ice over everything, nearing an inch in thickness. There still had been no perceptible rain, merely the silent creeping mist that hung in the air and froze as it settled on any surface. Trees bent low under the increasing weight of the thickening ice. The big cedars fared the worst. Their feathery foliage caught and held more moisture, which was silently converted into tons and tons of ice. Occasionally a loud booming crash, like the sound of an explosion, would rumble down the street. A heavy branch would break away from the main trunk, falling on the one below. Crushed by the double load, that one would give way, too. Tons of ice-covered branches would continue their rolling, crashing fall to the ground, ripping away each successive branch to leave a ragged, shattered trunk.

It was not a time to be outside. The ground was slippery in most places, unsure at best. Only in the muddy street itself could one be confident of his footing. There, it was uniformly terrible. The sheet of ice was not quite thick enough in most places to bear the weight of a man. So he either slipped on a treacherous surface, or broke through to plunge ankle deep into clinging mud.

The only sensible course of action was to stay inside. The big fireplace in the tavern lent welcome warmth, and a brisk business ensued.

Liberty and Andrews found themselves at a corner table, discussing final preparations for departure.

"Once we start, we cannot count on the weather," Liberty reminded. "We take what comes. It's good that we did not experience this ice storm on the trail."

"True. It seems our only choice in weather is the day we start."

"That's about it. We can choose that day, but take our luck on every other one."

"So, we are ready, except for that choice?"

"Yes. As ready as we can be. I'm thinking that these spring storms are always short, and there should be a few days of good weather before another. What would you say to the day after tomorrow?"

Andrews frowned. "Would it not be quite muddy, with the melting ice?"

Liberty pointed out the window at the soggy street. "The worst of the mud is right there. If we wait for dry footing it will be August. Besides, with a few days' sunshine, each day will bring *better* travel conditions."

"Seems logical . . . very well, the day after tomorrow, then."

Liberty had not been able to visualize Alexander Andrews in the wild. The man was always perfectly groomed, starched ruffles gleaming white, shoes polished, gloves and cane at hand. On the trail, he would be a fish out of water.

Liberty need not have worried. On the morning of departure when they assembled at the livery, he did not even recognize Andrews in the dim light of early morning. He was dressed in a frontiersman's buckskins, with a broad-brimmed slouch hat and heavy boots.

The other transformation that Liberty found difficult to accept was that of Washington. He, too, had abandoned the formal wear that had previously clothed him, for buckskins. On his head, however, was a fur cap, and in place of boots, moccasins.

Both men seemed quite comfortable and familiar with this attire. Andrews's buckskins, in fact, showed some evidence of previous wear.

Well, they would all learn much about each other in the coming months.

Travel was somewhat better than they expected. It was as if nature were repenting for the inconvenience of the ice storm. There followed a week of warm sunshine and the rebirth of all living things. Birds sang their territorial nesting songs, buds burst into glorious bloom. In the woods, the bright lavender of redbuds contrasted with the white of plum thickets and the larger white flowers of the dogwood. The smell of moist earth and growing things was everywhere.

Liberty's estimate proved correct. Once they were out of the churned-up mud of the city streets, the footing became better, and improved each day. The soft but firm loam, loosened by winter's alternate freeze and thaw, was easy on the horses' feet.

The six pack animals were led at first, tied one to the other in a long train. After the routine was established, it was found that the lead ropes were really unnecessary. The four mules would follow an old pack mare. The sixth animal, a stocky bay gelding, was thought to be her colt, and easily followed, too.

"Let me lead ol' Fanny, there," Zeb Williams suggested. "I think the others will follow her."

This proved to be quite practical. In fact, in a few days the mare did not even need to be led. She was an old hand at the trail, and followed Zeb's horse without the lead. One rider to the rear of the pack train was all that was needed to keep things moving.

On the fourteenth day of travel they reached a sizable village of log-and-mud dwellings, and camped there for a day. The natives proved to be Missouris, and seemed eager to visit with the travelers. The distribution of gifts may have helped a great deal, but there was also a familiarity and friendly demeanor that was unmistakable.

There were enough signs of beaver in the area to intrigue the potential trappers. Andrews assured them that this was not a practical idea. This was directly on the route that would be taken by every would-be trapper west of the Mississippi.

"We must move into new territory," he insisted. "Well beyond the fork where the Kenzas River enters the Missouri, I think."

There was another feature at this camp that impressed Andrews greatly. On the north side of the river, across from the village, were some tumbled log ruins. Andrews became excited, asked many questions of their hosts, and finally arranged for a canoe to take him across for a look. He asked that Liberty accompany him.

They walked among the rotting logs of several large structures, and what seemed to be a palisade wall, now fallen in most places. Andrews's excitement was replaced by wonder. He stood touching the weathered silver-gray logs with an awe that bordered on reverence.

"Liberty," he said softly, "I believe that this is Veniard's fort. Fort Orleans, his gateway to the wilderness. If so, we are only a week's travel from the city of the Kenzas."

A thought struck Liberty, and he turned to one of the boatmen who had brought them across.

"How many sleeps to the Kenzas' town?" he asked in hand signs.

"Seven, maybe eight," came the answer.

"Yes," Liberty translated for Andrews, "this must be the fort."

6

They reached the town of the Kenzas, and were pleased by the welcome that they received. There was feasting and a council with speeches of welcome and exchange of gifts. It was much like their experience with the Missouris earlier.

"This is much as Veniard described it!" Andrews told the others. He was almost ecstatic with the progress of his expedition.

They could plainly see the junction of the two rivers at this point. The waters were of slightly different colors as they merged, not completely mixing until some distance downstream. Liberty had not really noticed this at the time of his travel with Lewis's Corps of Discovery. Possibly he had been preoccupied in his awe at the immensity of the project.

In a way, he still felt so. There before them lay the path to the great uncharted West, huge beyond imagination. He had seen a part of it, and a completely new part now lay before him, straight west toward the mountains. *How far?* he wondered. Andrews, who had studied the old French records, thought that the mountains would be considerably closer than those on the upper Missouri. But the expedition under Veniard had traveled more than three weeks after leaving

Fort Orleans before turning back. Andrews was led to believe that they had been no more than halfway. Then, too, there was Lieutenant Pike, whose party had not been heard from in a year. *They* had followed this route.

Liberty was quite satisfied with the way their own party was functioning. They had been on the trail long enough now to know what to expect of each other. At each evening camp there was no longer any need to discuss responsibilities and the minor chores of a campsite. Each man was finding his own niche. It was also pleasing to see that even Andrews thought none of the menial tasks beneath his dignity. He had shed the pampered-dandy image and appearance as he shed his fine clothes. In a remarkably short time he had become a frontiersman.

Washington, too . . . Lib had wondered how an educated former slave would react to the hardships of the trail. But he had judged his man correctly. Lib recalled now that in their first conversation the man had mentioned spending some time "in the woods." His frontier skills were many and varied. He moved gracefully, and seemed to anticipate well what was needed and how he could be of assistance to the others.

In many ways, except for his slightly darker skin, Washington at times seemed much like the Indians they met as they traveled. He seemed to relate well to them, in an easy, effortless manner. His entire attitude was one of easygoing confidence. He was proud of his status as a freeman, but did not belabor it, and was well liked by the others of the party immediately.

There was one possible exception, Zeb Williams's cousin from Tennessee. Charlie Williams was a lean man with a dour look about him. He was capable and quick, a good man with the pack animals, but rarely laughed. Liberty wondered if Charlie had ever really had any fun.

His attitude toward the former slave was not antagonistic. It was more as if he preferred not to notice Washington at all. Liberty wondered at first whether Washington saw this, but soon realized that he did, very strongly. It was no point of friction. A casual observer might have overlooked it entirely. It seemed to cause no problems in the group, and there was nothing to be done about it. Some men will never enjoy each other's company, but may work together productively. Still, Liberty was mildly uncomfortable about these two. Would this smoldering thing someday burst into flame? He did not know.

Andrews and Washington might have seemed the unlikeliest of friends. However, they quickly found areas of common interest. Both had a considerable amount of education, especially in literature, and quickly found common ground. Liberty was constantly amused by their exchanged quotations from Shakespeare, Plato, and Homer.

Possibly the biggest surprise in the party was Gustav Schmidt. Because of his immense size, it was easy to see the man as a bit slow-witted. It quickly became apparent that this was far from the fact. Here was a highly intelligent man, but with no book learning. He could write his name, but little more, and he appeared somewhat sensitive about it. This he concealed with bluster and intimidation.

The incident that convinced Liberty that this was the case occurred as they camped on the trail one night. Their camp was near a grove of heavy timber, and they had seen bear sign. Everyone was a bit uneasy, and there were nervous glances at the dark woods. There were a few attempts at jokes about bears, producing a little tense laughter. It was then that Charlie Williams spoke up.

"Schmidt," he said loudly, "if I was as big as you I wouldn't worry none about bears. I'd just walk out in them woods"—he pointed—"an' find the biggest bear I could, and just rassle him to death."

The big German took a stick from the fire, and carefully lighted his pipe. He blew a cloud of pungent blue smoke toward the evening sky before he spoke. His answer was gentle.

"Charlie," he said, "dere's a lot of liddle bears in dere too, yah?"

The others laughed, and Charlie Williams was embarrassed. He said nothing more that evening.

Liberty was startled at the depth and insight of Schmidt's remark. Of course he might have used it before, maybe many times. He had probably had plenty of opportunity. Lib himself had never stopped to realize it before. Yet a big man, no matter how strong, may still get tired. In addition, he may be carrying twice the body weight alone, to tire his already aching muscles.

Now he felt a certain regret that he had floored Schmidt with unleashed fury at their first meeting. Actually, Liberty realized, he had gone out of his way to provoke that fight. He was embarrassed and a little ashamed that he would have stooped to that. He was now gaining a healthy respect for the big man. Not only for his strength but also for his wisdom.

One of the pastimes around the fire each evening was the learning and practice of hand signs. Both Liberty and Zeb Williams had some degree of skill from previous experience. Andrews and Washington both progressed rapidly and with interest. Soon even Schmidt and Charlie Williams were gaining some practice. This could be very useful as they moved farther west.

They left the main Kenza town and moved westward along the river. They found it easier to travel on high ground overlooking the river itself, because of its winding course. There was a trail of sorts, made over the generations by travelers with similar ideas. At several smaller Kenza villages they stopped briefly, paying their respects to the leaders of each cluster of log dwellings.

They were in more open country now, traveling through flat-topped grass-covered hills. There was still heavy timber along the river, and along the smaller tributaries. Huge oaks, sycamores, and walnut trees mingled with cottonwoods and willows and elms. Liberty wondered why these trees had not covered the hills as well as the ravines and canyons. Maybe he could learn later.

At one of the Kenza villages they were told of a Pawnee town two days' journey to the north of the main river. After some discussion they decided to detour north to make that contact. If they were to be trapping in the area, it would be well to have met their neighbors.

They found the village, on high ground to the south of one of the major tributaries to the main river. They were met rather coolly, but the Pawnees became more friendly after some gifts were distributed.

Liberty had heard other tribes refer to Pawnees as the Horn People. In fact, the hand sign for this nation included a gesture that implied a single horn, growing out of the forehead. Now he was able to understand. The heads of the men were shaved, except for a circle of hair about four inches in diameter. This scalp lock was allowed to grow long. Treated with tallow and red pigment, it was twisted and plaited into the shape of a horn, rising out of the top of the head. *Of course,* he thought. *Horn People.*

One of the most striking customs of this group, however, was their housing. The large, semiburied lodges were roomy enough to house an extended family of as many as fifty or sixty people. In one, they noticed a horse, apparently brought inside for safekeeping while there were strangers in the camp. After all, a man must guard his most precious possession.

The Pawnees, like the other peoples they had met, were growers. Their fields were not yet planted, but it was apparent that corn, beans, and pumpkins were staple foods here. There was a puzzling difference here, however. In Liberty's experience, most farming tribes were friendly, trading with all. The more aggressive nations encountered by the corps had been the nomadic buffalo hunters—Blackfeet, Sioux, Crow. But here were farmers who also had characteristics of the warrior nations. Domineering, belligerent, at times almost threatening. It was no wonder that their neighbors seemed to live in an uneasy fear of these Horn People.

"I do not understand, entirely," Andrews confided. "Veniard spoke well of these people. He apparently got on well with them."

"He gave them gifts?" asked Liberty.

"Yes. Quite lavishly, it seems."

"Then we should do likewise."

"It would seem so."

More gifts brought more friendship. Liberty was uneasy about this approach. *What happens,* he wondered, *when the visitor runs out of gifts?*

Yet it had apparently worked for Veniard. They stayed two extra days with the Pawnees, attempting to cement the friendship. They explained in detail about their plan, to harvest as well as to buy plews. The Pawnees had been trading a few furs to the French for several generations, in exchange for guns and metal tools.

"This will save you much travel," Andrews explained.

Their hosts nodded, apparently pleased.

One of the unexpected benefits of the two-day stay was the opportunity to learn the council structure of the Pawnees. The idea of cooperation in the fur-trading venture was discussed in the village council, and generally accepted.

"But the other bands must decide, too," the leaders explained.

"Of course," agreed Liberty. "How many bands in your nation?"

"Four main tribes. Several towns in each. Leaders from all towns meet in council. But any one tribe can say no to the council's plan."

Liberty tried to translate for Andrews, who became fascinated. "You mean, any of the four has power of veto over the decision of the whole?"

"I think so, Alex. Let me ask further."

When that impression was verified, Andrews became even more interested.

"Remarkable! Franklin, this is quite advanced, politically. Fancy, an Indian government much like a republic."

A few days later the travelers encountered a lone trader and his wife on the trail. Both of the couple rode horses, and each led a pack horse.

"Arapaho. Trader People," the man signed in answer to Liberty's query.

"My woman, Cheyenne . . . Finger Cutters."

This familiar sign referred to the Cheyenne custom of gashing an index finger in the mourning ceremony at the death of a loved one.

Liberty nodded. "I know your people," he signed.

"How is this?"

Liberty had noticed that the man wore around his neck a thong with one of the "Peace medals" given as gifts by Lewis and Clark's Corps of Discovery. The coinlike token with its symbol of clasped hands was becoming an item of great pride, a prized possession. Now he pointed to the medal.

"I was with the Soldier Chief," he signed.

Instantly, it was as if old friends had met. Night was nearing, and they decided to camp together. The trader was quite helpful in describing the country ahead.

"The mountains? Maybe . . . a moon's travel. Not quite, maybe. But there is a place of danger. You will come to a fork of the river. The north fork is bigger, but do not take it. The other, the smaller, is the way to the mountains."

"Where will we find the Comanches?" Liberty asked.

"Anywhere. They will find *you.*"

They explained the purpose of this party, and the trader nodded enthusiastically.

"It is good. Good for trade."

"The Horn People seemed to approve," Liberty commented, fishing for information.

"Ah, you have met them!" the trader signed, very noncommittal.

Well, a trader must be a friend to all, reasoned Liberty. He must not form alliances, for the good of his profession and for his safety as he travels. He trades with all.

The traveler finally signed, "The Comanches have a saying about the Pawnees. 'The easiest to scalp.' Because of the scalp lock, you know. 'But the hardest to kill.' "

Liberty's heart quickened. "They are at war?"

"No, no! Not really. Sometimes, maybe."

How is one to know? Liberty thought.

"Franklin, let us ask him about the map," suggested Andrews.

He had been trying to map the area they traversed, and correlate their findings with those of Veniard nearly a century before. Now he unrolled his map and began to point to landmarks.

"Here, the Missouri River . . . there, the city of the Kenzas . . . the Kenzas River . . . here, the Pawnees . . ."

The trader responded eagerly. "I have seen such talking paper before. It is good."

"Yes," agreed Andrews. "Now, this river . . ." He pointed to a wandering line with no upstream end, joining the Kenzas River from the north, a major stream. "How is it called?"

The trader nodded. "Yes. I know it. It starts in the mountains. Shit River."

"What? What is the sign he used?" asked Andrews.

Liberty was puzzled. "The sign means 'shit' . . . dung. Can this be?"

"Say again," he requested in sign.

"Shit River," came the reply.

"But *why?*"

And in sign, the trader replied.

"Buffalo. Many, many. Thirsty, from dry travel. Stand in water, shit in water."

"You mean," Liberty asked, "the water is too fouled to use?"

The trader nodded. "No good to drink, no good for horses."

But the river had seemed clear, and Liberty signed to that effect.

The trader agreed. "Yes, now. But when they come in the fall, come south to winter, many shits. Bad taste."

"How long a time?"

"Half a moon, maybe. Water is very scarce then."

"But how do people live?"

"Not drink much. Move upriver. Find little waters. Springs."

"Do you believe him?" asked Andrews.

"Yes . . . I think so. There is no reason not to, is there?"

"I guess not. You saw 'many, many' buffalo on the Missouri, did you not?"

"Yes. Not enough to foul a river. But we were on the Missouri. A much bigger river."

"Well, so be it." Andrews shrugged.

That night, by the campfire's glow, he carefully lettered in the name of the previously unnamed stream: Shit River.

7

All in all, the night spent with the traveling trader and his wife proved very beneficial. After the initial communication with hand signs, it was found that the trader was fluent in several tongues. Liberty recalled having met such men before. Those traders traveled widely, were useful to all, and quickly acquired means of communication. Some people are gifted in the use of language. This man, like others, was very quickly able to acquire enough understanding in a new tongue to carry on his profession.

Often such a trader would have a wife of another nation, and in turn she too might be skilled in language. It was so in this case, Willow Woman speaking Comanche, Kenza, Osage, and passable French. Andrews was delighted with this discovery, and made use of his abilities in the latter language.

Part of the expertise of the traveling trader was also to carry news and to entertain. This would create goodwill and confidence among his clientele, and his stories were many and varied, from contact with many cultures.

Crow, this man was called, an inside joke. "For does the Crow not also carry trinkets?" he asked.

He was immediately well liked by the travelers, and it promised to be an interesting evening. The conversation and stories would be in a rich mix of native tongues, French, English, hand sign, and a dash of Eastern trade language. Even the problems involved were a source of amusement.

Liberty and Zeb Williams had enough experience in such situations to see the possibilities. They had become aware during the expedition to the Pacific that the stories of different nations are of interest to each other. When two parties or bands from different tribes camped together, they would become acquainted through the legends of each. The undercurrent of curiosity, expressed in hand signs to establish acquaintance, could be easily seen: *Who are you? How are you called?* And these questions could often be answered in depth by the recitation of the legends and the Creation stories of each group. *"In the beginning our People lived in darkness, inside the earth. . . ."* A common thread of many Creation stories. *In the beginning . . .*

From there, the stories usually progressed into legends of Old Times. Almost universal, the tradition that once all humans spoke the same language, which was also spoken by all animals. There were stories of deities and semideities, good gods and bad gods, the spirits governing wind and rain, cloud and sun.

There were stories of how Man got Fire from the Sun, with the help of Coyote, Buzzard, and Spider. How Bobcat lost his long tail, in several versions . . .

This trader had a magnificent store of such stories from his wide travels, and told them well. Liberty could not recall such an evening in the two years he had traveled with the corps. Of course, during that campaign, there had been the primary interest of exploration and science. There had been little thought of storytelling.

Shortly after full darkness descended, Liberty oriented himself with the North Star, locating it by alignment with the two stars in the bowl of the Big Dipper. It was a habit learned long ago from Samuel, back at Miss Madge's.

"When it gets dark, no matter where you be, you look for the drinkin' gourd, an' it point to dat north star, an' you know where you be."

As a boy, Liberty had not realized the significance of this simple orientation. As a runaway, it had become more important. Now, as a guide to those who would explore the wilderness of the West, it had become all-important.

"The Seven Hunters," Crow signed.

Liberty roused from his meditation. "What?"

"The stars," Crow went on, pointing to the Big Dipper. "They are the Seven Hunters. Each night they circle the sky. See, the second one, there, has a dog at his heel."

Liberty could see the faint glow of a smaller star, near the next-to-last star in the handle of the dipper.

"His dog is always with him," Crow went on. "Their lodge is there. . . . At the Real-Star, which never moves."

"Remarkable!" spoke Andrews. "He knows about Polaris, the fixed star! It is used in navigation."

Andrews turned to the trader, and with some help in hand signs, tried to explain.

Crow nodded. "It tells where I am," he agreed.

Andrews became more excited. "My people call your Seven Hunters 'Ursa Major,' the 'Great Bear,' " he said.

Crow looked confused, and Liberty tried to translate. The dipper, a drinking gourd, a bear with a long tail, Seven Hunters . . .

Now Willow Woman laughed. "A bear? It looks more like a skunk, with his tail arched, so. . . ."

Yes, it does, thought Liberty. *It is many things to different people!* To him it would always be Samuel's drinkin' gourd, the long-handled dipper.

"Look!" said Washington suddenly, pointing.

They all turned, to see the arching rim of the moon sliding majestically into view above the eastern horizon. Blood red and huge in its illusion of nearness, it slid into view as they watched in awed silence. The openness of the big sky and the far horizons made it a unique experience, and Liberty felt a primitive stirring in his heart. He wanted to sing, to dance, to do something, to commemorate such an event.

The moon rose completely above the horizon now, just a little past full. Just a slight flattening of its perfect circle at the upper right. It must have been full a day or two ago. Why had he not noticed? Oh, yes, it had been cloudy.

There was no such problem tonight, one of those priceless rare nights on the prairie when all creation seems in tune, vibrant with excitement. One does not want to seek his bed, because there is an unspoken anticipation that something is about to happen. At any moment, all the secrets of the universe will be revealed, and to close one's eyes and miss the moment would be sacrilege.

The moon's color was becoming paler now. Orange, then rich cream, as the party watched. The face of the man in the moon was especially visible as the background color changed. Someone remarked on it, and Crow answered.

"A man? Oh, yes, the face . . . some see a standing woman. See, she looks left, her hair flying out behind to the right. She sings and holds a small drum in front of her, to the left."

"I have been told of a rabbit," said Washington. "My mother's people see a rabbit, dancing on hind legs. Rabbit looks to the left, and his ears point to the right. The part that forms the flowing hair of Crow's woman . . ."

His mother? wondered Liberty. She must have been a slave. He had always thought that Washington's father must have been white. It was only a passing thought, interrupted by another member of the circle.

"Mein people," said Schmidt slowly, "see a boy and girl. They carry a pail of vater between dem. See?"

Andrews chuckled. "Like Jack and Jill?"

Schmidt looked uncomfortable. "Dey schpill it sometimes, und der moon gets liddle."

"Aha!" said Andrews. "Marvelous! This accounts for the waxing and waning of the moon, no?"

Again, Liberty marveled at the variety of stories. A man, a woman, a rabbit, a boy and girl. Everyone's background caused him to see a slightly different picture. There was a puzzle here, though. The rabbit seen by the people of Washington's *mother.* Had she been *other* than Negro? Or were her "people" one of the many African peoples raided for slaves? Could it be that the rabbit was a traditional legend that came from Africa on a slave ship? Or do rabbits even exist in Africa? He had no idea.

Lib lay awake a long time after they finally retired. He turned restlessly in his blankets, or simply lay on his back, staring upward at the immensity of the starry sky. Finally he sat up, leaned his back against his saddle, and surveyed the vast rolling prairie before him.

The moon was high overhead now, silver instead of red-orange. Its light bathed the entire scene, like a picture he had once seen, painted all in black and white. Lib was amazed at all that could be observed by this lesser light. The fire had died to powdery white ash, with a dull red coal or two glowing softly through. Soft snores came from the blanketed forms around the camp.

A little farther away, Zeb Williams, squatted on his heels Indian fashion, stood guard. Beyond Zeb, the hobbled horses contentedly grazed. In the far distance, a shifting mass of dark forms indicated the small buffalo herd they had seen just before dark, no more than a few hundred animals. They had already shot an antelope, and did not try for a buffalo. Antelope had been quite satisfactory, though not in the same class as a fat yearling bull. His mouth watered at the thought of well-browned hump ribs, cooked Indian style over a bed of buffalo chips. His stomach was full of antelope, but his soul craved buffalo.

What a strange thought . . . maybe it was the association with the Arapaho trader, and the stories. Buffalo were sacred to the people of the prairie. Or maybe it was the land itself, the prairie calling, reaching out to draw the soul, like a moth to the candle.

In the distance a coyote called, and another answered. It was good to hear. He had not realized . . . all during the two years in the West with the corps he had longed for civilization. Then, during the winter in St. Louis, he had fretted restlessly. He had considered going back to Philadelphia, but never got around to it. There was nothing there for him anyway. He had drunk too much. He had not understood what was happening to him, and had even thought he might be going crazy. Now the world seemed simple and pure, even though dangerous, and he found himself at peace.

A great owl swept noiselessly overhead, marked mostly by the patch of stars it obscured for a moment. *The messenger* . . . where did *that* idea come from? One of the many native people with whom he had been in contact, probably. He had not realized until now the profound effect that their ways had had on him. He could be quite content, he thought, trapping beaver from here to the mountains and back, with maybe a visit to St. Louis occasionally. . . .

A quiet figure came and sat near him. Crow, the Arapaho, who nodded a greeting, and then sat, looking at the night, sharing its beauty. Finally, without breaking the silence, he spoke in hand signs.

"It is good."

"Yes," Lib returned the sign. "It is good."

8

Between that meeting of the spirit with Crow and the morning, Liberty had conceived an idea. Would it not be good to enlist the trader and his wife to accompany them on their mission? The couple knew the country, were fluent with language, and were good company. It would give a great advantage as they established a network of fur trade in the central and southern mountains.

In a step such as this, he thought that he should consult with Andrews. He broached the subject as everyone was rising, yawning, and stretching to greet the day.

"Alex," he began, "step aside here for a moment."

The two men strolled a few steps toward the stream, and Liberty quickly outlined his idea.

Andrews nodded. "Capital idea, Liberty! Have you spoken with him?"

"No, I felt that you should be consulted."

Andrews dismissed that with a wave of his hand. "Go ahead. I see no problem. It could be a good introduction to new tribes and their areas."

The problem proved to be not the agreement of Andrews, but of Crow. He said nothing for some time after Liberty explained his proposal, but sat staring off into the distance. Finally he spoke, in broken English accompanied by hand signs.

"No . . . many ways, it would be good. But I am trader. We have just come from Comanches. Why go back?"

He paused and smiled, and there was regret in his expression.

"I am made to think," he went on, "that your heart is good. But you follow your trail, I must follow mine. When you reach Comanches, ask for Spotted Dog. My friend. Tell him I said it."

Liberty nodded. "I know your heart, Crow. Tell me now, what other peoples will we see?"

The trader thought for a short while, and then answered. "Cheyenne, Apache, Kiowa, maybe. Tonkawa. *They* eat people, some. How far you go?"

"To the mountains. Maybe south to Santa Fe."

"Trade in Santa Fe?" Crow's face showed surprise.

"Maybe."

"Long trail . . . you like Spanish?"

"I do not know. Are they friends?"

"Sometimes. Maybe, maybe not. Taos is good."

"The Spanish are there?" asked Liberty.

"Not so much. Mud-house people. Adobe."

"They have furs to trade?"

Crow shrugged. "Maybe."

Liberty asked a few more questions, but learned little, beyond the fact that there were furs but also unpredictable warrior peoples in the southern mountains. Those who lived in adobe towns, Crow seemed to say, were more peaceable. Maybe there would be enough furs to keep them busy closer than that, anyway.

They parted, the trader and his wife heading east, the others west.

"May our trails cross again!" signed Crow.

Liberty nodded. "May it be so!"

They traveled on westward, into a country that appeared drier and the grass shorter. The river's course was somewhat unpredictable now, wandering, growing smaller as they traveled upstream. Several times they came to points where small tributaries joined. All of this was favorable, of course. The existence of a series of smaller and smaller streams, spreading out across the wide country, meant the possibility of beaver. They saw beaver sign, in the form of sharp-pointed stumps of willow and cottonwood. But basically, there were fewer beaver here.

There was a marked difference in the construction of the beaver lodges they saw here, compared to those on the upper Missouri. Lewis's expedition had seen huge lodges, some as tall as a man, made of sizable sticks and logs. Lodges here were, by comparison, much smaller.

"There is a lack of material here," joked Zeb Williams.

"You may have hit upon it!" exclaimed Andrews. "There are so few trees, all they cut are needed for food."

"Are these really *beaver*?" asked Washington, "or some smaller species?"

"Like the muskrat?" agreed Liberty. "Maybe."

There was also an almost complete absence of any of the dam-like structures of the mountain beaver.

"Should we trap a few to see?" Andrews suggested.

"No. No use trapping summer fur," Liberty mused. "Let us just camp and look around for signs. The horses are getting thin anyway. They can use a day or two to rest and eat."

That had been a constant problem since they left the tallgrass country. The horses never seemed to have enough time to graze enough of the shorter grass. Buffalo grass, they had begun to call it. The short, curly grass seemed to furnish enough nutrition for the great herd, but why not enough for horses? They discussed it at their camp that evening, while they watched the horses greedily cropping the blue-green growth.

Washington tasted a few of the jointed stems. "Sweet . . . it must carry good food value."

"But for buffalo and not horses?" mused Andrews. "Wait . . . what is the difference here? Cattle, or buffalo, gorge and swallow without chewing, then rechew the cud later, after they move on. Or *while* on the move! The horse has to chew at the time he eats. More hours must be *spent* in eating!"

It was something to consider, and they decided to observe with such an idea in mind.

Meanwhile, the two days' rest not only benefited the horses greatly, but answered some of their questions about beaver. They found many tracks in a marshy area beside the stream that appeared identical to those in other beaver country.

There was another question, posed by Andrews. "You have seen the mountain country, Franklin. The beaver are active in winter, no? They would have to be, to trap them."

"Yes . . ." Liberty was confused by the question.

"How do *these* winter?"

That was a puzzle. There was no deep water here, to remain unfrozen. The animals did not seem to build dams.

"The streambed is too flat to build dams," said Zeb Williams, always practical.

"But there are no big lodges to provide warmth," Andrews observed. "We have seen very few since we left the bigger rivers."

"The really big lodges on the Missouri are in the water, or protected by it," mused Liberty, still confused.

"Aha!" chortled Andrews. "Maybe that is it! Look . . . a big lodge, right here. It would be vulnerable on open ground. Bear . . . I suppose other predators . . . man, even. With no water, no place to escape. Which brings me back to my question: How do they *winter* here?"

That question was partly answered by the discovery of a burrow in a cutbank above the marshy area. It appeared to be in use, and by an animal the size of a beaver. There was none of the carnivore sign that would be seen around the den of a coyote or wolf. No scraps of bone or fur.

Zeb cautiously stuck his head into the opening and sniffed. "Smells like beaver!"

The others tried it. Yes, there was a definite musky animal smell, but not like that of a carnivore. This appeared to be the answer to Andrews's question as to how the creatures could winter here.

"But they're pretty defenseless," said Liberty. "And how would you trap them?"

That was a question. Both the snares used by the Indians and the Newhouse steel-spring traps now coming into use were usually set underwater.

They discussed the situation at length around the fire that night. Was there any use in further exploration?

"But remember," Liberty reminded, "the trader spoke of fur trade with the Spanish in Santa Fe, and the Indian city of Taos. There must be trapping in the mountains."

"True," Andrews agreed. "But this appears to be an area where it would not be practical. Did you cross such a region on the Missouri?"

"A treeless region, yes. But remember, we were on a larger river. Here, we are nearing the headwaters, and the streams are small. There are fewer trees on the stream, even."

"How far do you suppose it may be to the mountains?" Andrews asked.

"Who knows? I wish the trader had agreed to guide us. But he did say to head straight westerly."

"He has done it?"

"So he said. He spoke of a dry two or three days," Liberty answered.

"It would appear dangerous to me," Andrews mused. "Are we equipped to carry enough water?"

"Depends on how many days' travel."

"Well, let us go on. There is still water in the streambed."

"Yes, and the sand is damp. Crow said the river runs 'upside down.' I did not understand," Liberty said.

"I am still not certain," Andrews agreed. "It seems there will be an area where some water flows, then disappears, then flows again a mile downstream. Does it flow into the ground and back up again?"

"I don't know, Alex. It is strange country."

"Well, let us follow the stream another day or two. If it appears to become too dry, we can turn back."

It must have been a tremendous disappointment for Andrews even to consider such a thing. Liberty said nothing. He, too, was disappointed. There was good trapping behind them and ahead, but not in this area. Well, so be it.

The night was dark, the narrow splinter of new moon having set almost with the sun. The coyote chorus had begun to tune up, one well off to the south, another to the west. One or two could sound like a dozen, Liberty mused. There must be at least three or four out there. . . . *wait!* A few too many!

They had become somewhat careless in recent days. In an area where one could see for a day's travel in any direction, it would seem redundant even to post a guard. But they had continued to do so, although not in a very convincing manner. What was the purpose?

The guard at the moment was Charlie Williams. He was sitting on the higher bank of the streambed, perhaps a foot above the other bank. He was not actually inattentive, merely careless. Thus it was not Charlie, but one of the others who first spotted trouble.

"Mein Gott im Himmel!" muttered Schmidt.

The others turned to look where the German was staring. There, just inside the dim circle of illumination from the buffalo-chip fire, stood a tall warrior. Immediately behind him, several more shadowy forms moved in the semidarkness.

9

L iberty sat very still as he raised his right hand, palm forward, in a hand sign of greeting. An open hand, no weapon . . . "I come in peace."

Even as he did so, he spoke to the others in a calm and even tone. At least, that was what he intended. It was only partly successful. His voice sounded high and tense to himself.

"Do not move, or move very slowly. Do not touch a weapon."

He continued to sign, even as he spoke. In sign, "Come and join us. We have meat." He pointed to a haunch of antelope near the fire.

The half-naked shadows drifted into the camp. Liberty tossed a couple of dry sticks on the coals and a cheery blaze broke into the darkness, pushing a circle of light outward. The newcomers eyed the seated travelers with suspicion.

"You are Comanche?" Liberty signed to the leader. "We are looking for a man called Spotted Dog. Our friend Crow, the trader, sent us."

The big warrior seemed to relax a little. He gave the universal sign for a question, which might mean nearly any query. In this case, almost surely "How is this?"

"We have brought gifts," Liberty went on. "We would talk with your people."

There was a moment of silence and lack of response that seemed to last forever. Finally the Comanche signed, hand signs that brought tremendous relief to the travelers.

"It is good. I am Spotted Dog."

It took a little time to become really relaxed in a situation that could have been explosive in nature. It had been a great help to have the name of one of the Comanche leaders. Even more, the leader of this hunting party. They were looking for buffalo, but the great herds had not yet moved into the area in their annual migration.

"We saw buffalo farther east," Liberty signed. "A few. Not the big herds."

"It is so with us," agreed Spotted Dog. "An old bull or two. Very tough to chew."

"If they found a big herd," asked Andrews, "how would they transport their kills? They have no packhorses."

"It seems this is not a party to carry out the hunt," Liberty guessed. "This is probably a search party. When they locate the herds, they will move their main camp to an appropriate area and carry out an organized hunt."

"Maybe," suggested Zeb Williams, "this party is to watch *us*."

This was a disconcerting thought, but Liberty knew that it was quite possibly accurate. There was little doubt that they had been under observation for at least a few days.

They distributed some of the small gifts that they carried for that purpose, and everyone began to relax a little. Conversation became easier as they learned each others' mannerisms. Liberty was beginning to explain their purpose in being here, when Spotted Dog bluntly introduced another subject.

"This man," he said indicating Washington, "paints himself so for a ceremony to find buffalo? And how does he curl his hair?"

It took only a moment for Liberty to recognize this reaction to a Negro. He had seen it before on the Missouri, as the Lakota, Absaroka, and Blackfeet reacted to Clark's man, York.

"No," he explained, "this man is born so. The skin and hair are always this way."

He was prepared for the response, but possibly not to the extent that resulted. There were looks of astonishment, and even a sort of admiration.

"This is not a ceremony he does to find buffalo?"

"No, no. It is the way he is."

Spotted Dog rose and walked around the fire toward the Negro.

"Sit still," said Liberty quickly. "He means no harm."

Washington nodded his understanding. He was becoming quite skillful with hand signs as they traveled, and had been following this conversation. It also occurred to Liberty that York might have described such scenes to his friend Washington.

The Comanche touched the dark skin of Washington's face, then his hair, and looked suspiciously at his own fingers. He spoke rapidly to his companions in Comanche. They reacted with excitement, and a couple of the others came to touch and verify their leader's claims.

"You speak truth," Spotted Dog signed to Liberty, who nodded, pleased.

"It is as I said."

"So . . ." Spotted Dog went on. "It must be very useful."

"What? Say again?"

"It is good, when you look for buffalo, to have this one with you. He does not even need to stop and paint himself before he prays for the hunt."

Liberty had never before quite reached this level of understanding. He had seen the respect with which York was treated, but Spotted Dog's signs brought new understanding.

"They consider you a sort of priest," he said to Washington. "Spotted Dog has the impression that you are with us to help find buffalo."

Charlie Williams laughed aloud. "They think that's what a nigger's for? To hunt buffalo?"

Andrews spoke sharply. "Be still, Williams! This is a serious matter."

The Comanches looked around curiously at this exchange, but quickly turned their attention back to Washington.

It was apparent that the Negro did not particularly enjoy having the warriors touching and feeling his hair. Maybe his stiff dignity as he tolerated it helped to further their attitude. Whatever the reason, it soon became apparent that to the Comanches he must be the most important person in the party. He was respected as a holy man, given special status, and treated with honor.

They spoke around the fire of their plans for trapping and trading, and the warriors nodded agreeably. It was plain to see, however, that this was a minor thing when compared to the wonder of Washington, the Black White Man, buffalo priest.

They awoke at dawn to see the prairie to the southeast teeming with life. The very land itself looked alive, shifting and rolling, squirming almost, with the motion of slowly moving buffalo, as far as the eye could see. The herds had arrived.

"You have done well, holy man," signed Spotted Dog to the Negro.

"But I—" Washington began. Then he saw the importance of the moment, and drew himself up with dignity. "It is nothing," he signed modestly. "I do my best."

"Jesus Christ," said Charlie softly. "He's takin' credit for it!"

Regardless, it was apparent that the prestige of "Black White Man" had increased enormously. By extension, the prestige and importance of the entire party was enhanced.

"We would be honored," Spotted Dog signed, "if you will go with us."

Liberty nodded. "You will bring your people to the herd?"

"Yes. We need not go all the way. See, Lizard there will ride to tell them. We meet them tomorrow, plan the hunt."

Lizard was already grabbing a few bites of meat from the previous evening meal, and swinging up to ride and carry the word.

"We will move slowly, watch the herd," Spotted Dog went on.

He called to Lizard, what must have been a wish for good luck, and the horseman waved an answer as he wheeled away.

The meeting with the Comanches was unique. Liberty and Zeb had, of course, seen bands of nomadic buffalo hunters on the move before, in the northern plains. For the others, it was a new experience. The column stretched for more than a mile, raising a thin plume of dust. Lodge covers and other assorted baggage were piled and lashed on pole drags, pulled by horses that were led or ridden. The drags, called "travois" after the French custom, utilized the very poles that would support the lodge cover when the camp was erected. Riding horses, travois, or running alongside with the dogs were the children.

A band of several hundred horses, herded by young men, brought up the rear, raising more dust. Around the entire caravan circled outriders, watching for danger, choosing the route. They would make certain that the traveling column did not accidentally encounter and startle the buffalo into a stampede of panic before the hunt could be planned. "Wolves," these scouts were called. Their constant circling of the moving band was like that of the circling gray wolves that followed the herds.

The travelers met on the appointed rise, and a campsite was selected and pointed out by an informal council of leaders. It appeared that Spotted Dog was a respected subchief. There were brief introductions, with a clear understanding that there would be time for visiting later. But first things first. Camp must be established.

The column turned toward the designated area, a grassy area along the stream, with water for horses and people, and behind a low rise to the south. From that vantage point the scouts could observe the movement of the massive herd.

Already it could be seen that Lizard, the messenger, had spread the word about the great holy man who accompanied the light-eyes. Black White Man had taken only overnight, it was said, to bring the herd to the area. He understood modesty, too, unlike most white men. Black White Man denied any personal credit for the gifts of the spirit that enabled him to find the buffalo and bring them to him. Consequently Washington was treated with great respect and honor, which reflected prestige on the whole party.

Again, this was met with mixed feelings on the part of Charlie Williams. He seemed astonished that a "freed nigger" would be accorded such respect. He had kept his true attitude under control until now, but he seemed to hold such resentment at Washington's status here that it was about to boil over. He would make a demeaning comment, a snide remark, a belligerent glance. Washington, from a lifetime of practice, managed to ignore the mildly hostile tone.

It was not unnoticed, however, by some of the Comanches. After a particularly cutting remark at the evening fire, Lizard rose and walked around to where Washington sat. There was an exchange of hand signs, and at one point, it was apparent that Lizard pointed a finger directly at Charlie.

Williams had scorned the idea of learning hand signs, and was perhaps regretting it now.

"What was that about?" he demanded of Liberty.

But it was Andrews who answered, with an indignant chuckle. *"That,"* he said, "was something like this: 'Is the skinny one annoying? I would be glad to kill him for you!'"

Charlie Williams paled in the firelight, and swallowed hard.

"You're jes' funnin' me, ain't you, Cap'n?"

"No," Liberty interjected. "That's what Lizard said."

"Wha—What did the nig—What did Washington tell him?"

"That you are a little strange, but to never mind, you're really his friend."

"Is that true?" asked Williams in a hoarse whisper.

"Yes, something like that. Charlie, he probably saved your scalp."

It was noticed from about that time on that Charlie Williams began to treat Washington with a great deal more respect.

He also demonstrated a renewed interest in learning hand signs.

10

The buffalo hunt among the Comanches was to be one of the most memorable of a lifetime. Liberty had seen and even participated in such hunts before, during the two years with Lewis and Clark. But that had been different, somehow. Here, they were a handful of outsiders, guests of a people who hunted buffalo as a vocation, a business. It was not until now that he fully realized the extent to which the entire existence of these people revolved around the buffalo.

The Comanches, by comparison with the northern nations, were generally short in stature. Lakota, Absaroka, Blackfeet, Northern Cheyenne, all had a tendency to physical height. It had not been unusual to see warriors who were well over six feet tall. One or two whom they had met along the upper Missouri had been taller than any of the expedition. Taller even than York, who was often considered a giant of a man.

There were occasional Comanches who showed some height. Spotted Dog was one. Intermarriage had some effect, Liberty supposed. But the general body build of these people had a tendency to shorter legs and longer torsos. This led to a rather odd rolling gait as they walked. Some of the warriors appeared almost clumsy on foot.

But only on foot. Once on horseback the same individuals seemed to become a part of the animal, or vice versa. The visitors watched the young men preparing for the hunt that first evening, readying horses and weapons. Some used a lance, which required that the horse approach a running buffalo from the left side, for a right-handed thrust. A hunter using a bow must shoot to his left. Therefore, it was desirable that his horse approach the quarry from the right side.

"Some horses like the right, some the left," Spotted Dog explained.

Thus, a hunter's mount was chosen according to which weapon he would use. To further complicate the matter, a few hunters possessed smoothbore muskets of French pattern, obtained in trade. These could be used to either side, at least theoretically. In actual use, they had a tendency to be impractical. Many were in poor condition, and misfires were common. Even after a successful shot, the hunter must reload. To reload a musket with loose powder and a cloth-patched ball while riding a galloping horse became somewhat impractical. To stop and reload would put the hunter far behind the fast-moving hunt. A short, sturdy Comanche bow and a handful of arrows was a better solution.

As they watched the preparations for the hunt, Liberty realized that the ownership of a musket must be mostly for prestige. It might be useful for a hunt or a battle on foot, but in this type of mass hunt, a bow or a lance would be far preferable.

The planning of the hunt seemed rather informal, compared to the military style of the corps.

"The wolves will cut off a small part of the herd," Spotted Dog explained. "A few hundred. Get them to circle. If they break away, we run after."

Liberty did not fully understand the hand-signed description until the next morning. The hunters drew up in a long line just over a low rise from the selected area, moving slowly forward at a walk. The visitors had been invited to join, and were now interspersed among the hunters. Lib's heart beat fast and his palms were sweaty with the excitement of the coming chase. Was it so at the dawn of time when the first hunters approached herds of now long-extinct animals of unknown description?

He glanced to his left, where Spotted Dog rode a magnificent stallion. Dog carried a lance, and he saw that its point was of flint. Many were now of iron. The sight of the stone spearhead reinforced Liberty's flight of fancy. The first hunters might well have carried such weapons.

His attention was drawn back to the present. The line of riders was topping the rise. He could see the grazing herd below, scattered in a little valley a mile or so in diameter. The wolves had done their work well. There was an empty expanse of prairie beyond this small band of a few hundred buffalo. A rider or two moved slowly back and forth to prevent these animals from trying to rejoin the main herd, which blackened the prairie beyond.

Now he saw the logic. When they started to run, if this nearer band could be induced to circle by turning the leaders back into the milling mass, then the wolves were in a dangerous position. But even one or two circuits would afford much greater opportunity for the hunters, and a better kill. And young men take pride in danger.

The line of hunters drew nearer to the herd, and an old cow raised her head, questioning. Her long-range vision was poor, but the keen sense of smell and instinct for danger compensated. It was a calm morning, but a slight shift in the air brought the scent of men and horses. Now she could see moving forms.

With a snort she whirled to head for the main herd on the far prairie. There was safety in numbers. But one of the wolves shouted and turned his horse to intercept her, waving a scrap of blanket to shoo her and her calf back toward the smaller herd. A yearling bull followed. In the space of a few heartbeats the now-alarmed buffalo were running, milling in a counterclockwise circle.

The line of hunters approached at a run and joined the circle, outside the dark mass. Eager horses crowded toward their quarry. Bowmen began to ride alongside chosen animals to loose their arrows, and buffalo began to stumble and fall. There was the occasional boom of a musket above the thunder of the thousands of pounding hooves.

Now Liberty could begin to see in action the marvelous skills of these Comanche horsemen. A hunter could handle the short stout bow and several arrows, fitting a feathered shaft to the string, shooting, and fitting another. All this while riding at breakneck speed and guiding the horse with his knees.

A young bull broke away and made a run for the prairie, and Spotted Dog kneed his mount after it. The horse required little guidance. Once it had identified the quarry, there was a singleness of purpose. Ears flattened, the stallion dashed after the yearling, straining to come alongside. From the *left,* because Spotted Dog used the lance. An accurate, efficient thrust, just behind the ribs, ranging forward into heart and lungs. The young bull stumbled. Dog drew his horse in to allow the stricken animal's momentum to withdraw the bloodied spear shaft.

Almost lost in the excitement, Liberty realized that he had not even thought of shooting yet. He thumbed back the hammer of his musket and pointed it at the broad side of a fat cow hardly an arm's length away. The gun boomed, and the cow fell behind. Liberty pulled away from the circling herd and looked back. Thick dust was rising to shroud the entire scene, giving an otherworldly glow in the morning sun.

Andrews swept past, aiming one of his twin dragoon-style pistols at the base of a running yearling's skull. White smoke blossomed with the boom of the gun, and the animal dropped. His face alive with excitement, Andrews stuck the empty weapon back into his waistband and drew the other.

But now a determined rush by a few animals broke through the circle of hunters. A dash for open prairie . . . one of the wolves seemed undecided whether to try to stop the rush or to get out of the way. He deliberated a moment too long. Horse and rider were tossed high on the shiny black horns of a huge bull. The horse screamed in pain and terror. Its soft underbelly was ripped open, spilling loops of white intestine into the dust. The rider, thrown high into the air, landed on the bull's back and bounced to the ground under the feet of the stampede.

The circle was broken, and the entire band that had been the object of the hunt swept away. A few riders started after them, but Spotted Dog called for a halt.

"Let them go! We have enough!"

The riders turned back. The dust was settling, and hunters moved among the dead and dying buffalo. A final death blow here and there, each claiming his own kills as marked by his specially painted arrows. Miraculously, the hunter whose horse had been tossed and gored was found alive. Battered and with a broken leg, but alive. He was carried from the arena of the hunt to the care of friends and family. His horse was dead.

Butchering parties began to straggle over the rise, and now the real work would begin. It had been a good hunt. No deaths, only a few injuries, and of those, none life-threatening. There had been many kills, and meat and hides would be in good supply.

Liberty watched the process of butchering with new interest. He had not had an opportunity before to see such a large-scale process at his leisure. The women worked in pairs or trios, with the men helping with the heavier work. One side of a buffalo would be skinned, and then the carcass rolled over to skin the other side. Usually this was accomplished by hand, but with the larger animals, a horse was sometimes employed.

As the women gutted out the carcasses, one would occasionally slice off a bite of the warm raw liver and pop it into her mouth.

"Why is this?" Liberty asked in hand sign.

A young woman smiled at him through bloodied teeth.

"Good!" she signed. "Here, eat!"

She held out a bite. Liberty was about to refuse, but realized the possible importance of such a ceremonial bite. He accepted the tidbit, and even with misgivings, began to chew. After the initial revulsion, it was not really bad. He had certainly eaten more repulsive things. But this fresh liver seemed to be considered a delicacy. *Why?* He tried to inquire again, but found little response. The women were too busy to answer. Well, maybe he could ask later.

Just then, he noticed Washington at his elbow.

"You wondered why, Mr. Franklin? It is their spring hunt. They are hungry for fresh food. Nothing but dried meat and dried vegetables all winter. Their bodies crave the freshness."

"How do you know this?" Liberty blurted, surprised.

The Negro shrugged. "It is so with my people. Many have little good food through the winter."

"I had not thought of that. . . . But for your people there is no spring hunt, Washington."

"True. But when they butcher a hog for the 'big house,' they take a bite of the liver in this same way, sometimes. For the same reason, I suppose. They talk of 'life juices.' "

As the work progressed, people would pause in passing to smile and nod and sign their thanks to the dignified Negro. It took the others a little while to realize that Washington was being credited with the success of the hunt. The hunt had resulted in an even greater prestige for Black White Man.

"They asked me to pray for success," Washington explained. "I saw no harm in that, so I did. Apparently, they think my 'medicine' is good."

"Medicine . . ." A word coming into use on the frontier. A makeshift word, to cover the gap that exists in English. There is no English word that adequately expressed all that is implied. Religion, healing, body, spirit, supernatural, world and universe, all one in interaction with the human soul.

Undoubtedly Washington's background included the southern Christianity with its African influences, as well as some of the religion of his mother, whoever she was. Whatever it had been, Liberty felt that Washington's understanding of the native religion here came quite easily.

Well, as he had expressed it himself, Black White Man's medicine was good.

11

It was undoubtedly the hunt that solidified the relationship of Liberty and his party with the Comanches. They were a part of the hunt, a part of the celebration. But first and foremost was the part that Washington had played in the appearance of the buffalo. And his prestige carried over to the rest of the party. They became honored guests, and were showered with the choicest food and with exquisite gifts. Small articles of clothing or ornamentation like moccasins covered with designs in beads or quill work, a pendant, a pipe, a small bag for carrying tobacco, small fur skins, well tanned.

There were offers of female companionship for those so inclined. Andrews declined, apparently feeling it beneath his dignity. He questioned Liberty about the risk of disease, which had become a problem for the men of Lewis and Clark in California.

"There is no way to be sure," Liberty guessed. "In the far West there had been much contact with the Spanish. Captain Lewis placed the blame on that. Here, contact with Santa Fe and with Texas. I am not sure, Alex."

It made little difference. The risk was mentioned to the men, but there is little use in attempting regulation of such matters. A determined man, or woman, will find a way. Here, as in California, the exploring party listened to the warning and did as they pleased.

The discussion itself managed to deter Liberty, however. He had been looking with favor on the advances of a handsome young woman. The questions raised by Andrews caused him to recall the suffering of some of the more promiscuous of those in the corps. The recollection of a man or two, suffering with draining abscesses in the groin, was enough to cause him to lose interest. Probably less risk here than in the houses of St. Louis, he figured, but . . .

A slight problem arose that was certainly unexpected. The comely young woman who had singled him out was somewhat offended at his lack of interest. After clumsy attempts at refusal were met with even more advances, he struck on an idea.

"You are very beautiful," he signed, "and I am honored. But I have made a vow."

The young woman smiled and nodded in understanding. A vow of any kind is to be honored.

"I am sorry," she signed, and patted his hand.

Her expression of sympathy, her gentle smile, the ardor in her eyes . . . but it was too late now. He had publicly told of a vow of chastity and he could not change his mind. *Damn that Andrews,* he thought. *Why did he have to bring that up about the disease?*

The others were less inhibited, and soon paired off for the evening, or the night.

Spotted Dog was quite helpful with the planning of the next portion of their trip. Liberty and Andrews sat with him, visiting and smoking the next day.

All around them, thin strips of meat hung on the drying racks. Children, even very small ones, could be of help now, shooing flies away with fans made of turkey wings.

It had been little short of a miracle, how rapidly the tons of meat had been butchered and handled. "Jerking," the frontiersmen had begun to call the process. A tendon at the end of a large muscle would be isolated and detached from bone. The muscle itself was loosened, pulling it free by the tendon, often with a quick jerk. Then it could be cut in thin strips for drying, sometimes in smoke or with salt to discourage insect damage.

This dried jerky then became a staple item of food. Liberty had seen its versatility before. Strips of jerky may be carried in a pocket or pouch. It is chewed in that form or stewed with vegetables. It can also be pounded to a meal and mixed with melted suet and any available dried fruits, berries, and nuts to become pemmican. This was stuffed into buffalo intestine, much like the sausages of the white man. Liberty had found during the two years with the Corps of Discovery that there was good pemmican and bad, depending on the ability of the women involved in its manufacture and on availability of ingredients. At its best it was excellent eating. Keeping qualities were not quite so good with the mixture as with the plain dried jerky, however. Suet, although adding flavor, turns rancid over time. Jerky keeps its quality much better in storage. They would take a supply of both as they headed on westward.

"How far to the mountains?" Andrews asked their host.

Spotted Dog puffed his pipe for a moment before answering. "Maybe half a moon," he finally signed. "You know about the fork of the river?"

Andrews answered. "Crow told us. The south fork is the true one?" he asked.

Spotted Dog nodded. "But even on that trail, very hard. No water, maybe for three sleeps."

"Is there a better way?" asked Liberty. Where there is no water there are no beaver, either.

Spotted Dog seemed lost in thought, but finally began to sign. "Go north to the river, then west."

"The Platte?" asked Andrews aloud.

"I think so," Liberty answered. He signed again to Spotted Dog. "Called by the French the Platte?" he asked, speaking the last word aloud.

Dog nodded. "Yes, that one. Or you could go south, to the Arkenzas, then west."

"What nations live there?" Liberty questioned.

"Cheyenne. Kiowa. The north trail, Arapaho."

"Yes. Crow's people."

Dog nodded. "Trader People."

"Are there any who would be our enemies?" Liberty asked.

"No . . . Not really. Mostly Comanche, my people, on the southwest trail. Tonkawa, farther south. *They* are enemies. Bad. Eat people sometimes."

"Your people are at war with them?"

"Of course. Is not everyone?"

The discussion continued, and Andrews and Liberty agreed that their best plan was to return to a river. The stream that they now followed was becoming unreliable. So, the Platte or the Ar-kenzas?

Eventually they decided on the more southern route. There was the possibility of trade with the pueblos of the southern mountains, and the area was more familiar, at least by reputation. If the exploration proved favorable to the possibilities of fur trade, they could return by heading north along the mountains and then back eastward along the Kenzas, or even the Platte.

"We will see what the summer brings," said Andrews.

It had been interesting to Liberty to see the change in Andrews as the days and weeks passed. It was as if the well-groomed and highly educated dandy had undergone a change, a metamorphosis into a different being. Caterpillar to butterfly. An odd simile, actually. Liberty pondered that thought a little while. No, not quite accurate. The man had been more of a butterfly when they met. Yet this was not a reverse evolution in any way. It was an upward step, up and onward. The educated butterfly had not devolved backward, but on and upward to a higher stage, that of a hardened, skilled frontiersman.

Liberty could see a change in himself, too. He was not certain why. Maybe this trip had given him more opportunity to observe the country, the customs of the natives. Perhaps it was that the goal was a more personal thing this time. In the Corps of Discovery, it had been merely a job for pay. This trip was bringing him a great deal more personal pleasure. The beauty of a prairie sunset, a cooling breeze across the high plains at the end of a hot day's travel. The roll of the hills, the whisper of the cottonwoods and the answering whisper of cool water from an underground spring.

He shook his head at such strange thoughts. What was happening to him? He was becoming fascinated with this strange country, its creatures and its people. The buffalo hunt had made him realize a larger pattern, and brought an understanding. The sun and rain produce grass, which in turn feeds buffalo to produce meat, which feeds people and wolves and bears and coyotes. Yes, and many others. At their deaths, all return to the earth again, and to grass. . . .

Almost everyone in the party, however, had exhibited a major change in attitude in the past few weeks. Schmidt, the Williams cousins . . .

Liberty had found that he rather liked Schmidt. It was easy to reach false impressions where this big man was concerned. His size was threatening, as was his strength. It took a little while to realize that here was an extremely sensitive man. Schmidt had tried to hide this sensitivity behind bragging and bluff, as a sort of protection.

Zeb Williams was a known quantity. He and Liberty had been to the Pacific coast and back. Steady, dependable. Cousin Charlie was still an unknown. Bigoted, impulsive, a little immature . . . but learning. It would be of interest to see if his good behavior continued after Charlie's come-uppance about Washington's prestige.

Ah, Washington! The greatest change of all . . . always dignified, respectful since he first turned up in St. Louis. Still there was a major change. The dignity and respect remained, but now there was a self-confidence that had been unnoticed before. In the Negro's eye there was now a "look of eagles," a pride and confidence that made him seem taller.

It could be only one thing. The prestige that had come to him as Black White Man, holy man, bringer of buffalo. Washington had been respected, honored by these people.

Liberty was glad for him. He knew that the black man had modestly accepted all the attention, the gifts, and probably the favors of at least one of the comely young women who were attracted to him. Even so, it was something of a surprise when on their third evening with the Comanches, Washington approached him.

"Mr. Franklin, may I speak with you?"

"Of course. What is it, Washington?"

"Sir, I would ask permission to leave the expedition."

"*What?* You were hired to go to the mountains and back!"

"That is true, sir. And if you and Mr. Andrews wish it, that is what I will do. But hear my thoughts before deciding."

Liberty nodded, still confused, and waited for the Negro to continue. Washington took a deep breath and plunged ahead.

"You may have noticed, sir, that these people accord me a certain amount of respect."

"Yes, I—"

Washington gestured him to silence.

"Let me continue, Mr. Franklin. I once mentioned my mother's people. She had run away, long before I was born. She was taken in and adopted by natives, and married into their nation. I do not know which. She had a child, and was pregnant with me when their village was raided by men looking for escaped slaves. Her skin was dark. . . ."

He shrugged, sighed deeply, and continued.

"She died when I was about six, but she told me stories of her adopted people, and of how it was to be free. We were fortunate, to have a Mastuh who was kind and somewhat understanding. He saw to my education with his own children, and then gave me freedom. Freedom for what?"

Liberty was uncomfortable. He had never heard so long a speech by Washington. Besides, he found the subject unpleasant. He waited.

"You have no idea," Washington went on, "how it is to be considered someone's livestock. And what if I should lose my papers, or have them taken from me? Then there is the attitude of other people of color who are still slaves. They have called me 'white man's nigger,' *because* of my education.

"Now *these* people"—he swept an arm to indicate the Comanche camp—"treat me with respect. Yes, you have done that. But theirs is an *honor*. . . . They call me 'holy man' *because* of my color! I am made to feel that these are my people, and those of my mother. Not the same tribe or nation, true. But those of the same spirit, and I would join them."

"Well, I . . . ." Liberty stammered. What could he say? "I must speak with Andrews. We both work for him."

"I am aware of that, but you hired me, so I spoke to you first. You wish me to speak to him?"

"No, no. Let me, Washington." He paused in thought. "Is there a woman, my friend?"

Washington smiled sheepishly. "Well . . . maybe. But that remains to be seen. I am not being insistent, you understand. If you and Mr. Andrews are not completely in agreement, I will fulfill my contract without hesitation. But then I will come back. Either way, it shall be as you say."

12

When the party moved on two days later, Washington did not accompany them.

Andrews, although as surprised as Liberty had been, could see the logic in Black White Man's reasoning.

"I might well make the same choice in his situation," he confided to Liberty.

They had considered asking the Negro to continue with them to the mountains, and to leave the expedition on the way back. But the disadvantages seemed to outweigh the benefits.

"We may not come back the same way," Lib reminded.

"True!" Andrews agreed. "*Probably* not. And the Comanches move around. Where would *they* be?"

"We let him stay, then?"

"It seems the most practical for him, and no harm to us."

"True . . ."

"Besides," Alex went on, "it could be of great benefit to us. Think of the advantage to our fur trade! A representative of the company actually *living* with the Comanches. It gives us a leg up on any other trading company."

Liberty laughed. "Alex, it seems we are trying to convince each other. I'll tell him."

Washington was pleased, of course. Still, Liberty was certain that if the decision had gone the other way, the man would have kept his word and his contract to the best of his ability. A remarkable and highly intelligent man. Under other circumstances he might have been . . . well, almost anything. Liberty smiled to himself. *Now,* he thought, *he does have other circumstances.* Maybe it would be interesting to see how this turned out.

This brought Liberty to thoughts of his own future, a subject that he had never really explored. Since the day he had fled from the custody of the Reverend Whitworth, he had had no real direction.

There had been a while that he bitterly resented Madge for pushing him out. Now he realized that she could have done nothing else. In another year or two he would have become permanently entangled in "the business" in one way or another. Madge, in the tribulation of her own life, wanted something better for him. As that realization sank home, he thought of fledgling birds he had seen, preparing to leave the nest. Fully feathered yet still not having flown, they would stand on the edge of the nest, fluttering and calling out for the food the mother bird should be bringing. The parent, meanwhile, kept a discreet distance, continuing to cry calls of encouragement. Finally in desperation the fledgling would make the try. Usually successfully. True, sometimes the failures became a meal for some small predator. But is that not the way of the world? Nature's selective process is cruel but effective, and the weak seldom survive to reproduce. The mother bird must finally and with qualms allow her child to leave the nest. As Madge had done . . . and Samuel . . . he could recall now the pride that Madge had shown when one of her girls *left* the business to marry.

Maybe someday he would go back to Philadelphia to see Madge. . . . To thank her for making him a man. But not now. He *would* write her a letter. She would be pleased to know that he had been with the Corps of Discovery, doing something worthwhile.

All of this deep thought did not do much for the deeper thought about the unsure status of his future. He had been a runaway, had done some odd jobs for a meal here and there. Then the corps, a temporary job . . . this was another, the present arrangement with Andrews. There was a need to know where he was going. Maybe the army . . . *no,* he thought. He did not believe that he would take kindly to the regimented discipline.

He now remembered how unsettled and frustrated he had been in St. Louis, the winter after the corps. He had been restless, wanting something but not knowing what it was.

He still did not know. Well, another few months of this . . . there was really no need to worry about it until then, when the exploration was finished. There would be a sense of satisfaction, because they *were* accomplishing a lot. Andrews's maps continued to grow, both in area and in detail. They had met and established relations with several of the major Indian nations. They had seen sights not seen before by European eyes. And there was more to come. But soon he must make those deeper lifetime decisions. . . .

He lay awake a long time, that first night after they left the Comanche camp. He watched the Seven Hunters make a part of their nightly circuit as he pondered. It was a beautiful summer night. The night sounds that had become so familiar now seemed a comfort to his thoughts. The owl in the thin strip of timber along the creek, the coyote calling to her mate beyond the rise.

His thoughts turned to his conversation with Andrews, the one about Washington. Liberty had been so intent on Washington's future that he now realized that he had missed something. Could he have been mistaken? No, Andrews had plainly said "of great benefit to *us* . . . advantage to *our* fur trade . . ."

What was his meaning here? Andrews had never said much about his fur venture. Liberty had always assumed that this expedition was in behalf of an organization based in St. Louis, or possibly back East. He had never really wondered who "the company" might be. It had been of no concern to him. When he finished this job there would be something else. Maybe he could be a guide or scout for some other faceless company as the West opened and the territory encompassed by the Louisiana Purchase was explored.

Now his curiosity was aroused. Andrews's use of the terms "us," "we," and "our fur company" now made him wonder. What sort of men envision such things? Bankers in three-piece suits in a posh club in New York or Philadelphia? And how did Andrews know such people? True, he *had* misjudged Alex at first, had mistaken *him* for one of those. But the man had adapted well, and seemed quite at home on the frontier. Liberty's concept of Andrews's function had now changed. Andrews was an ordinary man, the frontier representative of a faceless company back East. Yet he spoke with an easy familiarity as if he were a part of it. Liberty determined to ask him about it when opportunity offered. Surely Alex would not mind explaining how such things work.

Liberty relieved Zeb Williams on watch at midnight, and spent more time in thought. Not such directed thought now, but more general matters of wonder. What makes it possible for the owl in the timber below to see in the dark? Is the coyote's cry simply a call to his mate, *I am hunting here,* or a warning to identify his territory? Or is he only singing to the moon and the night sky to celebrate all of creation?

None of these questions were resolved that night. In fact, it was several days before Liberty had a chance to talk to Alex. He almost abandoned the idea, but his curiosity finally wore him down.

"Alex," he began when the others were occupied elsewhere one evening, "may I ask about something?"

The other man looked at him closely for a moment, puffed his pipe, and finally answered.

"You look very serious, Liberty. Is there a problem?"

"No, no. I hope I am not being presumptuous. I was only curious."

"About what?"

"About your fur company. What sort of people are they? Your backers . . ."

Andrews chuckled. "Is *that* all? I thought it was something serious!"

Liberty was mildly embarrassed and a bit irritated. He had gone too far, maybe, asking about something that was no concern of his.

"Well, I . . ." he stammered.

"Liberty," Andrews interrupted, an amused smile on his face, "you are *looking* at the fur company."

"You are . . ."

"Yes. I had a little family money when I graduated from Harvard. I was expected to practice law like my father and grandfather, but I wanted to see the new West. I'm seeing it."

"Then there *is* no fur company?"

"Oh, yes, Liberty, there *is*. *We* are the fur company, you and I. If you will consent, that is."

"But . . . but Alex, I have nothing to invest."

"Oh, but you do, my friend. Your skills. I thought you were my man, but I was not sure. Now I am. We'll know, in a season or two, whether our fur company is practical. I furnish the capital, you the expertise. I should have approached you before this."

"Why did you *not?*"

"Well . . . I had to watch you long enough to decide. Then I found that I was enjoying the watching. It would not have been the same if I had forced you into a decision too early. Then, when we talked of Washington . . . I considered speaking of it, but that was Washington's moment. I *would* have brought it up soon. Maybe I was afraid you would say no."

Liberty sat in stunned silence as Andrews took a stick from the fire to relight his pipe.

"Well, what do you say?" he went on. "The Andrews and Franklin Trading Company? I can run the St. Louis end, the corporate papers and all. You can handle this end, with the help of Washington and all our other contacts. Shall we try it for a season or two?"

Liberty took a deep breath. "Why not? As long as I can do my end out here somewhere."

There, he'd said it. With some surprise, he suddenly realized that this was the question he'd been dodging all along. What would he do when he was forced to return to the world of cities and city people? Somewhere along the line he had fallen in love. Not with a woman, though he felt that was yet to come. His love was for the prairie. . . . For the wide sky and the far horizons, the promise of untold mysteries over the next rise and beyond. For grasses, taller in autumn than a man on a horse. For clear cool streams over white gravel. For smells of broiling hump ribs of buffalo over a fire of buffalo chips, after a successful hunt.

Andrews interrupted his reverie. "So be it! Now, let us plan. I think we should at least contact the Southern Cheyenne, no? We can do that, maybe reach the mountains, and head back before autumn. Agreed?"

Liberty nodded. Already he was planning what supplies he might need, and wondering where he would spend the coming winter. At least, not in the saloons of some city.

AFTERWORD

A ndrews was not the only traveler to note the unique political structure of the Pawnees. The Pawnee-controlled area between the Platte and the Kansas rivers became known as the Indian Republic. By 1814, the name of the northern stream that enters the Kansas River at Junction City had been euphemistically changed to the Republican River. Cultured mapmakers were unwilling to use the more earthy Indian name. It survived for some time, however, in a frontier expression. To be in an extremely bad situation was to be "up Shit Creek without a paddle."

Several smaller trapping and trading companies such as the Andrews and Franklin helped to establish the fur trade in the southern mountains. Manuel Lisa's and the later Rocky Mountain Fur Company of William Ashley overlapped this territory in the ensuing decades.

There was constant, though not major, contact with the pueblos at Taos and at Santa Fe. The international border remained for some time along the course of the Arkansas River, Spain claiming all land south of that boundary.

BOOK V

❖

A.D. 1814
LONG WALKER

1

The old man shifted his position slightly in the chair to catch the warm October sun on his right shoulder. There was a time when, on a day like this, he'd have been running the woods. It was his favorite time of the year, the autumn. There was an excitement about it. Not the same as the foot-itching spring excitement, with the geese moving and the buds bursting, and the driving mystery of what might be over the next hill or around the bend.

Now the geese were moving back south, to winter in warmer climates. It was good to walk in the ripe woods on a warm sunny day in Indian summer, to smell the scents of autumn. He could see the colors turn by the day. By the hour, almost. The maples and red oaks and sweet gum trees were coming on in a blaze of color now. Reds and yellows, gold and orange. Trees a little different from those back home in Pennsylvania and even in Kentucky . . . that had been the frontier then.

He wondered about some of the friends they had left behind when they came here to Missouri, more than sixteen years ago. Lord, what an interesting life he'd had! A Quaker, born of English parents. Moved around some, drove a supply wagon for General Braddock's campaign against the French in 1755. Back home in Carolina, he'd married a neighbor's daughter. Ah, he and Becky had had a good life together. . . . Almost as good with a rifle as he was himself. He missed her now. She'd been tolerant when the call of the wild geese would get under his skin and he'd have to go. She'd complain, but she'd go along with his need to wander. She'd thought him dead, sometimes. She'd even gone back East when he'd been captured by Shawnees that time in Kentucky. He'd had to find her after he returned to Boonesborough with a shaved head, an adopted Shawnee in his own right.

But all that was a long time ago. His aching joints reminded him of that on cool mornings now. The snows of many winters lay on his head now, as Blackfish, his adopted Shawnee father, would have said. He'd pretty near killed himself a few seasons ago, trying to trap beaver on the Missouri River and its branches. Felt like a young man trapped in a creaky old body, he had. After all, he *had* turned seventy-seven that February, in a shanty on the river. Yet only sixty beaver plews to show for the season . . . *times ain't what they was,* he thought.

But all that had happened—the war with England . . . Washington and the new country, the "United States of America"—when he'd been about forty. That looked *young,* now.

He shifted his position again and scratched his left ribs with his right hand. Maybe he'd take ol' Tick-Licker, his favorite rifle, down off the wall and try for a deer a little later. Or maybe not. He *had* seen a nice buck though, down by the spring, the past few days. Maybe a ten-pointer.

A figure came into his field of vision on the distant road, and he studied it as the traveler came nearer. Resentment flared in him for a moment, as his eyes refused to see the detail that they once had. That, and the way the country was getting so crowded. This was the third traveler to pass down the road today, and it was hardly noon.

A few years ago, he'd have moved on west. He'd done that a few times. To Kentucky, and then when that got too crowded, just a few years ago, he'd walked on out here. His family, most of them, anyway, had come by boat down the Ohio and up the Missouri. The Femme Osage region, claimed by Spain. The Spanish authorities had been glad to welcome him. Well, he'd always gotten on well with most folks. They gave him a grant of land and made him a magistrate. He hadn't really had the book learning to be a judge, but folks respected his fairness. And he'd been younger then, of course. Only about sixty, he reckoned.

Then a lot had happened. Spain had ceded their land to France, who sold it to the United States. That might have been good, except that his land grant title was from Spain, and he had no papers. That had happened to him before, the trouble with titles and deeds. The lawyers always tried to make a simple ownership too complicated with all their papers and whereases and therefores. And this time, he was just too old to move on. He sighed. Well, it *was* comfortable here in the sun.

Of course, there was that doin's in the Congress. Some of his friends had gone there to try to help him get his land back. Maybe part of it, anyway. No tellin' how that would come out, but he appreciated the effort.

He wasn't really comfortable with the idea that he had become a hero to a lot of people. It was embarrassing to have folks write about his deeds on the frontier, calling him a trailblazer and an Indian fighter. He had no claim to such. All he'd ever tried to do was stay alive and to feed his family.

As for killing Indians, he took no glory in that, like some folks. Maybe it was his Quaker background. They didn't hold with killing at all. *Reckon I don't either,* he thought, *unless they was tryin' to kill me or mine.* Sometimes he'd had to kill folks, but never relished it like some.

But most of that was long ago. Now here he was, nearing eighty winters, resenting the limitations that time had put on him. But today was good, the sun was warm. . . .

A young woman came to the door and smiled at him.

"Are you all right, Daddy?" she asked.

"Oh, yes . . . jest watchin' that feller on the road."

"Another traveler? Yes, they're getting pretty frequent. The country's settling down."

She turned back into the house. *Drat,* he thought. *She talks almost like she thinks that's good.*

Still, Jemima was a good daughter. And her husband, Flanders Calloway, was a good man. They had made him know that he had a home with them if he needed. And his son, Nathan, was living nearby. He could visit there sometimes . . .

The figure on the road drew nearer, and now he could tell by the way the fellow moved that it was a man. A young man, who carried a pack on his shoulders. The momentary pang of resentment struck again. No, not so much resentment as jealousy, maybe. Jealousy that such health and the strength of young manhood should be wasted on the youth. Then he smiled at himself for such an idea. *Ah, well,* he admitted, *I had my time. And, such a time . . .*

The young man now reached the short path up to the cabin, and hesitated. Then he turned and strode purposefully up toward the dooryard.

"Mr. Boone?" he inquired politely.

"That was my daddy's name," replied the old man with a twinkle in his eye. "Mr. Boone, or Squire Boone. I'm jest Dan'l. Dan'l Boone. Could I help ye?"

"Well . . . well, yes, sir . . ."

The voice had tones that told of affluence and culture. Some education. Boone had learned to size up folks pretty well. Here was a spoiled young man who'd never done much hard work. Gone to one of them colleges, likely. Still wearing expensive clothes, though a bit trail worn now. And he'd been right, the fellow was young. Of course, everybody looked young now. But what did this young man want? Maybe he was a writer, looking to write a story about "the great frontiersman," or some such nonsense. It had been a few years, though, since one of them had sought him out.

"I . . . I wanted to meet you, sir," the young man blurted.

"What fer?"

"I'm not sure. I just felt the need."

Now here was a new idea. This youth was straight out, up front. He didn't *know* why he was here, but he *felt a need.* The old man knew how it was to feel a need. It was what had driven him in his own youth. He could not have told, even now, what it was that had driven him away from the farm and into the woods, repeatedly. Kentucky . . . folks were calling the trail he had marked there Boone's Trail now. It wasn't, really, in his own mind. He'd just found the road used by the Indians for travel and trade. Yes, and for war. They'd used it for generations, he figured.

Florida . . . he'd spent some time there. . . . Really different country. He'd enjoyed its differences. Why had he gone there? He'd *felt the need.* He could have been happy there. Nearly decided to live there, in fact. But that had been the only time Rebecca really put her foot down. And he'd decided she was more important than Florida. She'd gone along with his "need" every other time, though. She had understood.

Boone pulled himself back to the present and looked at the young man with a new insight. This youngster had said that he felt the need to be here. He'd said it with a touch of confusion, as if he really didn't understand it himself, but wasn't ashamed of it. That was good in a man. *He reminds me of myself,* the old man thought. He pointed to a bench by the door.

"Set a spell," he invited. "Tell me about it."

He already knew a lot about it. The unexplored West, just beyond the sunset, yonder. He envied the young man the road ahead of him, the sights he'd see, the experiences he'd have. Even the dangers, because that was part of the excitement of it. Boone had been out on the prairie a ways, a time or two. Different, but he'd loved that, too. Big sky, horizons three days' travel away . . . buffalo by the millions . . . deer, antelope, turkeys, grouse, beaver, bear. Mountains beyond, they said. He'd talked to a couple of men who'd been with Lewis and Clark. Lord, the tales they told! Even allowing for their tendency to brag it up some, it must have been glorious to stand and look *west* at a sun setting in that far ocean. This young man might see that. But in the meantime, so much else to see.

The traveler shrugged loose the straps of his pack and slid it from his shoulders. He worked his muscles a little, dropped the pack on the bench, and leaned his rifle against the wall of the cabin. Then he sat down.

It was a new rifle, Boone noticed. Probably bought it in St. Louis, and paid too much for it. But the young man noticed his glance and spoke.

"I hope you'll approve of my weapon, sir. I got the best advice I could in Kentucky."

"Well, let's get acquainted first. You have the advantage of me. I don't know your name."

"Oh! Forgive me, sir. Jed . . . Jedediah Sterling, from Baltimore."

"Howdy, Jed. Reckon we can do without the 'sir,' though."

"If you wish."

"I do. Now, you know about me. Some, anyhow. Tell me about you."

This was going pretty slow, but now the young man, Jed, kicked his tongue into a lope.

"Well, I've been in college for two years. My father wanted me to follow him into law, but I didn't like it much."

That speaks well for him, Boone thought.

"My mother died last fall, and the judge . . . my father . . . remarried. She's young, pretty, but . . . well, she doesn't like me much. I can't very well go home. I'd be in the way. So I headed west."

Boone had a strong feeling that there was much more to that story. It wasn't the main story, though. That was the excuse. The reason why Jedediah Sterling had headed west wasn't back in Baltimore. It was here. In spite of his inexperience, the young man was here because he belonged here. He felt the need.

2

Jedediah Sterling could hardly believe his good fortune. Here he sat, on a rough bench in frontier Missouri, talking with Daniel Boone himself. All of his young life he had heard or read about the exploits of this man.

In fact, he was here now, probably, because of his fascination with the adventures of Boone. He had read of the dangers, the miraculous escapes and the tests of courage and skill. He found such reading much more interesting and exciting than the stodgy old textbooks and lecturers in the ivy-covered halls of the university. His mind was constantly elsewhere.

It had been his mother, he now realized, who had spurred his interest. She had been a dreamer and a visionary, and above all, a reader. The household had never lacked for books, tall shelves of them that reached the ceiling in the library of the big house in Baltimore. His mother had read aloud to him when he was small, and helped him to select appropriate books when he began to read on his own.

His father, Judge J. T. Sterling III, had not been a major figure in his youth. Jedediah remembered him as a stern patriarch, held in awe by the Negro house servants. The few visitors who came to the house for formal occasions or on business showed great respect for the judge, but there was little warmth. Jed and his younger sister were a bit afraid of the imposing figure, though they had no real reason to be so.

It had always been assumed that Jedediah would follow his father and grandfather in the profession of the law. He had little interest, yet attempted to master the fundamentals out of respect for his father's wishes.

There had been two escapes from the routine. One was the escape into his books, living the adventures of others through the pages of fine literature, guided and encouraged by his mother.

The other, only partly understood by her, was his escape to the woods along the river that bordered the estate. There, he would be transformed into Robin Hood, or one of King Arthur's knights, or perhaps Beowulf, stalking dragons. Sometimes his sister Sarah would accompany him, to become a maiden in distress for him to rescue. But Sarah, several years younger, failed to join fully in the spirit of the thing. Besides, their mother never totally approved. He felt an odd dichotomy there. His mother would have enjoyed that fantasy escape, he knew. Yet she considered it beneath her position as the wife of Judge Sterling to behave in a manner so unladylike. Jed had always felt sympathy for her because of this stifling responsibility that held her in check and prevented her from really enjoying the things about which she loved to read.

He had been away at Princeton when it happened. He had stopped to pick up his mail after an especially boring lecture. The clerk flipped through a bundle of letters, not yet completely sorted.

"Mm . . . Sterling, right? Let's see . . . *oh!*"

The tone was one of surprise. The man paused, and carefully drew a single envelope from the stack in his left hand. It bore a stark black border a quarter inch wide, all around the margin of the envelope on both sides. There was almost a tone of reverence in the clerk's voice as he handed the letter to Jed.

"Sorry, sir."

His heart pounding, Jed ripped open the envelope to draw out the letter itself, also edged in black. Something had happened to Sarah. . . . It had not even occurred to him yet, but now he realized that the handwriting was that of his father. It was usually his mother who wrote.

It is with deep sorrow that I must inform you of the death of your mother, who has succumbed to pneumonia last night. . . . From that point on the words blurred and became meaningless. There were a few more details, but no comfort.

He stumbled out into the street, trying to formulate plans to return home for the funeral. It was beginning to snow, great fluffy flakes that floated silently to the ground like soft feathers. It was almost Christmas.

He returned to school after the holiday with even less interest. He had always been something of a loner, but now became even more so. His reading for escape had taken a slightly different direction, away from the classics. There had been a small shop a few blocks from the campus where one could buy various kinds of reading material, much of it frowned on by the university administration. There were French postcards and small tracts with smutty stories and sketches. But for a few cents, he discovered, he could buy a pamphlet with stories of the frontier and the West. Some were of poor quality, some well written, but his interest was in the content, not the skills of the writer. In this way he learned of the exploits of the brave settlers who were opening the wilderness—Kentucky, Tennessee, Ohio, Louisiana. He read of explorers and trappers and hunters, such trailblazers as Daniel Boone. Boone had become a hero in the young man's eyes.

The following summer he had spent the holiday from school in his father's office, acting as a law clerk. It was a boring task, mostly copying documents with a quill pen on parchment. His father was as distant and uncaring as ever.

The judge was also engaged in a dalliance, or possibly a courtship, with a young woman named Phoebe. She was only a few years older than Jedediah, and reminded him of the girls on the French postcards, though she wore more clothes. There was a flirtatious manner about her that he found quite offensive. It was apparent that her cap was set for the judge. Jed resented this, so soon after the death of his mother. His father, he felt, was acting in an undignified manner, more like a silly schoolboy than a respected attorney.

To make matters worse, Sarah seemed completely under the spell of the scheming young woman. The two of them would draw aside, giggling together in whatever secrets must be involved in girl talk.

He sensed that the servants disapproved, too, of Phoebe's obvious schemes to become mistress of the estate. He saw it in their eyes, along with a dread of what might happen if she gained authority over them. The hopeless expression as they looked to him for the help that he could not give lay heavy on his heart.

Jed would, at every opportunity, slip away by himself, to walk the river paths with one of the hunting dogs. Not hunting, it was not the season. Just to get away from the house.

Possibly worst of all was the way that Phoebe shamelessly flirted with him, Jedediah, when there was no one else around. He was attracted to her physically, of course, his young maleness being on the rise. Under some circumstances he might have considered a roll with such a woman exciting and even worthwhile. In this situation, however, he thought her actions not only inappropriate but downright disgusting. She would probably actually bed with him, Jed thought, even while scheming to catch his father.

He returned to the university, and in October learned by letter that Phoebe and the judge had married, in a small private ceremony. There was also a note from his sister, Sarah, who was excited and wildly enthusiastic about this development.

Jed was heartsick. He dreaded the Christmas holiday, and all the memories that it would bring. But he would try to consider his father's happiness and his right to do as he chose.

It was a night or two after Christmas that he woke, having heard a noise in the house. Someone was in his bedroom. Startled, he sat upright, and as he did so he caught a slight scent of perfume. Phoebe's . . . she lifted the covers and slipped into bed, stroking his body with her long legs as she snuggled next to him.

"No!" he whispered, horrified. "This is not right, Phoebe!"

Even as he spoke, he was becoming aroused. It was like a dream, or a nightmare.

"I know you want me," she whispered. "Who will know?"

She kissed him full on the mouth, her lips warm and moist, and drew her leg over his hips. He was being sorely tempted.

"No!" he said firmly, pushing away. But he was weakening.

"I *could* scream," she whispered, "and say you lured me in here." She paused and chuckled seductively. Then her demeanor changed. "But never mind. Next time, Jed!"

She kissed his cheek in an almost sisterly way, slipped out of the bed, and was gone.

He lay there staring into the darkness until the pale gray light of the winter dawn began to filter into his window. It was snowing, and his whole world had turned cold. Of one thing he was certain. There must be no "next time."

He contrived to return to the university as soon as he could, but he did not really do so. He picked up a few personal things from his rented room, and withdrew the money from the bank account he had opened at Princeton.

"*All* of it?" asked the teller.

"Yes. I have to leave school for now. A death in the family."

"Oh. Sorry, sir."

Jed had been building up the bank account ever since his mother's death. He could not have told why, until now. He must have realized that he might need a means to escape. An escape to the West. Boone's West, the blazing of trails . . . adventure, danger, and thrills.

For a while, when the weather turned bad, he had stayed in an inn on the Cumberland, impatient to be moving on. He talked with men who had been West, hungering for any scrap of information. He began to sort out that which seemed valid from that which was mostly talk.

When spring came, he had followed Boone's trail to Kentucky. Had actually seen a birch tree with a carved message: *"D. Boone cilled a bar on this tree."* It had made his heart race and his skin tingle.

At Boonesborough, he had bought a rifle. Until then he had been armed with only a pocket pistol, and had not had occasion to use it.

The gunsmith who sold him the rifle professed to know Boone.

"Dan'l says," the man offered, "that you need a bigger ball for the game out West. Buffler, bear . . . thirty to thirty-six might be all right for deer and such, but I'd pick a bigger rifle if you're headin' west."

Jed settled on a .45 with a somewhat shorter barrel than usual, to keep the weight down. He bought powder, lead, flints, and a bullet mold, and moved on. He considered a horse and some buckskins, but his money was running low. He decided that he'd better walk.

And now, here he was, all the way to Missouri territory. He'd asked about Boone in St. Louis, and kept moving west. He was not certain what would be next, or where. But he had already fulfilled one of his goals. He was actually sitting here, talking to Daniel Boone, at the gateway to the West.

3

oone studied the young man as they talked. He had seen a lot
of them. Sons of "gentlemen" who had headed west looking
for excitement. Some were robbed, or worse, and never even
reached the frontier. Some families, he was sure, never even learned
what had happened to their sons and heirs.

Occasionally, though, there would be one who was a bit different. One whose spirit had called him on this kind of quest, whose
"heart was right," old Blackfish would have said. That one would
become a hunter, trapper, a woodsman. And despite the well-worn
gentleman's clothes that hung on the lanky frame of this youth, Boone
felt that this was one of the good ones. Somehow their spirits reached
out, touched, and met, and it was good.

For one thing, maybe, it was that this boy *was* wearing such
clothing. A greenhorn wearing fancy store-bought buckskins with
long fringes would be suspect. All clothes and no man. A man who
wore and used what he had, with no pretense, must be respected.

"How come you ain't wearin' leather?" Boone asked, testing.

The young man flushed, embarrassed.

"Well, I . . . I thought I should save my money till I knew more about what I'd need."

Boone nodded. "But ye're carryin' a new rifle."

"Yes. I had some advice on that, in Kentucky."

The old man knew precisely the source of that advice, but did not say so. It *had* been good advice. Large-caliber bore, short barrel. Unless he missed his guess, the young man would also be carrying about the right amount of lead, powder, and flints, too. A few things still lacked. Maybe he could make a few suggestions. A hat for instance.

Boone pushed his ancient black felt hat back on his forehead. He'd always preferred this hat. A lot of his friends had gone to wearing a coonskin hat with the tail hangin' down the back. That was all right, if a man came across an especially nice pelt with a long tail, he guessed. It had always seemed to him, though, that if a man got caught in the rain, more water would run his neck from a fur hat. Not that it was a problem. Not bein' made of sugar, a man ain't goin' to melt, he reckoned. But his wide-brim black felt shed quite a bit of rain, as well as shading his eyes from the sun when it weren't rainy. Particularly he'd found that to be true out on open prairie. A bit different from Kentucky woods, more open and less shade.

"You walked all the way from Baltimore?" he now asked.

"Yes. Again, I thought I should conserve my resources," Jed Sterling answered.

And wouldn't spend it to ride when he could walk, Boone thought. *Yep, this 'un may make it.*

"I wanted to see you, sir . . . uh, Mr. . . . uh, Daniel. . . ." the young man stammered hesitatingly. "First, just for the honor of it. But I also hoped to ask for advice. Any hints you might give me."

He paused, looking embarrassed.

Wants to ask about everything west of sunrise, Boone thought, *but don't know where to begin. That's all right.*

For starters, the rifle . . . "have you tried your rifle?" he asked.

"Just a few shots, in Kentucky where I bought it."

Yes, the old man thought. Out behind Ephriam Doty's shop was the stump a hundred paces away where he'd let a customer try a new rifle.

"Shoot purty straight?" he asked.

"Yes. Probably better than I can point it."

Good. He's some modest, too.

"But where's yer powder horn?"

"Don't have one. I figured I could make one when I have a chance."

"So, yer powder's in your pack."

"Yes. A can . . ."

"Mm . . . handy for carryin', an' it jest don't get wet."

"I know. I've been lucky with the weather so far, too."

"But ye can't count on it. Let's see, now. Ye need a horn. A left horn, if ye can."

"A left horn? Why?"

Boone smiled to himself. *Well, he ain't afeared to ask,* he thought. Aloud, he explained.

"Well, the curve fits around yer body some better. You use yer right hand to pour, so you want the horn on yer right hip, with the spout end forward. Yer right-handed, I reckon? Yes. Now, if you were *left*-handed, you'd want the right horn fer yer powder. Let's go back to the shed, here. . . ."

He rose and led the way round the cabin to a small lean-to in the back. There hung or stood a clutter of tools and hides and pieces of leather harness, a dilapidated saddle. An ax was stuck in the flat surface of a chopping block, and a cord or so of firewood was stacked against the wall.

Boone rummaged among some steel traps of various sizes and drew out a trio of mismatched cow horns. He brushed dust from them and squinted carefully, evaluating the choices.

"Not the best," he murmured, "but mebbe this one'll do."

He handed the horn to Jed, and tossed the others aside. "Try it on yer hip," he suggested. "Fit purty good?"

The young man held the horn to his hip and found that yes, it did seem to lie well. "I guess so."

"Good. Now let's cut off the pointy end."

He took a fine-toothed saw from the wall, carefully sawed off about two inches of the horn's tip, and handed it to the young man.

"There," he said. "Hang onto that. You'll use it later."

"For what?"

"A powder measure. Ye ream out inside to hold a charge jest right fer yer rifle. But fer now, ye need a plug fer the open end, and a stopper peg for the pourin' end. Here . . . you got a jackknife, ain't you?"

"Yes . . ."

"Good. Take yer smallest blade and start reamin' out the pourin' end. Make it round inside, and here's a stick of ash to make the stopper. I'll find a plug for the big end."

By the time the sun began to hang low, the horn was nearly completed. The outside was still rough, but as Boone said, "Ye can scrape on that a little bit at a time so's to smooth it. Now fer yer measure. Hand me one of the balls from yer mold."

Jed fished a round lead ball from his pocket and handed it over. Boone examined it with approval.

"Good. About forty-five, ain't it?" He went on without answering. "Here, hold it in yer palm."

Jed complied, and the old man began to trickle black powder from the horn, to fall on the silvery surface of the bullet. The powder slid off, of course, beginning to form a circular pile around the sides of the bullet in the young man's palm. When the ball was nearly covered, he paused and replaced the stopper in the horn.

"There," he said. "Thet's yer charge. Now take that horn top and begin to ream out the hollow. Ye quit when the powder will fill it. You'll find the charge thet's jest right for yer rifle as you use it. A little less, a little more. Start a bit light and work up. When it ain't just a bang but a *crack,* yer rifle's talkin' to ye."

The old man patted the new rifle affectionately. "This'll be yer best friend, son, so treat her right. Now, I've an idee. You need to stay the night, 'cause it's late. You kin spread yer blankets in the shed here or anywhere. Then at daylight we can let you try for a big buck I been seein'. Are you game?"

They ate, a rich stew prepared by Boone's daughter, and Jed spread his blanket under the stars. He slept little that night, because when dawn came, he would actually participate in a hunt with the legendary Daniel Boone.

Even so, he had managed to doze off for a little while when he was wakened by a hand on his shoulder.

"It's time," said Boone simply.

Jed sat up, to find the sky in the east turning from black to a muddy yellow-gray.

Boone led the way down a path that seemed virtually invisible in the dim light.

"Here," he whispered. "We kin set on this rock. The creek's yonder. He'll come in from the north there, likely."

They watched, not speaking. The light grew and spread, and the scattered stars began to disappear.

Jed did not see the approach of the big buck. One moment he was not there, and suddenly he was, head raised in all his glory. There had not been a sound, or a hint of motion. At least, not that Jed had seen.

"Ssst!" whispered Boone softly.

Jed began to position his rifle, very slowly. The buck appeared suspicious, Jed was certain that the animal was staring straight at him. The ears were spread wide and the head high. He could even see the ragged shreds of velvet hanging from the great rack of antlers. It was early in the season, and this year's growth of antlers were not quite polished yet in preparation for the rut. But it was a truly magnificent buck, with at least five points on each antler. Boone had described this head last evening as "lookin' like a room full of rockin' chairs." Not until now had Jed fully understood the simile.

Jed carefully brought the flint from half-cock back to the fully cocked position. There was a soft click, not louder than a single tick of a well-oiled clock. But the buck heard. He had not reached this stage of proud maturity by ignoring the small things. His white flag of warning to other deer stood erect and bright in the growing dawn. He snorted, the soft whistling snort of alarm. Another heartbeat and he would be gone. Jed's finger tightened on the trigger, as the sights aligned on the desired patch of hair. Just behind the foreleg, low in the chest, a heart shot. The flint struck the frizzen, opening the priming pan and showering sparks into the waiting powder. Jed's vision was obscured by a cottony puff of white smoke as the rifle cracked. He caught a glimpse of the buck bounding away.

"Ye got him!" Boone chuckled at his elbow. "Now jest wait a minute. He can't go far."

Jed had assumed that he had missed. But of course, a stricken animal would attempt to flee.

Boone rose now, and moved forward, his glance sweeping the ground ahead of them. It was not twenty paces, a few desperate leaps by the dying buck. The animal lay where he had fallen, and the hunt was over.

Then Boone did a strange thing. He stepped to the fallen monarch, took the antlers and turned the head to a more lifelike position, facing forward. He addressed the creature in a series of syllables, an unknown tongue, with an attitude of respect. His ritual finished, he stooped to cut the throat, "bleeding out" the meat.

"What . . . what was that?" asked the confused Jed.

"What was what?"

"The words you said. A ritual of some sort?"

"Oh, thet . . ." Boone seemed a trifle embarrassed. "An Indian thing, a kind of ceremony."

"But what does it mean?"

"Well . . . I reckon it means a lot to them. I sort of got the habit, mebbe. It says somethin' like . . . let's see, now . . . somethin' like, 'I'm sorry to kill you, brother deer, but I need you for food.' They figger that keeps the other deer from holdin' a grudge, I reckon."

"They do that for every kill?"

"Prob'ly not. Mebbe some do. Mostly at the first of the season, or the first kill of a hunt. Some special situation. Like this."

"Why this?"

Boone smiled. "Well, I dunno. I sort of thought this was a purty special hunt for you. First one with a new rifle . . . the beginning of your move into the prairie. I dunno," he finished lamely, "sort of like a table grace . . ."

4

"Y e've got to be plannin' fer winter," Boone admonished a day
later. "It's a bit late for the season, but you'll do all right."

"Should I try to partner up with one of the fur companies? I heard tell of them in St. Louis."

"Reckon I wouldn't, son. One thing, there's too many of 'em on
the river now. Ashley and his bunch . . . then come the Astorians
. . . Manuel Lisa's out of it now, I think, an' good riddance. But, tell
you what . . . you strike me as a loner, anyhow. Whyn't you try the
other river?"

"The *other*?"

"Yep, the Kansas River. Most of the big trappin' outfits are
goin' up the Missouri. But the Kansas flows into it about three days
west of here. There's a town there, Kansa Indian town. They're
friendlies. 'South Wind People.' Thet river runs pretty much straight
west, it appears, purty near clean to the mountains. An' there's a
tradin' company in there, I heard. What was it? Feller name of Franklin . . . yes, Lib Franklin. Never met him, but heared he's honest.
But wait . . . you know hand signs?"

"No."

"Drat, boy, have I got to learn you everything?" But he said it with a smile. "Look . . . stay a day or so. I can get you started on the signs, and show you about traps and such. Are you goin' to use steel traps or snares?"

"Well, I . . . I don't . . ."

"Money? Yes . . . snares, then. After a season or two, mebbe buy some traps. Now, yer best cash crop is beaver. Ye kin hunt, with yer rifle here, not only for meat but some furs. Fox, wolf, 'coon, bobcat. An' ye really ought to have some buckskins. There's an ol' Indian woman down the crick a ways who'll make ye some. She does good work."

Boone rambled on, pouring out his heart to a willing listener. He had always been thought quiet and something of a loner, and now was rather surprised at himself. He understood why. Here was a young man who felt the same urges as he had, the need to go and see and do. And out there it was vast and unexplored, a million miles of it, just waiting. It was as Kentucky had been in his own youth. Now settled . . . that was the troublesome thing. A fine land cried out to be tamed and explored and settled, and he gloried in the doing of it. Yet when it was accomplished, the tamed land was no longer desirable. Its spirit was broken to the yoke of civilization and to the will of people who did not understand.

The land beyond called out. He'd talked with John Colter and some of the others who'd been with Lewis and Clark and the corps. They'd told him what a fine land it was.

But he was too old now to answer the call. That last winter he'd trapped on the Missouri had been hard. Now he'd have to be content to sit in the sun and whittle and dream of days gone by. Well, trap a little along the creek here, maybe. Enough to keep his hand in.

And, for right now, teaching this youngster. He'd taken a fancy to the boy. Despite their different backgrounds, he knew that this was a spirit like his own. A few years ago, he'd have liked a partner such as this, to spend a winter with, on the traps. Too late now, but he could help this one get a start, maybe. Teach him things that could save his life out there.

Boone was concerned that new buckskins and rifle would identify Jed as a greenhorn. They had spent the better part of a day to remedy that situation. There was no thought of attempting to age the rifle, but they concentrated on the buckskins, obtained from the Indian woman. The old frontiersman carefully rubbed sand and mud into the knees of the leggings and the elbows of the shirt. Then he dipped the garments into the creek, wrung them out and rolled them in the dust of the path.

Jed shivered in a breechclout while the garments dried over a smoky fire in the yard. Boone took a little bear grease from a gourd in the lean-to and smeared it artfully on the buckskin sleeves and fringes.

As a final touch he advised Jed to shoot a squirrel and they "blooded" the new clothing for luck, smearing the front of the thighs and a blotch or two on the shirt.

"Now here could be a problem," the old man mused. "We wouldn't want the bloodin' with squirrel to make ye good on nothin' *but* squirrel. But we cover yer tracks, here."

He sliced a strip of flesh from the carcass of the buck, hanging in the shade on the north side of the cabin. With the raw meat he reannointed the buckskins with the venison.

"There, ye're blooded fer both big and small game. You shot both, no? Now nobody'll take you for a tenderfoot."

Jed had to agree. He not only looked but *smelled* like a frontiersman.

"Now, as to Injuns," Boone continued, "ye'll see Missouris right away, and Kaw, or Kansa. Their big town's yonder. Well, we talked of that, didn't we? Both of them are pretty friendly, and your sign talk is comin' along. I reckon you'll see Osage, and farther west, Pawnee. The Osages are prob'ly *okeh,* but Pawnees a little doubtful, so be careful.

"Farther west and south, Comanche. Don't know much about them. They move around, live in them skin tents. But by that time, you'll have met some folks, Injun an' white, that kin tell you how the wind's blowin'. . . ."

It was a few days later that Jed Sterling moved on westward. His appearance was changed considerably now. He wore well-conditioned buckskins and moccasins, and carried an extra pair of the latter in his pack. His hat was of fur. He had considered a boughten hat like Boone's, but there was no place to buy one, even if he'd had the money.

"Ye could consider a horse, later," Boone had advised. "But for now, ye won't be travelin' much longer. A horse would jest be a nuisance in winter camp. See how it goes for a season. Drat, I'd admire to go with ye!"

The two shook hands warmly.

"I . . . I can't thank you . . ." Jed mumbled.

"Ferget it, son. But don't be a stranger, now, hear? You know where I'm at. Stop by!"

He watched the lanky figure until it was out of sight around a turn in the road. The long road west . . .

Jed met other people on the road, but fewer than there had been farther east. Boone had warned him to be wary of association with strangers.

"They's all kinds of people out here now, good an' bad. Mostly, folks tend to help one another when they can, but they's always scoundrels, ready to take advantage of honest folks. An Injun, now, might feed ya or try to kill ya, but he'll be honest about it, generally. It's the whites to be wary of. They smell money out here, furs, gold. . . . Makes 'em crazy, seems like. . . ."

From time to time Jed recalled those words as he sized up the travelers he encountered. Ill-kempt, shifty-eyed individuals, poorly equipped; a few who appeared to be farmers. Boone had advised him to "look quiet but confident. Ye learn more from listenin' than from talkin'."

It was not long before he realized that his appearance was commanding a certain amount of respect. A tall man in stained buckskins had to be considered skilled in survival. One pair of ruffians whom he met approached with a swagger and haughty airs. They appeared to have little to swagger about. Worn clothing, bad teeth, several days' growth of beard on each. One carried a heavy belt knife, the other an old shotgun. Neither had a pack, which said that they must live, or at least camp, nearby. Then why were they appearing to travel? They looked him over, and immediately the manners of the two changed. From the domineering approach they backed off to a position of almost fawning respect, which seemed equally inappropriate. They talked of the weather and the game and the trail. Then they parted again, the strangers following the trail the way Jed had come.

A time or two he felt that he was being followed, but saw nothing. Still, he was uneasy as he camped that night. He took great pains to lay out his camp and his fire in plain view. His best guess was that they wanted his gun. He was obviously not carrying money, and was heading *out* to trap furs. His pack held only a small supply of dried meat and a little sugar, tea, and tobacco. Well, possibly there were those who would kill for those few supplies.

Actually, he realized that he probably had been lucky as he traveled up until now. Surely there were those who preyed on travelers back East, too. But law was stronger east of the Mississippi. Here, there was virtually none. If these road agents meant him harm, he was on his own.

He built a good-sized fire, but used only sticks of small diameter, so it would burn down rapidly. He fed it carefully, keeping his circle of light large until it was fully dark. Then, as he let it die, he made a big show of spreading his blankets and lying down, settling in for the night with his rifle beside him. His bed was between the fire and a large squarish boulder some six feet high and the same across. It had tumbled from the hillside long ago to land here near the trail.

As the last flame flickered out and plunged the area into darkness, he slipped out of his blanket and around the rock, and up the back side of the rock, carrying his rifle. There he stretched out prone and waited.

In the trees a whippoorwill called, and a pair of owls carried on a dialogue from points on either side of him. It was more than an hour before anything else occurred. Then it was only a suggestion of movement below, near the trail. The dim form in the starlight materialized into a human figure, stooped over as it moved toward the little camp. Jed was congratulating himself on his cleverness, when he heard a slight noise behind him. Instantly he realized that the best place from which to observe his camp was here, on the flat top of the boulder. The other ruffian was coming up behind him now. *But,* he thought, *he may not know where I am. They think I'm in bed.* At the same time the man's heavy body scent assailed his nostrils.

He gripped his rifle and turned his head carefully to watch the rear. He visualized in his mind the smaller boulder he had used as a stepping stone to climb the rock. The other man would do the same. Maybe he *had,* many times. The shaggy face, poorly visible in the dark night, thrust up over the boulder's edge, exactly where Jed expected. *Now!*

With all his strength, he thrust backward with the butt of the gun, striking into the looming face. There was a crunch of bone and a thud as the limp form struck the ground below. Quickly he looked around. The other man was bending over the blankets, but now straightened.

"George?" he said in a stage whisper. "That you? You get him?"

Jed, almost amused by the stupidity of the man, grunted and mumbled an unintelligible answer.

"Well, come on down!" the other exclaimed.

Jed slipped backward and slid down from his rock, stepping over the still form on the ground and around to the other side. The man was bent over, pawing through his pack when Jed hit him. Not with the rifle. He'd hated to use the rifle butt before. It would be easy to damage the slender stock. But he quietly stepped forward with a stick of firewood and a full-arm swing. The man started to turn and the chunk caught him just below the right knee. Jed felt the bone crack. The man fell, almost into the dying coals of the fire.

Jed tossed some dry grass and small twigs, saved for the purpose, into the coals, igniting a cheery blaze. Soon the clearing was light again. A few more larger sticks . . . he dragged the groaning form away from the fire, took the knife from the ruffian's belt, and went back around the rock for the other.

This man was much heavier, but Jed managed to drag him around into the light of the fire. He was semiconscious, floundering around, and pawing at his smashed nose and broken teeth. Jed almost felt sorry for him, but not quite. These two would have shown him no mercy. They'd have likely killed him just for his rifle. He checked it and found the stock intact. Good. But now . . . *the shotgun. The big man had carried it.* He glanced at the two and then stepped back around the rock. Yes, there where it had been dropped. A lucky break. He'd have to be more careful.

He discharged the shotgun into the air, swung it by the barrel and smashed it across the rock. Then he tossed the pieces into the fire. The lock mechanisms would be useless with the temper of the springs destroyed.

There seemed no point in remaining here. He would sleep little tonight anyway, with excitement still coursing through his veins. He might as well travel. He began to repack his pack and roll his blankets.

"You cain't leave us here alone like this," whined the man with the broken leg. "It ain't human!"

"You don't deserve any better," Jed snorted. "Either of you would have cut my throat for what I was carrying. You'll recover, more's the pity."

He started down the trail, his temper still fuming. He was a little surprised at how hard he had become. And how quickly.

5

The town of the Kansa, or Kaw, Indians was exactly as Boone had said, near the fork of the river. The stream that bore their name entered the somewhat larger Missouri River near the town. It was plain that any traveler following the river system, whether by water or by land, would pass this way. It was a veritable crossroads, a gateway to the West.

He spent a day or two there, practicing his hand signs and observing the customs. In a way, he was disappointed. Many of the Kansas spoke a fair amount of broken English, and some spoke French. Somehow that seemed incongruous to him, for a primitive tribe on the frontier to use a tongue that he had studied at the university. Yet he understood. The French had been in this area for over a century. People who spoke English were the newcomers.

There were several white men in the town, some camped in makeshift shelters around the edges. Some were living in the partially buried and earth-bermed houses of the Kansa, apparently with Indian wives. He visited briefly with some of them, but his presence actually drew little attention. Everyone here, both red and white, seemed quite uninterested. Jed Sterling was merely another trapper heading upriver, and there were many of those. And Boone had been right. Most of them were heading up the Missouri.

He talked at some length with an older man whose Kaw wife and children stared at him in shy but friendly silence. To this man he mentioned that his intent was to follow the Kansas River. The man drew a puff or two on his pipe and seemed more interested.

"Why?" he grunted finally.

"Seemed like a good idea. Maybe too many going up the Missouri."

The man nodded.

"Yer right. Them as has been there come back with great tales, but ain't nothin' wrong with trappin' the upper Kansas."

"Have you been there?"

"Shore. Both rivers."

"Which is best?"

"Don't matter none. You trappin' alone?"

"Yes. For now, anyway."

"Thet's mebbe the best. Unless you git hurt or somethin'. I like to died when I broke this laig, here. Thet's why I don't trap no more. My gimpy laig. I hunt a little near home here. I got a fine wife an' two kids I kin be proud of. What more kin a man want?"

Jed could see that here was a man who was content. His wife *was* quite attractive, and the children bright and alert.

"Do ye know anybody on the river?" the man asked.

"No. I'm new in the area."

"Mm . . . let's see . . . ye know hand sign, an' that's good. I was thinkin' about who ye might run acrost. Several livin' with the tribes, like me. Some of the come-latelies call us squaw men. Oh, yes! Black Fox. He lives with the Comanches, mebbe three weeks west of here. Comanche wife."

"Why 'Black Fox'?"

"Thet's his name! Oh, I see. Most of us have a name they give us. Mine translates somethin' like 'Crippled Bear,' on account of the laig. Now, Fox, you'll like him. He talks educated, like you. Seems like I heard he was first called 'Black White Man'."

"The 'Black' part?" asked Jed, still puzzled.

"Oh, *thet*. On account of his color, I s'pose. Not really black, get right down to it. More brown, like."

"But I don't . . ."

Realization came to him in a rush, just as the other man spoke again.

"He's a nigger. The hand sign is 'black white man.' "

"An escaped slave?" Jed asked.

"I don't think so. No, seems I heared he's got his papers an' all. Yep, I think Franklin told me that, years back."

"Lib Franklin?"

"Shore. You know him?"

"No. A friend told me to look for him." Jed did not mention that the "friend" was Daniel Boone. He didn't want to appear to be name-dropping.

"Well, he told you right, Andrews and Franklin. Fur buyin', traders. Franklin's this end of it. I reckon Andrews runs the business end in St. Louis."

"You know where this Franklin is?"

"Well, he was livin' on the upper Arkansas. Built 'em a little tradin' post there. He's got a Comanche wife. Good-lookin' woman. You look him up ef you get that far west."

"How far west?"

"I dunno. Mebbe a month. The country gets drier out west a ways, an' the upper Kansas smaller. When it peters out, you head straight south a couple days an' hit the Arkansas. It's the bigger river at that point."

Once again, Jed was impressed that in this country distances were expressed not in distance but in *time*. The time required to travel from one point to another. He had heard one man speak of looking at something "a day yonder," which he took to mean a day's travel. He had also noted that one of the Indians referred to a long distance as "many sleeps" away.

As yet, he did not quite understand this concept, or *why*. Maybe later it would become clearer to him.

Another thought . . . "You mentioned the Pawnees. I've heard tell that they're sometimes unfriendly?" Jed inquired.

The old trapper sucked his pipe for a moment, seemingly lost in thought. Finally he spoke.

"Reckon everybody gets unfriendly sometimes. Pawnees are sort of different, I reckon. You have to understand their ways, which are some different from their neighbors."

"Different? How so?"

"Lessee . . . well, they plant crops, but they have a big summer hunt, too. Buffalo. But their lodges are different. . . . *big!* Hold maybe fifty people."

"*Fifty?*"

"Shore. Mebbe more. Whole family, aunts and uncles, brothers and sisters and their families; one big room, dug into the ground, and mounded over. Well, you'll see. . . . Now, another thing. Most of these tribes, growers and hunters both, figger the sun is about the most important thing there is. Likely they're right, of course. Makes the corn grow, an' beans and pumpkins and all. For the hunters, it makes the grass grow, and that brings back the buffalo. So, generally the religion of most any Injuns is sort of tied in with the sun."

"But what—"

The old man held up a hand in restraint.

"Wait! I'm tryin' to tell you. The Pawnees you asked about . . . for them, it ain't so much the sun, but Morning Star that's their god."

"What does that have to do with anything?"

"Quite a bit, sometimes. Mainly, they're *different,* and I reckon folks is suspicious of anybody that's different. 'Course, some things *everybody* does the same, like doorways facin' east."

Jed was puzzled. "Why is *that*?"

"Oh . . . well, you ask 'em, it's a religious thing, mostly. Greet the sun for a new day, welcome him like a guest, all that. Start the morning with a prayer to Sun, thanks for his warm light. Or *hers* . . . some of the tribes figger the sun is a *she,* you know."

"No, I didn't know that. But about the door facing east. You started—"

"Oh, that . . . yes, there's another reason. So the fire will draw better."

Jed thought for a moment that the old trapper was teasing him. Then, from the twinkle in the eye, he saw that he was being teased, but that the *reason* must be real. But what possible connection could there be? Just a trifle irritated at the teasing, he waited. When the trapper was ready, Jed supposed he would be initiated into the joke.

"The *wind!*" the old man finally stated with the air of a conspirator.

Jed still did not understand. What was the joke? Or was there one? Maybe this old man was a little bit crazy.

"*Wind?*"

"Shore! The wind is a lot more important here than wherever you come from. I'd reckon you're used to more trees, no?"

"Well, yes."

"Uh-*huh*! But out here, and more so farther west, there's not much timber. Nothin' to stop the wind, except right along the streams. *Now* it gets real important to have the door of yer tent or lodge downwind. Quarterin' downwind is even better."

"I don't see your point," protested Jed.

"Well, the wind's generally from the south, here. That's what it *means*—Kansa, 'South Wind People.' When it ain't from the south, like if there's a storm brewin', she comes in from the west or northwest. Sometimes even due north. Hardly ever from the east. So, if doors an' smoke holes an' such are all on the east, downwind or quarterin' down, the smoke draws better, and it don't rain in much."

Jed was not completely convinced but it did make sense. At least, it seemed to.

"You'll see it, easy, when you're in a skin teepee in a storm." The old man chuckled. "Folks shore swing them smoke flaps aroun'."

And how, Jed wondered, *does one survive a winter in a skin tent?*

The wind already carried a chill, and made him realize that he had considerable planning to do, and some travel.

He knew he was nearing the Pawnee village by the haze of smoke hanging low in the crisp autumn air. The setting was not quite what he had imagined. This town, by contrast to several Kaw villages he had passed along the river, was on a hilltop, well above the stream.

At first, in fact, he had mistaken the rounded tops of the earth lodges for grassy hummocks. Then he realized that the haze of smoke was actually rising from *inside* the hummocks, through holes in the roofs. He paused to study this phenomenon, and to get a general impression of this setting, completely new to him.

He had been told by the Kansas to whom he had talked on the previous evening approximately where he would find the Pawnees. And again, he had received the same impression: *Pawnees are very different.* Maybe one of the vague differences that seemed so important to everyone was this, their location on an exposed, rolling hilltop. *Why?* he wondered. They were growers, and growers usually traded freely with the hunter tribes, he had been told. Corn, beans, and pumpkins for dried meat and hides. It was good to be on good trading terms with everyone. In addition, ripening crops in the fields are very vulnerable to raids or to destruction by an enemy. Hence, it is better to have no enemies, and growers are peaceful people.

Yet the Pawnees, he had repeatedly been told, are more warlike and aggressive. Their big summer buffalo hunt, after the second hoeing of the corn, had been mentioned by several. They possessed some of the domineering qualities of the nomadic buffalo hunters. Now he realized that this might explain the location. A more warlike people might well have more enemies, and be more subject to attack. And certainly this cluster of buried lodges on an open hilltop was quite defensible. Any approaching enemy must climb a steep slope from the river, or approach across open prairie. A sentry or two to give the warning could easily make sure that the village was well defended. The only problem would be water, and that could be carried from below.

Just as Jed had been thinking of sentries, a well-armed warrior now rose before him. He was startled. He could have sworn that only a moment ago he had looked at that very clump of dry grass, and there was nothing there. The landscape was deceptive, though. He had passed through several areas where the seed heads of autumn grasses were taller than his head. It was from behind one of these clumps that the warrior stepped.

Startled though he was, Jed managed to raise his right hand in the sign of peaceful greeting. Hand open, showing no weapon: *I come in peace.*

The Pawnee studied him for the space of a few heartbeats, while Jed did the same. Even though he had been told of the unique Pawnee hair style, he was not quite prepared. The entire head was shaved or plucked except for a patch of hair three or four inches in diameter on top. This long lock was twisted and tied, greased with tallow and red paint and drawn up into a horn-shaped appendage. *Like a unicorn,* Jed thought. *Of course* . . . their hand sign was "Horn People."

6

"How are you called?" signed the glowering Pawnee. "What are you doing here?"

Jed had decided, at the suggestion of Daniel Boone, that he should have a name that could be hand signed. "Jedediah Sterling" would mean nothing orally to any natives he might encounter. Likewise, there were no appropriate hand signs to approximate the phonetic syllables.

"Let's see," Boone had said, "somethin' that describes ye without puttin' ye down any. What hev ye done thet merits tellin'?"

Jed had been at a loss, and besides he felt that the frontiersman was teasing him, so he said nothing.

"I know!" Boone said suddenly. "Ye *walked* here. How about somethin' like 'Boy-who-walks-clean-acrost-the-country'?"

As it turned out, Boone had been only partly teasing. They talked about it, and finally came to an acceptable version that said much the same thing. He had used it several times, and now it came into good use again, as he answered the Pawnee who had challenged him.

"I am called Long Walker," he signed.

"What do you want here?"

"Nothing. I am only passing through. I come in peace," he signed again.

The Pawnee was not quick to accept. "Where are you going?"

"Up the river. Trap some beaver, maybe. Hunt."

"You have friends there?"

"Not yet. Tomorrow, maybe."

For some reason, this seemed to amuse the Pawnee. He smiled, or at least softened the hard lines of his grimace.

"Maybe . . . you bring gifts of friendship?"

Jed looked behind him as if he were surprised.

"Aiee!" he muttered aloud. Then he continued in signs. "I have lost my mules. Their packs were filled with fine gifts for my Pawnee brothers. Now I have only a little tobacco. But this I will share."

He pointed to his pack. There was a long pause while expressions of doubt flickered across the face of the other.

This was exactly the situation about which Boone had taught him.

"They'll expect gifts," he had warned, "and you'll have none. You'll have to carry a few trinkets an' such. Tobacco, mebbe. Ye make clear thet you'll share what ye have, but without losin' yer dignity. The other feller will try to face ye down. It's a game, like tradin'. Another thing, folks don't generally know an Injun loves a joke. Ef you can find somethin' to make him laugh . . ."

All of this now ran through Jed's mind as the Pawnee studied the situation. He was actually in a pretty dangerous position. There was nothing to prevent the warrior from killing him. It might be from disappointment that he carried nothing of value. Except for the rifle, of course. Or even on a whim, the other might challenge, just to prove his manhood. Jed braced himself for any surprise attack, still trying to appear calm and casual.

The game continued to play out. It must be apparent to the Pawnee that here was a man who had almost nothing, but was bold enough to challenge the wilderness and to accept the risks involved. Foolish, maybe, but brave.

Then the Pawnee threw back his head and laughed, and the tension broke. It was a relaxed, friendly laugh, and a quite welcome one to Jed's ears.

"How is it," the warrior signed, "that you carry such great gifts?"

"Because of my great wealth," Jed signed seriously.

The Pawnee chuckled. "My heart is heavy that you lost them. Shall we go and look for your mules?"

Jed brushed that suggestion aside. "No, there are plenty more where those came from."

This appeared to be going well. Now if he could just avoid a misunderstanding.

"Wait!" signed the other. "You *did* speak of tobacco. Let us smoke. Come."

He led the way toward the cluster of mounded dwellings. Jed could see the dark doorways facing them as they approached.

"Sit," the man offered, pointing to the sloping earth roof of one of the lodges. He called something to a group of children who had gathered to stare, and a boy scampered on an errand of some sort.

Both men now took out their pipes and pouches. Jed also drew out a twist of tobacco and cut it in half, handing one part to the Pawnee while he replaced the other in his pack. It would later be mixed with other plants for smoking. Now Jed handed his pouch to the other man, who nodded and handed Jed his own. Both pipes were filled and the pouches returned.

"How are *you* called?" Jed signed.

"I am Red Horse," the other answered.

The boy returned with a burning stick, and both men lighted their pipes, each using the other's tobacco.

"It is good," Jed signed. "Cedar?" He did this by indicating a nearby tree.

"A little. Some other things."

At this point the sign talk lost some of its effectiveness. It is difficult to have a universal sign for each of the hundreds of plants, birds, and insect species. It had been easy to identify the aromatic cedar that Jed had tasted in the smoke, and to point to one that grew nearby. But there were subtle tastes like grape, corn silk, and sumac, even catnip, often blended with tobacco. There might be signs for these, but Jed did not know. That line of conversation was at an end.

"It is good," he signed again.

"Yours, also," answered Red Horse.

They talked of the weather and the game, and children and a few curious adults watched. The sun moved toward the western horizon, bringing a bit of autumn chill to the air.

"You will stay with us tonight?" asked Red Horse.

"I am honored. But I would pay my respects to your chief."

"No matter. I am the one. You did not know?"

"No, I am a stranger here."

The gathered children found this quite amusing, laughing and chattering away among themselves.

Now Red Horse rose. "Come, let us go in. It grows cold."

Jed, who still struggled with the idea of a lodge that could hold fifty people, was unprepared for the size of the room they entered. It must be at least twenty paces across. The rafters rested at the center on a pedestal of four poles set in a square. A fire pit in the middle of this square with the corresponding square smoke hole above furnished light, heat, and cooking facilities for inclement weather. Jed supposed that as with other tribes he had encountered, most of the cooking was done outside on small fires when weather permitted.

Around the periphery of the room could be seen the living space of individual couples and their families. There seemed to be little opportunity for privacy, and he wondered at that. Darkness as the fire died, of course, but . . . would this closeness not inhibit romance?

A dog got up from near the fire to sniff the newcomer. "The dogs stay inside?" Jed asked.

"Sometimes," answered Red Horse with a shrug. "In really bad weather I bring my best buffalo horse in, too."

Jed wondered whether the warrior was joking, but he seemed quite serious.

A woman approached as the two men sat down on robes near the wall.

"My woman," explained Red Horse.

Jed nodded a greeting and the couple engaged in a short conversation in their own tongue.

"She will bring food," Red Horse signed to his guest.

Now Jed noticed an attractive young woman who appeared to be staring at him. It was a bold, somewhat flirtatious stare, a studied evaluation.

"Raven likes you," signed Red Horse.

Jed was embarrassed. He had heard of the forwardness of Pawnee women.

"She has no man?" he signed.

"It does not matter. It is her choice," his host answered.

Among any other people he knew, it *would* matter, a great deal.

He felt insecure, a little panicky. The young woman smiled and ran the tip of her tongue across her lips. She *was* beautiful.

He was rescued by the arrival of the food, and they ate. Three of the children who had gathered outside previously appeared to belong to Red Horse and his wife. They joined the family circle with their mother, and the meal proceeded.

Jed could not avoid an occasional glance toward Raven. Each time he found her looking back. He tried to think, to remember what he had heard about Pawnee customs. Beyond, of course, the ribald stories of the aggressive attitude of their women in matters of romance. It seemed that any behavior initiated by the woman was acceptable. He had heard these tales, but was still unprepared. His strict Episcopal upbringing was surging back into his consciousness.

In conflict with these feelings was the urgent call of his young manhood. He was relatively inexperienced, but the urge was certainly making itself felt. Jed could not take his eyes from the beautiful face and figure, the sensuous smile across the room. He realized that her flirtation was calculated and deliberate. There would come a time very soon when he must make a decision. . . .

The fire had died now to a few glowing coals in the fire pit. A single shaft of silver moonlight slanted through the smoke hole to give vague shape to the room. Soft snores came from robe-muffled forms around the walls. Jed lay awake, straining his eyes into the darkness. He had spread his blankets in the indicated spot, and was unsure now. What was expected of him? No one had given him the slightest hint of expected or even acceptable behavior. What was he supposed to do now?

An amusing thought struck him. Maybe he was expected to sleep. Everyone else was certainly doing so. Had he completely misunderstood the behavior of the beautiful young woman?

In spite of himself, Jed began to feel drowsy. It had been a long and exciting day. He had reached a dreamy point somewhere between sleep and waking when he was roused by a movement near him.

A figure crouched over him, and instinctively he reached for a weapon to defend himself. But a gentle hand touched his. As he focused his consciousness he could discern a female form. A very well-molded and graceful female form. Her long hair hung down toward his face. She tossed it back and bent to kiss his lips, and it was good.

Gently, she lifted the edge of the blanket and slipped in beside him. There was a moment of panic as he recalled his reason for leaving home. This scenario was much like the advances of his predatory young stepmother. That thought was driven from his mind by the realization that this situation was completely different. The unscrupulous Phoebe had been violating every precept of her own culture. Here, by contrast, although using the same technique, was a woman acting completely within the ethical boundaries of her own people. Very strict boundaries, he was to learn later.

He had no power to resist, and in the final analysis, no reason to resist, he thought. Oddly, a line of scripture flitted through his mind, a bit of advice from St. Paul in one of his letters to somebody. "When in Rome, do as the Romans."

That seemed to resolve a lot of torment in his mind. He was able to relax, to accept the warm embrace of the beautiful Raven as she enfolded him in her arms and kissed him again. He returned her advances, now with enthusiasm.

7

He traveled on west the next day. The morning's chill reminded him again that winter was coming, and that he really had no plans. Maybe this was far enough west. There was plenty of beaver sign, sharp stumps where the animals had felled willow and cottonwood to store for winter food and to build their lodges and dams.

But something drove him on. He began to understand the feel of the land, even the strange way of expressing distance in the time it would take to get there. On a sunny morning he could easily select the general area where he would spend the coming night, because he could *see* it ahead, a day's travel upstream.

Sometimes he was fooled. A hill or ridge, purple in the distance, might seem only a day away. Yet, even after a good day's travel, twenty miles or more, there would be his landmark, seemingly as distant as ever. At times he even considered the disturbing idea that he was walking in one place and the distant landscape was moving. Of one thing he was certain. The next time he traveled this trail, he would have a horse. Not having seen the wide skies and far horizons of the grassland, there had been no way to understand its distances or its subtle beauty.

At night he lay in his blankets, the velvet dome of starry sky arched over him, marveling at the vastness of creation. Night sounds were music to his ears. On moonlit nights he had difficulty sleeping. There was a feel of magic, as if at any moment some marvelous event might occur that would reveal all the secrets of the universe.

Sometimes he thought of the raven-haired Pawnee girl, Raven. . . . was that how she got her name? He imagined her warm body next to him. Would she share his wonder at the beauty of the moonlit night?

Then he would shake his head in despair at his own childish simplicity. He would probably never even see her again. Even if he did, their worlds were different. They could not even communicate. Except . . . they *had* communicated for a little while, very deeply and closely. *Ridiculous,* he told himself. *That was only animal pleasure.* Any man would have done as well for her, and in her culture, she would have her choice of men. Probably even now . . . he did not like that thought. And she *had* chosen him. Forcibly, he drove her from his mind.

There was a period of a few days when the weather provided a virtual heaven on earth. Warm, still days were followed by cool nights. He had heard this time of autumn called "Second Summer." It did not happen every year, but when it did, the result was a marvelous experience. Leaves turning color, geese high overhead, excitement in the air mixed with a lazy comfort that said the world was good.

Yet in all his experience, there had never been a Second Summer like this one. The sky wider and bluer, the days warmer and the nights more comfortably crisp for sleeping. The colors of the sumac and other shrubs and trees whose names he did not know colored the slopes along the streams. Their reds and orange and pink were a contrast to the golden yellow of the cottonwoods. The prairie grasses themselves were changing color, too. More muted colors, but interesting in their mix of soft gold to dark burgundy. To each grass species its own color, he noticed. The tallest, which Boone had called "turkeyfoot" because of the shape of its seed head, had changed now from blue-green to a reddish color as it cured.

There was less of the tall grass now, however. He was traveling into the shortgrass plains. Here, he encountered buffalo. He had seen the creatures before, but only in small bands of a hundred or fewer. It was with some degree of surprise, then, that he topped a low rise to see the country ahead black with the massive bodies. His first reaction was shock that he had not realized that the great herds were there. After all, he could *see* three days' travel ahead. But the land was somewhat different here. It was flatter, with fewer of the rolling hills that he had encountered earlier. And with no high ground from which to view the terrain, there was a certain sameness in distance.

Now he realized that possibly he *had* seen the dark blanket of slowly moving buffalo, but from a day's travel away. Distance destroys color, and faraway objects take on a sameness. He may even have realized that the distant prairie appeared darker, but did not attribute the shifting shadow to the multitude of grazing bison. And he had seen areas that took on different colors at a distance. A range of low hills to the south of his line of travel, which presented a smoky appearance. A grove of giant cottonwoods a day's travel away had looked for all the world like a puff of gray smoke until he drew closer.

There was no doubt about the sight that now lay before him. Millions of buffalo, the herd stretching to the south as far as the eye could see, clear to the horizon. The great herd was thinner to the north and nearer to him. He could make out individual animals, all grazing their way slowly to the south. Around the edges of the herd circled the gray wolves, stalking, searching for a sick or injured straggler or a calf separated from its mother. He saw individual animals of lighter and darker shades, some a yellowish dun, some almost black, with an occasional bluish or mouse gray specimen. Most, however, were a fairly uniform dark brown.

He saw another moving form and studied it for a long time. Finally he sat down and propped his elbows on his knees, to cup his hands into two tunnels through which to look, a trick Boone had described, to shut out light except that on the object to be observed. Jed had not tried it before, but was pleased at its effect. It was almost like looking through the tube of a spyglass, but without the magnification.

He could see clearly now, this creature that followed the herd. It was a light-colored bear, followed by two cubs. It took a moment to realize that he was watching his first grizzly. He had heard such tales of the great bear's ferocity that a shiver of fear ran through him. Night would be coming, and he would need a fire. He would make camp early. He could not safely walk through even the fringe of the herd anyway.

Jed turned toward the stream to locate a spot to camp, only to find it muddy and foul smelling. That problem had not occurred to him but yes, a million buffalo had trampled and fouled it upstream only a short while before.

This presented a serious problem. He thought of trying to strain the water through his blanket, but it did not seem practical. It also might be possible to fill his wooden canteen and allow the contents to settle overnight. He was not certain that would work, and if it did, the sludge and debris would then be accumulated in the bottom of the container. In his pack was a tin cup, which he had bought in St. Louis. It had been on a whim, and he really regarded it as a luxury rather than a necessity. But now would be a time to test its usefulness. He dipped a cupful of the cleanest water he could find and set it aside while he made camp.

One of the most important steps was to build a fire. He had seen the predators circling the herds, and had no desire to become a meal for a grizzly that had been unable to make its kill. Besides, there could be danger from the herd itself if some chance shift in direction brought the buffalo this way. A fire would be his best defense against any of these problems. All animals except man shun the fire.

He managed to find a quantity of dead wood and some buffalo chips that were dry enough to use as fuel. He smiled as he thought of all the buffalo-chip fuel that would be available here a month from now. He struck the spark from his steel and nurtured it, blowing gently until his tinder began to glow, then continuing until it burst into flame. Carefully, he fed twigs. The warmth was good. It might be a chilly night.

He checked the tin cup, and found the contents still murky and foul smelling. A touch of alarm crept into his mind. What if he was unable to clear this water enough to drink? If he were dying of thirst he would drink it anyway, he supposed. Would that kill him? He did not know.

Panic gripped him. Now that he had come to realize his predicament, thirst descended on him with a vengeance. His lips felt dry and sticky, his throat so parched that he could hardly swallow. There was no question of sleep. He lay awake, listening to the murmur of the distant herd, the occasional bleat of a calf separated from its mother, the cry of a distant coyote. Once, the deep-throated howl of a gray wolf, follower of the herds.

He tried to think of everything he had ever heard about thirst, and how to deal with it. He remembered that sucking on a smooth round stone was said to moisten the lining of the mouth. With a little searching, he found such a pebble along the stream, and tested the theory. The result was disappointing. Saliva did increase for a little while, but soon became sticky. Maybe he was worrying too much.

He tried to avoid such thoughts, but it was no use. How long could a man survive without water? It seemed to him that three days had been mentioned somewhere, sometime. . . . He was already well into the first day. He could not remember exactly when he had emptied his wooden water bottle. He had thought of refilling it at the time, but he had been some distance from the stream, trying to take a shortcut.

Could he start downstream now and reach clear water? He doubted it. He had no idea how far downstream the pollution had carried by this time. No, he should stay here or go on *upstream* to where the river might be fresher. Yet again, he had no idea how wide was the swath that the buffalo had cut through the river. He had seen before dark that the herd reached southward clear to the horizon, two or three days' travel. Might it not also be that *wide?*

He remembered a tale of a lost frontiersman drinking the blood of a deer that he was able to kill. Or was it his own horse? Yes, maybe. The subject of that story had cut the animal's throat to survive on the moisture in its blood. He had no horse, but there were a million buffalo out there. In the morning he would shoot one and drink its blood.

Now that he had a plan, of sorts, he felt better. Not *much* better, but some. He built up his fire and rolled in his blanket. He had dried meat in his pack, but ate none. He knew that it would create more thirst. He was glad now that he had not tried to filter the scummy water of the stream through his blanket. Then his blanket, too, would have been wet and scummy.

He finally drowsed and slept fitfully, rising occasionally to feed the fire. It was on one of those occasions that he happened to think of his incongruous situation and chuckled aloud. Only a few months ago he had been safe and warm in his rented room at Princeton. That had been before . . . ah, how many things! He thought back. Would he have done anything differently, had he known?

But one does *not* know, Jed realized. He cannot know. He might have left home anyway. He would have been forced to do something.

As he drifted back to sleep he wondered about his father and what seemed to be a disastrous remarriage. He felt a sorrow for his young sister, Sarah.

8

Jed woke with the sun in his face, the first bright rays peeping across a distant rise to the east. He jumped up, startled and a little stiff. His fire was dead. No, a few warm coals, he discovered. He fed it back to life as he studied the distant prairie in the growing light.

There were only a few scattered animals nearby now. The bulk of the herd had moved on. This brought about a sense of urgency. He must approach and kill one of the stragglers before they were *all* gone. His dry mouth reminded him of this crisis.

The grizzly he had noticed last evening had made a kill, about a mile to the west. The bear crouched over it, feeding with her two cubs, while a circle of coyotes waited at a respectful distance. A little closer crouched a pair of the larger wolves. But even they were careful to honor the property rights of the great bear.

Jed began to search for a suitable quarry for his own use. He had wondered a little, whether he could bring himself to drink the blood of a fresh kill. Now his dry mouth told him beyond a doubt. The thought of the warm moisture, soothing the parched surfaces, was pleasant to imagine.

The edge of the herd was perhaps a mile or two to the south. He would move in that direction, he decided. Maybe he would have a chance at one of the stragglers before he reached the main herd. He was becoming anxious now. What if this scheme proved unsuccessful? For the first time since he had departed Princeton, he began to have some real doubts. The vastness of the grassland, which had been exciting and stimulating, now seemed overwhelming, a little frightening. The distances were so great. What if, as he approached one of the lone buffalo out there, it simply ran away before he could shoot? How long would he have the strength to pursue time after time as his quarry retreated, just out of range?

He vowed to himself that he would never again be in such a situation without a horse. If he were mounted, he could ride toward a chosen animal, even pursue it if it retreated. In his present predicament, he might never come close enough for a kill. His depression deepened. He found it puzzling that he had received misleading advice from none other than the great frontiersman, Daniel Boone. How had that happened? Boone had clearly considered it a disadvantage to try to sustain a horse during the winter months.

The thought of winter called his attention to yet another problem. With the warm lazy days of Second Summer, it had been easy not to realize that he must plan for the coming season. If, of course, he survived the present crisis. There was a fur of white frost on the prairie grasses, and a crust of ice along the edge of the stream. Plenty of water, but useless water . . . he considered that he might even try again to drink it. He tasted, and spit out the foul stuff in disgust. He would have to be in greater distress before it would be worth the try. Even then, he wondered if he could gag the foul liquid down.

He wasted a little time in experimenting with boiling some of the foul water in his tin cup over the fire. That experiment was a total failure. The simmering fluid smelled bad and tasted even worse.

As he rolled his blankets and tied his pack, a slight hint of motion *downstream* caught his eye. He turned to look, expecting a coyote or some other, smaller creature. But no, three antelope stood at the stream, pawing at the sand and lowering their heads. Can they drink the fouled water? he wondered. In the confusion of wondering about that, he nearly overlooked the obvious. He need not pursue buffalo if he could kill one of these.

Dropping to a crouch, he reached for his rifle, checked the pan, and drew the hammer to full cock. No, maybe . . . the range was questionable. He must move closer. Carefully he held back the hammer, pressed the trigger, and eased back to the safer position at half cock. Then he began to move toward the antelope. He had not gone more than a dozen steps when one of the animals threw up its head with a snort and turned to look at him. Maybe a chance shift of the light breeze had carried a scent of smoke. Or maybe it was a glimpse of his movement. The rump of another antelope that was facing away from him suddenly turned snowy white, as if someone had shaken out a linen cloth. Jed had never heard of this alarm signal by antelope, and was caught completely by surprise.

The morning seemed to take on a dreamlike quality, with the frosty grasses and a thin mist rising from the deeper pools of the stream to disperse into the colder air. In addition, he was looking toward the east, not quite into the rising sun. The relative position of light and shadow, mist and frosted earth created an otherworldly effect, and enhanced his dream. The antelope, now completely alarmed, bounded away. Their white rumps seemed to float through the mist until they became a part of the dream state. Belatedly, Jed cocked the rifle and snapped off a shot that he was sure would be useless.

Nevertheless, he stumbled forward to see. He was right. He had missed completely. He found the tracks of the antelope in the sandy bank, much farther from his camp than he had estimated. How deceiving the distances. Yes, here was where the antelope had been standing before they whirled to run. Moist sand, thrown up by that first leap. The puddle where they had been drinking . . . *Wait* . . . The water in that puddle was *clear*! He cupped a hand and tasted it. Not the best water he had ever drunk, maybe, but today, the finest on earth.

He pawed away the sand, digging a little deeper, enlarging the puddle. While he waited for the water to settle and clear, he went back to his little camp for his tin cup. As he did so, he looked at the sandy shore near his camp. It was much like the spot where the antelope had pawed. Experimentally, he used his cup to scoop out a depression in the damp sand, and watched the water seep into the resulting basin. The antelope had known the survival skills that he had lacked!

Hurriedly he started another of the seep wells, and a third. The resulting water was clean and clear, filtered from below by the sands. His confidence began to rise as he sipped the life-giving fluid from one seep and another. It seemed that he could never get enough. He made the short trip back to the place the antelope had pawed, and drank deeply from its now clear water.

He rose, turned, and with the sun at his back, looked toward his campfire. There, looking casually at his pack and his rifle, sat three horsemen, warriors in buckskin shirts and leggings. His first impulse was to run toward them, but he realized quickly how stupid that would look.

Yet how could he possibly appear any more stupid than he already had? Here he stood, armed only with a tin cup. His rifle, which he had not even reloaded, lay across his pack. The words of Daniel Boone came back to him. *When ye shoot, reload. No matter what, reload first.* He had not even thought about it.

He walked, slowly and deliberately, back toward his camp. It was perhaps the longest two hundred paces he had ever crossed. His heart was racing, his palms sweating. The warriors waited. One had dismounted, and Jed was greatly disturbed to see that he casually picked up the rifle from where it lay. This could be a dangerous encounter, and quite possibly his last. He decided that his best bet was to try to bluff it out.

He raised his hand in the sign of greeting, and casually tossed his cup aside near the pack. He had taken time to evaluate the appearance of the three as he approached. The one on the ground was short and stocky, possibly middle-aged. That was hard to tell, though, among natives. The man's legs were short, his body long.

The other two were younger men. The skin of one was somewhat darker than that of the other, though he had found that not unusual. But there was something about the darker warrior . . . a fullness of the lips, a slight broadening of the nose . . . could it be?

"Black Fox?" he asked in sign, and hurried on before the other could answer. "Welcome to my camp!"

There was a look of total astonishment on the faces of all three. Jed took the opportunity to make another bold move. He stepped over to take his rifle from the hand of the warrior.

"Here," he signed. "I must reload. I had tried for some meat to welcome you, but I missed."

The surprised warrior released the weapon.

"There is water, there." Jed gestured toward the stream bank where his seep wells lay.

"You saw us coming?" It was the darker of the warriors, and he spoke aloud and in English.

"Of course," Jed lied, also in English. "And you *are* Black Fox?"

"That is true. Do I know you?"

"No," answered Jed. "But . . . forgive me. I am called Long Walker. I was told to look for you."

"Why? What do you want?"

The question was direct and to the point. Jed struggled for an answer.

"Well . . . I came west to trap. I was told that you have connections with the fur company, Andrews and Franklin."

There was still considerable doubt in the eyes of the dark man. Jed began to realize that he did present something of a puzzle to an experienced frontiersman. His clothing and equipment were proper, but there was much about survival on the prairie that he did not know. This realization was emphasized by the next words of Black Fox.

"You lost your horse?"

"No, I had no horse. I had been advised against it."

The other spoke to his companions in their own tongue. One was just returning from the seep well, and the three talked excitedly for a moment.

"Who told you such a thing?" the dark man now asked.

"A man in Missouri," said Jedediah. It made no sense, even to him, that he would have been told such a thing by Daniel Boone.

Black Fox now swung down from his horse and stretched his legs. He was chuckling.

"By a man who never traveled the prairie, no?"

"I guess not. He has trapped some."

Jed was having mixed feelings. He felt a loyalty to Boone, but was beginning to realize some facts about the prairie country. The next words from Fox helped to put it into perspective.

"But back in the forest country or on the rivers, right? It's a different story here, Walker."

Of course. Even in the past few seasons, Boone's trapping had been along the Missouri. The great frontiersman had never experienced the far distances and wide skies of this country. Here, it was often more than a day's walk to the nearest landmark.

The newcomers drank and then watered their horses.

"I have some dried meat," Jed signed. "Do you want to eat?"

The others accepted, and they sat or squatted. Jed was pleased with himself for this move, which was based on a conversation with Boone.

"It's hard to kill a man ye've shared a meal with, son. So, if ye're not sure of somebody's intention, offer him food. When ye've et together, ye see one another different."

Such advice proved good in this case. In a few minutes, Black Fox was relaxed, talking freely and openly.

"Yes, I can put you in touch with Lib Franklin. But you don't need that until you begin to collect furs. Now, I see no traps. . . . You'll use snares?"

"Yes. The rifle, too, maybe."

"And you know snares, care of plews?"

"I think so."

"Good. You've been taught some, then. Now the fur's about ready to trap, but time is growing short. You need to know where you'll winter. And oh, yes . . ." He smiled broadly. "I can see why you are called Long Walker. But we really must get you a horse!"

9

J ed stayed for several days with the Comanches, a guest in the lodge
of Black Fox. He found that he was at ease with the man and his
family. It was incongruous that here he sat in a Comanche lodge,
discussing Shakespeare, Shelly, and Keats with a freed slave who
was also a Comanche warrior. But within a short time it seemed quite
logical, merely one of the strange contradictions of this wild and exciting country. It was good to talk again with an educated person of
some refinement.

He hunted with the Comanches, using a horse belonging to his
host.

"Keep him," offered Fox. "You can give him back or buy him
after your season of trapping."

This band had been "following the herd," hunting around its
edge. There was not much need for further winter stores, but when
fresh meat was easily available it was only good sense to use it. There
would be long moons ahead with only dried meat and pemmican.

He discovered that most of the Comanches preferred a bow or a
spear for hunting buffalo. Many of them had guns, but set them aside
for the hunt.

"With your rifle you have only one shot," Black Fox explained. "Some of these hunters can reload on horseback, but I never could. Even so, the bow gives them more shots, and faster. Many times, the hunt is over very quickly, and the number of shots one can make in a few moments is important."

"You use the bow, then?"

Fox laughed. "No, no. I am made to think that one must begin that at about the time he learns to walk. It is the same with horsemanship. These people use a dependable old mare to look after a baby while the mother is busy. Simply tie the child to the horse's back and turn it out to graze."

That, decided Jed, must account for the remarkable feats of horsemanship that he observed. Young men, showing off for the girls or merely for each other, could twist and turn and throw themselves over and around and across virtually every part of a running horse. They rode bareback, mostly, or with a single cord as a surcingle around the withers. One youth, hanging by his heel on the side of his horse, shot an arrow *under* the animal's neck to strike a target that had been placed for the demonstration.

"He says a running buffalo is easier," laughed Fox. "The horse can run *with* the buffalo, and he has more time to shoot."

Jed was familiar with the English longbow, as tall as a man. Young men of his station in life had been taught archery as well as swordmanship and fencing. The short, stout Indian bow seemed strange to him. He had been inclined to scorn its primitive appearance, but now was quite impressed. He remarked on this to Black Fox one evening as they talked.

"Yes," the dark man chuckled, "I had the same feeling." He paused for a little while, and then spoke again, hesitantly. "Walker, you have obviously a gentleman's education. Why, then, are you here?"

Jed smiled a little sadly. "I might ask the same of you, Fox."

"Of course. Forgive me if I was too forward."

"No, it is a logical question. In brief, my mother died and my father, a judge in Baltimore, remarried. I did not get along well with his new wife."

Fox nodded. "It is reasonable. Then you are not running from the law?"

"No, no . . . are *you*?" This idea had not occurred to him.

"No!" Fox became very serious. "I was freed. I have my papers!"

Jed saw that this was a very intense subject for the Negro. He had heard of free Negroes who had been robbed of their papers and carried back into slavery. A man such as Black Fox, whatever his name might have been, would be at great risk back in civilization. He had never thought of this before, but it made good sense to him now. Living as a Comanche, among people to whom the shade of one's skin had little meaning, would be a logical course of action. He felt a great empathy and understanding toward this man, and felt compelled to explain himself a little more.

"My name," he said thoughtfully, "is Jedediah Sterling. The name Long Walker is so that it can be said in hand signs."

Black Fox nodded solemnly. "I have heard of your father, the judge. A just man, it is said." After a moment, he continued. "My name is, or was, Washington. No first or last, just Washington. My father was an Indian. I do not know the tribe. My mother, a slave. A long story . . . but these are my people now. My owner saw to my education and then freed me. Another good man."

They smoked in silence for a little while, and Fox spoke again. "Walker, if you don't mind, who advised you not to have a horse? All of your other advice seems to have been good."

Jed chuckled. "You may not believe this, Fox. It was Daniel Boone."

"*Boone?* You know him?"

"I met him, in Missouri. He helped outfit me."

The Negro threw back his head and roared with laughter. "Boone! I *heard* he was in Missouri. But why? About the horse, I mean."

Jed became a little defensive now, feeling that he had somehow been untrue to his teacher.

"He helped me immensely, Fox. I spent a few days there, and most of what frontier knowledge that I have, I got from him."

"I see. He taught you about the 'Indian wells' you were digging when we found you?"

"No . . . I . . . well, an antelope taught me that."

"Yes . . . it is good, Walker. You see things. But about Boone . . ."

"Yes, I have given that much thought, Fox. I think it is this way. He came to Missouri from Kentucky a few years ago. Walked all the way. And he trapped beaver, up until the last year or two, he says."

"Remarkable! He must be past seventy, Walker."

"Yes, nearer eighty, probably. But think about it. Most of his experience is in the woodlands, where a horse is impractical, because of trees and brush. Even his recent trapping has been along the lower Missouri, in the forested area. As far as I know, he has never seen this prairie country and its distances."

Black Fox nodded thoughtfully. "I am made to think you are right, Walker. And I sense that you feel a need to defend him. That is good. Loyalty."

Jed was embarrassed. "He was my mentor, Fox!"

"Good. So be it . . . a great man by any standards. Now, you have not spoken of your plans for the winter. Where will you winter and trap?"

"I do not know. I am guilty of poor planning, maybe."

"Maybe, some. But even Boone did not know, Walker. It is new country, with new problems. We learn as we go."

"Where will *you* winter?" Jed asked.

"That is why I brought it up," said the Negro. "Soon, the People will move south for the winter. South of the Arkansas River somewhere. You could winter here, or along the Arkansas. Lib Franklin is living down there. He'll be buying furs, come spring. Or come with us. Our lodge is warm."

Jed was touched by this demonstration of friendship.

"I know. I must decide, Fox. I appreciate your hospitality and your friendship more than you know, but . . . when will the People move south?"

Fox shrugged. "When it is time. A few days, maybe."

Jed nodded. "When the time comes, then, I will be ready. Ready to decide, that is."

Black Fox nodded, knocked the dottle from his pipe into his palm, and tossed it into the fire.

"It is good. So be it!"

Jed lay awake that night in the darkness of the big lodge, undecided. It was pleasant here, the warm glow of the dying coals the only light. The smoky odor of the fire mingled with the similar scent of buckskin garments and that of the lodge cover itself. It was blackened toward the top, from the smoke of many camps. A narrow strip of sky, criss-crossed by the pattern of the lodgepoles and studded with a few stars, marked the smoke hole.

He could hear the quiet breathing of the children, the gentle snores of Black Fox and his wife, Kitten. That was not exactly the translation of her name, Jed understood, but often names do not translate well. Kitten was a sort of pet name used by her husband.

She had returned from her few days' stay in the moon lodge only since Jed's arrival. The devotion of the couple was apparent, and they made no secret of their resumption of romance after their time of separation. The soft noises of rhythmic joy struck a responsive chord in the young man's being. Inescapably, he recalled his last night among the Pawnees, when the beautiful Raven had come to his bed.

Once more he was tortured by the question that burned at him. At the time it had not mattered, in the ecstasy of the moment. It had been only later, as he thought of that night and of its significance to him: had he been only another man to her? Or had she, too, felt not only animal pleasure but some sort of spiritual oneness, as he had? Or thought he had, anyway.

He remembered her shy smile as he left the village. Red Horse was telling him of the trail ahead, bidding him good travel, and wishing him well. Jed had happened to glance beyond his host, to see the girl watching them from a few steps away. He smiled at her, unsure of protocol, and turned his attention back to Red Horse and the information about the trail ahead. *I should have gone to her then,* he had told himself many times. And always the thought came back at him that it might not have been proper. Maybe, even, a breach of etiquette. It was the woman's place to make the first move, and Raven had done so, in a very memorable way. He had no idea what was supposed to come next. He had assumed at the time that this had been simply a night's pleasure. He had treated it so. Now, in his memory, it had become ever so much more important. He was still unsure as to what it had meant to the girl, or what he *wanted* it to mean to her. There was even some uncertainty what he wanted it to mean to himself. *I should have asked,* he told his tortured self. Here in the darkness of his friends' lodge, their ecstasy affected him powerfully. Finally he fell into a troubled sleep, filled with erotic dreams. The smiling image of Raven shimmered indistinctly, just out of reach. . . .

10

The Comanches moved south a few days later, and Jed with them. He had still not decided entirely where he would winter. He amazed himself sometimes. He had had no trouble with the decision to leave home and the university. His decision-making capacity had been good. But now, he seemed unable to arrive at any definite course of action. It was easier just to drift along from day to day, postponing the obvious.

The big lodges came down, the covers folded and rolled. Some of the lodgepoles were used for travois, to transport rolled lodge covers and other baggage. Some were merely dragged, to be used again. In this country of few trees, lodgepoles became a valuable commodity.

They passed over a low, rolling upland, heading generally southwest. The caravan stretched for nearly a mile. Outriders, "wolves," as Black Fox called them, preceded the column and rode alongside to act as sentries and scouts. The horse herd, several hundred in number, was kept together by young men on horseback. This, their first duty as men, seemed to be considered more an honor than a task.

Some of the elderly rode on travois platforms, and in some cases women or small children rode the animals that pulled the travois. Innumerable dogs ran alongside. In a hard year with poor hunting, Fox explained, dogs would be a staple source of food.

"We will try to avoid traveling directly behind the herds," he went on. "At this season, the buffalo will have eaten the grass down, and there will be none for the horses."

Jed had never thought of that. The necessity of winter fodder for the hundreds of horses in this band must be enormous.

"A buffalo-hunting people such as this must spread out, summer or winter," he went on. "That limits the size of a band. Not only enough game for food, but enough grass for the horses. This, too, is another reason to keep moving, no?"

Of course. Jed had never thought of these things. He had had no reason to do so. He was just beginning to realize, here was an entirely different way of life. Complex, intricate, suited to this land and climate. One who did not understand it would find it hard to survive. He still could not see how one could winter in a skin tent.

On the fourth day, they saw a distant line of trees snaking across a broad valley to the south.

"The river," observed Black Fox. "The Arkansas. We will follow it west a little way, then cross and head south."

"How far?" asked Jed.

"A few days. There are oak thickets for shelter, good for winter camp."

"You mentioned Liberty Franklin?"

"Oh! Yes, he'll be downriver, a few days east of here. You want to find him?"

I don't know, thought Jed, *what I want to do.*

"Maybe," he said aloud.

"You could do that, and return to winter with us," suggested Black Fox.

The thought was inviting. It would at least be a decision. But he was not sure. There was still a wanderlust, an urge to go somewhere and do something, a vague and poorly defined goal out there.

"Maybe," he said. "Let us see what the day brings."

Day followed day, and the band moved into an area characterized by wooded hills with areas of grassland between. The trees were primarily a scrubby type of oak that was new to him. None were taller than fifteen or twenty feet, but they grew in a dense thicket. The leaves were dead and brown, yet still on the trees. Jed began to see the advantages of this area for a winter camp. The oak thickets would provide shelter from howling north winds.

"Here," stated Black Fox, "we will camp."

The site was chosen, and families began to scatter along the south slope of the ridge, selecting the most desirable spots to erect their lodges. A winding stream a bowshot away would provide water, and to the west of the camp was more open grassland with more scattered patches of oak thicket.

Each woman chose the exact location for her lodge, and supervised its erection, the men assisting with the heavier parts of the work. Jed had seen this procedure before, and helped as he could. It was soon apparent, though, that more care would be taken in the setting up of a winter camp. Kitten chose a level spot protected on the north and west by the curving edge of oak thicket a few paces away. The door must face eastward, of course. She drove a peg in the ground where the fire would be, and dropped the loop of a rope over it. Then she shook out the rope and with the help of a previously placed knot, staked out the circle, several paces in diameter, where the lodgepoles were to be placed. First a tripod, tied together at a marked spot on each pole, then other poles, secured to the first three by walking around with the dangling end of the rope. One last pole, opposite the doorway, was used to hoist the big skin cover into place. With the front laced tightly, the lodge was ready for occupancy.

There came the lighting of the first fire, a solemn ceremony. There was a sort of announcement, Black Fox explained, a prayer to whatever spirits might inhabit the place: *Here I intend to stay, to establish my lodge for the present.* There was also a prayer of supplication, a request for tolerance and help on the part of the spirits. Black Fox tossed a pinch of tobacco into the fire to honor and appease them.

"Its smoke is pleasing to the spirits," he explained without apology.

Jed was startled at such a statement from an educated man. But he found it easy, himself, to slip into the comfortable ways of these, "the People."

After all, he reasoned, this rite of the first fire was much like the housewarming of a new home among his own. Even the blessing of the hearth by a priest as the first fire warms it.

This, however, was only the beginning of the preparation for winter use. Jed had previously seen, on a warm day, lodge covers rolled up to allow a breeze. Now the opposite effect would be needed. The lodge lining, a curtain of skins nearly as tall as a man, was tied to the poles and hung to the floor as a circular wall around the sides of the lodge. The space between the cover and the lining, he saw, was used for storage. Extra space was stuffed with dry grasses, gathered for the purpose. He began to see that the lodge *could* be winterized to a degree, and with a central fire reflecting heat back down from the slope of the sides . . . yes . . .

Black Fox interrupted his observations.

"You are wondering if it will be warm enough?" he asked with a chuckle.

"Yes . . . well, I *was*. I can see, now. Is it really comfortable?"

"Quite, actually. If there is snow, it helps. They bank snow up around the lower edge outside."

"The heat does not melt the snow?" asked Jed.

"No, no! The lodge lining and the space between hold the heat in, the cold out. I have been quite impressed with their expertise. I had thought these a quite primitive people."

"I, too," Jed admitted. He was a little embarrassed that he had looked with scorn on such a culture.

"It took me a little while to realize," Fox went on. "You or I could not survive a winter on the prairie without such knowledge."

"Or build a house," Jed added.

"Of course. But could you or I have built a dwelling that would be livable between now and winter?"

It was not actually a question but an observation, and Jed did not answer.

"Come," Black Fox suggested. "Let us try for a turkey before dark."

The first snow of the season roared out of the north only a few days later. Ice crusted the edges of the stream, and the ground was white when they awoke. *I have waited too long to decide,* thought Jed. *It has been decided for me, where to winter.*

He mentioned this to Black Fox.

"Not necessarily," the dark man answered. "This will not last. The ground is too warm. There will be days, several at a time, when you could travel if you like." He laughed, the rich, deep-throated chuckle of his heritage. "Believe me, my friend, I know your dilemma. In bad weather, one cannot or does not want to travel. In good weather, he does not need to!"

"That is true," Jed admitted.

"Another thing," Fox went on. "I am made to think that you are beginning to look at life as these people do. Why worry about something that may happen in the future? They live from one day to the next. Time means nothing. And I readily admit, I not only respect this, I *envy* it, and try to adopt this attitude. And I see you doing it, too."

Jed nodded. It was good to feel that here was someone who understood and actually approved of his indecision.

"It is good," he said, hardly realizing that he was adopting some of the phrasing and expression of "the People."

"But for now," Black Fox suggested, "why not trap a little? There are beaver here. Then decide. Or not . . ."

But not to decide is to choose to stay here with the Comanches, Jed realized. He wondered if Black Fox might be hinting that he should move on.

"Is it a bother to have me here?" he asked bluntly.

"No, no, that is not it! I have treasured someone with whom to talk, Walker. Kitten, too, welcomes another hunter in her lodge. We have eaten well, no? But if there is any way I can help you with your plans . . . could we find you a woman?"

"No. But I am made to think . . ." *There I am, talking like Fox,* he thought. "I should do something. Maybe find Franklin? How many days do you think it is?"

"Maybe a week. Probably less. Certainly you could do that. He can tell you of the fur market, help you get started. Then come back here if you like."

Jed nodded absently. "Maybe. How do I find Franklin?"

"Head north and east. When you strike the river, head downstream. Lib Franklin has a house, a log cabin, on the north bank. You'll find him."

"It is good, Fox! I will start tomorrow!"

But Fox's mention of a woman had set his mind to racing. Thoughts of a long-limbed Pawnee kept flitting through his mind.

"What if I decide to winter with some other people?"

"As you choose . . . you have someone?"

"Friends, among the Pawnee . . ."

"Aiee!" Fox laughed. "Well, don't say much about your Comanche friends. We're usually at war."

"So I heard. But I was well received there."

"Of course. You had no Comanche friends yet."

Both laughed, and Black Fox continued. "Seriously, Lib Franklin will know the situation, and who is angry at whom. A trader must stay neutral."

11

He had no trouble finding his way back to the Arkansas River. He traveled light, and with a good horse under him, he was surprised at the territory he could cover. His previous travel had been on foot or with the moving band of Comanches, necessarily slow.

In three days he struck the river and turned eastward to follow it. He was a bit uneasy about the weather, and as he rode, planned in his mind. If a storm threatened, he would hole up in heavy timber on the river. A lean-to shelter of brush and a fire to warm it, until the storm passed.

He did not know how far it might be to the cabin of Lib Franklin, but kept an eye on the other bank of the river. The north bank, a good setting . . . He was beginning to understand the importance of direction in this country. A cabin on the north bank would have timber behind it for winter shelter, cool south winds from across the water in summer. Black Fox had assured him that he would have no trouble recognizing the place. He could visualize it in his mind already.

On the second day he saw a haze of smoke ahead. His horse became more alert, and called out an inquiry. An answering whinny told him that this was the place. He rounded a thicket and looked across the stream to find that he was mistaken. There was no cabin, but a cluster of lodges, similar to those of the Kansas. He tried to remember. . . . He had heard of no such tribe in this area who might be warlike. These were obviously growers.

He thought of passing on, but knew that he must have been seen, and hated to leave a question in the minds of these people. He might want to trade here sometime. There was a shallow riffle just above the village, and he turned his horse into the water. Several people now emerged from the lodges. The men carried weapons, but apparently only as a precaution. Their faces reflected merely curiosity.

Jed drew his horse up before them and signed a greeting.

"I am called Long Walker. I am searching for the lodge of a trader."

"Yes," signed one of the men. "The Trader's lodge is downstream."

"How far?"

"Maybe two sleeps."

The others nodded.

Jed thought of stopping here, but it was only a little past noon. He could travel far before dark, even though night was falling earlier as winter approached. He moved on.

It was snowing when he awoke the next morning. This was no roaring storm, like some on the prairie, but a soft and silent occurrence. Big fluffy flakes drifted down through the branches of the trees overhead as gently as the soft underfeathers of an owl. "Breathfeathers," Black Fox had called them.

Jed pulled himself awake and out of this dreamy whimsy. He must decide whether to move on, or to stay here and improve his camp against a possibly worsening storm. He built up his fire, warming hands and feet, and chewing on a strip of jerky as he did so. It was not uncomfortable here, with virtually no wind. He decided to stay a little while to see what the day might bring as it grew lighter.

The snowfall became heavier, a curtain of white that completely surrounded the little world at his campfire. Then it would thin to an occasional flake. Just when he decided that the storm was over, the snow would thicken again. All of this, in complete silence. No bird songs, no sound of whispering wind in the trees . . . only an occasional creak of a branch as it became a tiny bit heavier with the weight of its burden of white fluff.

Toward midday the snowfall and the sky overhead seemed lighter. Jed decided to move on. He noticed that it seemed colder. The snow under the feet of the horse now made a squeaking sound instead of a soft swish.

That night was clear and cold, deceptively cold with no wind. He could not seem to get warm. He wrapped himself in his blankets and paced around the fire, stamping his feet to relieve the numbness. Finally he built a second fire and stood between the two.

As soon as it was light he started on, his feet numb and tingling. He reached the trader's in midafternoon, and almost fell when he dismounted. Liberty Franklin helped him inside.

"You spent the night out there?" the trader asked. "You are lucky, son. This was the coldest night I've seen. Now, thaw your feet some, and tell me who you are, and where you're goin'."

In a few hours, with hot tea and some warm food, Jed began to feel better. He had become acquainted with Franklin and his family, who were quite concerned over his condition. A couple of toes were frozen on his left foot, and the tips of his ears burned like fire. That was nothing, though, compared to the pain as his toes thawed and the sensation began to return.

"You might lose that one toe," Franklin predicted. "Maybe just the tip, though."

In the ensuing days, Jed told of his time with Boone, with the Comanches.

"Black Fox . . . Washington . . . he was good to me," Jed explained.

"Oh, you know him?"

"Yes. That is his horse. He told me how to find you."

"You were *looking* for me?" Franklin seemed surprised. "How do you know me?"

Jed could not remember. Was it the old trapper in St. Louis? Boone? Or the Pawnees? Or all of them?

"No matter. Was it something special, why you wanted to find me?"

"Yes . . . well, no . . . I wanted to trap, and was told that you could advise me."

"Mmm . . . well, I'd advise against winter travel," Franklin chuckled. "Settle down for the winter, fix a shelter, trap some furs. I'll buy them. Of course, you can't till your feet heal, now. You'll have to stay here."

"But I don't want to be a bother."

Franklin brushed that aside. "You have no choice, just now. And Washington likes you. Otherwise he wouldn't have told you how to find me."

Jed took another angle. "I was very foolish to try to travel, I guess."

"No, not necessarily. I might have tried it, myself. This was a very early cold snap. Maybe," he pondered, "this country is so new that we don't really understand it yet. Sometimes I think I know it less all the time. But you'll get a feel for it. And November . . . well, it just shouldn't have gotten that cold. Now tell me. Where were you going next?"

Jed had had some time to think about that, and now had managed to admit it to himself. In the back of his mind there still dwelt the memory of the beautiful Pawnee, Raven. There must have been, all the time, some idea of going back to see her, to learn of her status. To learn whether she, too, had felt as he did about that one wonderful night together. At the same time he was afraid of rejection. What if it developed that she had a husband and family? That could be, in keeping with the customs of her people. But now he was able to look at it more objectively. At least, partly.

"I . . . I wasn't sure. . . . I'm still not, maybe. But I guess I had in mind going back to the Pawnee town where I stopped on the way out. Red Horse, their leader."

"Yes, I know Red Horse. But why?"

"Well, there was a girl. . . ."

Liberty Franklin smiled, a look of amusement crossing his face. "This is about a *woman*?"

Jed heard a chuckle and turned to see the trader's wife. There was a knowing smile on her face, too.

"I . . . I guess so," said Jed, somewhat defensively.

Franklin's smile softened. "It is good, Long Walker. I once found myself in much the same situation. Now you must go and find out, no?"

"Maybe . . ."

"No, you will worry until you do. Your toes are nearly healed, and the village is closer than you think. Straight north, almost. Maybe two sleeps."

"No more than that?"

Franklin shook his head. "I can tell you about some landmarks, draw you a map."

Suddenly Jedediah felt that all the weight of the world was lifting from his shoulders. How simple, when it had come right down to it. He would go and find out!

There was still, of course, a gray cloud of doubt as to what he would learn when he arrived at the Pawnee village. However, he would at least know for certain the answer to the question that had troubled him ever since: Was Raven married or single, available or not? As he thought of this, a fear gripped him. What if she had been available at the time of the tryst, but had married since? It would have been her right, of course. She had no reason to believe she would ever see Long Walker again.

There remained, too, the possibility that she had been married, but had taken the visitor as a husband for that one month. A Pawnee woman could do that, he understood, as long as she guaranteed the parentage of any child she might conceive.

He did not think that was the case. He had seen no man who seemed to be associated with her. If it was true, he would be crushed in spirit, but would get over it. The worst was not knowing.

With a new sense of urgency, he seemed to recover quickly. It was not many days before he was on the trail northward. His feet were still painful after some time in the saddle, but he could stop to walk, rest, and massage the aching members.

"I wish you good fortune," Lib Franklin told him as they shook hands at parting.

Jed happened to glance at Franklin's wife just then, intending to thank her for her hospitality. She smiled, shook her head and spoke in hand sign: "I, too, wish you the same."

As he drew near the Pawnee village he nearly turned away. Maybe, even, she would laugh at him. But he would never know unless . . . he kneed the horse forward.

People watched curiously as he rode up before the door of the big domed lodge and dismounted. Several people, alerted by the children, stepped outside and greeted him. Red Horse welcomed him with the hand-signed gesture of greeting and beckoned inside.

But just then, from the doorway behind Red Horse, stepped Raven, more beautiful even than he remembered. He could look only at her, and she looked back, not in a coy, flirtatious way as a white woman might have done. Her look was open and honest and confident.

"I knew you would come," she signed. "What took so long?"

He came bluntly to the point.

"Have you a man?"

The onlookers laughed, and he was embarrassed.

But now the girl became coy. She came to him and placed a hand on his arm.

"Now I have," she signed.

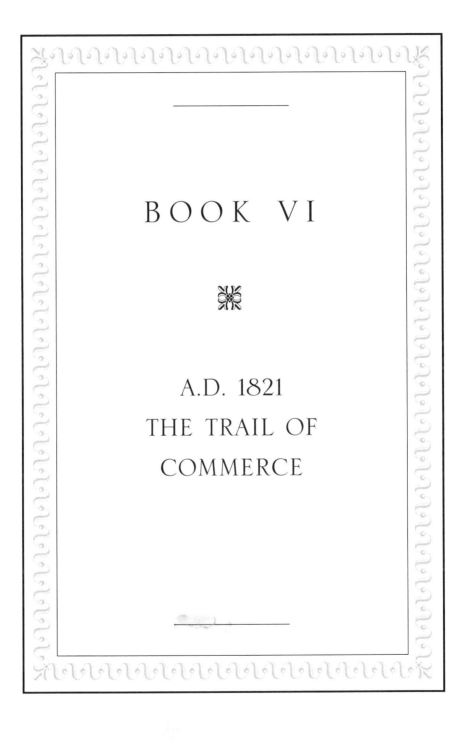

BOOK VI

❊

A.D. 1821
THE TRAIL OF
COMMERCE

1

Jedediah Sterling lay on the sloping dome of the earth-lodge roof, sleepily observing the rolling hills. Life was good, this late summer or early fall. Warm days, cool nights . . . the sun felt good on his buckskin-clad chest.

The warm smells of the season always intrigued him. The sounds of summer insects and of the birds who hunted them made a low hum of life across the cornfields and the grassy hill beyond. Below, busy squirrels in the timber were beginning to search out the best trees for acorns and walnuts. It was not quite time to begin to store the winter supply, but it was coming. The gray-blue haze over the distant hills foretold that.

He loved this season on the prairie. The profusion of early autumn flowers of brightest yellow was always spectacular. Yellow and purple . . . why? he wondered idly. With few exceptions, the wild flowers of this season were brilliant yellow-gold. Dozens of varieties, along the trails and the streams, where the timber was open enough to let the sun in. Sunflowers of several kinds, goldenrod, also of several varieties. Though not in such profusion, there was also a variety of smaller purple blooms in some areas. His adopted Pawnee people had names for them. They even used the roots of some of the sunflower types as food. But why all the same colors? he wondered, yellow-gold, purple. He had once mentioned it to Raven, who had simply shrugged.

"It is the way of things at this season."

The tall prairie grasses were beginning to send up their seed heads already. Turkeyfoot, the earliest. He could see clumps beyond the pumpkins to the east of the village that were almost as tall as his head already. Soon the plumed feather grass would make its move, nearly as tall, but with heavy yellowish fronds of seed. It was good. . . .

Raven walked past the lodge on her way to some minor errand, glanced up, and smiled at her husband. Five . . . no, six years . . . it must be, because their son was five, was he not? No matter, he was a fine boy, being instructed in the ways of the People by Raven's brother, as was their custom.

Jed had adopted many of their ways. He had not shaved his head. He had offered to do so, but Raven protested.

"I loved you as you were when we met," she had told him. "Hair on the head but smooth on the face."

That had been a choice. Most of the People had sparse facial hair, and plucked it with clamshell tweezers. Most of the incoming trappers and frontiersmen had heavier, European facial hair. Some did pluck it after the customs of their Indian families. Some shaved. Others simply avoided the choice and grew beards. A beard was good anyway.

A distant motion caught his eye, on the trail that led to the village from the east. A lone rider, in no particular hurry, not trying to conceal his approach. His arrival was some time away, and there were several low spots on the trail where the rider could not be seen. That would tell. If he disappeared in the first of those low swales and did *not* reappear, there might be cause for concern.

The rider dropped from sight and then reappeared as expected a few moments later. Good. Jed did not really want any concern to interfere with his enjoyment of the day. Now he could watch with no more than mild curiosity. He filled his pipe and called to Little Elk, who was playing nearby with the other children of the community lodge.

"Elk, could you help me light the pipe?"

Pleased with the responsibility, the boy hurried to the outdoor cooking fire, where his mother handed him a burning stick. The boy ran to his father, his momentum carrying him easily up the side of the low dome.

"It is good," Jedediah nodded, patting the boy on the head.

He applied the glowing stick to the pipe bowl. A few puffs, then a cloud of fragrant bluish smoke hung in the calm air around his head. He handed the stick back to the boy, who scampered back to the fire to toss it in.

The rider was closer now. A white man, by the look of him, and the size and angle of his broad-brimmed hat. Soon recognition dawned. One of the trappers whose acquaintance he had made, on a trip to St. Louis a season or two ago. It took him a moment to remember. Mose . . . Moses . . . the Indians had called him One-eye, because of an accident that had left that socket empty. A patch covered it. McCauley, yes, that was it! *Mac* . . .

The wiry little Scot rode up to the lodge and drew his horse to a halt.

"Howdy," he began, scratching the reddish stubble along his jaw. "Jed Sterling, ain't it?"

Jed nodded. "And you'd be McCauley. Get down."

"Right," affirmed the other, swinging from the saddle. "Can ye tell me where I might find a man called Long Walker?"

Jed was confused for a moment.

"*I* am Long Walker," he blurted.

"Oh!" the other laughed. "I didna' know. I know ye from St. Louis, no?"

"Yes. We met there."

"Ah! I was told to look for a white trapper livin' with the Pawnees, who goes by 'Long Walker.' I didna' know yer Injun name."

"Why were you looking for me?" asked the confused Jed.

"Ah, yes. A mon called Becknell. He's after plannin' a trip to Santa Fee to trade."

"Not a good plan, I hear. Everyone who heads there ends up in jail."

"Yes, he knows that. Even Joe Walker last year, I have heard."

"Walker, too? I'd have thought he'd know better."

Joe Walker was among the most experienced of scouts and trailblazers.

The newcomer leaned against his horse. "Well, there's a lot goin' on," he began.

"Come, sit!" Jed offered.

"Thankee!"

He seated himself, and the tired horse wandered a few steps and began to crop the grass along the path.

"You knew about Mexico?" the Scot asked.

"Mexican independence, you mean? There's been talk about it for years."

"Yes, but it's finally happened. Joe Walker jumped the gun. Couldna' wait, mebbe. He's out now, I'm told. But it seems it's *really* happened. The Mexican government freed from Spain. *Wants* trade with us."

Jed was not quite convinced. "Would it not be better to try Taos first?"

"Have you been therre?" McCauley asked, rolling the *r* on the end of his question.

"A time or two. Traded with the natives. I don't do much trapping now. Sell what furs I have to Franklin's company. Why does this Becknell want to go to Santa Fe?"

The other shrugged. "New market, I'd suppose. Yard goods, supplies, tools, for gold and silver from the Spanish mines. Why does a mon do what he does, anyway?"

Both laughed.

"But what has this all to do with me?" asked Jed.

"Oh, yes . . . Becknell's lookin' fer a guide. Your name come up."

"But . . . I've never been there."

"Who has? But ye're said to have a way with the Injuns, what with livin' here an' all."

"Franklin would be better, or Black Fox, maybe."

"The Nigra Comanche? I don't think he'd help. He'd have to be found, and they move around. Franklin won't want to leave the Arkansas with winter trade comin' on. No, you'd be our man, I'm thinkin'."

"How does he plan to go?"

"Pack mules. Oh! Ye mean what route?"

"Yes. The old southwest trail?"

"Now ye're catchin' on. The trade trail the Injuns hev used. It follers the Arkansas River and then turns south, don't ye ken?"

"So I've heard. He wants to start in the spring?"

The little Scot's eyes widened. "No, no, mon! He's on the way."

"Now?" Jed was astonished. "But it must be nearly September. Winter's coming."

"True, lad. But the uncertain part of the trip is at the other end, and the climate's warmer there. We could winter there if need be, no?"

Jed was not so certain about the climate. Farther south, yes, but more mountainous. But it would be possible to inquire. The challenge had begun to appeal to him.

"Then you're going, too?" he asked.

"Of course! I'm to meet the others at the Great Bend of the Arkansas, with you if ye'll come."

The adventure was tempting. He'd have to think it over, consult with Raven. . . . "Let me sleep on it," he offered. "Meanwhile, tell me the news from Missouri, and we'll eat after a while."

There was a considerable amount of news, even aside from the important event of Mexican independence from Spain. That was the big news, the possibility of opening trade to the southwest. But Missouri had just entered the Union as a state, and the Platte country suggested as a territory. McCauley was a bit vague about the boundaries.

"I don't know, mon! I'm thinkin' that the line's to run summ'at west from where the Kansas River runs into the Missouri. Drop another south from somewhere, there. Doesn't matter, does it?"

Well, it might, Jed reflected. Governments do strange things.

"And west to the mountains?" he asked.

"I suppose. There was some talk of the Divide."

Yes, the Continental Divide . . . the backbone of the continent, following the ridge of the Rocky Mountains from north to south. Jed had once been shown a spot by Lib Franklin that he claimed was the exact dividing line.

"You spit west, it'll run into the Pacific Ocean," Lib had insisted. "Spit east, into the Gulf of Mexico."

Jedediah had known that he was only half joking. But in theory, there must be such a point. A fitting western boundary for the Great Plains, he figured.

"The southern boundary for the territory is the river, then?" he asked.

"The Arkansas? Don't know . . ." McCauley scratched his chin. "I'd suppose, part of the way . . . likely, Mexico will claim what's been Spanish, don't ye ken? But no matter. Oh . . . ye know Boone is dead?"

A great sadness came over Jed. He had stopped once to see the old hunter on a trip to St. Louis. He felt that he owed much to the man who had taken him in, helped and advised him. There was a lot of water down the creek since then, as Boone would have said.

Jed tried to speak, and had to pause, take a deep breath and clear his throat.

"How . . . how did it happen?" he asked in a whisper.

"He died in bed, at his daughter's house in Missouri," the Scot related. "Strange, no?"

Yes, strange, Jed reflected. The man who had so many times looked into the face of Death and challenged it. Death had finally found him, but on Boone's terms.

"There," he said simply, "was a man. He was my friend."

McCauley nodded. "I saw him once. Never knew him. Must hev been past eighty, wasn't he?"

Jed nodded absently. He didn't want to talk about it. There was too much happening, too many people coming west. He could understand Boone's need to leave Pennsylvania and head out into the frontier. Now *that* frontier was gone, and Boone with it. It was the end of an era.

But he began to see an odd circumstance here. Boone, in his desire to escape civilization, had *led* it into the unknown wilderness. So had others. Pike . . . Lewis and Clark . . . Manuel Lisa . . . Colter . . . Franklin and Andrews . . . even he, himself. It was a trap. Somehow the urge to go, see, and do became entangled with the coming of more people, and destroyed that which had made it attractive in the first place.

Maybe it was like the moth that flies around the candle. Circling, unable to resist the excitement and the danger. To follow the light becomes more important than the risk. . . .

"I'll go with you," he told McCauley.

The end of an era, but the beginning of another . . .

2

History records that on September first, 1821, Captain William Becknell left Arrow Rock, Missouri, with pack mules laden with merchandise, including "calicoes and domestic cotton cloth." His goal was Santa Fe, and his route was to become known as the Santa Fe Trail. Becknell was assisted in this first successful American trade expedition by "four trusty companions."

The sumac on the south slopes was turning a dark red when they reached the Great Bend of the Arkansas. Becknell and the rest of the party had not yet arrived, so they made camp and waited.

It was only a day or two. Becknell was intent on moving swiftly. Jed had had some doubts about starting such an expedition at this time of the year. However, he found himself carried along on the wave of Becknell's enthusiasm. It was plain that the first American traders into Santa Fe would be in a very favorable trading position, and a quick, successful run would make a great impression. Provided, of course, that the rumors of friendship by the new Mexican Republic were true. That remained a point in question, and one that gnawed at the back of Jed's mind.

Fine weather held, a warm and lazy Second Summer, with bright days and comfortable travel. The trail was good, and easy to follow, wandering along the north bank of the Arkansas. At some points, the easiest path departed from the river by a mile or more, but the reason was plain. The river curled in loops and oxbows, and the obvious route was to cut across, approaching the stream again at the next bend.

By this time the pack mules were accustomed to the routine and gave little trouble. Most of the time Jed rode ahead as a wolf or scout. They saw elk, deer, turkeys, and some buffalo, although not the great herds of the migration. That had been a concern of Jed's, but this time it offered no problem. He wondered sometimes where the animals were, in seasons when the massive herds were not seen. *Where do they go?* There was no easy answer.

They encountered a band of Comanches, moving south toward winter camp, and camped near them for the night. Jed was delighted to find that this was a band that he had met before. He visited the leaders, exchanged news, and asked about various friends. More importantly, about the trail. He had seldom been farther west than this, and was unfamiliar with the country.

It was not difficult, he was told. *Go too far west, you run into mountains. Before that, there is a trail that joins this from the north. Both go south together.* He was far from confident, but resolved to give it a try.

As luck would have it, they encountered a traveling trader, an Arapaho and his wife. Arapaho, "Trade People" in hand signs, traveled much and knew the trails and the languages. They camped together, and Jed learned many details of the road south across the pass into New Mexico. The trader and his wife had just come from Taos, in fact, and would rejoin their own people for the winter. The new leadership in Mexico? The trader shrugged.

"Who knows? It may be better."

They had been to Santa Fe, but not recently, preferring to trade with the natives in Taos. The trader was quite fascinated with the bundles of trade goods in the mules' packs, and would have traded for some of the cotton cloth, but Becknell was not interested. His market was Santa Fe, he explained through Jed.

There was some concern about the weather. The trader warned of cold and snow in the higher elevations of the pass. Raton Pass, the Spanish were calling it.

"You might have to camp for a day or two to cross between snows," the Arapaho explained.

They actually had little trouble when the time came. There was a light snow on the ground and on the pines, but the sun was bright and the sky clear and beautiful. In later years, Jed came to understand that they had been extremely lucky. November 1821 was unusually mild. In many years, the trail would have been impassable.

But now the land of New Mexico spread before them in her glory. Jed did not know how far it might be to Santa Fe, but they were following a fairly plain trail. There should be native towns, and they could ask directions.

It was November 13, 1821, according to Becknell's journal, when they saw the Mexican patrol. A squad of dragoons, riding in formation, bright uniforms shining in the sun. A pennant fluttered from the guidon.

A cold hand of fear gripped Jed's stomach for a moment. What if the rumors were wrong? Here was a strong, well-armed patrol, who might well resent an intrusion on the territory of the new Mexican Republic.

It was too late now. The soldiers had seen the little pack train and altered their course slightly, spreading into a frontal advance at a trot. Becknell's party awaited their approach, nervously trying to maintain some semblance of dignity.

The officer in charge halted his dragoons a few paces away and rode forward, looking over the packs of the mules. Becknell kneed his horse forward to indicate that he represented the expedition. It must have been in the back of his mind that in previous attempts at trade, Americans had been jailed and their property confiscated. But he seemed to show no doubts.

"*Buenos días, amigo,*" the young Mexican officer now spoke, tossing an informal salute in Becknell's direction. "You have come to trade?"

The Americans relaxed a bit, but this could still turn sour.

"*Sí,* that is true, *Señor,*" Becknell began. "We have heard—"

But the officer silenced the explanation with a casual wave of the hand.

"Welcome, *amigos,* to the Republic of Mexico!" he said grandly. "Our patrol takes us back to Santa Fe. Will you travel with us?"

By the time they camped together that evening, it was apparent that the trade was to be welcomed. Some of the dragoons spoke a little English, some had a working knowledge of hand signs. Their commander was a friendly young man whose English was fluent, laced with accents that told of a good formal education. They talked far into the night, and the excitement of the trading ahead began to rise. Becknell had many questions.

"You have cotton goods?" the officer asked in disbelief as Becknell told of their cargo. "Ah, there will be great demand for that, *Señor*! All of ours has been shipped from Spain, and now yours will bring good prices in Santa Fe!"

This proved true. With the break from Spain, the inaccessibility of manufactured goods was being quickly felt. There was no haggling with the traders over price. Rather, prospective buyers were bidding against each other for the right to purchase. Santa Fe had become a traders' heaven.

Within days, Becknell was making plans for the next expedition. There had been some thought of wintering in Santa Fe, but it soon became apparent that the trader would not wait. As soon as their trade goods were exhausted, Becknell announced, they would start the return journey. In that way, he could be ready to travel in the spring for another trading venture.

He drew Jed aside one evening, and spread a rude map on the plank table of the cantina where they sat.

"I want your opinion, Sterling," Becknell began.

"If I can," Jed answered. "But . . . I have seen no maps of this area."

Becknell laughed. "Nor has anyone, really. I understand that Joe Walker, the mountain man, draws maps, but this one is mine. I have been gathering information for years. Well, look. You will see what I mean."

Becknell's map showed easily how he had arrived at the theory that he now advanced. They had traveled almost due west until they came to the front range of the Rockies. Then due south, across Raton Pass into New Mexico.

"Now," he pointed, "what if we had headed southwest from a point about here"—he indicated a spot on the trail he had penned in—

"about where we met the Comanches? That was fairly flat country, no? Now look at how much closer to Santa Fe, across that shortcut!"

Jed's mind roved back to his days in the university, which now seemed so long ago. His father must wonder what had become of him. He really should write, sometime. But now the diagram on Becknell's map looked familiar. Geometry, yes. The shaggy-haired professor, illustrating a diagram of a right triangle. *The square of the hypotenuse is equal to the sums of . . .* how did it go? No matter. This was a perfect illustration.

". . . and I figure a wagon train could cross there," Becknell was saying. "I'm thinking it would cut the distance by some two hundred miles! It would miss the mountain pass, too!"

"Wagons?" Jed protested. "I don't know that country. Is it possible to take wagons there?"

Becknell smiled. "I don't know. Of course no one does, because it's never been tried. But the route we traveled . . . did you notice? At most places, a wagon could easily pass along that trail."

"I did not notice," Jed admitted.

"Of course not. You were thinking of other sorts of effort and accomplishment. Yet until someone tries, no one will ever know. Wagons can carry far more freight, and far more easily, than pack mules. It would not be necessary to pack and unpack each day. And think of the profit! At the prices we are seeing here, it is hard to imagine what wealth there is to be gained!"

The man's enthusiasm was contagious, but Jed's doubts remained.

"But this shortcut . . . is there water?"

"There should be. This route must cross two rivers, the Cimarron and the Canadian. Exactly where, we do not know. No maps, you know. Probably about *there* . . . And *there*."

He jabbed a forefinger at the area of the proposed shortcut.

"It's Comanche country," Jed observed.

"Certainly. We came through Comanche country anyway."

"That's true," Jed admitted.

"Then you'll help me?"

"Wait . . . I have not said that."

"I'll pay well."

"It's not the pay, Captain. I'm just not sure I want to be away from my family. That's a long time."

"But much shorter, with the wagons and the shortcut. At any rate, please consider it."

Jed was longing to rejoin Raven and her people, to see his son. Still, the old restless urge stirred within him. New sights, sounds, new places and experiences. And there was an importance to these events, an excitement. The first wagons to reach Santa Fe . . .

"I will sleep on it," he told the captain.

On the thirteenth of December, the successful traders started home, arriving in Arrow Rock, Missouri, forty-eight days later. Afterward, it was realized that on this leg of the journey, too, they had been very lucky. It had been a mild winter.

3

When it came down to the choice, there was really no choice
at all. The moth to the candle . . . the West was calling
again and he must go.

Jed found that as the warming of spring began, he was becoming restless. March was the Moon of Awakening for the people of the prairie country. Buds were swelling. The twigs of the willows along the streams were turning a bright yellow, long before the green of the leaf buds began to unfold. The dark red flowers of the soft maples burst into bloom impossibly early, it seemed. Often they were coated with ice and snow while already blooming. "It is their way," Raven commented in answer to her husband's wonder.

On sunny days there began to be gatherings of the partridgelike birds that inhabit the tallgrass prairie. "Prairie chickens," the frontiersmen had begun to call them. Jedediah was reminded more of the ruffed grouse of his eastern woodlands. This similarity was enhanced by the strutting and drumming of the males in their elaborate courtship rituals. There were two distinct sounds involved, a chirping song and the deeper boom of whirring wings on air-filled neck sacks of bright yellow-orange skin. The birds gathered by the hundreds on a round-topped grassy ridge south of the village. *Why there?* Jed wondered. *Why not the next hilltop?* He was met again with the same explanation that was really no explanation at all.

"That is their dancing place," Raven told him. "It has always been, since Creation. *It is their way.*"

And that, he realized, was often the answer to such a question. For his wife's people, there are many things that need not be understood, only accepted. It is the way of things, and beyond that, no understanding or explanation is necessary. This was convenient sometimes. Raven had needed no explanation when he told her that he must go again with Becknell to Santa Fe. In another half a moon, there would be enough growth of new grass to support their horses and mules, and they could start.

"I am made to think that you are like the geese," she said, pointing to long lines of snowy birds high overhead. "They must go north in the Moon of Awakening. You must go west, maybe, for that is *your* way."

He had some deep feelings of guilt about leaving her again so soon, but Raven brushed aside his apologies.

"No matter! Elk and I might go with you, but I am with child again."

Now the guilt fell even more heavily on his shoulders. Already he missed her. The few weeks after his return from Santa Fe had been idyllic. It was no wonder that she was with child. Mixed with the guilt was an odd satisfaction. In his absence, by the customs of her people, Raven *could* find another man to warm her bed until his return. That was a custom to which his strict upbringing had never adjusted. Raven, flattered by his jealousy, had never taken that option, out of respect for his customs. She was amused by it, and liked to tease him about it. Just a little, not too much. He had to admit, though, that it was a comfort to know that during this absence she would be hindered from extraneous romance by her pregnancy. That in turn brought another wave of guilt. *Aiee,* life could be so complicated at times! But Raven only laughed at him.

"It is nothing, my husband. We will be here when you return! Is there not a reason you are called Long Walker?"

Jed smiled ruefully. Yes, the name by which he was known to the People was one that reflected his urge to travel and see new country. It had been given to him by Daniel Boone, after he'd walked all the way from Pennsylvania.

"It is good," he told her, though in his heart he was still uncomfortable.

Becknell had hoped to push through the first expedition
of the year 1822. But by early May another company
under the leadership of Col. Benjamin Cooper had hit the
trail with a well-equipped pack train and fifteen men,
headed for New Mexico, now a province of the Mexican
Republic.

Jed met the rest of the party at the Council Grove on the Neosho River in mid-June, the Moon of Roses, among the People. The Grove had been a landmark, a place of meeting on the trail for many centuries among the native peoples. Kansa, Osage, Pawnee, all knew the place. The trail crossed the Neozho, or Neosho River, here, a shallow ford across firm white gravel.

The primary feature of the landscape, however, was the Grove. Two or three square miles of massive hardwood trees, centuries old. White oak, walnut, hickory, maple, sycamore, and the ever-present cottonwoods. In later years, this would become known as the last source of hardwood for the repair of wagons before heading out into the treeless prairie. For now, it was a well-known camping place, and a place of meeting for council. There was plenty of fuel, water, and game. And, in an area used by several tribes and nations, the Council Grove had become a meeting place for any and all. In effect, a neutral territory.

Becknell was aware of the Cooper party ahead of them, but considered it no great concern. His expedition boasted two major advantages. The first, his proposed shortcut, which he estimated would reduce the journey by more than a hundred miles.

"The Coopers may even trade in Taos," he explained. "But by our route, we miss Taos entirely, avoid the mountains and come straight into Santa Fe, *around* the southern end of the Sangre de Cristos."

He had expanded his map, adding more details.

"The farther into Mexico we travel," he explained, "the more valuable our goods. So, we strike directly for Santa Fe and the towns to the south. Let others trade in Taos!"

The trade goods in the three big freight wagons were valued at five thousand dollars in St. Louis, and should be easily worth ten times that in Santa Fe. Drawn by big, powerful mules and protected by a force of some thirty men, this would be a historic event, the first wagon train across the Great Plains of Kansas. Becknell's excitement was contagious, and by the time they camped at Diamond Spring two days later, Jed was completely drawn into the esprit of the expedition.

Travel had been good, the wagons efficient, and much time saved by not packing and unpacking at each camp. Morale was high.

"With the shorter route, we may even reach Santa Fe *before* the Coopers," Becknell suggested.

The trail angled to the southwest, across rolling upland, toward the Great Bend of the Arkansas. Grass for the horses and the mule teams was good, and game plentiful. It fell to Jed and one of the other scouts to provide fresh meat. They would ride out ahead, looking for a suitable site for a night camp, then try to drop a buffalo or antelope near that area.

Another innovation on this expedition was the use of watchdogs. They would be in Comanche country. The time-honored custom of horse stealing to prove manhood might be a threat to the travelers, so the party was accompanied by several dogs to assist in detection of any night prowlers.

Travel continued to go well as they moved westward along the Arkansas. There were a few places where soft sand was troublesome for the wheels of the big wagons. It was necessary sometimes to double-team the mules to pull through, but it could be done.

The big decision became, very simply, at what point to cross the river and proceed due southwest. The level plain across the river looked inviting for travel, though it shimmered in the summer heat. The scouts, sometimes accompanied by Becknell, crossed and recrossed the river, looking for the best route for the wagons. Finally a place was selected, a long slanting route to take advantage of low banks on both sides. Becknell directed the procedure.

"Enter the water here, where the slope is easy. Slant across and upstream, straight toward where Sterling has marked the other bank. You'll be in the stream a few hundred yards, and *keep moving*. If you stop, the wheels will sink in the sand!"

Carefully, the first big wagon was readied, and a rider gripped the cheek piece on the bridle of the lead-off mule. A shout, a whack with the reins on the rumps of the wheelers, and the wagons lurched forward.

"Keep it moving! Keep going," yelled Becknell.

Splashing, rumbling, rolling, in a half minute the first wagon had traversed the treacherous crossing. The teamster urged his sweating mules up the bank and paused on solid ground to let them blow.

One by one, the others crossed successfully. There was a cheer from the watching horsemen as the third wagon rumbled up the slope to reunite with the expedition, now intact on the south bank of the river.

"We'll camp here," announced Becknell. "Rest the mules, let them graze. In the morning, fill all canteens, anything that will hold water. We don't know how far it is to the Cimarron, and that's a desert out there."

The worst was not knowing. The very thought made mouths dry. It had been three days now. The last drop of water from the last canteen had been used the night before. The horses and mules, dry now for two days longer than the men, were suffering. The dogs, straggling alongside the discouraged column, could no longer muster even enough fluid from their bladders to mark their passing on each rock or bush. Animals and men plodded on, sweating and exhausted.

There had been a time of short-lived joy the day before. A cool lake of shimmering water was sighted in the distance. Riders gathered canteens and loped ahead. It was a little while before they realized that they were drawing no closer to the lifesaving waters. Then, a slight shift in the furnacelike breeze, and the whole thing dissolved from view in a shimmer of silver. A mirage . . . the dejected riders sat on their exhausted mounts, staring numbly at the parched desert under a molten sun in a brassy sky.

That night they killed the dogs, to attempt to use the moisture of their blood and flesh. It was only partly successful, and thirst quickly returned.

The next day one of the teamsters slashed open a big vein in the ear of a mule to suck the precious fluid. Others followed the example, but in a short while the thirst was worse than ever.

At evening camp, it was decided to go back. They had seen no sign of the Cimarron, and nothing ahead as far as eye could see. Even in the clarity of dawn, before the day's heat produced the now-familiar mirages, there was nothing ahead but more sand. They must attempt to turn back to the Arkansas and its cool waters.

The decision was met with some degree of optimism, but Jed, as well as the more experienced of the others, said nothing.

The facts were apparent. They would have as far to travel as they had now come, with not even the two day's supply of water with which they started. Both men and animals were in weakened condition. There was little chance that everyone could even last out the day, much less survive the blistering return trip to the river.

That night, Jed went alone into the desert a little way. On this, the last night of his life, or close to it, he prayed. It was a prayer for help, to the God of his Episcopal upbringing, the gods of his wife's people, and to any chance spirits who might happen to dwell in this burning hell on earth. He listened to the cry of a distant coyote, and then returned to his blanket, to sleep fitfully and to dream. The night vision, as Raven's people would have called it, was one of a supernatural creature who looked like a buffalo. The beast, or spirit, whatever it might be, rose up out of the burning sand and led them to water.

He awoke to face the blinding sun, more discouraged than ever.

4

Jed was familiar with the sensations brought on by fasting. A sharpening of the senses, a clarity of understanding. He had experienced it on occasion. Raven's people used fasting to induce visions. He had doubted, at first. Yet it seemed that visions and dreams were quite common among the Pawnees. Furthermore, they were taken quite seriously. One's future often depended on the validity of such mystical experiences. A dream of green grass during the moons of winter could be a prediction that the dreamer is destined to survive until the Moon of Greening.

Even so, his mystical night vision of the buffalo and water was completely inappropriate to the situation. He did not even consider that it might have significance, beyond the suffering they were experiencing. On this day, quite possibly the last of his life, he did not think of his dream as anything other than further torture.

The worst torture, of course, had to do with thoughts of his family. His beloved Raven, pregnant with their second child. He would not be permitted even to know that one, and would never have the satisfaction of seeing either of their children grow to maturity. They would do well, of course. Raven, even with two children, was young and beautiful. She would never know what had happened to him, but in a year she could take another husband. Maybe some traveler would find their bones and find a way to identify the dead.

The scouts decided to ride a little farther before turning back, just in case. . . . The shimmering heat waves were beginning to become silvery with the water mirage when it happened. Up out of the burning sand ahead rose the head and humped shoulders of a buffalo. Dully, Jed recognized it as the creature of his dream.

The lone bull stood looking at them, head raised. The image was blurred and distorted, and seemed to dance and ripple, sometimes almost disappearing, only to become solid again. Was it real, or only a figment of tortured imagination?

The breeze shifted a little, and the image seemed to become more solid. Yes, a buffalo bull, a gaunt old loner, driven from the herd by younger and stronger bulls. Still there was an unreal appearance. A spirit creature? Jed was still staring when McCauley's rifle cracked, bringing him to his full senses. The bull sank to its knees and toppled to one side, kicking feebly. It *was* real, then, not spirit. He looked at Mac, a little surprised at the man's action. And the leaden ball would not have struck down a spirit-being. . . . Or, had they *already* crossed over, and this action was taking place on the Other Side?

McCauley was mumbling unintelligibly. "Water . . . paunch . . ." as he stumbled forward. He had dropped his rifle and drew his knife as he moved.

Jed now realized. *There is always a little moisture in the stomach of a grazing animal.* Deer, antelope, buffalo . . . *it is their way.* . . . Raven's words from another context came to him in this time of need.

McCauley had already realized the possibility of a swallow or two that might be life-giving. He had slit the skin and was cautiously cutting, now about to enter the paunch. Not too big an opening . . . Mac tossed his hat aside and thrust his head into the cavity, noisily sucking. Now he rose and motioned to Jed.

The greenish slime was bloody, malodorous, and warm. The best drink he had ever tasted. He could feel the parched tissues of his tongue and his cracked lips responding to the moisture. After a long suck, he rose to give the next man a chance. There had been more fluid there than he had expected. Now, if his shrunken stomach could hold it down . . .

He swept his glance around the area, a little alarmed at the narrow margin of survival. But he could see more clearly, think more clearly now. He must have been beyond the clarity of fasting, and into the confusion and dullness that comes from dying by thirst. He began to observe things that had gone unnoticed a few moments before. There was a shallow depression in the flat desert, where the bull had apparently been resting. Their approach had disturbed it, and as it rose, it seemed to come right up out of the ground, exactly as in his vision. *But in the dream,* he thought, *the bull led us to water.* More water than there would have been in the paunch. No, he had clearly seen a *stream* in his vision. Something was wrong. . . . Had McCauley destroyed the outcome by shooting the bull? Jed's anger flared for a moment, and then he calmed as he realized the futility of such an emotion.

He looked again at the carcass of the old giant. A mossy-horned patriarch, past his prime, an outcast. Unable to compete with younger bulls, but still in pretty good shape. Not dry and shrunken, like some he had seen, pulled down by wolves in a last futile defense. This dethroned monarch had at least met a swifter, kinder end than that.

But now he was puzzled. *How* had this rogue bull maintained such condition, here in the desert? He knew it to be true that a ruminant, a chewer of the cud, can digest nearly any plant material. Cattle or buffalo can survive where a horse would starve, and there *was* saltbush and scanty growth of other kinds here in this godforsaken hell. *But what about water?*

He looked more closely at the still form in the sand. The moisture in the paunch had come from *somewhere.* And the muscles, the skin, were in passably good condition, well rounded, the hump firm and rounded, the legs seemed sound. *Wait!* Between the toes of the cloven hoof that extended toward him . . . Jed knelt to touch and examine the sandy dirt, touched and rubbed it between his fingers. *It was moist!* Only a short while ago, this animal had walked in *mud.*

Jed almost jumped to his feet, searching the surrounding plain with his eyes. Only sand, and the shimmering silver of the treacherous mirage, promising water everywhere. But maybe . . . could he backtrack the buffalo? He stepped into the hollow from which the animal had risen, and searched the circular rim. *Yes,* there, tracks leading into the depression. He stumbled in that direction, trying not to be careless in his excitement. The trail wandered a little, but had been used before. There were dried buffalo chips here and there. He had not realized until now that there was ahead of him, as he moved on, a very slight roll to the land. Not much of a rise, and even that partially hidden by optical illusion and by mirage. But it had been enough to hide that which they sought. There before him, scarcely a rifle shot away, was a sandy stream bed, with scrubby plants growing along the edges. In places, even, a clump of cattails. At this time of year, the stream was nearly dry. The dry sand stretched smoothly from one low bank to the other, perhaps a hundred paces in width as it wound across the desert. But near the center of the broad flat snaked a narrow ribbon of silver. He thought at first that it was another mirage, but slowly, deliberately, the truth finally sank home.

"*The Cimarron!*" he murmured.

They drank their fill, carefully at first, and allowed the horses to drink, a little at a time. It was amazing how quickly the gaunt, tired skeletons of man and beast were restored to life by the precious fluid. Then they filled canteens and waterskins and hurried back to those left behind.

The entire company then moved to the river, leaving the wagons for a short while until the mule teams could be watered and their strength restored. It was nearly sunset by the time they had returned to haul the big freighters back to the new camp.

It was remarkable, the change in attitude in the space of a short hour or two. They had been expecting to die, if not today then surely the next or the day after that. Everyone had been listless, hopeless, moving slowly, exhausted by the mere effort of breathing in and out. The animals had stood, heads drooping, dying on their feet. Except, of course, for those that could not stand.

Now all men and animals were refreshed, active, and alert. Jed watched as men stood in the narrow rivulet that was the Cimarron, laughing, splashing, and cavorting like children. Horses and mules, now having drunk their fill, wandered along the banks, browsing contentedly on sparse vegetation. For some reason there flitted through his mind the words of an old hymn from his childhood, "Shall we gather at the river, Where bright angel feet have trod?"

There was a much deeper meaning, now, to those words, so puzzling to him as a child. No guidance by bright angels, here, but by a lone rogue bull buffalo. He began to realize, then, a similarity. Angels? He had always visualized angels as beautiful blond women with huge snowy wings, like the pictures in some of his mother's books. He *had* puzzled over the fact that some of the angels in Bible stories were men. For some reason there were no pictures of them.

Now he began to think about some of the customs of his wife's people, and others of the prairie. Their supernatural helpers and spiritual guides were usually animals. They might appear in human form, though, and could speak, on occasion.

It was nearly dark when he rose from his seat by the campfire. Taking a burning twig, he walked back toward the place where they had encountered the buffalo. A coyote slipped away in the dusk, to stand watching, a bowshot away. Jed had gathered a small handful of dry twigs and weed stalks, and now selected a spot in front of the dead buffalo's head. Here, he ceremonially lighted a tiny fire, and added a pinch of tobacco to honor the spirits. He did not know what to say, so he first offered the traditional apology. He was a bit embarrassed as he thought of the times he had neglected this ritual over an important kill.

"We are sorry to kill you, my brother, but on you our lives depend, as yours depend on the grasses."

This was falling short, he realized, and was not quite appropriate in content. Uneasy about this, he decided to extemporize.

"I thank you, my brother, for the lives of our party," he said aloud.

The distant coyote called, and there was an even more distant cry from another. They would soon gather for the feast. He turned back toward the river.

Becknell looked at him inquiringly as he stepped back into the circle of firelight, but said nothing.

"Something I forgot," Jed muttered self-consciously.

Becknell nodded, and then called to the others to gather. "We must decide," he began. "Do we go on, or go back?"

Discussion was obviously to be limited by the fact that no one really knew what lay ahead.

"How far to the next water?" someone asked.

"We don't know. The Canadian is out there ahead. Mexican settlements to the west. Sterling, what do you think?"

"I can't say for sure, Captain," Jed answered. "This is new country to me, too. I am told that the Comanches use this route."

"But they can go without water," a man protested.

"So it is said," Jed agreed. "But they are people, too. And *we* have just gone without water!"

There was a mirthless chuckle.

"Look," said Becknell, "how could it be any worse than the past few days? We may as well go on, no?"

Becknell reported later that they were able to find enough water beyond the Cimarron to reach the village of San Miguel. They had crossed the upper Canadian River and other tributaries. Other accounts add that from San Miguel "the road to Santa Fe is seen quite easily." There were several towns called San Miguel, but this one was apparently located forty to fifty miles southeast of Santa Fe, near present-day Las Vegas, New Mexico. A few miles to the north is the site of Fort Union where ruts of the Santa Fe Trail and the Cimarron Cutoff join, and may still be seen. In that area, they are referred to as the Mountain Trail and the Desert Trail.

5

August 1825

Jed sat on his horse at the edge of the bluff overlooking the Council
Grove and watched the activity below. He could scarcely believe all
the changes that were taking place. The Grove, so quiet and restful
only a few years ago, now hummed with a hustle and bustle like
that of a town. No, a small city, even.

There were people resting in the shade, visiting, gambling.
Some even trading horses, and others racing. There was a flat treeless
area just west of the river where horsemen could organize a match
race while others placed bets on the outcome.

At the south edge of the Grove the army had erected a few
tents. The company of dragoons who represented the interests of the
United States government camped there. A somewhat larger tent
served as the headquarters for the officers and staff who would consummate the treaty.

He could see the camps of the various Indian groups, mostly
brush shelters, but a canvas tent here and there. That would be the
Greater Osage, or Big Osage, camp, near where the trail crossed the
river at the ford. Just to the north, Little Osages. A delegation of Kaw,

as the Kansas were now being called. They would sign another treaty later, but were here as observers, he'd heard.

Jed was there with a handful of Pawnees, also as observers. It had been decided that a small delegation should be present. Not too many, that would only be asking for trouble with the Osages, their traditional enemies. But a few could make their interest known, both to the Osages and to the soldiers.

Scattered through the Grove were camps of white men, usually marked by fires that were too big. A white man builds a big fire, Raven's people often said, and cannot get close enough to cook or to warm himself. There was much truth to that, Jed knew. It was certainly illustrated this morning.

"Ah! So many wagons!" said One-eyed Horse, next to him.

It was true. Only a few years ago the wheels of the first freighters had drawn their narrow stripes in the dust of this ancient trail. Now they were commonplace. Dozens of wagons stood along the road or by the camps among the trees.

That in fact was the reason for the gathering today. There had been no major problems on the trail to Santa Fe. None with Indians, anyway. Plenty with heat, cold, mud, dust, thirst, breakdowns. There were always those who, in the interests of a quick dollar, would start the long drive ill equipped and inexperienced. Someone was always organizing a wagon train, to travel together for safety and mutual help. Jed had seen some of the handbills, tacked to trees in the Grove, though most trains organized in Franklin or Liberty or Independence. Teamsters were recruited in this way, as well as independent wagon owners.

"Each man shall be required to have a good rifle," one of the handbills had read, "a dependable pistol, four pounds of powder, and eight pounds of lead. Provisions for three weeks . . ."

Requirements for other equipment or for experience and judgment were not so stringent. Jed was certain that there would eventually be some problems. Inept and ill-equipped amateurs, crossing Comanche hunting grounds with horses and mules to be stolen—a design for trouble. Yet there had been very little. Probably, he reasoned, because most of the travelers on the trail *were* seasoned and experienced. This was a business to the organizers, like Becknell and Cooper and Baird. To the teamsters, a job. A hard, demanding job but one that paid well.

Jed had acted as a guide for another expedition. By this time, though, the route was well established. There was little need for a guide, and the position amounted to little more than hunter, to furnish meat for the travelers. Occasionally he had acted as interpreter when they encountered traveling bands of Comanche or Cheyenne.

There had been no casualties, as far as he knew, on the Santa Fe Trail. But the traffic was growing heavier, and there was some concern. Enough to alert the Congress, in fact. An army officer, the one who had told him about this council, had spoken of the great interest in the Kansas land and the growing trade with Mexico. A surveyor had been placed under contract to survey the road and mark it. There was a concerted move to protect the commercial traveler by treaties with the Indians along the way. Let the Kansas Territory, reaching from Missouri to the Continental Divide, remain Indian Territory. . . . There was even a theory, the captain had told him, that it would be advisable to move permanently many of the eastern tribes to Kansas, to give them more room. Shawnee, Delaware, Potawatomi, Ojibwa, Wyandotte . . . they would be happier here in this wild country, away from white man's encroachment, it was theorized. Already there was legislation pending to declare Kansas "Indian Territory."

Jed had his doubts. No one had bothered to wonder what the present occupants of Kansas might think of the scheme, the Pawnee, Osage, Comanche, Cheyenne. Nevertheless, the wheels of progress had begun to turn, like the wheels of the freight wagons on the Santa Fe Trail.

This council was for the signing of a treaty to try to avoid trouble, he understood. A payment to the Osages to allow crossing of their territory. But Jed questioned whether such a document was practical. The army was negotiating with the wrong people, he figured. The Comanches would be the ones with whom to treat.

"They may be approached later," the officer had said. "After all, what we need is not their territory, just the right to cross it. A narrow strip, along the road. That's all."

A sum of money would be paid to the "chief and headmen," he explained, for the right to use the trail.

Jed had been astonished. "A toll road?"

"No, no!" the officer replied. "A one-time payment."

Maybe Jed's presence here today was partly to see how that was going to work. A bag of money, paid to a few of the chiefs and subchiefs of a nation as large as the Big Osage? It was likely that it might be years before all of the widespread Osages even heard of this treaty. Well, they had not been aggressive toward the flood tide of whites. Not yet, anyway. Comanches might be another matter. Or Kiowas. Did the government expect to buy the right to use the trail from every nation from here to Mexico? It appeared so. A meeting with the Kansas was planned for next week.

He turned his horse down the steep trail that hugged the west face of the bluff, and started to descend toward the river. One-eyed Horse fell in beside him, and Big Tree, with his nephew Lean Dog behind them. They crossed the river at the ford, and found themselves among the clutter of wagons and campfires. Men looked up curiously, and from time to time Jed nodded a greeting or spoke to an acquaintance. The horn-shaped hair of his companions marked the little party as Pawnees.

There was a sudden exclamation from young Lean Dog. "Look! Spotted buffalo!" he gasped in astonishment.

Jed turned to see a yoke of oxen tied to one of the wagons among the trees. The big animals were calmly chewing their cuds, awaiting what the day would bring. Lean Dog looked as if he might want to loose one of his arrows at such an easy target, and Jed hastened to forestall any trouble.

"The white men sometimes use them like horses or mules," he explained.

"They *ride* buffalo?" Lean Dog was incredulous.

"No, just to pull wagons. They are not buffalo, Dog. They are different."

"Yes . . . spotted. Red and white."

"That, too. But these are cattle." He started to explain about milk cows, but decided that it might be too complicated. "Come, let us talk to the man."

Jed greeted the suspicious teamster, who relaxed a little when the newcomer spoke English.

"We have seen no oxen on the trail. My brothers, here, are curious."

"About what?"

"Well, I, too. Why oxen? Why not mules?"

Now the man grinned. "I reckon them better. Wait a bit . . . you be that Pawnee squaw man, no? Long Walker, ain't you called? You were with Becknell on the cutoff?"

"That's right. But tell me about the oxen."

"Oh . . . well, I was with the Baird party in '23, and I seen some of the trouble different ones had since. When it rains, the mud is pure hell. You know that. There's a wagon this summer, a bit east of the Caches, mired to the hubs. I don't know ef they've gotten it out yet."

"But the oxen?"

"Shore. I drove oxen as a boy in Pennsylvania. Fer some things, they're better than horses or mules."

"How so? Aren't they slower?"

"Well, yes. But not as slow as bein' stuck in the mud. An ox pulls better."

"He's stronger?"

"Well, yes, but thet ain't it. It's the shape of his foot. Put weight on it, it spreads to give better hold. Then when he starts to lift it outta the mud, it folds up, pointy-like, and is easy to pull out."

The man illustrated with his hand and fingers.

"Now a horse or mule," he went on, "his foot is solid. It don't give none. Mud sucks it down."

It seemed logical, Jed had to admit.

Now Lean Dog interrupted the conversation, which he had not understood. Dog spoke in Pawnee.

"Ask him if these taste good, like mules."

Jed relayed the question, and the teamster laughed.

"More like buffalo, I reckon, but tougher. Hold on . . ." His face became serious. "He ain't thinkin' of tryin' *these*?"

Jed smiled. "No, I think not. I'll tell him, though."

He now shifted to Pawnee, and spoke to Dog and the others. "The man says these spotted buffalo are not very good to eat. Very tough and stringy."

"Then mules are better?" persisted One-eyed Horse.

"Yes . . . well, no. A man eats what he must, in bad times, no? But it is better to eat good meat than poor, is it not? These are very tough."

There were tentative nods.

"I like the meat of the long-ears," Big Tree stated, nodding toward a mule team tied a few steps away.

At this point Jed decided that it was time to move on. He thanked the bullwhacker and wished him well. It would be interesting to see how the oxen would prove over the long haul. He could see one other advantage with oxen. They could browse rapidly, gulping without chewing, and then move on to regurgitate and chew the cud later, as they traveled. A horse or mule must spend much more time in grazing. That was one of the major problems of the long trail. The teams lost weight rapidly if the day's travel became too long. Well, time would tell.

They moved on toward the tent under one of the huge white oaks, where a table was set up and the dignitaries were gathering for the council.

6

The Osages, both Great and Little, signed the treaty on August 11, 1825. Basically, the agreement provided that traffic on the trail could proceed unhindered. It was also provided that travelers should have access to adjacent territory on each side "for a reasonable distance," to gather required fuel and to hunt for provisions. Five days later, the Kansas signed a similar treaty.

It appeared to Jedediah Sterling that this opened the floodgates. It had seemed a good idea at the time, a nonaggression agreement that could help to avoid much trouble. In a short while, however, it seemed that the treaty had stimulated an overwhelming interest in the Mexican trade.

Sometimes it seemed that everyone east of Missouri had been afflicted with the madness and had joined the rush to Santa Fe. Teamsters, impatient with slower-moving wagons ahead of them, would pull out and around. There would always be this situation. Now, with the occasional ox team being used, that factor became important. They could pull heavier loads, but their speed of travel would never quite equal that of a well-matched span of mules or horses. This constant passing of slower wagons or wagon trains quickly developed parallel sets of wheel ruts. The fickle weather of the prairie contributed, too. Rain in the deeply churned dust of the ruts created a muddy, slippery soup. Teamsters would seek out the more solid undisturbed sod of higher ground. In places, west of the Great Bend, it was possible to follow the ridge to the north side for miles, still keeping the river and the muddy trail in sight. In effect, the Santa Fe Trail became not a wagon road but a sprawl of parallel ruts, sometimes spanning half a mile in width.

In addition every teamster, proud of his own abilities, might choose to try his own alternate route. There came to be dozens of branches and spurs and shortcuts, some more practical than others.

Despite the variety of ideas, skills, and temperaments, there came about a tendency to standardization. What seemed to work well for one was tried by others. Originally the wagons themselves were whatever could be obtained. Many were made on the Missouri frontier by backwoods smiths and mechanics. But the lure of trade was powerful. Manufacturers in the East, recognizing a market for the heavy freighters, rushed to meet the demand for wagons. Conestogas, with upturned ends like those of a boat, were among the earliest. They were, in fact, built like boats, with the expectation that they could be floated across the wide prairie rivers. The low center of gravity would keep the load shifting toward the middle, to increase stability. These semiamphibious vehicles, with their tall white canvas covers stretched over hickory bows, did resemble ships under sail when seen at a distance. Writers and poets leaped upon the simile, gushing about the "prairie schooners" of the trail.

It was soon found that such a marked upward curve at the ends was not needed. There was seldom an opportunity to float the wagons anyway. A more modest low curve in the center would stabilize the load. This made construction easier. Studebaker and other manufacturers pushed construction, and wagons rolled to the growing town of Independence, Missouri, whose main industry was the outfitting of expeditions heading west.

Due to the difference in terrain, the hand or foot-brake lever then in use became not only ineffective, but a nuisance. Many wagons were now equipped with brakes of a different type. This consisted of a length of chain dangling from the wagon bed itself. When a steep downslope presented that could not be handled by mules leaning back into the breeching, the chains were passed through the spokes of the rear wheels and fastened to rings or hooks to prevent the wheels from turning. This "putting on the brakes" proved so effective that many were installed locally.

More wagons heading west required more animals to pull. Some of the earliest traders to Santa Fe discovered that cheap horses and mules were available in Mexico. They would trade their goods in Santa Fe and buy jack donkeys, horses for breeding, and Mexican mules, driving herds of as many as four hundred animals *back* to Missouri. For some, Jed understood, this had been more profitable than the trade goods.

Eight animals, it seemed, became the standard hitch for the freighters, four span of mules or four yoke of oxen. This was quickly expanding Missouri's mule-breeding industry. Any farmer who could was breeding the best draft mares he could afford to Mexican jack donkeys to produce heavy draft mules. Belgians, Clydesdales, Percheron . . . those in greatest demand were big, red mealy-nosed mules from the Belgian cross.

The mule teamster rode the left wheeler and handled the lines from his saddle, after the manner of artillery soldiers. He also carried a short-handled whip of braided leather several feet long, with a "popper" of string at the tip. The lash was seldom applied to the animal itself. The pistol-like crack over the back of a malingerer was sufficient incentive. Jed heard an experienced teamster boast that he had "made it all the way to Santa Fe and back without havin' to draw blood" with the cutting lash of the whip.

The ox drivers, by contrast, walked beside their teams. Yoked oxen required no reins, but responded to yelled commands. If the "gee!" or "haw!" of right or left was insufficient, the whip might be used in a similar fashion as with mules. This whip was of different design, however. Usually of second growth hickory, it was a pole six or eight feet long, with a two-foot leather braid at the end and a popper at the tip.

There was considerable yelling by either ox or mule drivers, which led to an odd situation that Jed found amusing. His wife's people, as well as other native tribes, especially Cheyenne, Comanche, and Kiowa, were not only astonished at the flood of traffic, at the wheeled vehicles, but especially at the use of draft animals. This was entirely new to them.

After watching from a little distance the efforts of a few teamsters whose wagons were mired in mud or sand, and listening to the shouts of the teamsters, they understood more. Not only the use of teams and wagons, but the terminology employed. Already they had known a mule as "long-eared horse," or simply "long-ears." A draft mule pulling a wagon was obviously called a "long-ear som-bitch." These draft animals were to be distinguished from the spotted buffalo, also pulling wagons, but designated "gee-haw som-bitch." The strange wheeled vehicles pulled by either team were much the same and were called "goddams."

One more thing Jed noted about the use of oxen. On the expeditions to Santa Fe he had seen the Mexican use of oxen for pulling carts or for plowing. The yoke was tied to the horns of the animals, and a tug line to that. American oxen wore the yoke on the neck and shoulders, held in place by a bent-wood bow under the neck.

"They kin get a better pull," an old teamster told him. "Pull with the shoulder instead of the neck."

One problem with oxen was that their hooves wore down faster than those of a horse on the dry, sandy western plains. This was partially solved by putting rawhide shoes on the feet, much as the Indians sometimes shod their horses with rawhide.

"Only thing is," the teamster complained, "an ox cain't stand on three legs, like a horse. You got to th'ow him, which ain't easy, just to put a shoe on him."

Jed, along with his wife's people and others of the area, watched with amazement. The prairie would never be quite the same.

In the same year as the treaties, the Congress in Washington also declared the area "Indian Territory." Eastern tribes and nations were assigned areas in which to settle, and were moved to these reservations. Wyandotte, Delaware, Kickapoo, Potawatomi, Ojibwa, Sac and Fox . . . each of these nations, as well as others, were assigned specifically mapped regions in the eastern portion of the new Indian Territory. Traditional occupants were shoved aside or assigned new territory farther west, to be held "as long as the rivers flow and the grass grows."

And the wagons still came, and more, and soldiers to protect the wagon trains. A settlement, Cantonment Leavenworth, was established in 1827, on the west bank of the Missouri River some thirty miles upstream from the confluence of the Kansas and Missouri rivers. It had been intended to establish the cantonment on the east bank, but Colonel Leavenworth, in command, wisely saw that the east bank would be subject to flooding. He later explained to his superiors, and the orders were changed after the fact.

In 1828, two men were killed by Comanches on the Santa Fe Trail, the first mortality to traders. A troop of dragoons from Cantonment Leavenworth set out in June of 1829, to escort a large wagon train to Santa Fe. Against his better judgment, Jed hired on as hunter, and joined the train at the Council Grove.

There was no trouble until they reached a point on the Arkansas River where a sizable island had become a landmark, Chouteau's Island, after the French fur trader. This was one of the places that had become a crossing for trains electing to use the Cimarron Cutoff, or "Desert Trail." The leader of the wagon train was determined to use the shortcut, and Major Bennett Riley, commanding the troop, was equally reluctant.

"You simply don't understand," he told the civilians. "That is *Mexico* on the other side of that river. We are at peace with Mexico, and I cannot enter her territory with armed forces!"

After much argument, a compromise resulted. The army would camp here, on the trail, for the summer, and wait for the return of the train. It was now August, and allowing time for trade, the army would wait until October 10, and then depart for the cantonment, whether the train had returned or not.

Jed was increasingly bothered by the whole expedition and his part in it. Where protection was needed, he believed, was primarily in the Comanche country of the cutoff. That, of course, was inaccessible to the army, and he was in their employ as a scout.

After a hot night, the soldiers watched the wagon train cross into Mexico and disappear in the desertlike distance. Jed sought out the commander.

"Major," he said, "you don't need me. I'm thinking I should head back to my family."

The major stood, thoughtfully considering the request. Finally he nodded.

"As you wish, Sterling. When will you—"

His words were interrupted by a yell from the desert. A handful of riders were lashing sweating horses back toward the river. Now above the shouts and hoofbeats could be heard distant shots.

"The train's been attacked!" one of the riders screamed. "One man's dead!"

Major Riley hesitated only a moment. He would be violating international law, but . . .

"Mount up!" he yelled. "We're going across!"

7

Jed jumped to his horse and splashed across the river with the troopers. The mounted warriors, in hot pursuit of the fleeing traders, hesitated a moment, then wheeled and fled, in turn pursued by the dragoons.

The direction of flight was back toward the wagon train, where the teamsters had managed a partial circling of the wagons. There had not been time to accomplish the wheel-to-wheel fort that had become nightly routine on the trail, with wagons chained together. This was a loose bunching of the caravan for such defense as might be possible. Men were firing at the circling Comanches from behind or under the wagons. Here and there an Indian pony lay dead on the sand or struggled feebly, struck down by the heavy lead balls from the guns of the beleaguered teamsters. One teamster lay still, outside the forted cluster of wagons. Jed remembered the first yells of those who had ridden for help.

"One man's dead. . . ."

He could not tell whether there were others.

Now the attackers found themselves outnumbered by the soldiers. The long, yipping war cries were replaced by shouts of communication, and the Comanches circled away, out of range of the dragoons' pistols. There was a cheer from the wagons, and a last final shot.

Major Riley ordered his troops not to pursue. There was no sense in trying to play another's game, especially on his playing field.

Casualties were few. Only the one death, the first man to fall at the initial attack. It was impossible to tell much about the Comanches' losses, because they had carried off their dead and wounded. Several told of seeing attackers fall, but that meant little. Jed was quite familiar with a Comanche trick in such circumstances. A warrior would appear to fall, but actually only slip to the far side of the horse, to continue the circling siege unseen.

Now what? There was a brief council between Riley and the leaders of the wagon train. The traders insisted that they go on, protected by the troops. Major Riley was equally adamant. He had already violated the international boundary by crossing the river. It would compound the act to take troops on toward the Mexican town of Santa Fe.

After some discussion, a compromise was reached again. The dragoons would ride as escort for the train for a day, and it would be seen whether the Comanches appeared to remain a threat. Then another decision could be made.

There was no further sign of the attackers. Riley and his officers gave some suggestions for organizing a defense if it should be needed, and then turned back. They would remain at the previously established camp until October 10, as agreed.

As it happened, there was no further trouble. On the return trip, the wagon train was escorted by Mexican troops, who met with their American counterparts at the Arkansas River, the international border. The two military units spent three days in friendly celebration together, and then went their separate ways.

Meanwhile, Jed Sterling had resigned his position and headed for home. He missed his family. The children were growing rapidly, and he felt a need to be with them.

He was uneasy, perhaps, about all the changes sweeping across the plains. More people . . . soldiers, traders, new tribes and nations displaced from the east to land formerly occupied by Kansas and Osages . . . he longed sometimes for the earlier days. The fur trade, men like Ashley, Lisa, Franklin, and others. Only a few years ago, yet so many changes. He had heard of a new fur company, a pair of brothers named Bent, and a French partner, what was his name? Oh, yes, St. Vrain . . . Jed had met one of the Bents at Liberty Franklin's trading post last year. At least, he thought that was the man, when he heard later about the venture. Well, maybe he should consider a winter of trapping, paying a little more attention to it than he had. With more people coming in, though, trapping might be harder.

His thoughts roved back to family. His son, his and Raven's . . . Little Elk would be six now. . . . Or would it be seven? *Aiee!* The boy's teacher, by custom among Raven's people, was her brother, Swimmer. A good man, he would teach Little Elk well.

Their daughter had been born shortly after his return from the desert crossing three years ago. A beautiful child, so like her mother. Cherry Flower . . . he smiled as he thought of her quick glance, her mischievous smile. Ah, how good it would be to be home.

There were times, of course, when he became restless. The life of the Pawnees, with a whole extended family of fifty or so living in a communal earth lodge, was still strange to him. The close contact in bad weather when no one could be out and around, the animal smell of large numbers of human bodies in a small space . . . but he had managed.

And there was Raven. Ah, how she could make everything worthwhile! And how fortunate he had been to find her. Many of the mountain men and trappers he knew thought little of wintering with a different tribe each season, with a different wife. There were many who felt otherwise, whose attitude was more like his own. Lib Franklin was firmly attached to his Cheyenne wife. One of the Bents, too, was married to a Cheyenne, it was said. And Washington, the former slave. These men all felt more as he did, apparently. It was a responsibility, but what a joy such responsibility became, when its object was such a wonderful partner as the lovely Raven.

He thought of her more and more as he rode. It would be good to see his friends. He would tell his stories of the skirmish with Comanches to One-eyed Horse and Big Tree. They would laugh at the strange preoccupation of the white man with borders, lines in the dirt that could be seen by no one. In this case, a river, but *aiee*! A river often changes its course, no? Yes, they would think his account of the crossing of the Arkansas extremely amusing. He began to imagine how he would tell it, each phrase and gesture.

But mostly he thought of Raven. The flash of her smile, the quick sideways glance, with a hint of flirtation and a promise . . . he thought of the way she moved, her long legs, the sway of her hips, the warm curves of her body, pressed against his in the sleeping robes. He nudged the horse with his heel and moved from a walk to a gentle trot.

He avoided the Council Grove, to prevent any distraction that might delay him. If people knew of the skirmish with the Comanches on the border, there would probably be questions and endless retelling of the event. If there were troops at the Grove, which seemed likely, he would be obligated to report to their commander, because of his recent employment as scout. Major Riley had not given him specific orders to do so, but Jed would have felt it. However, if he did not encounter any soldiers, he needed to make no report. Consequently, he crossed the trail near Diamond Creek, and headed on toward the Pawnee towns.

A storm held him up for a day. He camped in heavy timber along one of the smaller tributaries of the Neosho, and waited for the rain to stop. It was a noisy, windy storm, with large hailstones and much lightning, which always made him uneasy. *Don't camp under a lone cottonwood,* he had learned. They attract lightning. He was not sure *why,* but had found it true. Heavy timber was safer, and gave better shelter anyway. He could not complain, he realized. After all, it was July, the Moon of Thunder on the prairie. Nevertheless, he was impatient to travel. As soon as the rain stopped, he was ready to move on.

Water still dripped from the leaves overhead as he saddled and mounted, but the sky was a clean-washed blue. He reached the top of a low rise and glanced around the horizon. To the east hung a blue-gray mass with flickers of orange, the now-retreating storm. Its roaring thunder was now only a low mutter in the distance. All seemed calm. A herd of buffalo, a half day's travel to the west, grazed calmly now. Their dark forms appeared almost black against the bright green of new-washed grasses. Soon their seed heads would make their annual spurt of growth.

To the south, a band of wild horses moved at a lively trot down the long slope. He watched them for a little while to see what had quickened their gait. He had come that way a few hours earlier, and times were unpredictable. The horses had not seemed really alarmed, but . . . was he being followed? *Ah!* A gray wolf appeared on the crest of the ridge behind the horses. In a few moments, another, apparently its mate. The two hunters sat on their haunches and surveyed the prairie. No real threat to a band of horses, but enough to explain their actions. The wolves would be hunting easier game at this season. Rabbits, small game, deer, maybe. All was normal and right on the prairie, at least here. He turned his horse and moved on, eager to reach home. And Raven . . .

It was midafternoon, two days later, when he approached the town. Corn was ripening, and pumpkins were growing round and plump on the vines. He wondered whether they had held the summer hunt. He hoped not. That would provide an exciting diversion. But he would not need a diversion for a little while. He smiled to himself as he thought of the waiting arms of Raven.

Children ran to spread the news of his return when he approached the cluster of mounded earth lodges. Raven straightened from one of the outdoor cooking fires, and ran to meet him. He folded her in his arms, smothering her face with kisses.

It was a few moments before he sensed that something was wrong. There was a tenseness in her body. Her smile, although loving and eager, held a tinge of sadness where there should be only joy. He held her at arm's length, and fear gripped him.

"Raven . . . what is it? The children?"

She laughed nervously. "No, no! They are fine. It is nothing, my husband. But I did not expect you home yet."

"There was a change. The soldiers did not go all the way to Santa Fe. What is wrong, Raven?"

"Nothing, Long Walker. It is only that we cannot be together for a little while."

He smiled. "Your moon time, no?"

"No . . . not quite yet. But I am with another, this moon."

Anger swept over him. "Another man? Raven, how could you?"

"It is nothing, Walker. You are my husband. It is only a few days until I can be back with you."

"Who is it?"

"Big Tree, your friend, Walker. His wife has just birthed. He was in need, and you were not to return yet."

Jed knew that this was the way of the People, and that it was a woman's privilege to do so. Yet it had not happened before. Or had it?

"Raven, when I have been away before—"

"No, no, Walker. Never before. I would have told you. I would have told you this time. I *did*!"

His head was whirling in confusion. This was a clash of his own upbringing with the ways of his wife's people. The circumstances of his leaving his home, the infidelity of his father's cheating wife, all came flooding back over him. He wanted to strike out at Raven, though he knew in his heart that he could never strike a woman. His mother had taught him that.

"Walker!" Raven was saying. "It is all right. It means nothing. . . . a few days . . ."

"Where is Big Tree?" he asked. At least he *could* strike his former friend, who had betrayed him. Kill him, maybe.

"On a summer hunt."

She seemed to sense his thoughts, and spoke firmly.

"No, Walker! This is not between you and Big Tree. He has done you no wrong! It is *my* choice."

He shoved her roughly aside and turned toward his horse.

"Walker," she yelled, "you are acting like a white man!"

That was perhaps the cruelest cut of all. He mounted, without looking at his wife, and jerked the rein to turn his horse. The surprised animal rolled white-rimmed eyes and opened her mouth wide to relieve the unaccustomed pressure. Jed nudged the flank with a heel and the horse moved into a trot, back toward the prairie. His pulse was racing, the blood pounding in his ears. He felt weak and light-headed. That which had just happened to him was impossible. The bitter exchange with his beloved Raven was like ashes in his mouth, and his heart was very heavy.

8

Jed sat staring into the purple twilight, yet not seeing. He had dismounted when the horse stopped, but only after sitting numbly for a long time. The animal finally caught his attention with a deep sigh. He stepped down, removed the saddle and bridle, and set them aside without really caring. He did not even make a fire, or perform the ritual invocation for establishing a camp.

Now he sat staring into the deepening dusk, his mood matching the growing darkness. Usually the twilight was a pleasant time for him, or always had been until now. He had enjoyed the quiet relief from the brightness of day to the cool of evening, the change from the sounds of the day to the songs of night creatures. Insects, birds, the coyote beyond the hill . . . the stars appearing, one by one . . . tonight he did not even notice. His world was shattered, the fire of living turned to ashes, bitter in his mouth. Raven had betrayed him. What was there to live for?

He did not know how long it was that he sat there. He had not even noted the position of the stars to locate the east for the routine camp chores. What did it matter? The passage of time, marked in the night by the rotation of the Seven Hunters around the North Star, was meaningless tonight.

That was how he failed to notice the approach of a rider. His horse, grazing near the stream, suddenly lifted her head and whinnied, long and loud. Jed's instincts took over, regardless of his dark mood. Another horse must be approaching.

He crouched, drawing his knife, and moved closer to a fringe of dogwood near where he had been sitting. It would prevent the outline of his silhouette from being easily seen against the night sky. The muffled clop of the approaching horse's hooves came nearer. He could tell by the way it walked that it carried a rider. Yes . . . there, against the stars, was the dim outline of a warrior's figure. A Pawnee. He could see the scalp lock sticking up like a horn from the top of the head.

The thought swept over him in a burning wave of anger that it might be his former friend, Big Tree. If so, he would kill him. He quickly realized that it could not be Big Tree, who was away on a summer hunt. His anger cooled a little. Maybe the man would move on and not bother him.

"Long Walker?" the warrior called.

Jed did not answer, but the two horses now spoke softly, and the rider spoke again.

"Walker? It is I, Swimmer. May I camp with you?"

Raven's brother, teacher to Jed's son. One does not refuse such a request, even from a stranger, under usual circumstances. But this was not a usual circumstance.

Jed heaved a deep sigh. "As you wish," he said finally as he rose. "What do you want?"

Swimmer did not answer, but dismounted and stripped saddle and bridle from his horse.

"You were hard to find," he said as he sat down. "Not even a fire. If it had not been for your horse . . ."

"What do you want?" Jed repeated.

"Nothing. Only to tell you, my sister's heart is very heavy."

"It should be," Jed snapped. "Maybe she can find someone to comfort her."

Swimmer was silent for a little while.

"Swimmer, she called me a white man!" Jed blurted.

The other man grunted, a muffled chuckle. "You *are* a white man, Walker. But there is no need for you to behave like one."

Jed's anger flared. Twice he had been the brunt of this insult today. But he held his tongue.

"You know our ways," Swimmer went on. "You have become one of us." He paused for a moment. "Look, Walker, can we have a fire here? I want to smoke."

Jed glumly agreed, and Swimmer took out flint and steel and in a short while had tinder and small sticks blazing. He offered a pinch of tobacco, tossing it on the fire, and then filled a pipe. After a long draw and a puff to the four winds as if this were a council, he handed it to Jed.

It was a good feeling. To share a pipe is much like sharing meat or breaking bread among other cultures. It brings people closer together. At least, Jed felt, here was a good friend.

"It is good," said Swimmer, blowing a fragrant puff of smoke toward the sky. "Now, let us talk."

"There is nothing to say!" Jed snapped hotly.

"Maybe not," Swimmer agreed. "Maybe so." And he fell silent.

The pipe passed back and forth a time or two, and Jed began to cool a little, though not much. There was still a tight, gnawing pain in the pit of his stomach.

"My sister's heart is heavy," Swimmer said, after a long time.

"You said that, Swimmer. *My* heart is heavy."

Swimmer nodded thoughtfully. "Your white man's ways are different. But I do not understand. To many white men, this would not matter."

"I know. But this is my *wife*, Swimmer."

Swimmer nodded again. "True. But you know our ways, Walker. It is a woman's privilege. You were not expected home until autumn."

"I have been away before," Jed pointed out. "Has she—?"

"No, no. Never!" Swimmer stated. "Everyone thought that strange. But Raven always explained that it was the way of your people."

"Then why this time?"

Swimmer shrugged his shoulders. "Who knows how a woman thinks? I am made to think that Raven felt Big Tree was in need. His wife just birthed, you know. But it is her right, of course. Raven's. Big Tree is your friend. His wife would do the same for you."

Jed's temper flared again. "I do not want *his* wife! I want *mine*."

Swimmer nodded calmly. "Of course. In a few days. And if you had been expected back this would not have happened at all. Walker, my sister asks you to come back with me."

"To *forgive* her?"

Swimmer's eyes widened in surprise. "Forgive *her*? No, no! She is willing to forgive *you,* for behaving like a white man!"

"*Forgive me*? I am still trying to decide whether to kill Big Tree!"

"Ah, that would be a mistake, my friend! You are one of the People now. It is forbidden to kill another."

"But he—"

"Big Tree is in the right, Walker. So is my sister. My heart is heavy for you, but I can only tell you how it is."

Jed pondered a little while, as Swimmer smoked.

"I . . . I am not sure that I can go back," Jed said at last. His anger still burned, and it was worse that of all the people involved, only he, Jed, saw anything unusual about this depressing turn of events.

"My sister is still your wife, Walker," said Swimmer.

This did not help in the least, but only brought feelings of guilt, as if he were neglecting her. The customs of the two cultures were at complete odds in this, and he did not know what to do. He did not know, even, what he *wanted* to do. He had been ready to forgive, only to learn that Raven and her people thought that *he* was the one who had broken the marriage pact. Each time he ran that through his thoughts, it infuriated him.

"I do not know, Swimmer," he said finally. "I cannot come back now. I must think on this."

They parted the next morning. It was plain that Swimmer disapproved of Jed's decision, though he said little in criticism.

"What shall I tell my sister?"

Jed hesitated for a moment. "Tell her," he said finally, "that my heart is heavy. That I must think on this."

"When will you come back?" Swimmer asked.

There was a strong possibility that he would *not* come back, Jed knew.

"I do not know," he said as he turned his horse toward the west.

·   ·   ·

He had no clear idea where he was heading. He could hire on again with the army as a hunter and scout. And there were other things going on, big changes.

Joseph Brown, the government surveyor, had finished mapping the trail. That project had been a bigger job than expected, and had taken three seasons. Jed had encountered the survey party several times. But no, that was finished, and Brown had returned to civilization.

He considered going back himself. Just for a little while, to see his father. If, in fact, his father was still alive. He should have written. He'd always intended to. . . . This line of thought proved unproductive. It always led to the memory of the circumstances of his leaving. In turn, the heart-wrenching perfidy of women, and the reason for his present aimless wandering. He forced his thoughts back to consider some of his other options.

He might trap for a winter. In a way, he enjoyed the solitude. Yet he had solitude now, and was not enjoying it much. Besides, his traps were back at the Pawnee lodge with Raven.

Something different . . . the Bents and Ceran St. Vrain were building that big trading post on the mail trail, just before it turned south toward the pass. At least, he had heard so. They might hire a few men.

One night he encountered and camped with a party of three men who seemed to be frontiersmen like himself, trappers and traders. He would have preferred to camp alone, but he knew the country, and this was the best, maybe the only, water in half a day's travel. One of the men looked familiar. From the early trapping days? Yes . . . Smith.

"Jed Smith?" he asked as they dismounted.

"Right! Don't I know you? Let's see, you're Jedediah, too. Long Walker, no? Pawnee man?"

"Yes, sir. Jed Sterling. We met at the Grove, I think."

They talked of old times and of mutual acquaintances, some now gone, and of the changing times. Jed was still in awe of the reputation of a man such as this. Smith had traveled widely in recent seasons, and had access to much of the latest news and gossip. He had been to St. Louis.

"Ye'd never know her, son. Really boomin'. Steamboats, goods comin' in. Not like the old days. The trail is opening up trade. Exciting times! Oh, you knew the town of Franklin washed away?"

"I heard something. Was it true?"

"Yes! Whole town site, just slid into the Missouri River, last season!"

"Many people lost?"

"Don't know. I wasn't there. But there's a town rebuilding there now. Other side of the river. Booneville, they call it. Doesn't matter. Independence is the outfitters' town. That and Westport, where the ferry is."

Booneville . . . Jed wished he could talk to Daniel Boone again. Boone had taught him so much in such a short time. Life had been so much simpler then. At least, had seemed so.

Before they parted in the morning, Smith took him aside from the others.

"You haven't said what you're doin', son. Would you be interested in a trading company?"

"I . . . I'm not trapping much."

"No, I mean . . . *in* it. You know the country, better'n most. We'll need a good man or two."

"That's what you're doing here?"

"Yes. This is in confidence, Sterling."

"Of course. But *you*—"

The old frontiersman nodded. "But a lot of my experience is farther north, on the Missouri. You know this country better."

It was high praise, and the flattery was effective. But . . .

"Think on it, son. If you're interested, ask for me in Independence!"

"I'll do that, sir."

9

Somehow the encounter with Jed Smith gave him the boost that he needed. His confidence mounted. There were several options open to him, and his skills would be in demand as the trade continued to boom along the trail.

This enabled him to stretch his imagination. A course of action he had not even considered came to mind. Settlers were beginning to move into the northern part of Mexico, the province known as Tejas. It was not all as dry and desert as the cutoff, it was said. He could seek a new life there, settle down, and build a homestead. But that implied a wife. . . .

Maybe he should go and talk with Smith about becoming a trader. Or go and at least take a look at the big trading post the Bents were building out on the upper Arkansas.

Yes, that would be good. He could go to the Council Grove and hire on as a scout with one of the trains forming there. That would be something he knew, a solid rock in a quagmire of doubt. He rose early the next day, and set out in his new direction.

It was easy to attach himself to a departing wagon train. He had been up and down the trail enough times to be acquainted with many of the teamsters and wagon masters. They moved out the following day.

Riding ahead and on the flank of a well-organized, efficient train, Jed's spirits rose. From time to time he almost forgot his inner pain as the train stopped at old familiar camping spots. Diamond Springs, Three-mile, Six-mile, and Camp Creeks, High Bank Creek, Cottonwood River . . .

They were beyond the rolling hills of tallgrass country in a few days, nearing the Great Bend where they would first encounter the Arkansas River. Jed noticed a smudge of smoke to the south, and decided to investigate. A band of Cheyenne or Comanche, probably, on a summer hunt, but it would be well to know. There had been no trouble on this part of the trail.

Since the smoke was half a day's travel away, he explained to the wagon master what he had in mind.

"Just keep moving. I'll find out, and rejoin you before you reach the Great Bend."

It was growing late when he approached the camp. Ten lodges, Cheyenne . . . judging from the brush shelters, they had been here for a while, because the leafy branches were drying. Also drying, in the heavy heat of August, were racks of jerky. Yes, a successful hunt.

He rode in boldly, holding up his right hand with palm forward in the sign of peaceful greeting. A young warrior stepped forward to meet him, cautious, well armed.

Jed knew a little of the Cheyenne tongue, but chose hand signals.

"I am Long Walker," he signed. "I am Pawnee, Horn People."

"What do you want?"

"Nothing. I saw your smoke. You have had a good hunt?"

"You are a white man," the other answered.

Now an older man, who had been sitting beyond a brush arbor, rose and came forward. He spoke to the younger man in Cheyenne.

"It is good. I know him."

Then, in hand signs, "Long Walker. I know you. Join us, we have meat."

"Thank you. Running Elk, no?"

The other man nodded, and Jed stepped down, unsaddled his mare, and turned her loose to graze.

The two acquaintances talked, in a mixture of Cheyenne, hand signs, and English. Curious children gathered around the two men as they sat smoking and talking. Small talk, of the weather, the game, and the Cheyennes' recent hunt.

One child came close. Probably a son or grandson of Running Elk, Jed guessed. He smiled at the boy, and received a shy grin in return. Big dark eyes stared at him, cautious yet friendly. This child would be about the age of Little Elk. A wave of guilt swept over him. In his anger he had left without even speaking to the children. How could he have?

He suddenly realized that Running Elk was speaking, had asked a question.

"What? Forgive me, Uncle. My thoughts were somewhere else."

Running Elk nodded, unperturbed, puffed his pipe and leaned back on his willow back rest.

"I only asked if you ride with the white man's goddams now, Long Walker?"

"Yes, sometimes. Like now. Many of them do not know the trail."

"They have only to follow each other," chuckled the old warrior.

"Yes. They know the trail, but not how to walk it."

"Well said, Walker. You think like one of us."

Jed was confused.

"Cheyenne, you mean?"

"Cheyenne, Pawnee, Arapaho." Running Elk used the hand signs. "All are different, but the walk is much the same, no? Yet the way of the white man is different."

Jed puzzled a moment over this. He was honored that the old man had accepted him as one who could understand. And how quickly he had been accepted! He felt a closeness here, a comfort. Now he remembered that he had once noticed a similar feeling on the part of other whites living with various of the Indian nations. Washington, Lib Franklin. These men were, in a way, more red than white. They were comfortable with it. Jed had never quite felt this, until now. Odd, that Running Elk could see it in him, when he had not yet seen it in himself. What did it mean?

Now Running Elk changed the subject.

"You heard of a fight last moon?" he asked. "South of the river, maybe ten sleeps west of here?"

Jed nodded. "I was there."

Running Elk's eyes widened. "Comanches and Long-Knives?" he asked.

"Yes. That was the one. On the desert trail. One white man killed. I do not know about Comanches."

Running Elk laughed. "They said *three* whites, two Comanches. If they admit two, they probably lost more."

Both men laughed, and settled back to smoke. It was good.

A young woman came over and handed food to the two men on flat wooden or bark trays. Broiled, fresh hump ribs, cooked to perfection. She smiled. Jed thanked her and could not help but watch her as she walked back to the cooking fire. He tried not to stare, but her build was tall and willowy, like that of many Cheyenne women. Her legs were long, well shaped, and moved in a most attractive manner with her swaying stride.

Cheyenne women know how to dress to good advantage, he thought. Their skirts were styled somewhat shorter than those of some other nations. It occurred to him now that maybe this was no coincidence. Through the generations, the Cheyenne woman's dress may have been intentionally designed to show their long and sensuous legs.

He looked back to his food, a bit embarrassed at his thoughts. One more quick look . . . he glanced up and in the deepening shadows of the coming evening, his eyes tricked him for a moment. He was seeing not the graceful form of the pretty Cheyenne but of Raven. He blinked, and when he opened his eyes the illusion was gone. The young woman was now handing food to her husband and her children.

A great longing swept over him, and tears came to his eyes. Had he thrown away something equally precious? He looked at his host, who was wolfing down a huge mouthful of well-browned meat.

"It is good, no?" Running Elk asked.

The next morning he rose early, and took his leave of Running Elk and his family. The young woman was Elk's daughter, he had learned. He could overtake the wagon train before they reached the Great Bend. He must talk to the wagon master.

"Look, Sterling," the wagon master protested, "you hired on for Santa Fe, not somewhere out here on the river. You leave now, there's no pay!"

Jed nodded. "I understand that. But you will do well. You had planned to take the main trail, and to follow it is easy. Not the danger you'd find on the cutoff. You'll pass the Bents' new post before you turn south. You could probably hire someone there if you think you need a scout, but I doubt that you need one."

He swung to his saddle and turned the mare's head to the back trail. He would follow it only part of the way, and then head across country. He was trying to count days. It is only a few days, Swimmer had said. It had now been a few days. He hoped that his timing was good. He was sure that Raven would not take up with another so soon, but . . . well, it would do no harm to hurry. The moon would be nearly full for a few nights now. He could travel long and far.

As he nudged the mare into a trot, he heard a muttered remark from the wagon master.

"Damn squaw man."

At some times in the past, he might have taken offense, but just now it did not matter. He was going home, and the heart of Long Walker soared like the eagle.

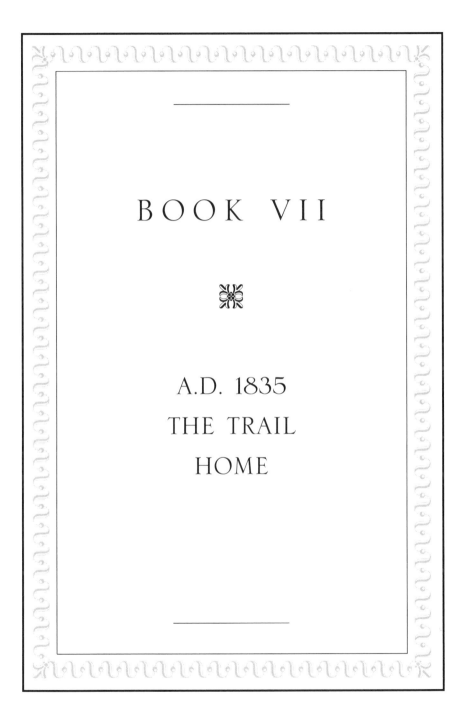

BOOK VII

A.D. 1835
THE TRAIL
HOME

1

"May you travel well, Long Walker. Be careful with the white men."

Jed smiled and extended a hand to his friend. "I will try."

Swimmer turned his horse away and started back toward the west. Jed finished his preparations to break camp, glancing at the retreating figure with good feelings. His best friend, also his wife's brother. How appropriate, that little shared joke as Swimmer turned back. *White men* . . . Swimmer had always teased him a little about it. Just enough to put the situation in proper perspective.

He tied his blanket roll behind the saddle and smiled to himself as he swung up. He was remembering the time that he and Raven had quarreled, and Swimmer was trying to mediate.

"She said I think like a white man!" Jed had blurted angrily.

"You *are* a white man," his friend had reminded. "My sister will forgive you."

For being a white man, he had realized. But with the help of Swimmer's gentle sense of humor and understanding of human nature, he had adjusted. The powerful love that he and Raven held for each other had grown and ripened through the years. It was now more comfortable, like the well-worn buckskins that he wore.

He could hardly believe the years that had passed since he left home to come west. Sixteen . . . no, seventeen, was it? That would make him some thirty-six winters. *Aiee!* But then his son Little Elk, his and Raven's, was becoming a man.

The time on the trail would provide him an opportunity to think. His mind wandered back to his childhood, his parents and his sister. Sarah would be a grown woman now, probably with a family of her own. His father, who had seemed old to him when he was small, must be sixty, at least. Judge J. T. Sterling III . . . another world . . . if he had not left home and college after his mother's death, he might now be a prominent Baltimore attorney himself. J. T. Sterling IV, Attorney at Law . . . *no, probably not,* he mused.

He was not certain what had made him decide to return now, if only for a visit. He had always intended to write to his father. He had done so once, in fact. It had been early in his career in the West, in St. Louis. He finished the letter and inquired where to post it, and then a thought had struck him. What if his father, knowing where to find him, hired a man or two to pursue and bring him back? He had burned his letter. Someday he would try again. But he never had.

So he had lived with the guilt of *not* communicating. Most of the time he had managed to divert his thoughts to more urgent matters, such as survival. He had trapped beaver, traded, acted as a guide and hunter for the wagon trains on the Santa Fe Trail. He had married Raven and had been accepted as an adopted member of her people. Their relationship had weathered some uneven times, but was now better than ever.

He could not have explained this present sense of urgency to see his father. Maybe it was the dream. . . . Raven's people held a great reverence for dreams as an aid in making decisions. He had dreamed of his father, who had appeared old and weak and ill. Jed had wakened with a start, disturbing Raven at his side.

"What is it?" she whispered in the darkness of the big earth lodge.

The soft snores of the other people in the extended family told that no one else had been wakened.

"It is nothing," he said. "A dream."

Now she was wide awake. This could be important.

"What did it reveal?"

"Nothing. It was of my father."

"Then you must think on it!" she insisted. "Your father, back among the whites? What was he doing, Walker?"

"My father wasn't doing anything, Raven," Jed answered her. "He looked old and sick."

"*Aiee!* It is a sign! You must go to him!"

Jed had fought the idea at first, but Swimmer agreed with the meaning of the dream.

"You should go, my brother. Your father may be in need. I will look after your family."

"I know you will, Swimmer."

It was already Swimmer's function, as the uncle of Little Elk, to see to his upbringing. And Swimmer understood the past problems between his sister and her husband. Problems now long ago settled by compromise. Maybe he *should* show concern, and allegiance to the family he had left behind when he fled.

It had not taken long for him to be convinced. One does not question the urgency of a dream. It was only three days later that he left the town to start the long back trail. When he had traveled it before, from the other direction, it had been on foot, and he had worn a younger man's clothes. Proper clothes, too, those of an affluent family's son and heir. Now Swimmer rode with him for a day, and had turned back. Jed rode alone with his thoughts and memories, his joys and regrets.

It was a bright morning in late spring. The prairie grasses were greening and trees were bursting into full leafy canopies of shade. Spring blooms scented the air. An especially delightful aroma wafted his way for a moment, and he recognized the perfume of wild grape blossoms, one of his favorites. Yes, there . . . he was on a stretch of the trail that followed close to the river. At this point there was a strip of dense timber, with massive old grapevines festooned among the branches.

The trail itself was more well traveled now. That saddened him, in a way. So many people coming in. Jed had rather enjoyed the isolation. But in the ten years since the whole area had been designated Indian Territory, there had been many changes. The federal government, he had been told, was moving more than thirty native tribes and nations from back East into the region along the Platte and Kansas rivers. It seemed to make no difference that the area was already occupied with the Kansa, Osage, Pawnee, Missouri. Some were moving on westward to avoid the influx of people. This, of course, would intrude on still others to the west, the nomadic Cheyenne, Comanche, and Arapaho. There was sure to be trouble.

On top of it all, the massive commercial trade on the Santa Fe Trail continued to grow. Treaties of nonaggression had been signed, but no one subchief could speak for all the wandering bands and individuals. There had been killings along the trail.

These attacks in turn brought more soldiers into the area. Some understood native ways, some did not. Jed had worked with some of these patrols as guide and interpreter, but he preferred the less regimented life of a hunter or trapper.

Trapping, too, was changing. Beaver pelts, once the standard of commerce, had fallen in value so badly that the fur companies in the Rockies had found commercial trapping unprofitable. They had withdrawn their outposts, discontinued the annual rendezvous. William Sublette had led what proved to be the last big fur expedition into the Rockies, and found it to be unprofitable. A few freelance trappers still stubbornly refused to accept the fact that the market for beaver was disappearing.

Jed understood it a little better than most. In the civilized world, fashions change. There had come a time when men in Europe stopped wearing beaver hats.

On the upper Arkansas River, William Bent's trading post, now called Bent's Fort, was still flourishing. The Bents were more adaptable than other traders. Other furs were still in some demand, and there was an increasing market for buffalo robes. In addition, Bent's Fort was in a position to furnish necessary supplies for travelers on the Santa Fe Trail, as well as blankets and trade goods for the Indians. On the few occasions when Jed had been there, the fort was always busy. The broad area between the massive adobe walls and the river was dotted with campfires, freight wagons, and the lodges of Cheyenne, Kiowa, and Arapaho. No one stayed long at Bent's, because there was no grass for the animals. The earth had been grazed bare for a wide radius around the post.

But now Jed's thoughts were turning in the other direction, back toward civilization. Here, too, he saw change in the now well-traveled trail. On his fourth day of travel he approached the old crossing on the Kansas River. The Kansa town on the north bank seemed larger than he remembered. As he neared the settlement, he saw that among the traditional half-buried Kansa lodges were several frame houses. He wondered if these were dwellings of whites, or if the Kansas were adopting white men's ways. Or both. The Kansas had been relocating westward for a decade or two. Their town at the junction of the Kansas and Missouri rivers was now occupied by others.

To his surprise, there was a ferry in operation near the crossing, a big flat boat that could take a wagon or two, and a number of people and horses besides. He turned his horse away in distaste and headed for the ford. He must save his money anyway. It would be a long trip.

The horse had to swim only a few yards at the main channel, and they soon struggled out on the south bank. He moved on to a likely campsite and stopped early to dry his outfit before dark. Nights could still be chilly.

The warmth of his little fire was good. He tossed in a pinch of tobacco, mostly from habit. He had long told himself that he did not really believe in this ritual in a new camp. Yet it had become a habit. And what harm could it do, this gesture to appease the spirits that might inhabit a place? It was merely a statement, *Here I camp tonight,* was it not? Now he thought little of it. It was a part of being one of his wife's people.

Just before dark he spread his blankets and sat, chewing a strip of jerky as he listened to the changing sounds of evening. The creatures of the day were quieting and retreating to their lodges, their songs replaced by those of the denizens of the night. A coyote called, and it was good.

"Hallo, the camp!" a voice called in the twilight.

A rider was approaching, a disreputable-looking figure on a spavined mule. Jed resented the intrusion, but one cannot choose the travelers one might meet on the trail. There was no other good camping place with water and grass for some distance, he knew. Unless, of course, the stranger intended to go on into the Kansa town. But no, he was dismounting and stripping saddle and bridle from the mule.

"Howdy," the man said cheerfully. "Nice night, ain't it?"

Jed grunted noncommittally.

"Which way you headed?" the other asked.

"East."

The stranger now studied Jed at some length.

"You a trapper, huh?"

Somehow this was a most irritating individual, though Jed could not have said why. Maybe it was that he had become used to the more private and reserved approach of Raven's people. Well, other tribes, too. Cheyenne, Osage, all resented personal intrusion from a stranger.

"I've trapped some," he said tightly.

"Yeh. Say, I seen you before! You're a squaw man, ain't you?"

This was becoming more and more irritating. He did not remember having met the man before, but he had encountered many through the years. This was certainly one he would have tried to forget.

"My wife," he said as calmly as he could, "is Pawnee."

"Yeh," the stranger answered with a leer. "I heard about them Pawnee women. Purty good in bed, huh?"

Jed's distaste rose to a near-boiling point. There was a moment when he was actually tempted to cut the man's throat and take his scalp. But no, that would create more of a threat of violence in an already violent border area. Some of his Indian friends or relatives would be blamed. Besides, the scalp probably would carry lice. And he was heading back into civilization. It would be good to behave in a more civilized manner.

"I am one of my wife's people now," he said.

"Yeh," the other chuckled. "How come you ain't shaved yer head to nothin' but that scalp lock?"

There *was* a reason. Raven had discouraged it. She had always felt a certain erotic pleasure in his long, loose hair, as it had been when they met. He tied it back part of the time, as it was now. But there was no way that he would explain such a reason to a lecher such as this. He drew his belt knife and ran a thumb along its keen edge.

"Friend," he said tightly, "I cannot keep you from camping where you like. But I want my sleep, and if you camp here, it will be without further talk. I need to add to my collection of scalps anyway."

He lay back on his blanket, knife still in hand, and openly watched the stranger.

"I . . ." the man began, and then fell silent. In a little while he turned again. "But . . ."

Then his eyes met the steely stare of the buckskin-clad figure. He turned back to begin throwing together his few belongings, which he tossed on the mule before he mounted.

"Damn squaw man!" he muttered as he jerked the mule's head around and kicked its ribs.

Jed built up the fire, his anger cooling. Would it be like this as he associated with whites?

On the off chance that this scavenger might have the nerve to try to harm him, Jed left the fire, retreated to a spot overlooking the campsite, and caught and picketed his horse near where he spread his bed. The animal would wake him if anyone approached.

But he saw no more of the stranger.

2

When he approached the settlements around the junction of the rivers, Jed had a hard time orienting himself. The familiar landmarks that he remembered from previous visits here were obscured by the expansion. There were so many people everywhere. Teamsters, Indians, tradesmen, carpenters putting up frame structures, smiths shoeing horses and mules for the trail.

He paused to watch a couple of men who were shoeing oxen. Since an ox cannot stand on three feet like a horse to allow shoes to be fitted, they had rigged a winch. The animal was led under a frame of logs, and a canvas sling placed under its belly. A winch lifted the entire animal off the ground, and each foot was available to the farrier. He was nailing an iron half-shoe on each toe of the cloven hoof.

Jed moved on, past Independence and Blue Springs on the now well-beaten trail. He hardly recognized those towns, which had mushroomed in population. He stopped a few days later at a town he did not recognize at all. It had not been there before, and he asked its name.

"Booneville!" snapped the man he had asked.

The man's bloodshot eyes swept over Jed's buckskins with a superior air.

"Ain't you ever seen a town before?" he asked as he moved on down the street, laughing. It was not really a question, but a joke, and a poor one, Jed thought.

But *Booneville?* He did not remember such a town. At about this point, there had been a town on the *north* side of the river, hadn't there? Then he remembered. He had heard about it several years ago. The town of Franklin had simply slid off into the river. Survivors had built a new town, farther from the bank, but it was now overshadowed by this new settlement south of the river.

Booneville. The name sent a pang of nostalgia through him. It seemed a world away and ages ago that he had encountered Daniel Boone in this area. Jed had been an inexperienced greenhorn and Boone had helped him. But Boone was gone now.

His heart was heavy as he moved on toward Columbia. It was larger now, no longer a sleepy town on the frontier. On to St. Louis.

That town, too, had grown. Riverboats and barges plied the channel, and there was all the hustle and bustle of a city. And the smell . . .

Now Jed had some decisions to make. Should he board his horse at a livery here and travel by stage to Baltimore? After much thought, he decided against it. Though he carried money, saved from the past few years of trapping, he was uneasy about how far it would go. The horse's feed at the livery would be an ongoing expense, and he did not know how long he might be gone.

His other decision was perhaps more complicated. He was beginning to notice more attention to his dress and his long hair by the civilized gentry of the towns. The interest had increased steadily as he traveled farther from the frontier. There were not many men in buckskins here. He was also carrying a large-bore plains rifle, which helped to label him somewhat. Many of the men here dressed like landed gentry, in waistcoats and tall hats. From here on, he would be traveling in progressively more civilized areas. Should he dress as the men here did?

He decided against that, too. *Who am I?* he thought. Not a pompous townsman, but a man of the prairies. He doubted that Daniel Boone, his mentor, had ever changed clothes just to look like somebody else.

He boarded the ferry with his horse, almost defiantly, ready to meet any challenge, but none came. There were a few curious glances at his attire, but he ignored them and studied the current of the broad Mississippi.

Once across, he hit the road toward the east. The last time, traveling the other direction, he had been on foot. He smiled as he thought of his Indian name, Long Walker. It was better to have a horse this time.

Illinois, Indiana, Kentucky . . . it was easier with the horse, but even so it was midsummer before he reached Baltimore. He had noticed as he traveled that the farther east he went, the less change there seemed to be. The eastern cities looked much the same.

By the same token, a frontiersman in greasy buckskins attracted more notice. By now, however, he did not even care. He actually was enjoying the reaction to his unusual garb, and even flaunted it a little.

There was another moment of indecision when he considered stopping to buy some more genteel clothes before meeting with his father. He shoved the idea aside. *I am what I am,* he thought stubbornly. *What they think is their problem.*

Even so, his heart beat faster as he rode up the curving drive, in Baltimore, stepped down, and tied his horse to the hitching post. A young Negro servant girl opened the door to his knock and gasped in alarm, staring at him, speechless.

"What is it, Jessie?" asked a woman's voice from inside.

He heard footsteps on the hardwood floor, and the door swung wider.

"Hello, Phoebe," he said, removing his fur cap.

She had not changed much. A little heavier, maybe, but still pretty. There was a question in her eyes, and a bit of distaste in her expression.

"Do I know . . . *Jed?*" she blurted.

Then, before the astonished eyes of the servant girl, she flew into his arms.

"You came back!" she whispered, actively pressing her still shapely body against him.

Jed found that he was aroused in spite of himself. He had not known what to expect when they met again. He had firmly rejected her illicit advances before. In fact, he had always recalled that incident with revulsion, the night she had crept into his bed. He wondered how much she had strayed from the home pasture in the intervening years, and how much his father knew of her behavior.

"We thought you were dead," Phoebe was saying, as if there were no underlying thoughts. "Your father tried to trace you after you left Princeton, but you could not be found. My gracious, Jed, you smell like a dirty fireplace. Where have you been? But come on in."

He stepped inside. The rooms were not as big as he remembered.

"A lot of places, Phoebe. Missouri, Kansas Territory. But how is my father? And my sister?"

"Oh, my . . . aren't there Indians there? But your father is well. He suffers from gout. He is at home today with it, in fact. And Sarah is married, has a family of her own."

This struck him hard. He still thought of his sister as a gangly teenager, but it had been a long time.

"Whom did she marry?"

"Peter Van Landingham. Oh, Peter wasn't here yet when you left, was he? A young lawyer from Harvard . . ."

As she talked, she led the way toward the judge's library, and swung back the wide doors.

"Look who I found!" she announced.

Judge Sterling sat by a crackling fireplace, his left foot wrapped heavily and elevated on a hassock. He held a book, and his spectacles perched on his nose. He glanced up and peered over the glasses. Jed saw that the snows of the intervening winters now sifted against the dark of his hair, a bit more over the temples. It enhanced the distinguished look that had always symbolized the dignity of his father's position.

"Who . . . Jed? Come in, boy! Where have you been? We thought you were dead!"

The judge started to rise, then thought better of it and sank back, wincing just a little with the pain in his foot.

"Damnable ailment! Doctor wants me to give up wine, cheeses, everything good. But sit down, boy. What in heaven's name possessed you to leave? To the frontier, apparently. God, your clothes stink! Phoebe, have the girl get him a bath and some clothes!"

Jed felt his resentment rising. He was not accustomed to being called "boy." He was respected among Raven's people for his mature wisdom, and was even called "Uncle," a term of respect for an elder, by some of the younger men of his acquaintance. Now he had been challenged, not once but twice, about the smell of his buckskins. The whole attitude rankled him. Even new buckskins, tanned with animal brains and smoked in the curing, smelled of the wild and of lodge fires, of sage, and far horizons. They continued to accumulate the scent of a hundred campfires and broiling hump ribs of buffalo or steaks of elk and antelope. He had always rather enjoyed the aroma, though it was not something about which one thought constantly. And one's nose does become accustomed to familiar scents, and does not notice.

He had noted the smells of the towns, and more especially the larger cities as he traveled. Sewage, rotting garbage, a livery with poor maintenance and piles of manure . . . he had forgotten these.

Now, in the warmth of his father's study, he found that he could very powerfully recall the familiar scent of leather-bound books and chairs, and the tobacco of his father's pipe. On top of this, the delicate sweetness of Phoebe's perfume. The sense of smell, he now realized, is more powerful in the stirring of old memories than any other of the senses.

Back to the present . . . "I'll take that bath," he agreed. "Maybe a shirt and trousers if you think they'll fit."

"You can have your old room," Phoebe cooed, looking him directly in the eyes. That was where she had attempted to seduce him before.

She picked up a little silver bell from the desk and shook it. The still-startled house servant appeared, and Phoebe began proclaiming instructions about the room, the bath, and dinner.

"And send Samuel to Miss Sarah's house. Tell her that her brother has returned," she finished.

Dinner was a strange experience. He had arrived shortly after midday, and servants scurried to prepare a repast to welcome home the wanderer. The Van Landinghams and their two young children joined them as the dinner hour approached.

Jed was uncomfortable in a white linen shirt and somewhat oversize trousers of his father's. He had shaved, but his hair was still long, tied at the nape of his neck. He tried on a pair of his father's boots, but they were far too small. He was still wearing his plains moccasins with their rawhide soles.

Sarah accepted him fairly well, although slowly. She had changed a lot, but so had he. And his sister had never really taken to the outdoor games when they were children, as much as he would have liked.

Her husband, Peter, was a bit haughty and self-impressed. He seemed to be constantly peering down his nose at everyone in the room, and gave curt orders to the servants. That was startling, because it was completely inappropriate to order servants who worked for someone else. Jed was surprised that his father would tolerate it, but he seemed to have a great admiration for the young lawyer, an admiration that Jed found difficult to share. Besides, there was something he could not quite define, a sidelong glance, a flirtatious smile between Phoebe and Van Landingham. Was there something there, an illicit understanding? He knew Phoebe all too well.

"So, you have actually been living among the savages?" Peter inquired in a patronizing tone.

"To an extent," Jed admitted in much the same way. He found it easy, in these surroundings, to revert to the stilted formal conversational style to which he had been exposed as a student. This conversation could be quite interesting.

"It must have been very trying, to live in such conditions," Peter offered sympathetically.

"Sometimes," Jed agreed. "But to a degree, are we not all savage in some respects?"

His brother-in-law ignored the invitation to a philosophical discussion.

"Is it true that they are cannibals?" he asked.

"Some are," Jed agreed. "Mostly farther south, in Tejas. I myself have eaten very little human flesh."

He had intended it as a joke, but it was not taken as such.

"Jed!" barked his father. "There are women and children present, and we are at table, for heaven's sake!"

Jed mumbled an apology. This was going to be a long evening.

3

After they had eaten, the three men retired to the library. Judge Sterling offered the younger men cigars and brandy.

Jed noted that here was a ritual that his wife's people would have understood. A social "smoke" by the men, while the women socialized elsewhere, discussing their own problems. Cheyenne, Comanche, Osage—all had similar customs of the informal gathering to smoke. He had not thought of it before, but it now interested him that in each case, a part of the ritual was tobacco, incense for the spirits. He doubted that these men would understand the spirit connection.

The room filled with heavy blue smoke. He would have preferred to smoke his pipe, with some of his own mixture of tobacco, sumac, a little catnip, and just a pinch of the leaves of cedar. But as a guest in the culture of Raven's people, he would have smoked the host's tobacco, and he did so now, scarcely thinking about it.

It did occur to him that after the first pipeful he would have offered a refill from his own pouch. But they were not sharing a pipe. The simile that he was running through his head seemed to break down when applied to big black cigars. Surely there must be a point at which the spirits are no longer pleased but offended by the overwhelming clouds of tobacco smoke. At least, he thought so.

They sipped brandy, making small talk about the weather and politics and the economy. Jed had become rather amused at the conversational antics of his brother-in-law. Van Landingham was obviously longing to ask questions about the great western frontier. Yet the man just as obviously looked down on a long-haired frontiersman as one of somewhat lower status. Jed amused himself for a little while by assuming an illiterate frontier drawl. Then, when least expected, he would toss in a phrase in cultured French, or quote a bit of Shakespeare. He would not let the pompous Harvard lawyer forget his Princeton education.

As they talked, it became apparent that Peter Van Landingham was a much more complex individual than Jed had thought at first. Some of his ideas and questions showed a great deal of thought and understanding. Against his initial judgment, he found that in some ways the man's thinking was quite sound. He felt quite uncomfortable to find himself agreeing with someone whom he had expected to dislike completely.

To further complicate his thinking, his father the judge seemed to have a great deal of respect for young Peter's ideas. Jed was most nearly at ease when the other two talked and he was able to listen. It soon became apparent that both were interested in the expansion of the United States into the frontier. Two main topics emerged relating to that, politics and investment.

Van Landingham seemed well versed in the political arena, and had obviously been following the proceedings of the Congress quite closely.

"It's only a matter of time," he observed, "until more states are added west of the Mississippi. Think of the investment possibilities, Judge. Look at the international trade with Mexico. Santa Fe Trail, don't they call it?"

He turned to Jed, only slightly condescending. Jed nodded.

"You've been there?" Peter continued.

"Of course. Several times."

"But isn't the fur trade over?" asked the judge.

"That's true," Jed answered, a little surprised that the collapse of the beaver market would be known to his father. "But the Santa Fe trade is still growing. Mexico needs a source for not only manufactured goods but staples. Flour, coffee, tea."

"Yes, as I said," Peter went on. "But tell us, Jed. Is there not a lot of danger from the Indians?"

It was at this point that the understanding of these men began to appear flawed, Jed saw.

"Well, there have been some incidents, yes. Mostly Comanches resent the wagon trains across their hunting grounds."

"But hasn't that been settled? Haven't the Indians ceded certain areas?"

Jed sighed. It would be hard to explain to someone like Peter Van Landingham.

"Look at it this way, Peter," he began. "We're talking about dozens of different tribes and nations, with different customs and languages. Some are as different as French and Chinese. You can't treat them all alike. Some live in towns, some move around, cover several hundred miles in a season."

"So I had understood. But the language problem . . . how do they communicate?"

"Hand signs. You can talk to anyone with signs."

"Ah, yes. I had heard of that. And it really works? *You* use it?"

"Of course."

"But then you lived with the savages, did you not?"

His manner became a bit more patronizing. Jed's temper began to rise.

"I did, I do, live among my wife's people. I had not thought of them as savages, exactly."

"You have a *wife*?" his father blurted.

"Yes, Father, and two children. Had you thought me celibate?"

The subject had not come up, he now realized. This angered him further. His entire family was so self-centered, so wrapped up in their own affairs, that they had not even wondered.

"I am a man of the Pawnee nation," he continued. "My name is known also among Osage, Cheyenne, Kansa, and a few Comanche. I am called Long Walker."

There was a stunned silence. Oddly, it was Van Landingham who spoke first.

"Pawnee? Is that not the Indian Republic?"

Jed was surprised. His brother-in-law must know a little more about the frontier than it appeared.

"It has been called that," he admitted. "Not quite accurately."

Van Landingham, with his political interests, now seemed fascinated.

"How different?" he asked.

"Well, the Big Council makes decisions affecting the nation. But any one band has veto power."

"Ah! How many bands?"

"Four. Several towns."

"And where is yours?"

"Near the river the whites call the Republican, after the so-called Indian Republic. My wife's people have a more descriptive name for it."

"How is that?"

"Loosely translated, 'Dung River.' The migrating buffalo foul it badly sometimes."

The other men chuckled.

"But," protested Peter, "did not the Pawnees cede the area south of the Platte to the government?"

"Something of the sort. You would have to be there to understand. The whole area is designated 'Indian Territory,' clear to the mountains in the west."

"So I have heard. But are there not treaties? Passage on the Santa Fe Trail?"

Van Landingham apparently had more knowledge than it had appeared about the status of things in the Indian Territory.

"That is true. But Peter, the government has moved many native tribes and nations from the East into this region. This crowds those already there farther west. The tribes *there* resent the intrusion from their neighbors, and so on."

"I see. But what is the future of the area?"

"What do you mean?"

Even as he spoke, Jed realized that he had refused so far to think of the future of the territory. He did not want to see the questionable progress of civilization. He would have much preferred to hunt and trap as Boone had done, as he had done himself when he first came west. Big skies, wide prairie, shining mountains . . . shining times.

"What will happen when statehood comes?" Peter asked.

"Statehood?"

"Certainly. Look, Jed, it will come. There's only one state west of the Mississippi now, Missouri. Well, part of Louisiana, of course. But there will be more. The territory to the south of Missouri is applying for statehood now. Arkansas, they call it."

Jed was familiar with the name. In the tongue of the Kansa Indians, *ar,* below or "downstream from" the Kansas. The river along which the Santa Fe Trail followed bore the name. It had occurred to him that it was odd to call a territory below *most* of that river "Arkansas." The river had flowed some six hundred miles before it reached that land of wooded hills. The river was still an international boundary with Mexico. Well, the area was certainly "downstream."

He noticed, however, that Van Landingham used a strange pronunciation. He knew that the area along the Mississippi had been French, and that the French language traditionally drops some of the final consonant sounds of a word. Thus Peter was pronouncing the name of the river or the proposed state with a soft ending: "Ar-kansah," rather than "Arkansas." Actually it sounded almost like "Arkansaw," which Jed found rather amusing.

"What is your interest in the area?" Jed asked.

"None, really. Parts of the West will be good for investment. Some of the rivers are navigable, I suppose. But essentially, I was thinking of politics."

"How so, Peter?" asked the judge.

"Well, sir, how will it be decided whether new states are to be admitted as slave states or free?"

Jed had not even considered the admission to the Union of states in the West. Maybe he had refused to consider such encroachment of civilization. And whether slave or free had no meaning for him. Some states were slave, others not. The proposed "Arkansas," being southern in location, would probably permit slaves. The native tribes in Kansas Territory usually had slaves, and so did some whites. Missouri, already a state, had many slave owners.

Now Van Landingham was pushing on, answering his own question.

"You are aware, of course," he said, with perhaps some sarcastic superiority, "that there is a division at the thirty-sixth degree of latitude? North of that line is to be free-soil."

"Where does the line fall?" asked Jed. He was impatient with such artificial demarcations. There had been many such technicalities to interfere with his trips into Mexico and Tejas.

"Between the state of Missouri and the Arkansas Territory. Nothing would be changed by the admission of Arkansas as a state."

"But . . . Missouri is north of that line, and has many slaves," Jed puzzled.

"True, by special compromise," the other admitted. "But Missouri had to amend her constitution to be accepted. And even a child born of slave parents in Missouri is a free-born Nigra."

Judge Sterling entered the conversation. "Wasn't there something about the state of Missouri denying free Negroes the right to enter the state?" he asked.

"That's true," Van Landingham agreed. "I doubt they can make it stick. It denies the right of a child of slave parents to be born."

"In Missouri, at least," the judge chuckled. "But gentlemen, I see a bigger problem here than the question of slave and free-soil." He became quite serious. "The last four or five states to be admitted to the Union have been northern. This gives a majority of voting power to the industrial bloc, as opposed to the planters of the South. This is now true in both House and Senate, because of population density.

"Now, look at the line Peter mentioned. Thirty-six thirty, to be precise, dividing North from South on the basis of slave or free-soil tendency. Do you notice anything else about it?"

Both men waited, and the judge continued.

"Look at any potential new states!" He leaned forward and squinted in a conspiratorial manner. "Let's look at a map!" He sat back and reached for a rolled paper on his big desk. "Here." He unrolled it and weighted the corners with an inkwell and a container of blotting sand.

"Now, look . . . here is the latitude thirty-six line. Nearly all of the Louisiana Purchase is to the north of it. Most of the area south of it belongs to Mexico."

"But Tejas—" Jed began, interrupted by his father.

"I know, Jed, they're talking independence, but that's between them and Mexico, and who knows what will happen? They may even form their own state *outside* the Union, if they succeed in splitting away, which looks doubtful to me. Isn't the population pretty thin there?"

"Yes, sir, I would think so. But go on."

"Oh . . . well, that was my point. Each new state admitted, after Arkansas, will necessarily be a free-soil state."

"But you seemed to say it is not a question of slave or free, sir," Peter said.

"True. Not slavery, but *power*. With each new state admitted now, the power of the central government is increased, that of the individual states *weakened*. I doubt that this was the intention of the founding fathers, who considered each state a sovereign nation."

There was silence for a little while, as the two younger men digested this idea.

"There's room for debate," said Van Landingham finally. "It depends on the intent of the Constitution."

"Agreed!" said the judge. "But gentlemen, I believe that this interpretation is the greatest threat that our young nation has faced thus far."

There was a sadness in his tone, and he looked old and tired.

"But sir," protested Peter, "we have, as a nation, defeated Britain twice. We are a rising world power."

"That is true," agreed the judge. "But those threats were from outside. This greater threat is from within."

4

The evening had not been bad at all, Jed thought as he prepared to retire. The dinner was good, although not to compare with broiled hump ribs over a fire of buffalo chips. It was odd, how familiar foods of his childhood now seemed foreign and strange. Well, he had told himself on many occasions where offered strange foods, when in Rome, do as the Romans do. He smiled at the manner in which he had come full circle.

The discussion with his father and brother-in-law had been interesting. He was surprised at their knowledge of the frontier. Not a practical knowledge, but an understanding of the political situation. He had learned useful things.

While he now felt closer to his father, his sister seemed like a stranger. Sarah was completely absorbed in her children and the duties of household management. Jed could hardly see in her the sister with whom he had played in the woods, and rescued from dragons and savages. Her entire life seemed centered on her children and her husband.

Peter Van Landingham was an enigma. His first impression had been that here was a spoiled, conceited, overly educated rich man's son. Then, talking over cigars and brandy, he had realized that Peter had some insight and thoughtful wisdom. He almost began to like the man. Jed had long since learned that it is possible to like and even admire someone, and still detest some of the things they do.

He was relatively certain that there was something in the nature of an illicit romance between Peter and Phoebe. The sidelong glance, the seemingly accidental touch. Jed felt some sadness for his sister, but she must know. It was something that civilized women often tolerated. He knew that many even accepted, as one of life's little disappointments, a philandering husband. Peter was a good provider, kind to the children. Sarah must have arrived at an acceptance, if not actual peace of mind.

But my God, he thought, *Phoebe is his mother-in-law!* Not biologically, of course, being Sarah's stepmother. There was only a few years' difference in their ages. No actual incestuous relationship, although it would never be tolerated in any of the tribes whose ways he had known. And Peter considered *them* savages. Jed smiled as he undressed and prepared for bed. It was a joke that few people whom he knew could understand.

This was the first time that he could remember, when he and his father had actually sat down and talked, man to man. The judge had never got along well with children, Jed realized only now. His was a world of adults, of laws and courts. It was apparent that the judge was not close to his grandchildren at all. A pat on the head, an admonition about behavior. It was as if Jed were watching his father's reaction to his own children. He remembered that distinctly. It was odd that now, on an adult level, they had communicated quite well. This had been the first time that the judge had ever really listened to his son.

Jed finished undressing, blew out his candle, and sank into the luxurious softness of the feather bed, wondering whether he could sleep. His bed was usually much harder, either on the trail or in the earth lodge among Raven's people. His thoughts turned to her and to the children for a little while. Here, seeing his sister and her children, he missed his own. Among the Pawnees, it would have been his responsibility to instruct Sarah's son. An odd thought, which made him more homesick for his own family far away.

It was late summer. The People would be sleeping outside, mostly. He thought of the gentle south wind of the prairie at this season of daytime heat and cooler nights. By comparison, this room seemed hot and stuffy. By morning, the prairie's chill would be cool enough to necessitate a blanket, and the warmth of Raven's body would feel good. Here, as he remembered, there was little relief from the heavy heat of summer.

A board in the hall's floor creaked softly, and his door opened and closed quietly on well-oiled hinges. A shadowy figure glided to the bed. If he had been more nearly asleep, his reaction would have been one of self-defense. As it was, however, he was still wide awake, and was certain that this was a different sort of threat. He could smell the flowery fragrance of Phoebe's perfume as she lay down beside him.

"You came back," she whispered.

Jed was older and more worldly-wise now than at their last encounter. He had had some experience. There had been many times in his life when he would have welcomed this blatant seductress into his bed. Now he seriously considered it. It would be so easy to go along with her advances, and the temptation was great. She drew a bare leg oh so slowly across his thigh. Here was a desirable, attractive woman who was obviously ready and eager. He had been a long time on the trail, without female companionship, and his own wife was far away. *Months* away. Why not . . .

"I have always thought of you, Jed," she whispered. "I hoped you would come back."

It was flattering, of course. He was aroused, but could not help but wonder. Did she whisper the same sweet nothings to Peter Van Landingham? Or, for that matter, to others? A woman as predatory as this must have experience with many men, before and since she had married his widowed father. He wondered if his father even suspected. And what if the judge happened to wonder about the whereabouts of his wife tonight, and came searching to find the scene?

At such a thought, Jed's arousal faded somewhat. But Phoebe's breathing was heavy and quick, causing him to waver again. She kissed him full on the mouth, tongue flickering like that of a snake. Gently he pushed her away.

"No, Phoebe, it can't be," he said, more firmly than he really felt.

"Yes . . ." she breathed in his ear. "It must."

"Why?" he stammered.

"I need you. . . . want you . . ."

"No!"

"I will scream, and cry rape!"

He remembered now, she had threatened that before, so long ago.

"You dragged me in here, and I resisted as long as I could, but finally screamed in desperation. Your father would believe me, not you. Now come to me. . . ."

She rolled toward him, her body expertly stimulating his.

"Wait," he whispered desperately. "Something you do not know."

"Tell me after." She kissed him again.

"No, now!" He pushed her away. "Phoebe, I would like nothing better," he blurted, not entirely untruthfully. "But I . . . I have the . . . the disease. Will you take the risk?"

There was dead silence, and he wondered if his lie was a mistake. From what he knew of this woman, she *might* take such a risk. If so, he had virtually committed himself to her wanton escapade. But she now pushed him away and rolled to the side of the bed, where she sat up. He could see her dimly in the moonlight from the window. There was a tightness in her whisper, not from passion now, but from anger.

"Jed, how could you do this to me?"

He started to protest that he had done nothing to her, now or ever, but she hurried on.

"Yech! To bring such a loathsome thing into my home. Yech! You have the morals of a tomcat!"

Jed almost laughed aloud. She was accusing *him* of immorality. He wisely refrained from voicing a thought that flitted through his mind. *A bitch in heat, accusing a tomcat of promiscuous behavior!*

"I'm sorry," he said, stifling a chuckle. "Maybe later . . ."

With that last twist, he was afraid he might be overplaying his hand. But not so. He had guessed correctly.

"Yech!" she said through clenched teeth. "You can never be sure you are cured of such vile things!"

He did not ask her how she knew.

Phoebe rose and glided silently out of the room. Jed thought that in all probability, he would not have to be concerned again about her unwanted advances.

.   .   .

He stayed a few more days. Phoebe was polite and coolly cordial, but no more. She carefully avoided his touch. His father seemed not to notice anything unusual, which was reassuring.

But Jed was restless. At home on the prairie, it would soon be the Moon of Ripening. Next, the Moon of Falling Leaves. He must hurry to reach Raven and home before the Moon of Long Nights and the Moon of Snows.

It had been a good thing, this visit. He felt that he under- stood his father better than ever before. He felt some sorrow for the judge. An unscrupulous vixen had taken advantage of a lonely man in his bereavement. Even so, there were some good things. His father was not alone. Phoebe was apparently a good manager, and the judge could take pride in her appearance and her social graces. Jed hoped that his father would never discover her pro- miscuity.

Likewise, his sister had a stable marriage and two healthy chil- dren. Sarah would be well taken care of.

These observations lifted a great feeling of guilt from his shoul- ders. He had not realized it before, but his leaving must have troubled him greatly. Much of the time, he had been too busy with simple survival to realize it. Now he could put any questions to rest, and get on with his life.

He announced the day of his leaving, and began his simple preparations. He needed a few supplies, an extra blanket, because it could be quite cold before he reached the shelter of the big earth lodge overlooking the river.

He checked his horse carefully, and had the animal shod at the farrier's next to the livery. He might have to remove the shoes later, but they would be of help on the cobbles and gravel of the civilized roads and streets during the first leg of the journey.

On the morning of his departure, Phoebe managed to draw him aside for a moment. She had a strange expression on her face, and this time she took his hand.

"I just figured it out," she told him. "You lied to me!"

"I . . . but . . ." he stammered, "about what?"

She took his arm, and pressed close to him.

"You know perfectly well," she smiled warmly. "A skillful move, Jed. But I'll not take no again. Next time . . . you'll not regret it."

He doubted that there would be a next time. The trip would

have consumed an entire season, by the time he reached home. He would most likely not try it again.

Ready to leave, he kissed his sister, shook Peter's hand and that of his father.

"Don't I get a hug?" Phoebe asked coquettishly, spreading wide her arms.

The judge chuckled at the embrace, little realizing its significance.

"Come back to me," she whispered in his ear. "I love you."

Like a pig loves to find an apple, he thought. He hoped none of the others noticed how Phoebe thrust her pelvis against his.

"Sure," he murmured.

He swung to the saddle, waved, and turned away. Probably the last time he'd see any of them. Meanwhile, there was a lot of ground to cover before winter. In his calculations of the time he would have before winter's freeze, he had overlooked one fact. The final portion of his journey would take place during the month called November by the whites. There was a certain logic in the designation by the natives for the same month. For them, it was the Moon of Madness.

5

utumn had always been one of Jed's favorite times of the year, and he enjoyed it as he traveled. There were long, warm days, cool nights, the profusion of fall-blooming flowers. There was a bluish haze in the distance when he happened to be in a place where he could see a far horizon.

That was something he had not anticipated. He missed the wide sky and the distant vistas of the grassland. In the very area where he had grown up, the cities, the rolling wooded hills seemed to close in on him and he felt trapped. He longed for open prairie and the whispering song of the wind in tall autumn grasses.

Most nights he camped on the road. If the weather was threatening, he sometimes stopped at an inn, where he could have shelter for himself and his horse. Once, even, he slept with the horse in a livery stall. He did not trust a couple of shifty-eyed characters who seemed very interested in looking at the better horses stabled there. His horse wakened him once in the small hours, speaking softly in a muffled snort that may have been one of surprise or alarm. Jed rose, then crouched in a corner, knife in hand, but there was no further activity. The horse resumed eating hay from the rack. Quite possibly a sneak horse thief had thought better of an original plan. A tall frontiersman in well-used buckskins would not be considered an easy mark.

He saw the same two lingerers as he saddled to depart in the morning. They were watching him, but would not meet his eyes when he looked their way. Jed made a big show of checking his weapons, even testing the sharpness of his belt knife's edge with his thumb. He also lifted the hammer of his rifle and carefully felt the edge of the flint. Then he lifted the frizzen, dumped out the priming powder and replaced it with fresh priming from the horn at his waist. That would not have been necessary, but he knew that the two rogues were watching, and he wanted to impress them.

After he had warmed it up, Jed let the horse lope for a little while, to put some distance between him and the potential thieves. He considered setting up an ambush in case they tried to follow, but rejected the idea. In the territory farther west such a move would be understood, but here, in a relatively civilized area, it might be frowned upon. Besides, he doubted that the two scoundrels had horses that would be able to match the travel speed of his own without really pushing. Still, he kept an eye on the back trail and took extra precautions for a night or two. He did not see them again.

In St. Louis, he decided to stop by the J. & S. Hawken gun shop. He had some questions about a new firing system he had seen.

The Hawken brothers' establishment was easy to find by the sign, a huge effigy of a rifle, which hung out over the sidewalk. At "the sign of the big gun," a man had told him in answer to his inquiry.

"Mr. Hawken?" Jed inquired as he stepped up to the long counter in the front of the building.

The grizzled gunsmith behind the counter smiled. "One of 'em, Jake. Sam's in the back. Which one ye want?"

"Either, I guess. I'm Jed Sterling. Called Long Walker by some."

"Haven't I heard of you? Were you with Ashley?"

"No. I've trapped the Kaw and the Arkansas, mostly. Traded with Franklin and the Bents."

"Sure. Santa Fe Trail?"

"A few times."

"Well . . . what can we do for you?"

Jed laid his rifle on the counter, which was padded with carpet to protect the finish on fine weapons.

"I'd like to ask about the new caplocks. I've seen a couple, never used one."

"I see. That's a fine piece you've got there. Kentucky?" Jake Hawken ran his hands lovingly over the well-worn stock. "Who made it?"

"Fellow name of Ephriam Doty. He gave me good advice on what I'd need."

"Heard of Doty, never met him. Worked on some of his guns, though. A good workman."

"It has served me well. But what about the caplocks?"

Hawken put the gun he'd been wiping back in the rack behind him, and lifted down another. He laid it on the counter with the lock and hammer facing up.

"Now," he began, "ye see right off there's no flint and no priming pan, no frizzen. Your spark comes from one of these."

He opened a small round tin box and rolled some shiny copper caps out on the carpet of the countertop.

"Inside, there is a tiny bit of fulminate. When you hit it, the fulminate explodes and shoots fire down into the powder charge."

"That's all?"

"That's it! The cap fits over this little nipple here," he pointed. "You don't have to carry flints, no separate priming charge."

"So far, so good," Jed agreed. "But are they sure-fire?"

"Much more so than a flint," Hawken assured him. "Of course, you keep 'em in just this little tin. Oh, yes, you'll notice faster ignition. No pause between the primer and the main charge, so you'll shoot better. And any trader's goin' to have caps now."

"Yes, I know. I've talked to some who use them, too. But would it be practical to change my own rifle over to caplock?"

"Sure! We could put a new lock on it. But I'd suggest just change the hammer, take off the frizzen, which ain't needed. Then drill out the touch hole and thread it for a drum and nipple, here." He pointed.

"How long would this take?"

"No time a-tall. I can do 'er this afternoon. Pick it up later?"

Jed nodded. "I'll go stable my horse, find a place to stay. Why don't I pick it up on the way out of town tomorrow? I'll need some caps and some lead, too, and a can of powder. You have 'em, I guess?"

"You bet. Be ready for you first thing in the morning."

Jed tested his converted rifle at a range near the Hawken brothers' shop, as was the custom. He was pleased. The ignition was indeed faster and more reliable, and reloading much less complicated. The feel and balance were unchanged, but Jed felt that over all, accuracy would be improved. The puff of smoke from the priming powder, so disconcerting to a beginning shooter, was completely absent now.

He traveled on, as the autumn weather progressed. From lazy, warm Second Summer, there came a nip in the air and a rime of frost on dry grasses in the chill mornings. By the time he reached Booneville, the bright leaves were falling. Near Blue Springs he saw long lines of wild geese honking their way high overhead. It was in the same area that he began to notice signs of the Moon of Madness.

At this season days become noticeably shorter, and a restlessness settles over all living creatures. An ancient migration instinct urges birds to travel south to warmer climates. Not all birds—some species stay behind, and prepare for winter in different ways. A change of food selection, a complete change of plumage to a different color. Why? *It is their way,* Raven said.

For those caught by the migration urge but unable to fly strongly enough to go south, it produces a crisis. Grouse, quail, other upland birds, take on an erratic behavior in the Crazy Moon. They fly blindly, colliding with the newly bared branches of trees in the thickets.

Buffalo migrate, too, following the green of prairie grasses ahead of the frost line, south in autumn, back north in spring, with the Moon of Awakening.

Bears prepare to sleep, growing fat on the abundance of the fall harvest of acorns, nuts, and the animals on which bears prey. Those, in turn, have fattened for the lean moons ahead.

For deer, it is the rutting season. Bucks with their new antlers are feeling the powerful urge, polishing away the velvet wrapping and preparing for combat. Through spring and summer they have been shy and secretive, having lost their traditional weapons. Now, strength renewed and with new and better armament, they are prepared to challenge in combat. The strongest survive to win the favors of the watching does and in this way improve the breed. They challenge not only other bucks but sometimes other species, too, including man.

More than once, a lone individual in an unusual location has been attacked by a deranged buck in the Moon of Madness.

The bugling challenge of a bull elk echoes across the land. He, too, feels the restlessness of the season, and his trumpet call raises the hackles on the neck of the hunter.

All are restless, anxious as each day becomes shorter than the one before. Sun's warmth, which seemed oppressive not so long ago, barely warms the scene before sinking again below earth's rim. Its fire is dying, or seems to be. In the dim racial memory of humankind looms the age-old question of our heritage, which all are afraid to voice: *This time, will Sun's fire really go out?*

The question remains unasked, because it is too dreadful a possibility to consider. But it is there. A thousand different races through the ages have met it with rituals and celebrations. There have been dances and fires, sacrifices, drummings and songs and prayers of supplication to whatever gods might have influence, to bring back the Sun. All have been successful, at least so far. But who knows . . . maybe this time . . .

It may be the mere subconscious existence of this possibility that brings about the frustration and uneasiness which results in the Moon of Madness. Modern physicians who deal with the minds of people know that at this season there is more mental illness and more physical illness related to stress. There are complicated explanations, but after all, it is the Moon of Madness. There will be strange, illogical behavior, as people break under the strain of trying to understand: *The Sun is dying.*

Closely akin to this restless panic and illogical behavior of the wild creatures is the madness of man at such a season. Jed saw it as he traveled. Quarrels, argument, infidelity. Not that of the treacherous Phoebe, of course. Such women are always in season. But normally stable people were reacting to the season in strange ways.

Near Independence, Jed had heard the tale of a man who had suddenly bludgeoned his three children as they slept, then his wife, and finally blew his own brains out with an old fowling piece.

"He was quiet," said a puzzled man who lived on the next farm. "A good neighbor, but . . . Gawd, I never expected somethin' like this."

It was the Moon of Madness.

Jed saw it again when he reached the Indian Territory, Kansas. There was the intermixture of many different tribes, those traditionally located there and those being relocated by the federal government. Many had a traditional fall hunt in their former territory. Jed had long since realized that the ownership of land was a concept completely foreign to the American Indian. However, the idea of a right to live and hunt in a traditional region was deeply ingrained. Now, with the removal and relocation in progress, the traditional fall hunt must, in some cases, be carried out in hunting grounds traditionally hunted by others.

Add to this the overall restlessness generated by the season . . . was it a premonition that he felt as he rode, or was he himself only a victim of the uneasiness brought on by the Moon of Madness?

He touched a heel to the horse's flank and moved a little faster.

6

Jed followed the familiar trail westward toward the Pawnee town where he would rejoin Raven and the children. The road itself had changed. When he first came west, he recalled, the ancient trail had been little more than a footpath. It had probably been used for centuries by traders and other assorted travelers.

Now it had become a part of the network of trails used by the pack trains and wagons of the white man. The old road from the towns of the Kansas, or Kaws, to the Council Grove was a part of the Santa Fe Trail, still growing with international trade. In the few years since he had traveled with the pack trains of the first traders, the road had become scarred with the tracks of heavy wagons.

He passed many of them as he traveled. Some were better equipped and more experienced than others, as always. Some seemed to travel together, others as loners. It was now the growing custom to gather at the Council Grove for the final organization of the trains. That allowed for minor repairs and adjustments after the shakedown run from Independence and the Missouri River. It was also the last source of hardwood timber.

Jed left the commercial travelers there, where the trail began to bend southwest across the Flint Hills, and took a little-traveled branch to the north. There were no wagon tracks here. Only a couple of days, now. Soon he would be home, could take Raven in his arms.

There was a full moon, and he used its light to travel through most of one night.

He met travelers on the road, and several times saw hunting parties of riders in the distance. At least, he presumed them to be hunting parties. It was the time of the fall hunt, and the tribes new to the area were probably exploring the possibilities. Some, he was sure, were Kaws, who were being pushed westward these past few years. In addition, there would be the restlessness that comes with the Moon of Madness.

It was late in the day when he reached the hill that would allow him to see the smoke from the cooking fires of home. Still, it was some distance away. He might not arrive before dark.

His first hint of trouble was something that he could not have described. It was more of a *feeling* than of anything he saw or did not see. The faint smoky haze over the town site was possibly a hint. The *color* of the haze, maybe, darker than expected. Yet colors become indistinct and unreliable at a distance, so who could tell?

The big earth lodges, too, had the appearance of rounded mounds or hillocks, from a distance. Still, something, an ill-defined uneasiness swept over him. He kicked the tired horse into a lope.

There was no sign of life. He rode among the empty lodges, searching for answers, trying to piece together what might have happened. The village must have been attacked, and surely no more than a few days ago. Some of the ruined lodges still smoldered. Some had collapsed, their supporting timbers apparently burned through. The mounds had become shallow craters, still smoking from the buried coals. Even the lodges that were still intact showed the scars of fire on the timbers that formed the entrances. They would be unsafe, of course. With supporting timbers probably burned inside and still smoldering, any of these could collapse at any moment.

Even as he had this thought, there was a loud crack and an earth-jarring thump. One of the partly burned lodges had given way and fallen in. A shower of sparks rose from the central smoke hole and fluttered into the darkening sky like evil fireflies.

But where are the People? Jed's thoughts demanded. If they were killed, there should be bodies here. And, who would do such a thing anyway? It made no sense.

Then, as he thought, he realized that the Pawnees, his adopted people, were not on the best of terms with their neighbors. There were too many differences, besides the fact that the Pawnees were more aggressive than most growers. Their religion was based around the deity Morning Star rather than the Sun, like most groups in the area. That alone would not matter. Religion was one thing *not* considered a valid reason for hate or war.

But there were traditional enemies. They had been at war with the Comanches most of the time for generations, stealing children from each other to sell to yet another tribe as slaves. There was also the traditional Morning Star Ceremony, the sacrifice of a virgin to make the corn grow. The selected virgin was always from a neighboring tribe. Surely that could not be the cause of this attack. This town had not used a live bride for Morning Star for a generation. An effigy had seemed to work as well. As far as Jed knew, the only band of Pawnees still stealing maidens for the ceremony were the *Skidi,* or Wolf band, far away on the Platte.

It could be, of course, that some other tribe, such as Comanches, had lost a girl to the Wolf band. In frustration they might attack another Pawnee town, one completely uninvolved. It had happened that way to others. Whites had often attacked the nearest natives in raids to avenge a wrong by an entirely different group. But he was more inclined to blame Comanches for this atrocity.

These thoughts were racing through his head and his anger rising when he heard the sound. Almost by reflex he slid to the ground and away from his horse. He must avoid becoming a silhouette against the sky.

He heard the sound again, a soft rustle of the bushes that grew along the path to the river. It could be a deer, or an enemy. Gripping his knife, he skirted around the circle of a collapsed lodge, feeling for a moment the heat of its still-burning timbers. He crouched against the mound of a lodge that was nearly intact, and waited.

The approaching form was quiet and wary. It could easily be an animal *or* a skilled and stealthy enemy. He had just begun to realize that there was no reason for an enemy to visit a burned-out victim's town when a soft voice called.

"Walker? Long Walker?"

"Swimmer, is it you?"

The figure rose to full height and came toward him.

"Yes. My heart is heavy, my brother. . . ."

A chill gripped Jed's heart.

"Raven . . . the children?"

"Dead," said Swimmer simply.

Jed felt that his heart would pound out through his ribs. Then anger began to rise. He would have vengeance.

"Comanches?" he asked.

"No, no. Delawares!"

"*Delawares?* The newcomers?"

Swimmer nodded. "Maybe a few Kansas with them. Both are being pushed west."

"But why?"

"Who knows, Walker? Maybe vengeance for a wrong done them by somebody else. These are evil times."

Another question struck Jed. "*Your* family, Swimmer? Are they—?"

"Dead, too. I waited here for you."

Jed did not ask how Swimmer had known to expect him. Swimmer's people often sensed such things.

"I have sorrow for you, my friend," he said. "Tell me of what happened."

"Yes. Let us camp, share our grief. Then I will tell you all I know."

Swimmer's story was brief and to the point. He told it calmly, in a quiet, detached tone. It was as if all of this had happened to someone they did not know, strangers somewhere far away.

Six days ago Swimmer had been with several other men on a short hunt. Someone had seen elk along the river and a hunt would provide an interesting interlude and perhaps some fresh meat.

"No one even thought . . ." Swimmer paused, swallowed hard, and went on, his voice choking. "Walker, no one can even remember when an enemy attacked one of our towns."

"Yes, go on."

"We could not find the elk, so we went a little farther, thinking that there might be a few buffalo. Finally we turned back, and found . . . this. . . ."

He pointed toward the burned-out lodges.

"The people were gone?"

"No, no. There were dead scattered, some trapped inside burning lodges. . . . People looking for family . . ."

Swimmer seemed to be staring into the distance, seeing again the tragedy unfolding before him.

"They killed some of the young men who were standing guard, first," he rambled on. "The People ran away, down through the woods toward the river. Some turned to fight. . . . Your wife and mine were among those. . . . But they were too many."

"The children?" Jed asked.

"Dead, too. I helped bury them, Walker."

"Was there no talk of going after the attackers?"

"Yes, some, but we had so many killed or wounded, so many in mourning. Walker, they took scalps. Some, a strip clear across the top of the head, and both ears!"

Jed shuddered.

"After the People ran, they burned the lodges. Brush, piled on the lodge fire until it was big enough to burn the four posts of the center, and the rafters fell. There were some bodies inside . . . still there."

"Where are the People now? Those still living?" asked Jed.

"We buried, as well as we could," Swimmer went on. "Then we held a council. It was decided to join one of the towns of the People to the north of here."

"On the Platte?"

"Yes. They left two days ago. We had only a few horses. The Delawares took most of them. I stayed to wait for you."

"Thank you, my brother. . . ."

The two sat, staring into the fire for a long time. Jed had never felt more alone. He had now found himself detached from his father's heritage, and had longed to return to his wife's people, where he felt more at home. Now that, too, was destroyed. He wanted to stand and scream out his frustration at the starry sky overhead.

He might have done so, except that now his brother-in-law began to sing. Jed had heard the mournful, wailing dirge before, but had never had cause to feel it personally. He recognized the Song of Mourning. He began to pick up syllables, and in a few moments was pouring out his grief for his loss. Tears streamed down his cheeks as he wailed his heart out, seeking comfort in the manner of his wife's people.

It was far into the night when the two paused, hoarse from their singing. Jed looked at Swimmer, realizing that he, too, was lost and alone.

They rested a little, sleeping fitfully, and rose with the sun.

"What now?" asked Jed.

The dark look on his friend's face was almost frightening.

"What else?" Swimmer shrugged. "We kill Delawares."

7

Three men sat around the campfire, talking and smoking. There was nothing unusual about the situation. Just one of dozens of such fires that scattered small circles of light across the vast prairie each night. The season was growing late, and travel would soon slow almost to a halt for the winter. A few hunters and trappers . . .

"Who are they?" asked Jed.

"I cannot tell yet," Swimmer answered. "Let us go closer."

Jed glanced around the horizon. He saw only one other fire, a tiny pinpoint of light which was perhaps a day's travel to the west.

Swimmer dismounted and tied his horse in a thicket of dogwood along the little creek. He took a thong from his pouch and tied it around the animal's muzzle to keep it from calling out. Jed followed his example, and they slipped quietly toward the fire. Within hearing distance, they flattened to the ground to crawl forward and listen.

"Are they Delawares?" whispered Jed.

"Can't tell yet. Listen."

They listened to small talk in an unfamiliar tongue, growing more and more uncomfortable on the cold ground. "We can ask them," suggested Jed.

At the fire, the three were also aware of the chill in the weather.

"It will snow soon," observed one.

"No matter. We will be home tomorrow."

"What's the matter with the dog?"

The three glanced at the animal. It now rose and stared out into the darkness, a questioning growl rumbling in its throat.

"Coyotes, maybe."

"Maybe someone is coming," said the youngest of the three.

"So? We are camped where it was given to us by the great white chief, no?"

"But there are others . . ."

"Do not worry about it. They are moving out."

The dog now burst into a flurry of barking, and the three looked into the darkness, rising as they did so. One spoke to the dog to quiet it.

Two men stepped into the circle of firelight. One was a tall white man in buckskins. The other wore the hair style which identified him as a Pawnee warrior. Both were heavily armed with rifles and belt knives, and the Pawnee carried a throwing ax.

Now the two moved apart a few steps, as one would when expecting an attack. The white man raised a hand in greeting.

The tribes moving from the east had initially been unfamiliar with hand signs, but were learning quickly.

"Join our fire," the older man signed.

He did not like the expressions on the faces of these two.

"Who are you?" signed the Pawnee.

"I am Otter. This is Hawk's Tail—"

"No, what is your nation?"

"Oh. We are Delaware. We—"

"You burned our homes, killed our people," answered the Pawnee, still in hand sign.

The three looked at each other in surprise.

"What did he sign?" the young man said in their own tongue. "We *killed*—?"

"I am made to think so," the one called Otter said. "I will ask."

He turned back to the strangers. "We do not understand," he

signed. "You have said *burned* and *killed?* We know nothing of this. We have been hunting."

"You lie!" accused the Pawnee angrily. "You are Delawares. You are in our hunting grounds!"

"But this is where Delawares have been sent by the white chief!" protested Otter. "It is to be our home."

Otter did not like the way the anger was twisting the face of the Pawnee. He turned in desperation to the other, the white man.

"Is it not so?" he pleaded. Maybe there was a shadow of doubt in the white man's face.

Now that one began to sign.

"Our families are dead. Our women and children."

"We did not kill them!" Otter protested. He was having more difficulty remembering the signs as his terror rose. "We are men of peace!"

"You are Delawares," signed the Pawnee. "Our people who are still alive said that the killers were Delaware. You are in this place."

"But we were not, when that happened. We have been traveling."

"Then how do you know what day it happened?" demanded the Pawnee.

His face was distorted with rage, and his eyes were like those of a hunting wolf. Otter was still struggling to find the proper hand signs to answer when Hawk's Tail made an unfortunate decision. He reached for his knife and lunged at the Pawnee.

"No!" Otter yelled in his own tongue.

Things happened so fast then that there was no time to think, much less to act. Otter saw his nephew, Hawk's Tail, make his move. Unfortunately, Hawk had never been known for good judgment, and this mistake was his last. His full-arm swing with the knife met only empty air, just a heartbeat before the Pawnee's ax descended. There was a hollow thunk, like that of a pumpkin dropped on a flat rock, as the ax struck the skull.

There was a moment while the Pawnee tried to pull his ax free, and Gray Squirrel, the third Delaware, ran toward him with an upraised ax. A deafening boom from the white man's rifle blew Squirrel backward, eyes still wide with surprise.

The Pawnee's ax was pried loose, and he turned, almost without looking, to swing it this time at Otter.

"No!" Otter yelled again, but his protest was unheeded.

It felt as if someone had struck the left side of his neck with a club, knocking him to the ground. His senses were fading, and he felt the warm wetness of his life blood spurting along his shoulder. Over him loomed the raging Pawnee, ready to strike again.

"I . . . It was not . . ." the Delaware began in his own tongue, but was unable to finish the protest. His world darkened and vanished into black nothingness.

Jed stood, numb for a moment over what had occurred. He and Swimmer had just killed three men. Probably innocent men. Only a short while ago, his heart had burned for revenge. He had been as ready as Swimmer, maybe, to kill Delawares. But not like this.

He had killed before. Not many, and he had never tried to keep an actual count. It would have been impossible, anyway. Some of his hits had been on renegade whites or Mexican Comancheros in defense of wagon trains. The dead and wounded were usually carried off by their companions. This was different. He would never forget the look in the eyes of the older Delaware just before Swimmer struck him down. That one had never made a move toward them. The man might have at the next moment, of course. Swimmer had undoubtedly been right to kill him.

Jed recalled a remark by an old fur trapper he once met. The man had been a little crazy from loneliness, maybe. He spouted Scripture, and had a saying based on a biblical passage: *"There are two kinds of fighters on the frontier; the quick and the dead."* Swimmer was quick, the Delaware was dead. Still . . .

The flame of vengeance began to flicker lower, as he watched Swimmer scalp the two he had killed.

"That one is yours," Swimmer said, nodding toward the Delaware with the dark hole in his shirt. Jed's rifle ball had punched through flesh to reach bone. "You will want the scalp."

"No."

"I'll save it for you. You will want it later."

Swimmer deftly circled the crown with his knife, jerked the hair free, and tucked it in his belt. Then he rummaged through the camp, finding little of value.

"Let us camp here," he suggested.

Jed had no intention of camping next to the corpses of three men they had murdered.

"No, Swimmer. This is not the way of my people."

"But you are Pawnee now."

"True. But I am made to think that even so . . ."

Swimmer waved his protest aside.

"No matter. I understand. Their spirits might linger here. Let us move, then."

They retrieved the horses and moved to an area a few miles away.

Jed stared at the fire a long time, and at the still figure of Swimmer on the other side. Swimmer had quieted now, from his talkative excitement earlier.

"Swimmer, how many Delaware scalps will it take?" he asked finally.

"To do what?"

"To complete our revenge."

Swimmer shrugged. "A hundred, maybe."

"But Delawares will kill more Pawnees over these three."

"Let them try! Besides, how will they know who kills Delawares?"

"You will want them to know, Swimmer, who seeks vengeance. *You* will have to tell."

"You, also, Walker. You avenge your family, too!"

"That is true. But you know these were not the same people."

"They were Delawares, no?"

"True. But Swimmer, remember when the Cheyennes attacked some of our people because of the Morning Star ceremony?"

"We did not steal that girl!" Swimmer protested indignantly. "That was the *Skidis*!"

"That is true. But is this not the same? We killed these because of what *others* have done."

Swimmer thought about it for a little while, and finally nodded.

"I see. But Walker, we still need to kill Delawares!"

"How do we know *which* Delawares?"

"For now, *any* will do."

"Swimmer, I cannot do it that way. If I knew *yes, this is the one,* I could skin him alive, cut his body in pieces while he still lived—"

"But we cannot know, for sure. So, we must kill *any* Delaware."

"I understand, Swimmer. Because we cannot know, you would

kill any who *might* be guilty. But I would kill none, unless I know for sure."

There was a long silence, broken finally by Swimmer.

"I know, Walker, that this is not because you are afraid. I would be glad to have you at my side in any battle. I honor your feelings on this, but it means we must part."

"Swimmer, that was not—" Jed began.

The other waved him down.

"I know. But I will be hunting Delawares. You must either help me or stay away, and you have said you will not kill if you do not know whether it is the right one."

"I understand. Yes, we must part."

They went their separate ways when morning came.

"Good hunting, my brother," Jed told him.

"And to you," Swimmer answered.

Jed was at loose ends, not knowing what to do. He had no more ties to the Pawnees, now living on the Platte. To rejoin them would only bring back memories, and he wanted to escape those for now. Maybe someday he could relive the happy times, but for now . . .

How could he have been so wrong, to think that killing Delawares would make him feel better? That whole episode had not made him feel better, but worse.

Maybe he should go back to civilization. He had enjoyed parts of his visit. His reunion with his father and his sister, the visit with the other men in the library after dinner. He could adjust, maybe, to such a life. But not there, not in Baltimore. The treacherous Phoebe would be dangerous, having stated her intention to consummate an illicit affair with him. It was ironic that such a woman would have such power in his life. *Her medicine is strong,* Swimmer would have said.

He could go the other direction, farther out into the mountains. . . . No, he had been there, seen the wonders of it. Something new . . . something to make him forget. He had no family, no friends available to him for comfort. He had never felt so alone, and the taste of the day was like ashes in his mouth.

8

I n later years, Jed could never quite remember how he managed to survive that first winter alone. He found himself in St. Louis, without remembering much about how he got there. He drank heavily, hoping to forget, to rid himself of the guilt that descended on him whenever he thought of the loss of his family. If he had only been there, instead of on his trip back to Baltimore. He might not have prevented the burning and destruction and killing, but he could have fought in the defense of the town. It would have been better if he, too, had been killed, he thought now. At times in anguish he blamed himself for the entire attack.

He alternately became angry and vengeful. Sometimes he even thought about trying to rejoin Swimmer in his self-appointed mission to kill Delawares. Then the anger would pass and be replaced by guilt over his own part in the killing of the three innocent men. He wondered about Swimmer, and whether he was still alive or . . . there was a good possibility that Swimmer's vengeful career would have ended in his own death.

There had been also a good possibility that he, Jed, might not survive that first winter. Some of his drinking bouts left him with no memory of the past few days. One morning he awoke, half frozen, on the boardwalk in front of a saloon, and realized that he could easily have died there. Probably would have, except that he had no money to buy enough whiskey to drive away the demons of his guilt. In his heart, he knew that there was not that much whiskey in the entire West.

He had sold his horse and some of his other possessions to finance his drinking.

When spring finally came, the call of the migrating geese jolted him back into the real world. He still had his rifle. He could thank the good advice of Daniel Boone for that. *If ye still have yere rifle ye kin provide for yere needs.* He started back westward again.

He heard tales of fighting in Tejas, and altered his course southward. In the back of his mind was probably the thought that if he were killed, his suffering and guilt would be over.

He followed an old trail south, and encountered many American settlers, who welcomed him as another fighting man. Jed had no destination in mind, and before he decided on one, he learned that the war was over. Tejas had declared independence from Mexico, and had formed a new nation, the Republic of Texas.

There seemed to be no purpose in remaining to help settle a political situation, so he traveled westward for a few days. He encountered a band of Cheyennes who recognized him and welcomed him. They had wintered farther south than usual, and were heading north, following the buffalo herds. Jed accompanied them, crossing back into Kansas territory at the Arkansas River. There he struck the Santa Fe Trail and again turned west, heading for Bent's Fort.

Over the next few years he had little direction or purpose. He hired on at Bent's for a while, doing odd jobs and sometimes hunting for meat, and he hunted for the army as well.

Jed had been aimlessly subsisting for several years, and he was beginning to look for new horizons. His chronic dejection prevented him from doing much more than think about it.

He was in Independence in early May of 1842, halfheartedly trying to attach himself to some group of wagons heading to Santa Fe. There was not much interest. Most of the Santa Fe traffic was that of experienced freighters now. The road was plain, the route familiar. There was no longer a need for guides or hunters.

He had just stepped out of a saloon, and almost collided with another man in fringed buckskins. He murmured an apology and stepped aside. The other man started to move on, then paused for a second look.

"Sterling?"

"Yes."

There was something familiar about the man, a few years younger than himself.

"Carson. Chris Carson. They call me Kit. We met at Bent's, a couple of seasons back. You are called Long Walker, no?"

"Sometimes. What are you doing now?"

"Working for the army. Times are changing fast, aren't they? Fur trade's over. Look, let's have a talk. Have you eaten yet?"

"No, I . . ."

"Good. Let's have supper, and visit a spell."

Over plates of fried ham and beans and cornbread in a little café off the main street, they talked. It was good to converse with someone who could understand. They talked with regret of some of the change around them. Other changes were more acceptable, even interesting.

There was a new kind of traffic beginning to make its way across the territory. Settlers were heading west to homestead in the far reaches of Oregon and California. For the first two weeks or so of travel the settlers' wagons usually followed one of the several branches of the Santa Fe road. Then they would cross the Kansas River on the ferry at Topeka, head northward to the Platte, and follow that river westward.

"I talked to some of them," Jed told his companion. "I don't know, Kit. I'm thinking they don't realize the distance or the problems."

"Some do, some don't, I figure," said Carson. "But that's where I'm going."

"What? I thought you were working for the army."

"I am. There's a young officer. Fremont. Captain John Fremont. He's taking a survey party to map that trail. At least to South Pass. I'm their guide!"

"Have you been there?"

"No," Carson grinned. "But I can follow a wagon. Some have gone through already. My main job is to deal with the Indians we'll meet. They'll all use hand sign. Look, why don't you come along? Fremont's recruiting men to go."

"*Join* the army?"

"No, no," Carson laughed. "Recruiting civilians. About thirty. Frontiersmen, if he can find them. I'm to meet him at Cyprian Chouteau's. Come along with me. Talk to him, anyway."

In the dim interior of Chouteau's trading establishment, Captain Fremont had set up a table at which to do his interviewing. The room was stacked with crates, boxes, and kegs of merchandise, bales of blankets, racks of tools and implements. Still, the place was large enough to accommodate twenty or thirty men in the open space before the table.

Fremont, in blue field uniform, sat behind the table, which was littered with letters and maps and assorted papers. He was a slender, intense man, with dark curly hair and beard. His eyes burned with the intensity of his convictions.

To his right sat a well-groomed young man, whom Jed later learned was the captain's brother-in-law. To his left, a red-faced, very blond Nordic gentleman, busily trying to organize the books and papers on the table.

Carson led Jed to the table. "Captain, this is the man we spoke of."

"Ah, yes. Joe Walker, the mountain man, right?"

Fremont extended his hand.

"No, sir," Jed protested. "Jedediah Sterling. I've trapped some."

"He's called Long Walker by the Indians, Captain," explained Carson. "Joe Walker is another man."

"Yes, surely, Kit. I had confused the two."

"I'm usually called Jed, sir."

"Jed it is, then," smiled Fremont, shaking hands with a firm grip. "This is Mr. Preuss, our cartographer"—he indicated the blond man—"and Mr. Benton, of Missouri"—pointing to the other.

The three exchanged nods.

"Now, you are familiar with our route?" Fremont asked.

"Only part way, sir," Jed admitted. "I've been . . ."

"No matter," Fremont waved the protest aside. "Very few have been all the way and back. That's why we're going, right? And we won't go clear to Oregon." He chuckled. "But this is important. Some day the United States will stretch from sea to sea!"

"Well, I . . ."

"Think of it, Sterling! A great country, dozens of new states, a powerful Union! And it falls to *us* to explore it, to open it to settlement. It is our destiny to do so!"

Fremont struck a dramatic pose for just an instant, and Jed was reminded of the exaggerated gestures of an actor on the stage. It would have been easy to draw back, to reject such flamboyance as the misplaced enthusiasm of the inexperienced.

In this case, though, it seemed appropriate. There was a charisma about this man, a powerful emotion that reached out to grip the listener with the same excitement that the captain felt. Jed had seen this quality before in leaders of men, both red and white. It was rare, but effective. Such a man could enter a room and in an instant, make everyone there feel important. *His purpose here is to contact me,* one would think.

Jed recalled that one might reflect later, and wonder how he had been talked into carrying out the wishes of such a leader. Yet at the time, it had seemed not only logical, but an honor to be asked to do such a leader's bidding.

This time, despite the whisper of warning in the dim recesses of his mind, he was swept up in the sheer enthusiasm of the leader. It was the first time in several years that he had felt any sense of direction at all.

"Kit tells me you have lived with the natives," Fremont was saying. "What tribes?"

"Pawnee," Jed answered, through a pang of painful memory. "I had a Pawnee family."

"Excellent!" chortled Fremont. "We will be contacting them along the Platte, no?"

"I would expect so, sir."

"Good. You speak their tongue?"

"Fairly well."

"And Comanche? Cheyenne?"

"Some. Mostly hand signs can help out with the western tribes."

"So Mr. Carson says. How did you two meet?"

"Trapping, fur trading. Most of us know each other from the fur rendezvous. I was employed at Bent's Fort for a little while, too, and met a lot of people there."

Fremont nodded, paused a moment, and asked a puzzled question.

"Do I detect a cultured accent, Sterling? You have some education?"

Jed was startled. He was seldom asked such a question.

"Well . . . yes, sir. I spent some time at Princeton."

Fremont chuckled. "Excellent! You will make a great addition to our party. Will you join us?"

"He is everything you said, Kit, and more!" Jed told his companion later. "How did you meet him?"

Carson chuckled. "We were on the same boat from St. Louis, headed up the Missouri to here. Got to talkin'. I reckon he saw from my buckskins that I was the sort he needed. And . . . well, you saw how he is!"

Jed nodded, and then recalled a thing Kit had said earlier.

"A boat, you said, Kit? How did you happen to be traveling by boat?"

"Well," Carson said sheepishly, "I sort of wondered how it would be. I was in St. Louis, wanted to get here, and there was a river steamer, about to leave. Don't cost much. Faster'n a horse, and a lot easier'n walkin'. You'd ought to try it sometime, Jed."

"Maybe I will, Kit."

He had noticed before that Carson was always inquisitive, trying new ways. The little man had been one of the first Jed had seen to use the Mexican skill with a lariat. It had, in fact, earned Kit Carson his Indian name, Rope Thrower.

"I think you'd like it, Jed, the river travel. Smooth, like flyin', almost. Time to watch the water and think a little, instead of wonderin' about the trail and where to camp tonight. Try it!"

"Be a while before we get a chance, though. Right? Tell me more about this expedition, Kit."

"A lot I don't know, Jed. There'll be a half dozen wagons, some pack mules, about forty men, all told. Oh, yes, he's got some equipment to try out, see how it will work in the West."

"Equipment?"

"Yes. There's a folding rubber boat or canoe he wants to try in the mountain streams. I dunno about *that*. A lot of stuff for collecting plants and bugs and things to study. Preuss will survey and map the route. You met him at Chouteau's, the German."

Jed nodded. This might prove an interesting season. It had been a long time since he had felt this interested in anything.

9

They traveled a few miles south to use one of the feed-in branches of the Santa Fe Trail, heading west. It was the tenth of June, 1842. A day later they came to the point where the trails branched, and took the Oregon route northwest.

On the fourteenth, they reached the crossing of the Kansas River. Fremont had elected not to use the ferry at the Topeka crossing. That would involve several trips back and forth to transfer the forty men and horses, eight mule-drawn carts and their assorted cattle and extra horses. Instead, they would use a ford a few miles upstream. It had been recommended by the Chouteaus as a dependable crossing, with a good rock bottom.

However, it became apparent as they approached that the river was at flood stage. Fremont later recorded in his journal that it was running bank-full, "with an angry current, yellow and turbid as the Missouri," already nicknamed the Big Muddy. Jed, Carson, and other experienced plainsmen assumed that they would camp overnight and wait for the water to recede. It was already late in the day. But they were not yet accustomed to the flamboyant style of Fremont.

"We'll cross before dark," he announced. "Break out the boat. It will give us a chance to test it. We'll swim the livestock across, and we'll carry the wagons one at a time in the boat."

The flimsy rubber boat was unfolded and prepared for use, to the amazement of some of the men. There were quiet wagers as to whether it could possibly work. Jed had his doubts. The first wagon was pushed, pulled, and lifted into the boat, and inched away from the shore. The oarsmen fought the current with all their might, striving to head upstream to counteract the pull of the current. Even so, they touched the north bank several hundred yards below the ford. Fremont leaped ashore, shouted "Hurrah," and waved his hat to indicate success. There was an answering cheer. This, the first major obstacle met by the expedition, had been proved conquerable. Morale was high.

Seven more times Fremont's experimental craft crossed the flooded Kansas River. The cattle, mules, and horses had already finished the swim and were being loose herded on the north bank when the accident occurred. As the last of the wagons was nearly across, the collapsible boat did exactly that. It folded, throwing the loaded cart, which held most of the expedition's scientific gear, into the river. The current swept the wreck downstream, as men strained on the ropes that had been used for lashing and for handling the boat.

Fortunately, they were past the deepest and most powerful part of the current. It was possible to reach a footing in the shallow water, and swing the wrecked boat and capsized wagon to shore. There was no loss of life. When Fremont settled by the fire that night to record the event in his journal, he reported that most of the equipment was recovered.

The next day they moved about seven miles upstream to a better campsite on rolling prairie. There, they spent a day drying out supplies and equipment in the bright Kansas sun. On the seventeenth they encountered a party of Kaw Indians, apparently on a spring hunt. Jed and Carson conferred with them at length about the weather, the game, and the route to the Platte. They also learned that a large party of settlers was ahead of them, by maybe three weeks.

"This must be the party of Dr. White," Fremont commented. "Chouteau mentioned them. Sixteen or seventeen families, as I recall, and some sixty men. Heavy wagons, household goods and all."

The captain seemed displeased.

"What's the matter with him?" Jed asked Carson.

Kit smiled. "I'm thinkin' he wanted to be the first over the trail this season."

"But why?"

"I dunno, Jed. The captain sees this trip as a real important one." He paused, then went on. "He's sort of different, maybe, but you got to like his style. And he ain't afraid of *nothin'*."

Jed did not comment further. Somewhere, he thought, is a line between courage and foolhardiness. He had thought that crossing the river in flood stage was rather close to that line. It had been successful, but could have been a disaster. A prudent frontiersman would have waited a day and watched the river.

Jed soon realized a curious fact. When he was in the presence of Fremont, he became swept up in the excitement and enthusiasm of the man's powerful personality. Then, after a little while away from their leader, he began to change his perspective. At a little distance he could better evaluate the actual situation. He was also mildly surprised that Kit Carson did not seem to have the same objectivity. Carson, basically quiet and steady, seemed completely entranced by the colorful Fremont. Possibly the captain's broad background of knowledge and interest, as well as his education, fascinated the rough frontiersman.

Fremont, in turn, was obviously impressed by Carson's expertise, once referring to him as "this intrepid Hawkeye of the West." Jed was familiar with that colorful fictional character from Fenimore Cooper's *Leatherstocking Tales*, but was certain that it meant nothing to most of the men.

An even greater enigma was the cartographer, Charles Preuss. Each night he busied himself writing by the light of the fire. Each day Fremont seemed to give him more responsibility in the meticulous cataloging of the scientific collections. The captain continued to concentrate on his own journal.

Most of Preuss's writings were in Latin or English, but Jed chanced to see, one evening, that he was writing in German. Jed had a slight familiarity with German as well as Latin, these being the languages of academia.

"In *German,* Charles?" he asked lightly, thinking little of it.

"Ja . . . letters to my wife!" Preuss explained quickly.

A little too quickly, perhaps. The German's haste to explain caused Jed to take an extra look before Preuss concealed the page with another. There had been little time to recognize anything, but an odd phrase in the German had seemed to jump out at Jed's glance. He was almost certain that he had seen the words for ". . . that childish Fremont . . ." across the paper.

Does Preuss feel the same thing that I do? he wondered.

The incident was soon forgotten as they traveled up the Blue River. This upland would divide the watershed between the Kansas and Platte rivers.

At the mouth of the Vermilion River where it enters the Big Blue, they found the deserted ruins of a Kansa town. Jed recalled that he had heard of this destruction by Pawnees the previous year. He wondered if it was a part of the vengeance war of which he and Swimmer had been a part. And where would it stop?

On the twenty-first of May, Charles Preuss reported that they were crossing the fortieth parallel, out of the Kansas Territory and into that which was being called Platte, after the river. Fremont noted the border crossing in his journal.

Carson killed a deer for fresh meat, and they had noticed antelope in the distance for two or three days. They moved on toward the Platte.

By contrast to the Kansas and Arkansas rivers, the Platte was wide, shallow, and sandy. In a few days they had left the tallgrass region behind. There were no longer the rolling hills with heavily wooded canyons. The only trees as far as the eye could see were scrubby willows and giant cottonwoods along the river. These provided a reliable landmark when they occasionally veered away from the trail to seek a better roadbed for the wagons, or to hunt for fresh meat.

In one area, a strip of cottonwoods formed a sort of narrow grove along the river for a few miles. Here they saw hundreds of large nests of sticks in the trees. It was the largest heron rookery that Jed had ever seen. The large blue birds, standing nearly as tall as a man, appeared clumsy on the ground, in the trees, or wading in the river. But, once in flight, they became creatures of grace and beauty. Slow, powerful wing strokes gave the impression of swimming through the air.

They shot one of the birds, in the interest of science, and Preuss dutifully measured and recorded its height, weight, color, and wingspan. They moved on.

Traveling was fairly good. The weather held, and Fremont had a tendency to push for long distances each day, recording the mileage accomplished. If it proved to be less than his desired twenty miles or so, he would appear disappointed and frustrated. On such occasions, Jed would recall Preuss's phrase "that childish Fremont."

Fortunately, these moody spells were short-lived. In a few hours, the captain would appear rejuvenated, excited, and ready for the next day's run.

By contrast, Preuss had a very even temperament, always dour and gloomy. It was understandable. The bright sun burned his blond Nordic skin badly. His face was always lobster red, and his nose usually either blistered or peeling from the last burn. His whole personality was rather compulsive and fastidious, completely unsuited to the rough amenities of the trail. Preuss was not overly demonstrative about all this, but kept quietly to himself, recording his compass readings and surveyor's turning points.

Jed suggested a salve for the sunburned nose. It was a mixture of buffalo tallow and white pigment from one of the cutbanks they passed. He had seen it used by Raven's people for treatment of minor burns, and as protection from the sun's rays. Preuss was appreciative, and frequently used the ointment.

As they moved on westward, Jed knew that they would pass near some of the Pawnee towns along the Platte. While it was considered by the white travelers best to avoid such contact, he felt that an announcement of their presence might be diplomatic. He viewed this with mixed emotions. It had been several years since he had been in contact with his wife's people. At least, as well as he could remember. There were gaps in his memory, lost periods when he had been drinking heavily. He could have contacted Pawnees, and forgotten after he sobered up and returned to the real world.

But no, he had been mostly among whites, trying to forget. Now it was his function to contact the Pawnees as part of his agreement with Captain Fremont and Carson. A question flitted through his mind. How had he allowed Fremont's enthusiasm to influence him in such an undertaking? He smiled ruefully. He had been honored by the opportunity. He thought of Preuss, who must at times have similar feelings. No matter, it must be done.

Jed had a general idea that there might be a Pawnee town in this area. One morning he saw the familiar haze from the smoke of cooking fires hanging over an area to the south of their travel. He sought out Carson.

"Kit, I'm going over there to contact the Pawnees, tell them we're here."

"Hell, they know that! But yes. Want me to go?"

"No, I'll talk to them."

"Oh, yes, they're your wife's people?"

"Yes. Not this band, though."

Carson nodded. "Go on. You'll join us tonight?"

"Probably." He found himself being vague about time, like Raven's people. "Indian time," some called it. *"When will it happen?" "When the time comes."* Was he slipping back into the ways of his Pawnee family?

He waved to Kit and reined his horse to the south. There was a slight roll to the sandy shortgrass prairie here. From a rise, one could see for perhaps a half day's travel. But there were blind spots, low-lying areas where a man and a horse could not be seen, or see very far. Jed rode up the easy slope after crossing a dry stream bed and found himself face to face with three mounted warriors, no more than a stone's throw away. Their attitude was a bit aggressive, threatening, but curious.

Jed held up a hand in greeting and only now realized that he had no easy way to show his alliance to their nation. He was in a trapper's fringed buckskins, and his hair was long. If one of these warriors used poor judgment, Jed could be killed before he even had a chance to identify himself.

"I am Long Walker of the Southern Band," he called as clearly as he could, in the Pawnee tongue.

Just then the three gave a yell and kicked their horses forward. He was not sure whether they had understood, or even heard his call. There was nothing to do but stand his ground. He kept his right hand aloft in the sign of peaceful greeting, and waited.

"I am Pawnee, my brothers," he kept yelling as they thundered down on him.

10

t the last moment, the leader of the charging warriors jerked his horse to a sliding stop. Dirt and sand spewed from under the stallion's hooves and spattered on and around Jed and his mount. With some difficulty, Jed controlled his own horse, now excited by the others. The three circled him slowly, looking him over.

"You lie," said the one who appeared to be their leader. "You are a white man!"

"But my family was Pawnee," Jed insisted. "They were killed by Delawares."

The three exchanged glances.

"Where was this?" one asked.

"Near the river of the Kaws, as white men say. Our town was burned, my wife and children killed. Several years ago. You must know of this. Many were killed."

The three warriors nodded.

"It is true, that did happen," agreed the leader. "But who are you? Who are your people? Some are with us."

"My wife was Raven. Her brother, Swimmer, was on a vengeance war to kill Delawares when I last saw him."

"Yes, I have heard of him. A little crazy from his loss. Swimmer was killed, you know."

"No, I had not heard. . . . How?"

"Delawares. He was brave, but careless."

No, he did not care, thought Jed. "He had no one left," he said aloud.

"That is true. Where are you going?"

"I am with the wagons," he jerked his head in the direction of the trail. "Rope Thrower is with them, too."

The Pawnee nodded. "Why?"

"We show them the way to the mountains."

"White men cannot find *mountains?*" asked the Pawnee leader incredulously. All joined in laughter, including Jed.

"Maybe, maybe not," he agreed. "But this bluecoat leader wants to mark the way on the talking paper. Nothing else. He comes in peace."

"Does this bluecoat bring gifts, then?"

Jed thought quickly. It might be well to befriend these Pawnees. Their town was near the now more heavily traveled Oregon Trail.

"Maybe," he shrugged. "I could ask him. Yours is Wolf band?"

The Pawnee nodded. "Yes. *Skidi.*"

"I will tell him. Maybe he will come for a council smoke."

"It is good!"

Jed knew that Fremont carried some trade goods for the express purpose of establishing friendly relations with the tribes along the Platte. Probably he had been thinking of Cheyenne, Comanche, and the Arapaho, close allies of the Cheyenne. But the Pawnees, arrogant, aggressive, and unpredictable, were always a possibility for trouble. Jed knew them well. Maybe it would be good to plant some seeds of friendship here.

Fremont was amenable to the suggestion. They camped near the village, ate and smoked and held council. Carson demonstrated his skill with a lariat, to the delight of the Pawnees. Fremont made a flowery speech, translated by Jed, and some small gifts of trade goods were distributed. All in all, it seemed a worthwhile effort.

Jed talked to some of the survivors of the destruction of his own town. It was a bittersweet reunion, one he would have avoided. But he found a certain peace in the closing of that part of his life. Maybe the eager, forward thrust of Fremont's dynamic approach to life helped him some.

Regardless of the reasons, Jed found a new interest in living as they moved on. For the first time in years, he was able to go through days at a time without the memories of his tragic loss gnawing at his soul.

Fremont was greatly impressed by the mountains. He wrote long, descriptive passages about their majesty and height and beauty. He was equally unimpressed by the South Pass, which was the primary purpose of the expedition.

In truth, South Pass was *not* very impressive, a low saddle surrounded by majestic peaks. Preuss took his survey readings and glumly recorded his observations. Fremont, always ready to concentrate on the most spectacular features and events, had his eyes on the lofty peaks.

"I have it!" he exclaimed. "We will *climb* one . . . the tallest. . . . that one over there!" He pointed. "Let us plant Old Glory on the top of the world!"

The next few days proved interesting, although frustrating. Attempts were made on two or three days to reach the summit of Fremont's arbitrarily selected peak. He divided the party, leaving the main force behind with the wagons at the base camp. Jed was assigned there, while Carson accompanied Fremont, Preuss, and the climbing party.

The first attempt failed to reach the top, having bogged down in a snow field. Preuss took his survey measurements at the highest point he could reach, and Fremont added a few hundred feet to establish an estimated height for his mountain. But he was determined.

Another route to the top was attempted, frustrated when Fremont turned back with a headache. Several of the climbing party did find a better way to the summit, which was used the next day.

The party carried brandy with which to toast the victory, and a small American flag to plant ceremonially on the summit.

Fremont's journal recorded the scene, after his description of working his way across ice and snow and a vertical precipice. It was August fifteenth.

> I sprang upon the summit and another step would
> have precipitated me into an immense snow field five
> hundred feet below. To the edge of this field was a sheer
> icy precipice; and then, with a gradual fall, the field
> sloped off for about a mile until it struck the foot of
> another lower ridge.

"I heard some shots," Jed told Carson when the party reassembled. "What happened?"

"Fremont fired off his pistol, and a couple of the others followed. Just to celebrate, I reckon."

"What was it like, Kit?"

"Oh, purty high. There's a rock at the top, just big enough for one at a time to stand on the highest point. We had a sip of brandy, they shot their pistols, unfurled the flag, and hollered 'Hurrah' a couple of times. Then we came down."

It was time to return to civilization. They started on the long back trail.

When they reached the Platte, Fremont decided to divide his party again. The main party would continue overland, while Fremont, Preuss, and a few others would attempt to survey the river by shooting the rapids in the rubber boat. At this point, the Platte was high from summer snow melt, and churning alarmingly. Shortly after launching, the boat was sucked into narrow, foaming white water. The collapsible boat did so *again,* and many of the carefully compiled records of the expedition were lost.

Otherwise, the return journey was uneventful. They arrived back in Independence in September, with Fremont already organizing plans for another expedition in 1843. This one would take him all the way to the Pacific Ocean.

Fremont casually broached the subject to Jed, but Jed declined the opportunity to participate. He had not decided yet what he would do, but another such expedition did not seem to be a reasonable course of action. He had a little money from the effort that just ended. Maybe he would even go back to Baltimore one more time. His father was not growing any younger. Surely Jed could avoid the advances of the predatory Phoebe.

Meanwhile, he had been thinking about Carson's fascination with river travel. Why not try it? He could at least go to St. Louis, look around, see what was going on, and then decide where to winter; St. Louis, Baltimore, or back to the prairie.

It was on the river steamer that the event occurred that was to send his life in a new direction. He was approached by a well-dressed man who invited him to sit in as a fill-in for an impromptu card game.

"Just a friendly hand or two," the man assured. "My name is Buckminster. George Buckminster."

Jed was in no way deceived. This was a gambler, who had spotted the man in buckskins as one who had just returned from a journey. If this frontiersman had bought passage on the steamer, he had some money. Probably pay from a job at guiding, just finished.

Jed had enjoyed poker at college, and some of his fellow students were quite clever at it. He had learned much about the wiles of the gambler. He decided to have some fun. This gambler would assume that here was a backwoods bumpkin, easy for the picking. He would play the part, until he could determine how the game was to go.

He feigned ignorance, asking questions about the game as he evaluated the situation. There were three other players. One, a small quiet type, seemed to handle the cards well. Jed decided that this was a partner to the instigator of the game, and skilled at shady dealing. There was a well-dressed planter with a marked southern drawl, probably the gamblers' real target tonight, and a fifth man who seemed to be a young gentleman on an adventure.

Each was allowed to win a little at first to keep them in the game, and then the plot began to take shape. The planter and the young gentleman received better and better hands. When the pot was moderate, one of those two would win with only a fair hand. When either had a really good hand, the betting would go wild, and he would lose. Occasionally, even, to Jed. Jed realized that they wanted to keep him in the game, to keep his interest so that he did not drop out.

They were using him. A quick mental calculation told him that he was a few dollars ahead for the evening. It was a very skillful job of playing one player against the other and keeping them all interested.

By the end of the game, Jed was a small winner, the gambler was slightly ahead, and the dealer was a loser. *Clever,* thought Jed. *That removes suspicion.* Of the two other players, the planter was a modest winner and the gentleman a fairly big loser.

"Another game tomorrow?" asked the gambler.

All agreed.

Jed was surprised after the second game, when he was approached in a conversational manner by the gambler. He was again a small winner.

"You have played before?" the man asked. It was not really a question.

"A little . . ."

"Good to have you aboard," said the man.

Jed was puzzled. There was something more here, something implied but unsaid. Somehow there was an implied recognition: *You see our game, but have said nothing.* Or could he be wrong? Was this merely the conversation that it seemed to be?

The next day he was more certain, as they approached St. Louis. The gambler who acted as spokesman for the team again engaged him in conversation.

"We have enjoyed your company. A pleasant card player. Good to pass the time with," he smiled.

And they have let me win a little, Jed pondered. *Is he trying to enlist me?* It would be a good play, to have a harmless-looking shill. He was certain when the gambler spoke again.

"Where are you headed, Sterling? We are bound for New Orleans for the winter. I would welcome a chance to win back what you've won from me."

Jed smiled. He knew that the net profit to these two was quite considerable.

"But your luck may hold, too," Buckminster said cautiously.

"Do you think so?" Jed asked, surprised. "How could you know?"

"I'm sure! If you have no plans, I'm sure you would enjoy the river trip. Maybe make a little money at the cards."

"Are you inviting me to *join* you?"

"Did I say that?" asked Buckminster innocently. "Why, I hardly know you. But you are a pleasant player, and I would welcome the chance to become better acquainted."

There was a small warning voice in the dim recesses of Jed's mind, but he really had no plans. He had always wanted to see the French country. Even so, he surprised himself.

"Well, why not?" he said.

Buckminster extended his hand with a grin. "I knew it!" he chuckled.

11

In St. Louis, Jed indulged in a bath, shave, and haircut. Next he visited a haberdasher. He outfitted himself with a white shirt, woolen trousers, a vest, and a plum-colored topcoat. This dress was completed by a silk top hat, a cravat, and a pair of leather boots. He was not certain he could tolerate the boots, after many years of moccasins.

He bought a satchel big enough to hold his buckskins and his possibles pouches. Then, carrying his satchel, he went down toward the river to an outfitter where he was well known, and approached the proprietor.

"Sam, could I leave my rifle with you? I'm on a trip downriver."

"Sterling? My Gawd, Jed, I didn't recognize you! What are you doin' now?"

"Just want to see some country. Maybe winter where it's warm for a change."

Sam laughed. "You look like a gambler. Well, sure, you can leave your rifle. I'll take care of it. But you'll need a weapon, won't you?"

"I hope not. But you're right. A small pistol, maybe?"

"Got just the thing here."

The outfitter drew from under the counter a polished wooden case no bigger than one of the smaller books in Judge Sterling's library. He set it on the counter and opened it to reveal a pistol no longer than a man's hand. It was fitted into a carved compartment lined with red velvet. Other compartments held a bullet mold, a tin of percussion caps, a few ready-cast balls, patches, and a tiny powder flask.

"Your complete equipment. Forty-four caliber. The pistol will fit in your belt, or even in the top of your boot."

Jed nodded, palmed the little gun, lifted and pointed it. A strange feel . . . so short an arm, how could it be aimed? There was a tiny gold sight on the muzzle, but no rear sight. Then he realized. At the range expected for use of this weapon, one does not aim. One shoots, point-blank. Jed nodded, paid for the cased pistol, and put it in his satchel.

"I'll be back in the spring for my rifle."

He strutted down the street, rather enjoying his new persona. He glanced at the sun. A little time before dark. The boat did not leave until morning, so he had a little time. Wander around, have a drink, maybe. No, maybe not. He did not want to fall back into some of the old habits. Some supper, yes, that was it. See some of the growth of the city to stretch his legs, and then pick a place for a bite to eat. There used to be a good café on Gravois Street.

It was then that he noticed a pair of rough-looking young men following him. Odd, that had never happened to him before. He strolled on, trying to appear casual, but now watching them closely. Yes, they were definitely stalking him. Finally he realized, it was the clothes. He had never been in St. Louis dressed as a gentleman before. These street bandits would never accost a frontiersman in buckskins. But, dressed in his new clothes, he must look like an easy mark.

I might be *an easy mark,* he thought. Well, a confrontation would be on his terms. He continued to stroll casually, and led the two into an area he knew from long experience. There was an alley. He lengthened his stride just a bit to put a little more distance between them, and turned into the alley, still trying to look like a sightseer.

Once out of their view, he acted quickly. He dropped the satchel, reached inside for his belt knife, and then stripped off his coat.

He tossed it and his silk hat on top of the satchel and moved back toward the mouth of the alley. There, he flattened against the wall.

The larger and more aggressive of the two rounded the corner almost at a run. His gaze was focused down the alley, where he had expected their quarry to be. Probably he did not even see Jed before the first blow. A fist to the groin, and the stalker doubled over in pain, his descending face meeting a rapidly rising knee. Blood spurted from his broken nose and split lips as he sank half senseless to the cobblestones.

His companion, close behind, almost fell over the crumpled form. He took a clumsy step backward, turned, and ran for his life.

Jed nudged the moaning figure with his boot to make sure the rogue was out of action, and then turned to retrieve his coat and satchel. He hoped that he had not bloodied the knee of his new trousers.

The day was growing late now, and the October sunsets were arriving earlier. He turned back toward a more respectable part of town. It had not occurred to him until now that his new clothes put him in a new light. He would be more vulnerable to such attacks as the one he had just experienced. A strange world . . .

Back toward town, he encountered none other than Buckminster. The gambler sized him up quickly, and then his eyes lighted with recognition.

"Sterling! My God, man! No, no, this will never do!"

"What?" Jed blurted.

"No, you must appear what you are . . . what you were. . . . Oh, no!"

"I don't understand."

"Look, as a frontiersman you are good to have in the game. Honest, innocent, reassuring to other players. But this . . . I had no idea you were . . ." The gambler hesitated.

"A gentleman?"

"Yes . . . no . . . no offense, sir . . ."

"None taken. Then our association is at an end?"

Jed was somewhat irritated at this turn of events. He was becoming uneasy at the unfamiliar role anyway, at its exposure and vulnerability.

"Well," said Buckminster thoughtfully. "That's your call. In buckskins, you might be quite useful to us. But we must not associate.

You may have noticed that even Le Duc and I do not do so. Yes, I noticed that you connected us immediately. You are quick, Sterling. What do you say?"

Jed shrugged. "I'll change back to leather. Might as well see New Orleans for one trip."

The Mississippi River steamer was much larger than those on the Missouri. It boasted three decks, the lowest of which was devoted to freight, livestock, and general deck passengers. The upper deck was reserved for the officers, the middle deck for the first-class passengers. In one roped-off area of the forward lower deck, a handful of Negroes stood or sat. Most were well dressed, and Jed supposed them to be slaves of first-class passengers. House servants or personal servants, probably. Field hands would be on the aft freight deck with the rest of the livestock.

He had already purchased a first-class ticket before he understood how the gamblers' scheme worked. Now, though back in buckskins, he climbed the stairs to first class, carrying his gentleman's clothes in the satchel. As he glanced down, one of the young women in the roped-off area caught his eye. She was striking in her dark beauty. He had a momentary pang as he realized that she looked much like Raven. Her facial structure and high cheek bones suggested some mixture of Indian blood. Maybe from the Carolinas, he thought, Cherokee. Their eyes met for just an instant, and he turned back to the stairs. People behind him were waiting.

He was oddly affected by this chance event. Slaves were part of his background. His parents had always had a house servant. Both whites and the natives with whom he had lived considered this a part of the way of things. *If only this slave girl did not look so much like my Raven,* he thought.

He passed Buckminster as he topped the stair, nodded politely but without recognition, and found a place at the rail. The middle deck was shorter than the lower by a few feet, and he found that he could look down into the roped-off Negro section. He tried to tell himself that it was a mere coincidence.

The slave girl moved with grace and dignity. Her clothing showed simplicity and taste, and she might have graced any dining room. Her skin was no darker than Raven's. *Why do I keep making this comparison?* he asked himself irritably. He turned away to look at the river, but found himself drawn back. The girl's body movements, her mannerisms were so familiar. Could he be losing his mind?

Now the gangplank was winched up and the lines cast off. The engine shuddered into motion and the boat nosed away from shore and out into the current of the mighty Mississippi.

That evening, he "chanced" upon a meeting that led to a poker game. The makeup of the players was quite similar to that of the first game in which he had joined the gambler. The results, too, were much the same, except that his winnings were somewhat better. In one hand, when he drew three cards to fill an inside straight, he was convinced. Le Duc, the dealer, was quite adept. Jed took this as a guarantee that Buckminster could deliver as he said. Their eyes met for an instant in passing, and even then the cold blue eyes held a twinkle of amusement. *You see?* the gambler seemed to say.

On the next night, another player joined, six in all. This changed the game only a little, but it was plain that the expert handler of the cards would only be in control one hand in six, instead of five. The winnings would be larger on each hand, but any illicit card play could be more easily detected.

The sixth player was a pudgy little man in a brown suit and a derby hat who said that he was an "investigator." None of the others were certain of exactly what that implied. But then, it was considered impolite to ask about someone's work or background.

In the course of the evening, the little man's luck became worse, and he dropped out. However, he was back the next night. Jed knew that this was a very irritating circumstance for Buckminster and Le Duc. They must engineer around the man to concentrate on their quarry. And what manner of investigator? Did he work for the steamboat company, to keep everything honest, or at least acceptably so? Was he a private detective, gathering evidence on someone on the boat? Or was he, after all, merely talking to impress the others?

Despite the distraction, the gambling went well on the voyage. Jed's money belt was growing fatter, and he knew that the two gamblers were doing even better as they milked the passengers who rotated through the game.

On the last night aboard the *River Queen,* events reached a climax. A wealthy gentleman who had sat in the game every night and lost steadily, suddenly half rose and grabbed Le Duc's wrist.

"I saw it! I thought so!" he yelled.

"Sir, are you suggesting . . ." Le Duc purred.

"I am not suggesting. I accuse you of cheating! You should be horsewhipped!"

"I assure you, sir, I do not know what you are talking about," protested the dealer.

"Look in his right sleeve," the angry gentleman told the others. The investigator rose and reached forward. Spectators began to back away.

Jed sat unmoving. There were too many variables here. Not only must he avoid association with the gamblers but be prepared to defend himself if necessary.

Then the scene seemed to explode all at once. Le Duc produced a slender knife from out of nowhere, and made a slashing stab at his assailant. The wealthy gentleman's sword came whispering out of the scabbard in his gold-headed cane where it had been concealed. As he thrust it into Le Duc's belly, Buckminster produced a small pistol and fired it into the chest of the swordsman. A woman screamed.

Jed sat very still. Any movement might provoke an attack from almost anyone.

12

As the smoke cleared, the salon burst into a frenzy of noise. A ship's officer burst into the room accompanied by two well-armed crewmen.

"Everybody stay where you are!" the officer commanded.

The "investigator" had disappeared, and was not seen again. Apparently, he had been no cause for concern at all. Ironic . . .

The room quieted as the questioning began. There were two men dead. Fortunately, no more.

Jed had not moved since before the outburst. To do so would have been foolish as the swordplay and shooting began.

"Where, where?" a tall woman screamed.

She thrust her way through the crowd to stare a moment at the dead gentleman on the floor.

"Frank!" she gasped.

"Come away, Mrs. Sullivan," pleaded the officer, taking her arm.

He was too late. Her head fell back and she swooned, her fall only partially supported by the officer.

·   ·   ·

It was nearly morning before the interrogation was finished, and a little later before they reached New Orleans. The steamer dropped anchor and a small boat was sent ashore to report to the port authorities about the killings. Meanwhile, the passengers on the *River Queen* reacted in all the ways people react, with patient waiting, anger, frustration, confusion.

During the wait, there was a considerable amount of discussion among those in the salon. This allowed Buckminster to approach Jed quite openly, but to speak privately.

"We do not know each other," he said. "I never saw you until on this boat."

"Of course," Jed answered. He paused for a moment, then spoke in sympathy. "I'm sorry about the dealer."

Buckminster nodded, more emotion in his face than Jed had ever seen. "Thank you. He knew the dangers, but he was a friend."

They drifted apart, and never spoke again.

The findings of the hearing were simple. Two men had been killed in an argument over a poker game. It had been started by one of the dead men. Buckminster's shot had been fired in his own defense and in defense of others at the table. The conclusion was plain: A murder, committed by one of the dead men, and a justifiable homicide to rectify it. The aggravated assault committed by one of the dead men during the fracas had no legal meaning now.

It was past noon before the steamer was allowed to dock and the passengers to embark. The grieving widow was kept in seclusion, away from prying eyes of the curious onlookers.

Jed felt great sympathy for the woman. It had been a stupid fight, with a tragic result. He wondered where the Sullivans had lived, and what the widow would do now. He knew about bereavement, and his heart was heavy for her, but in a detached way.

He carried his satchel down the gangplank and followed the crowd toward the town. Now that he was here, he did not know exactly what to do next. First, he supposed, was to seek lodging. He did not know yet how long he intended to stay. A few days, maybe, possibly all winter. His brief experience in the gambling profession had left him with a substantial bulge in his money belt. He could afford to live well for a while. Already, though, he was wondering whether he would really enjoy it. He had a brief moment when he considered going straight on through the town to find open country and woods where he would feel at home. It was a strange idea, and it quickly passed.

He noticed now that the streets, at least in this area, were not laid out by the compass, but on the diagonal. This gave him an odd feeling, because the diagonals, the semicardinal directions, were of great importance to Raven's people. He walked northwest on St. Peters Street, thinking as he did so that northwest was the road of the Bear. Was this an omen of some sort? For no particular reason, he turned right on Bourbon, and traveled the Wolf path to the northeast. Here he was brought back to the real world by repeated offers of feminine companionship for a price. He brushed all of these aside with a smile and "Maybe later . . ." His first need was for lodging, and this was not the sort he had in mind.

He wandered on, glad for the chance to exercise his walking muscles. He was enjoying the unfamiliar, spicy smells of unknown foods and condiments, mixed with the tang of salt on the breeze from the Gulf. Walking back down St. Peters Street to Chartres, finally he happened on a small boardinghouse that appeared clean and well kept, and checked into a room there.

He had begun to notice curious and often disapproving glances at his buckskin dress, although it had not happened on Bourbon Street. There, it had drawn approval. Still, he thought that it would be more appropriate to change. His gentleman's clothing would be wrinkled, of course, but should lose some of the wrinkles in the humid sea air. He hung the coat while he bathed, using the pitcher and basin on the dresser in his room.

The proprietor, a middle-aged lady, gave him a startled look when he descended the stair, dressed now as a gentleman. It was strange, he now realized, what a difference it made, the extreme change in costume. She had seemed almost reluctant to rent him the room, but was now quite friendly. Not only was he perceived differently, but he *felt* different. He smiled to himself, wondering. Would the attitude of the girls along Bourbon Street now be different? He decided not to test that theory, and went to look for other places of interest.

"Supper's at six," Mrs. Thorpe called after him.

The next morning he walked the old town, enjoying the sights, sounds, and smells that attach themselves to an international port. He found himself in the market district, and saw a crowd gathering in an open square a block away. Curious, he sauntered in that direction.

"What's happening?" he asked a young man who passed him, hurrying toward the crowd.

"Slave auction!" the other called over his shoulder.

Jed had never seen a full-fledged sale of this type, and curiosity drew him toward the raised platform where an auctioneer chanted his cry. On the platform beside him stood a well-muscled, nearly naked young Negro.

"Tarn around there, boy," the auctioneer ordered. "Show 'em the muscles!"

The young man strutted a little, apparently trying to increase his value. This display struck Jed's heart very powerfully, in a way he had not expected. It was impossible for him to understand how one's immediate goal could be so hopeless and perverted that it revolved around trying for a higher dollar price to be paid by his buyer.

"Three hundred . . . once . . . twice . . . sold, to Mr. Oglesby, there. And a fine field hand he'll make you, sir!"

Jed started to turn away, but the next words of the auctioneer caught and held him.

"Now, this next lot is something special, folks. Due to the unfortunate death of her husband . . . I'm sure you all heard of that . . . Mrs. Frank Sullivan will be selling three nigras today. The first is a female, about twenty, I'm told. Friends, this is a high-yellow quadroon! No field nigger, but a high-class house servant or companion for a lady or children. She's strong, healthy. . . . Be a good breeder, even. Look at her, there! What am I bid?"

Jed was already looking, and his heart rose in his throat. It was the beauty from the riverboat. Her fine clothes were gone, and she wore a thin blouse and full skirt that fell well below her knees. She was barefoot. She looked as if she had been crying, but her head was held high, and there was pride and defiance in her eyes. *The look of eagles,* Jed thought. Now she reminded him even more of Raven.

"Let's see her legs!" shouted a man behind him.

Jed whirled, but stopped short of striking the man. Under the circumstances, it was a legitimate request. He clenched his teeth as the auctioneer nodded to the girl, and she raised her skirt to her upper thighs, showing remarkably well-formed legs. There were whistles and catcalls.

"Here!" scolded the auctioneer. "None of that! This is a dignified sale. If you want this lot, bid on it!"

Jed could think of nothing but Raven.

"Three hundred!" yelled someone.

The auctioneer paused and gave a grunt of disgust.

"Gentlemen!" he said pleadingly. "Let us not waste time today
on frivolous bids. I'll not accept such a bid for this fine piece of merchandise. No bids under a thousand for this lot. Ah, *there*! Thank you,
sir! I have a thousand. Now two? Two, two . . . over there? *Fifteen
hundred!* Now, two . . ."

Jed watched numbly, still awestruck by the girl's resemblance to
his lost love, the mother of his children. He watched the motion of her
body as the auctioneer made her turn for the inspection of the buyers.
She was ordered to remove her blouse and did so with dignity and a
degree of pride. *As Raven would have done,* he thought. His head
whirled, and his anger was rising, resentment at such treatment of a
young woman.

He had never been affected in this way by anything in his life,
and did not understand it. It was not a change in his political attitude
toward the slave trade. His thoughts were entirely removed from politics at the time. Here was simply a burning rage at injustice toward
this individual. He did not know her story, did not care, but in the
past few moments, this business transaction had become the most important event in his confused life. He began to elbow his way toward
the platform.

At this level of finance, bids were few. The early one-try bid-
ders had dropped out quickly, and there appeared to be only two
serious buyers left. The auctioneer was at twenty-one hundred now,
trying to raise the offered price in increments of fifty, and getting only
smaller amounts.

One of the buyers was a dignified elderly gentleman, well-
dressed, with well-trimmed hair and beard. A broad-brimmed
planter's hat shaded his face. His privileged background was reflected
in his grooming and in his confident manner. Jed quickly sized him
up, and turned to look at the other heavy bidder.

This was a burly, red-faced man with nondescript clothing and
a well-chewed cigar. He wore a large diamond pin in his poorly tied
cravat. Jed could not have explained specific reasons why, but he was
immediately impressed that the man was uncultured and crass. At the

same time, he decided that here was a trader, looking for bargains for resale. It took only another moment to guess the next stop for an attractive female such as this. Probably only after the trader had tested the merchandise to his own satisfaction.

He now saw a pattern to the bidding. The older gentleman was raising the bid by small increments, trying to stay in the game, while the trader was bullishly pushing for a sale. *The old man knows,* Jed thought. *He's trying to help her.*

The auctioneer was growing impatient as the bid reached twenty-five hundred.

"And ten," offered the planter.

"Twenty-five fifty!" called the trader irritably.

"Three thousand!" Jed's voice was tight.

"Ah! New blood!" chortled the auctioneer, delighted at this turn of events. "Now, gentlemen, let's settle down to serious bidding. Do I hear thirty-five, thirty-five?"

The trader whirled angrily on Jed, a challenge in his eyes. Jed was caught off guard, but his instincts, honed fine by long experience, recognized the situation. A bully, dangerous but not too bright. In poker terms, time to show a hint of your hand and run a bold bluff. He casually shifted his weight to both feet and half turned toward the trader. Very carefully, he drew the skirt of his topcoat aside. The hilt of the small pistol peeked above the waistband of his trousers. The angry look on the face of the trader changed to one of shocked surprise.

"Thirty-five, five . . ." chanted the auctioneer.

"Hell, she ain't worth that," snorted the burly trader.

Worth the risk of what you think I might do, thought Jed.

"Thirty-five . . . going once, twice . . . *sold*! To Mr.—?"

"Sterling, sir. Jedediah Sterling."

"Yes, sir. I assume you have credentials. Please see the clerk over there. He will assist you with the paperwork. Thank you, sir."

Numbly, Jed walked toward the clerk's desk.

What happened here? he asked himself. *I have just bought a slave!*

The elderly planter approached him and paused.

"Son," the planter said, "I hope you'll be good to her. She belonged to my brother. He thought highly of her."

"You . . . he was Frank Sullivan?" asked Jed.

"Yes. You knew him?"

"No. Not at all, sir. But I was on the boat."

He saw no reason to explain in more detail.

"I see. Well, it's over. He was in money trouble. Gambling, racing. Trying for that big win, I suppose. No matter now."

Jed felt a pang of guilt over his part in Frank Sullivan's last poker game.

"Mr. Sullivan." he said. "If you could spare me the time, I would like to know any more you could tell me about this woman. May I settle with the bursar first?"

"Of course. My pleasure, sir. I will be waiting here."

13

Charles Sullivan was waiting under the shade of a tree beside the street.

"Where is Suzannah?" he asked.

"That is her name?"

"Yes. It should be on your papers."

"True. I left her in the holding area until we talk."

"Good. Ah, where to begin?" the old planter mused. "Well, as I said, Frank had fallen on hard times. Miz' Jennie, his wife . . . you met her?"

"No. I saw her on the boat."

"Yes. They had only one child, Annabel. She'd be about the age of this girl. With no other children, they . . . rather, *he* brought a child and her mammy up from the slave cabins."

"And that baby was Suzannah?"

"Of course. Her mammy worked in the kitchen. But the two girls had a teacher, too. Both learned schoolin' the same."

"Wasn't that illegal?"

"I reckon. But they were like sisters, you see. Only thing, Jennie, Frank's wife, never did cotton to this. She always hated Suzannah, some."

"But *why?*"

"Don't know for sure, son. But those two girls were surely a pair. Like two peas in a pod. I thought it a happy situation for the girls."

He paused and enjoyed for a moment the memories of happy children on the lawn.

"Excuse me," he said finally. "When the girls were about fifteen, I guess, both took down with a fever. The doctor treated 'em with quinine an' all, but Annabel died. Then Jennie hated this girl all the more. Wanted to sell her or send her back to the cabins. Frank wouldn't do it. Seems like she became more precious to him, for losin' his daughter, you see."

"I can understand that."

"Yes," the old man continued. "When times got hard, it got worse. Frank was sellin' some of the darkies, some that had been in the family a couple of generations, even. Jennie demanded that he sell the girl. She'd bring quite a bit, you see. But he wouldn't. They been arguin' over that for some time. Frank always planned to free her, I know. Told me about it. He just never got around to it."

Jed was confused. Was the man suggesting that *he* free her?

"Why do you tell me all this, sir?"

"So's you'll know, I guess. I knew Jennie'd sell her, first thing. Always wanted to. I tried to buy her, to free her like Frank wanted. I couldn't have. Times are bad for me, too. I'm only proud to think that pimp didn't get her."

"What makes you think I won't do that to her?" Jed asked.

The old gentleman eyed him for a moment. "You wouldn't. You've got a good face."

Jed chuckled. "It's seen a heap of miles, sir."

"But honest miles, I'll warrant. Most of 'em, anyhow." He paused only a moment. "Now, what are you goin' to do with her?"

Jed took a deep breath. "Mr. Sullivan, I must tell you . . . I have no idea. I saw her on the boat, and admired her grace and beauty. When I saw her mistreated, I was angered, and . . . well, I bought her."

"See, I figured you right! It was meant to be. You have an outdoor look about you, but some degree of quality and education. Let me guess . . . a surveyor?"

"No. Pretty close, maybe. I was with Captain Fremont as a guide. Mostly I've been a trapper."

"And the culture in your talk?"

"A few years at Princeton."

"Where is your home now?"

"Kansas. I had a family. . . . They're dead now."

"My sympathies, sir. You're going back there?"

"My plans weren't complete. They'll need some changes now."

"Indeed! Let's see . . . what are your slave laws?"

"None, so far. Presumed to be of Northern trend because of location. I'm not certain, I guess."

The old man nodded. "Makes a problem, does it not? But isn't Missouri a slave state?"

"Again, I'm not certain, sir. There's an odd law, as I recall. Negroes born there are considered free, but no free Negroes can enter from elsewhere."

"Which brings us back to the original question," Sullivan smiled. "What will you do with her?"

"And still, I don't know. I don't know why I *bought* her."

"Well, don't free her here," the old man advised.

"Why not?"

"Well, you'd give her papers, but papers get lost or stolen. She needs someone to look after her. Not that she couldn't do it, but she'd have little legal status, you know. I'd buy her, but . . . well, you know. I really can't afford it, and there's Jennie. She's still family, and she'd hate me for it."

Jed nodded. "Maybe I'll just head back upriver and then decide."

"Might be good. But let me tell you about it. She's just dark enough to draw suspicion, so keep your bill of sale handy. Shove her around a little, to make it plain. Then folks won't ask questions."

"A good plan. By the way, sir, do you know how much Negro blood she has?"

"Doesn't matter. *Any* darky blood makes 'em darkies under the law. But I don't know. Her mammy was said to have some Indian blood. Now *there* was a handsome woman."

"She's dead now?"

"Yes. That same fever time. But back to the present . . . I'd think her slave status is a protection while you're in this area. When you get farther north, you'll have to play the cards as they're dealt, I reckon."

He paused and gave a long sigh. "Well, in Frank's behalf, I thank you for whatever you can do for her. I've done what I can."

The old man rose from the bench where they were sitting, and walked away without looking back. His pride showed in the ramrod-straight back and determined stride.

"Thank you, sir!" Jed called after him.

The girl was tense, apprehensive, and just a little defiant. She had obviously been crying. He wondered if she had been abused. He presented the necessary papers to take possession, and turned to where she sat on a rough bench in the holding room.

"Come on, girl!" he said, a little roughly.

She followed him out into the sunlight. She was dressed in the thin blouse and full skirt that she had worn on the platform at the sale.

"You have no other clothes?" he asked.

"They took them."

He stepped back inside. "Where are her clothes?" he asked one of the employees.

"That's all she was wearin', Cap'n."

"No shoes?"

"I didn't see none."

Jed stepped back outside. "Never mind. We'll get you some. For now, come on. Suzannah, isn't it?"

"Yes. Where are we going?"

"I haven't decided all that yet. I talked to Mr. Sullivan."

He saw the confusion in her eyes, but she said nothing. His heart reached out to her, and he smiled. The anxiety in her face relaxed a little.

"Come," he said.

They walked across the square and in the general direction of the rooming house. There were a great many immediate problems to be faced, such as where the girl could sleep and eat. But first, he felt a need to talk to her, to get acquainted, to reassure her.

He stopped at a bench on the street and motioned for her to sit. She sat at a respectful distance toward the other end of the bench.

"Now, Suzannah, let us talk a little. You obviously have some education."

A trace of fear appeared in her eyes, and she spoke quickly. "Oh, no, Massah!"

He realized her anxiety. "It's all right, girl. I know about it. Mr. Sullivan told me. Don't worry. Oh . . . my name is Sterling. Jedediah Sterling."

"Yas, Massah Sterling."

The girl would quickly catch on to playing a part, he thought. He had seen her dressed like a lady, and now like a house slave. But he had also heard her speak in cultured tones, and had just now heard her revert to the dialect of a Southern darky. This was a protective device, he realized, developed from necessity. There must have been times when it was *safer* to be an ignorant darky, and times when it was an advantage to show culture and class.

But don't we all do this? he thought. With something of a shock, he realized that he had done this himself, to a great extent. He had been quite at home socially, talking politics with educated men in his father's library in Baltimore. On the frontier or in the mountains, however, he had been able to converse easily with the other fur trappers at rendezvous. Some of them were completely unschooled, but some, like Jim Beckwourth, were well educated. *We are all playing a part, all the time.*

He began to feel better about the situation into which he had now thrust himself. The two of them *could* carry it off. He still did not know what he would do, or what he wanted to do. But if they could reach the frontier, he somehow felt that it would work out. Kansas Territory was rough and demanding, but forgiving, in a way. Social graces were less important than survival.

He studied the girl as she sat there on the bench, beginning to relax a little. Her long hair, which had first caught his attention, was wavy. Not straight like Raven's, but neither did it curl tightly like that of many Negroes. Her features . . . this was his first chance to look closely at her face. High, strong cheekbones, full lips, a straight, fairly slender nose. More like Raven's face than he had realized. His eyes roved over her well-formed body. He had seen her legs at the auction platform.

"Inspecting your purchase, sir?" she asked suddenly.

She had abandoned the drawling, fawning darky speech, and was again a cultured young woman with pride and dignity. Jed was a trifle embarrassed, and searched for words.

"Well, I . . ."

"Why *did* you buy me, Massah?" she said sarcastically.

It angered him that she could see through him this way.

"Never mind, for now," he snapped.

She seemed to sense his confusion, and retreated to a safer position.

"I'm sorry, sir. It was not my place to speak so."

This was an intermediate mood, somewhere between her sarcastic defiance and her fawning subjugation.

"Now," he went on, "let us start again. Mr. Sullivan . . . *Charles* Sullivan . . . told me some of your background."

"You talked to *him*? I thought you meant Mr. Frank."

Now she was confused and off balance.

"Look," Jed suggested, "let us not, either of us, jump to any conclusions yet. We have a lot to learn about each other, and some planning to do. Agreed?"

She nodded, with a tentative smile. It was only a tiny hint of a smile. It struck him that he had never seen her smile. She had had nothing to smile about.

"Agreed," she said.

"Good. Now, you are wondering about me. Where I live, do I have a family?"

"Of course, sir."

He hated the "sir," but for the present it would serve a useful purpose.

"I come from the Kansas Territory. I have no family."

Her eyes widened, and a certain doubt crept into her expression.

"My wife and children were killed a few years ago."

He saw her face soften in sympathy, yet that expression was quickly replaced by one of doubt.

"May I ask, sir, what is your business?"

"I have been a trapper, trader, guide, scout. . . ."

Her eyes swept quickly over his clothing and his new boots.

"But you are . . ." There was a question in her eyes and in her face.

"Educated? Yes, some. I left it behind."

"Then why—?"

"Later . . . were you fed this morning?"

"I was not hungry."

He nodded, understanding that the meal offered had probably not been very appealing.

"You asked me earlier," he went on, "why I bought you. We will talk of that later. For now, we will go back to where I am staying. You need some food, some better clothing, so that we can travel."

"To the territories?"

"Yes."

There was more to the question than he was prepared to answer yet, so he let it drop. They started back to the boardinghouse, with the girl obediently following him, a few paces behind.

14

"You can't bring her in here!" the landlady practically yelled at him. "I run a respectable house!"

"No, no . . . please listen a moment, Mrs. Thorpe. This is not what you think."

"I *know* what it is!"

"I think not, madam. This girl is a slave. Her owner was killed on the *River Queen*. I'm sure you heard. She was on the block, just now. I bought her, bidding against a trader."

"So's you could have her for yourself," the woman sneered.

Jed took a deep breath. "Mrs. Thorpe, this is really of no concern to you. I am not breaking any law and am not asking you to do so. You are mistaken in your assumption. I bought a slave, that's all. I need a place for her to stay, and meals for her while I make some arrangements and plans."

She eyed Suzannah suspiciously. "Is that right, girl, what he says?"

"Yes, ma'am."

There was a long pause, and finally the woman seemed to soften.

"Well, I guess so. There's a room in the barn, a corn-shuck mattress. It'll cost you extra, of course."

"Thank you," Jed offered. "Now, they took her clothes and her shoes. Where would you suggest we try to find her some things?"

Mrs. Thorpe was mellowing rapidly.

"Well, let me give that some thought. But she's likely hungry. Here, girl, come on in the kitchen. We'll find you something."

In an hour, the woman was puttering around like a mother hen. She found an old cotton dress that would be practical, a pair of rough but serviceable brogans, and a well-worn wool coat.

"Nights get cool sometimes," she observed. "And she'd probably best stay in the house. She can use John's room off the kitchen, there, where I can keep an eye on her. He don't mind sleepin' in the barn sometimes."

John, it seemed, was an aging Negro handyman who had been with Mrs. Thorpe for many years. "Since even before my husband died. I'd never have made this place go without John." He agreed to give up his room for a little while.

"She'll be safer there," he agreed.

Now Jed had almost more help than he needed or wanted. He had still not decided on any real plan. He had not had time to think.

That night he lay awake for a long time, staring into the darkness. He was still struck by the beauty of the girl, but even more by her marked resemblance to his lost love. Even the changing moods of the girl reminded him of Raven. The flicker of a smile, which was now becoming more frequent, was the same. So were her mannerisms, and the way she moved and walked.

He was not certain whether this was good or bad. She was his, bought and paid for. She was required by law to be anything he wanted her to be. That was his problem. He had no clear idea what he wanted from her. The physical attraction was strong, but he was well aware that it would be only that. To try to substitute such a thing for the love he had lost would only be a corruption of Raven's memory. He could not buy that love.

He could marry the girl, of course. But that, too, would be empty without the love that had been his and Raven's. It had been stupid, he told himself, to buy this girl simply because she looked like Raven. Then he would recall how she had looked, standing there in the sun on the auction block. To have let her go to the trader's bid would have been a betrayal of all he had felt for the wife he had loved.

Jed wondered what Raven would have said, under these circumstances. It was an impossible situation, and he somehow felt that even now, she might be laughing at him from the Other Side. He finally fell asleep, and dreamed of her laughter and of the way her eyes sparkled in the moonlight.

He woke, and it was not yet morning. This time his thoughts turned to more practical matters. He must begin to plan. Regardless of what sort of relationship was to develop, he felt that he must get the girl out of here. He recalled the advice of the old gentleman who had wanted to help her but could not. Treat her like a slave. Yes, to treat her too well in this area would be to draw attention. Farther north, it would be different. And in Kansas, the Indian Territory, the dusky hue of her skin would go unnoticed. There, she could be virtually anything, to him or anyone else. And that would give him time to discover the nature of the relationship.

Of one thing he was certain. He could not sell her. He might free her, taking the considerable financial loss. It would be only a bad bet in a high-stakes poker game. But he was not ready to do that yet, before all the cards were dealt. And even if he did make such a decision, it could not be here. A freed slave who was an attractive woman would be quite vulnerable in New Orleans, or anywhere in the area.

So each line of thought led him in the same direction, back upriver, back to the familiar land that had become home to his spirit . . . Kansas prairie. There, it might be easier to think. Besides, it would give him a chance to become better acquainted with this stranger who had accidentally become a part of his life. *But are there really any accidents?* he wondered. Maybe he had simply not yet been allowed to see how this was to work out.

He drifted back to sleep.

The sun was shining in his window when he woke, and he rose hurriedly. There was much to do today. He had missed breakfast, but Mrs. Thorpe poured him coffee in the kitchen.

"Reckoned I'd let you sleep." She laughed. "You and Suzannah had a big day."

Jed was amused at the change in attitude. This was the same woman who had refused to allow the girl in her house only a few hours ago. Now Suzannah was helping in the kitchen, quickly and capably. She was also smiling more. She set a plate of grits and gravy before him, and refilled his coffee cup.

"Well," he said as he finished the plate, "I've done some thinking. I want to head upriver, where I know the customs and the country better."

Mrs. Thorpe nodded approval.

"I'll see what sort of passage I can get," he went on.

He did not add that he had to think of how well his money was holding out. That was a matter of some concern. He had been quite affluent a day ago, but now he'd have to be careful.

He went to the port offices, and bought a first-class ticket on the *Mississippi Pride,* to embark two days later.

"Just yourself?" asked the man behind the desk.

"I've a slave."

"He'll have to go deck passenger. Another ticket, but it's cheaper."

Jed considered a moment. Maybe he, too, could travel deck. He abandoned that idea, and another struck him.

"May I ask, sir," he began, "if on another trip my wife asked to accompany me . . ."

"She'd need a ticket. She'd share your cabin, I suppose?"

"I suppose. We're usually on good terms."

Both men chuckled, and Jed turned away with his tickets. He had more information now that might come in handy later. Still, he was uneasy about deck passage for the girl. She had traveled that way with her previous owner, but had been dressed as a ladies' companion. Maybe she could tell him more about what might be expected. Or, feared . . .

There was no way to broach the problems of travel with the girl except to discuss them bluntly. She was becoming less suspicious daily. She shifted back and forth into what he had come to think of as her darky act less frequently. She would converse with him more easily now.

"Tell me, Suzannah, is there danger in your traveling as a deck passenger?"

"Of course. Not much, though. There are the darkies there, and that keeps people from bothering somebody else's slaves, in the roped-off part."

"Any danger from *them*?"

"Not really. There's usually another woman or two, and that helps. If there's not, I can handle it."

"How?"

"A woman learns such things, Mr. Sterling. There are ways. She can pick a big, shy, harmless-looking man to sit with. She can protest that it's her time of the moon. Don't worry about it."

He would have expected such straight talk from Raven, or from any other Indian woman. It was odd to hear this from a slave girl, and it puzzled him. He finally decided that the confusion in his mind was caused by the manner in which he had first seen her. She had been dressed in high fashion, as she had been raised, in the home of a white planter. Jed had perceived her in that light. It had never really dawned on him that her heritage came from the slave cabins below the hill.

"Tell me of your mother, Suzannah."

They were seated in two chairs in the kitchen. Tomorrow they would embark.

"I don't know much. She was a beautiful woman. Part Indian, she said. *Her* mother was kidnapped and sold as a little girl. Ended up on the Sullivans' plantations. They taught me pride. I don't remember my grandmother, but my mother taught me."

She was quiet a moment, and then went on.

"I don't remember when I didn't live in the big house. My mother had a room there, behind the pantry."

"You were treated well, then?"

"Oh, yes. Like family. Of course, Miz' Jennie didn't like me."

"Mr. Charles mentioned that. Why was that, Suzannah?"

"I don't know. Mr. Frank always treated me like a princess. As well as he treated Annabel, probably. Maybe it was that. Then, when I grew up"—she pointed to her shapely breasts "—I think Miz' Jennie was afraid he wanted me for his bed."

Again, Jed was startled by her frankness.

"It wasn't that, of course," Suzannah went on.

"Why not?"

"He just wasn't that way to me. He treated me like he treated his daughter. I used to pretend I *was* his daughter."

There was a long pause, and then she continued.

"I've never said this to anyone before, but he's dead now. Mr. Sterling, I've always thought maybe I am."

"His daughter?"

"Yes. The way he looked at my mother, took care of her. I think Miz' Jennie suspected something, and I think Uncle Charlie knows."

"Does it matter now?"

She smiled ruefully. "I guess not."

Both were silent for a little while. The twin wicks of the whale-oil lamp sputtered a little.

"Suzannah," Jed began, "we start upriver tomorrow. I want you to know a couple of things."

"Yes?"

"First . . . you asked me once why I bought you. I didn't know. Maybe I still don't. You look much like my wife, who was killed."

"*That's* why? But you haven't—"

"I don't know. It's partly that. But I saw you on the boat . . . the *River Queen*. Then I happened by the auction, and I wanted to help you."

"By *buying* me?"

"Well, yes. I still haven't figured exactly how. But you'll be better off where I came from than in Louisiana, I think."

"Does this make me a runaway?" she asked, her voice a little tense.

"Not if you're with me, and I own you. Now on the boat, I may rough you around or swear at you to show that that's the way it is. For your protection."

She flashed him her biggest smile yet.

"Of course . . . Massah."

"Don't do that!" he snapped. "I don't even know yet what's going to happen upriver."

15

The trip back upriver was much slower than the downstream run. The powerful current was deceptive to watch. It appeared relatively calm and gentle from the shore, but its mighty power could be felt when the steamboat nosed into the current. The heavy engine shuddered and groaned as the craft swung to face the full force of the great river. On a good day, they might make as much as fifty miles. On a day when weather or traffic or floating snags slowed their progress upstream, it was much less. The whole trip, some eight hundred miles, would require more than half a month.

The first leg of the trip, New Orleans to Memphis, was broken every few days by a stop at one of the busy port cities of the South. One long day to Baton Rouge, two more to Natchez, then Vicksburg, Greenville . . . from Greenville to Memphis was a three-day run.

Some river masters, Jed was told, made better time by traveling at night. The more conservative captains, fearful of night travel because of snags or other flotsam, preferred safety to speed. The captain of the *Mississippi Pride* was one of these.

They would change to another steamboat at Memphis. The remaining distance, some two hundred fifty miles, would be traversed in four or five days, with one major stop at Cairo, where the Ohio joined the larger stream.

On the first day of travel, Suzannah attached herself to a portly woman in the restricted area, as she had intended. Jed made his presence quite apparent, descending the ladder to the lower deck at least once a day to talk to the girl and establish his identity to the others. There were three men, all house servant types, with some degree of refinement. It occurred to Jed that it would probably not be practical to transport field slaves by riverboat. The cost of tickets for passage would be prohibitive. He was beginning to understand some problems involved for a slave owner with a small operation.

On the occasions when he went to the lower deck to make his presence and his concern known, he was careful to appear rough and domineering. It was difficult for him to do, but it seemed the safest way. Suzannah responded with an exaggerated darky talk to show that she understood the ploy. Jed also took pains to wear his pistol in his waistband and to show it openly to the deck passengers. This would indicate that he was ready and able to resist any insult or potential harm to the girl. At least, he hoped that it would leave a strong impression.

He had wondered if the difficulties and problems of their strange situation would cause him to resent the girl. He found the opposite to be true. His concern for her well-being only increased. In addition, he began to look forward to the short while each day that he could spend with her. These times became the most important moments of his day, times to enjoy and cherish.

Jed had paid for two meals a day for her, but it was apparent that the fare was poor. Soup or mush, and hardtack. He realized that to complain would single her out and attract unwanted attention and possibly resentment. Therefore, he contrived to take to her tidbits of food from the dining salon.

Suzannah was appreciative. He admired her appetite. A woman who ate well was likely to be a healthy woman. He realized that this principle was one that he had learned among Raven's people. The slave girl still reminded him of his loss, but it was now in a different way. Not a depressing memory, but a recall of happier days. And there were differences. Suzannah had a shy, flickering smile and sidelong glance that were hers alone. Jed found it very appealing.

He was, in fact, more and more attracted to her, not only physically but emotionally. The chance touch of her fingers when he handed her a bit of food from the first-class tables sent a thrill of excitement through him. More and more, he looked forward to their brief moments together.

Sometimes he dreamed of her, and sometimes of Raven. Sometimes they became as one in his dreams, an essence of pure womanhood that was beginning to obsess him. Often, though, he would lie for hours, wide awake. He watched the patch of moonlight that shone through the porthole on the empty bunk across the narrow cabin from him. The rhythmic lapping of the water against the hull both lulled and excited him. A romantic sound . . . how ridiculous, he thought, the contrived formality of his own culture. It would not be so among Raven's people.

Jed sighed and rolled over. He must be thinking about some upcoming decisions. He no longer wondered whether he wanted a physical relationship with the girl he had bought. That urge was overwhelming. Only the circumstances were in question. He did not think that she would object. Actually, under the law, she *could* not. He could demand her favors. But that would defeat the purpose. He doubted that he could take a woman who resented it. And in addition, there were legalities involved. Civilization could make such things so difficult. . . . Among the Indian Nations where he had traveled, lived, and trapped, there would be no problem.

Maybe he could return to Raven's people with Suzannah as his wife. No, it would not be fair to expect that of her. A neutral culture? Possibly one of the Civilized Tribes? The Cherokee Nation, now transported to the West, was in territory familiar to him. There would be no problem to them, if he joined them with a wife of questionable lineage. Or Cheyennes. But that would require this girl to learn the nomadic ways of the buffalo hunter. She had been brought up in an affluent white society, much like his own childhood.

He could, possibly, become a settler, open a store or settle on a farm. It would be necessary to verify the law wherever they settled. He was still unsure about that freed-slave ban in Missouri. Kansas Territory would be different. Few laws as yet, a land with which he was familiar.

Another possibility would be Ohio. He had been told by Mrs. Thorpe that freed slaves were safe anywhere north of the Ohio River. He did not presume to ask how she knew such things, but he had wondered.

He also thought of the danger to Suzannah if some accident

happened to befall him before they reached the relative safety of the Northern states. He obtained paper, pen, and ink and wrote a document that he hoped would never be needed.

> To any who may be concerned:
> I, Jedediah Sterling, on this the thirteenth day of November, 1842, do attest as follows:
> The person of color, known as Suzannah, a female Negro of about twenty years, having been purchased by me at auction in New Orleans, is hereby awarded her freedom from all encumbrances and indenture.
>
> > Signed,
> > Jedediah Sterling

He blotted the paper carefully, allowed it to dry, and folded it with his bill of sale. He started to place the documents back in his money belt, but then thought better of it. If he were killed, accidentally or on purpose, that would be the first item stolen. He placed the papers inside the lining of his silk topper. On his next visit to the lower deck, he whispered to Suzannah of his action.

"If anything should happen to me," he told her, "look for papers in this hat."

He tipped the hat to her in a flippant gesture, but the girl looked greatly concerned.

"Are you in danger?"

"No more than anyone, Suzannah. But you would be in a dangerous position if something *did* happen to me. Is there anything you need, now?"

She shook her head, and he walked away.

Somewhat later, the portly mammy who had befriended her broached a conversation.

"Honey, dat Massah Sterling of yours sho' be handsome."

"Yes, I guess so."

"I *know* so, child. Be you pleasurin' him?"

Suzannah blushed. "No."

"Lordy, why not?"

"I . . . he's not that way, Mandy."

"Oh. You mean he's different. Maybe he likes boys?"

"No, no. I don't think so. He's just a gentleman."

The old woman chuckled. "Yeh, I know about some of *them,* though!"

"Not that way . . . he only bought me a few days ago."

"Oh. He take a little mo' time than some, then. But he *like* you. Ol' Mandy kin tell. Best you treat him good."

"I . . . he has been very kind to me. . . ."

The woman nodded. "Tha's good. I'm thinkin' you got a good 'un there, honey. You be nice to *him*!"

Suzannah smiled. "If I get a chance."

The woman left the boat with her "folks" at Vicksburg, but by this time, the firm presence of Suzannah's owner was well established. There seemed little threat of harm to Suzannah. None of the men were likely to brave the wrath of her tall and capable-looking owner.

At Memphis there was a delay of an hour before the steamboat would depart. Jed transferred his satchel, and then suggested that they walk. Suzannah fell in behind him, but he turned and offered her his arm.

"I . . . I'm not dressed appropriately, sir."

Jed looked at her plain dress, her rough shoes. "That's true. Or maybe *I'm* not. But that can be fixed. Let's try something."

He turned into a dress shop, and spoke to the clerk.

"We'd like to look at some dresses, ma'am, and perhaps a pair of slippers."

In a short while they were back on the street, headed back toward the docks. A passing gentleman tipped his hat to the now well-dressed Suzannah, and she nodded in response.

At the boat, Jed gave her hand a slight squeeze as they headed up the gangplank. The steward tipped his hat, too, and checked his passenger list. He seemed confused.

"Will the lady's companion be coming, sir?" he asked. "You have a deck passage for a personal servant."

This appeared easier than Jed had expected.

"Servant? No, there must be some mistake. Just my wife and myself."

"Very good, sir. Cabin three, next deck up."

They climbed the stair and located the cabin. It was small, with a bunk on each side of the narrow space.

"I . . . I did not expect this," stammered Suzannah.

"Nor did I," Jed admitted. "It just happened."

She looked at the two bunks, a question showing in her face.

"We had to face this sometime," he said. "I did not expect it yet."

She laughed, embarrassed.

"Suzannah, anything that happens . . . well, I . . . look, you take one bed, I take the other. Your choice."

She smiled.

"After that," he continued, "we will talk. Still, you have a choice. I will not . . ."

He paused, feeling foolish and embarrassed. He was accustomed to a people whose ways were different. Among Raven's people the woman had a much greater role in such things.

"You mean, sir, you would not force yourself on me?" There was a twinkle in her eye.

"Well . . . something like that," he mumbled awkwardly.

"I would not have expected such a thing from you," she said seriously. Now it was her turn to be embarrassed. Her eyes dropped, and she fumbled for words. "Did . . . had you thought . . . that it might not be necessary?"

Now both laughed, and it was good.

EPILOGUE

The Santa Fe trade continued to grow. In the ensuing few years, a number of events brought about change.

Jedediah Smith was killed in 1831 by Comanches on the Cimarron Cutoff.

The fur trade was virtually over, as beaver hats for men faded from style.

Politically, the Republic of Texas declared her independence from Mexico in 1836. The international boundary at the Arkansas River was no longer Mexican, but Texan. The Main Trail still led directly into Santa Fe.

International ports of entry were closed in 1843, because of impending war between the United States and Mexico, and for a time the wagons ceased to roll.

Still, storm clouds of internal strife continued to gather over the expanding nation.